For Wells –

an awesome person

Fatal
Rhythm

with great values –

very best wishes

R. B. O'Gorman

Immaculada Books
Mobile, Alabama
2014

in your future endeavors

R.B. O'Gorman

For Susan

ACKNOWLEDGMENTS

Carolyn Haines and Kathleen Matthews taught me how to write. What I've executed correctly I owe to their guidance. The mistakes I've made reflect all that I still need to learn. I'm grateful to Alexis Lampley for creation of the book's cover, a work of art.

Many friends have read my work and offered advice. Special thanks to Dick Duffey, Marilyn Johnston, Michelle Ladner, Kaye Park Hinckley, Thomi Sharpe, Gus Palumbo, Jo Anne McKnight, Isabel Brown, Alice Jackson, and Pat Stanford.

Along the way, a number of professionals have offered encouragement. Thanks to Craig Thorn, Hope Neely, Lolly Waldron O'Brien, Patrick LoBrutto, Loretta Barrett, Elaine Cissi, and Peter Mongeau.

Dr. Michael E. DeBakey developed a Department of Surgery centered on a faculty par excellence. I owe all that I know about patient care to those teachers: Kenneth Mattox, David Feliciano, George Noon, Hazim Safi, Arthur Bell, George Jordan, Jimmy Howell, Charles McCollum, and many others, along with the chief residents that guided me from my intern year through the seven years of learning the art and science of surgery.

I've been blessed to work with a great group at Cardiovascular Associates in Mobile, Alabama. Special thanks to Doctors Maltese, Damrich, and Kyriazis, who along with Dawn Andrews and a dedicated group of office personnel are committed to service. To our patients, we'll always be grateful for their faith in us.

My family made this work possible and the effort worthwhile. Inestimable gratitude to Susan; Tom, Daisy, and Corinne; Mary and Rob Herbst; Matthew, Heather, Lotus, and Matthias; Amy and Joe Block; Joseph; Elizabeth; Keith and Eleanor; Tommy and Amy Sue.

FATAL RHYTHM

CHAPTER ONE

OLIVE GREEN SHEETS DRAPED THE YOUNG WOMAN'S body, except for a small area in the center of her chest. There, the sternal retractor spread apart the two halves of the sawed breastbone to reveal the beating heart. Dr. Joe Morales wasn't assigned to this room, but he had to check on his cousin Lourdes. So, he'd slipped into OR 19, the Mount Olympus of surgery, and staked out a position behind the curtain that separated the anesthesiologist from the surgical personnel.

Joe watched as Dr. Jacques De la Toure, head of the Houston Heart Institute, placed the last sutures deep inside the cavity. De la Toure put down his needle driver and looked to his faculty associate, Dr. Victor Carlisle.

"Good job," Carlisle said.

De la Toure had closed an abnormal hole between two of Lourdes's heart's pumping chambers. Serious stuff, but on the spectrum of procedures, it anchored the low-risk end, and Joe had encouraged Lourdes to proceed with surgery. She was not only his cousin, but also his best friend, his only friend from the neighborhood. She respected him, admired him, adored him. So, when he told her she needed the operation, she acquiesced like a gentle lamb.

Her father and his mother prayed to the Virgin for her recovery, but Joe did better. He arranged for her to have the finest heart surgeon in the world.

De la Toure turned in the direction of the heart-lung machine. "Start coming down on the pump, but don't give any volume."

"Yes, sir." The muted voice came from Kim Chiu, the middle-aged, Asian heart surgeon that De la Toure had brought to Houston to serve as his head perfusionist, supervising all of the technicians. Her reserved, subservient demeanor belied an intensity that Joe had witnessed more than once.

"Oh, Lordy," Marie Coleman, the scrub tech, said out loud.

Inside the chest, Lourdes's heart was ready to burst.

"I told you not to give extra volume," De la Toure said.

"I didn't," Chiu said. "I know how to run this machine."

Joe realized that, in fact, she knew how to perform the operation as well as any of his attendings, but her attempts to obtain proper credentials had been thwarted by the Board of Surgery and its laws protecting American trainees. De la Toure ignored her words and looked to the anesthesiologist, Dr. John Allgood, standing next to Joe at the head of the table.

"Go up on your epinephrine," De la Toure ordered.

Joe knew Allgood would pull Lourdes through if anyone could. Despite the double, right earrings and the ponytail stuffed under his surgical hood, this sixties holdout knew his medicine. Allgood glanced at the epinephrine pump and then leaned over the drape.

"We're already at 50 cc's, Chief," Allgood said.

"Then go to a hundred."

Allgood let out a sigh but did as he was told. Minutes ticked by.

She just needs time, Joe hoped.

As they waited, Joe noticed a band of sweat start to form across the front of De la Toure's surgical cap. Joe shivered as the air conditioning evaporated perspiration from his own skin. Finally, the increased epinephrine took effect. The heart began to contract vigorously, flogged by the dose of pharmacological adrenaline.

From under his mask, De la Toure offered a deep, low "thank you," and Marie chorused with a soft "Amen."

Allgood extended a congratulatory fist and Joe countered with his own. They bumped in midair.

De la Toure placed his open palms on Lourdes's chest and pushed away, as if he needed her help to stand erect.

"Now let's come down again," De la Toure said. He straightened his back, growing in stature right in front of Joe's eyes. "Slowly. And this time, Chiu, don't give any volume."

"Yes, sir," she answered curtly. "Two liters. . . . One liter. . . . We're off bypass."

"Chief, you're having some PVCs," Allgood said. "And some short runs of nasty-looking V-tach."

Joe turned to the monitor. Abnormally wide electrocardiogram complexes recruited others until groups of six or more filled the television screen: V-tach, a fatal rhythm. With these rapid beats, the heart produced no blood pressure. The arterial tracing flattened into a straight line.

"Check your labs," De la Toure said. "This is a young woman with pristine coronary arteries. There is absolutely no reason for her to be having V-tach."

"Everything's normal, Chief," Allgood said.

"Do not tell me everything is normal." De la Toure threw down his instruments, leaned over the surgical drapes, and glared at Allgood.

Allgood moved forward to confront De la Toure, their faces inches apart, their bodies separated only by the expanse of faded green fabric that marked the boundary of the sterile field. Allgood's right shoulder ticked to some internal metronome, a nervous habit Joe recognized.

Embarrassed, Joe turned away. He saw Chiu bowed low over the pump, pretending to check on the tubing.

The various operating personnel froze in their positions. Dead silence.

Finally, Allgood broke the standoff. He pulled back a few inches and spoke slowly and forcefully.

"Dr. De la Toure, the pH, oxygen saturation, hemoglobin, potassium, calcium, and magnesium are all normal." Allgood enunciated each item in a crisp rhythm, his right shoulder jerking upward with each word.

"Check them again. You are obviously missing something. And start some lidocaine. Or should I get another anesthesiologist in here?"

"Oh, Lordy," Marie said, returning De la Toure's attention to the patient's heart, quivering inside the open chest.

"She's in a sustained V-tach," Allgood said as he turned to his drug cart.

"I can see that," De la Toure said. "Give me the defibrillator."

Marie turned to the stainless-steel stand behind the surgeon.

"Now!" De la Toure shouted.

"Yes, sir." Marie handed De la Toure the two long metal lollipops, each connected by an electrical cord to the power source. Carefully, he slid them into the chest, and sandwiched the heart between the two paddles.

"Clear," he ordered. Then, he pushed the red button on the handle.

Lourdes's body jerked, knocking a tray of instruments onto the floor. A cacophony of metal against metal. The suddenness and volume of the sound elicited an involuntary gasp from the operating personnel, followed by an immediate embarrassed silence, but, like De la Toure, Joe remained focused on the exposed heart, the bloated muscular pump drowning in a pool of its own blood.

Lourdes's body lay still now. A sacrificial virgin at the apex of the pyramid, her chest split open, her heart exposed. For what purpose? To appease an unseen Quetzalcoatl, the feathered serpent? The idiocy that Joe's Aztec ancestors accepted as fact was indeed as logical as any reason Joe could fathom. Whether you believed in the myth of a merciful savior or a vengeful deity, what difference did it make? Dead was dead.

Piercing illumination from the four OR lights bore down on the center of the surgical field. Each one, like a satellite dish with hundreds of mirrors, focused its halogen light source into a unified beam that spotlighted Lourdes's distended heart. As Joe stared into the cavity, he couldn't prevent his eyes from watering. Beneath him, a crater with a glob of burgundy muscle plopped into a puddle of crimson fluid. Deep, dark, deathly red overwhelmed his vision. Joe couldn't look at it for another moment.

He raised his head but was blinded by the overhead lighting. A supernova strobed inside his brain. Reflexively, Joe closed his eyes, but within his cranium, throbbing gray matter threatened to erupt like an overdue volcano. He opened his eyes to look at the monitor, frantically searching for signs of life, but the red, green, and yellow tracings from the plasma screen stretched and twisted and twirled around him like a time-delayed photo of the Southwest Freeway during evening rush hour.

Why had he pushed Lourdes to have the surgery? True, the VSD had prompted the beginnings of congestive heart failure, but there were medications. And now, she might die because of his advice.

Joe started to sway. His vision blurred. Stepping back from the table, he stumbled over a cable on the floor.

Allgood took hold of his arm, providing support. "Yo, Joe, you all right? Need me to sit you down?"

Joe looked at Lourdes, sweet and pure. Inmaculada. His knees wanted to buckle, but his mind wouldn't allow it. He felt Allgood tighten the grip on his arm.

"Joe? Man, you OK?"

Joe pulled away. He had to be strong. Professional.

"I'm fine. Look, I have to get to OR 15. It's where I'm assigned."

Without turning back, he rushed out of the room, his hand covering his mask in case he couldn't control the bitter fluid rising in the back of his throat.

* * *

WHEN THE MECHANICAL DOORS opened into the ICU, Jacques De la Toure faced his head nurse, by no means a young woman, but still sensuous. Only weeks before she had helped him recapture his lost youth.

"Delia, where is Lourdes's father?" De la Toure asked.

"In the consultation room," she answered. "Do you want me to come with you?"

"Yes, that would be helpful."

"We heard she barely came off pump."

De la Toure didn't respond. As he walked, he felt Delia's hand gently grasp his elbow, guiding him past the waiting area where the families congregated. He avoided eye contact with anyone.

Stopping outside the closed door to the consultation room, Delia turned to face him. "You remember that Raúl Sanchez works as an orderly here in the ICU?"

"Yes, I know Raúl," De la Toure said.

"And with him is Dr. Morales's mother, Lupe. She works in the hospital, too."

"I know her, but I didn't realize she would be here."

"They're cousins," Delia said. "Raúl is the reason Lupe got her job here. Years ago, when I was a student nurse."

"I remember when he brought Lourdes to me to consider for surgery."

"Yes. Raúl and his wife took care of her and since Raúl's wife died, they've been very close."

Delia pulled open the door, but De la Toure paused at the entrance. He detested this place. He'd complained so much about the industrial, cold space that one week ago his wife Susan marshaled the auxiliary to perform a complete, while-you-were-out makeover. They accomplished a luxuriant transformation, but the antique Persian rug and the Mary Cassatt reproduction failed to soften the space. Neither did the faux-stucco walls with trompe l'oeil accents diminish the distress of the messages to be delivered here.

For years, De la Toure came to this tiny space, not much larger than a modern Catholic confessional, to convey unpleasant news, and these last weeks he had to offer apologies for results that he couldn't explain. He admitted his failures, but there was no reconciliation. He never left feeling forgiven or renewed, and he expected today to be no different.

De la Toure felt Delia's firm hand in the hollow of his back, as if to push him across the threshold. The family conference couldn't be avoided.

Inside, he found the couple huddled in the center of the settee, a mauve, velvet Queen Anne sofa with curved cherry legs. The two squeezed in tightly, as if to draw comfort from their closeness, to form a shield against the anticipated storm. They sat underneath a copy of Cassatt's Two Children at the Seashore. His wife knew how much he admired the impressionist who renounced a privileged existence in America for a lifetime of study in Europe. For a moment, he relished the copy of the lush oil work that hung in the National Gallery of Art. This reproduction captured the strong brush strokes, vivid hues, and lustrous light of the original.

On the canvas, two girls played in the sand. In the background, a sailboat floated on calm water. Serene. De la Toure could almost smell the salt in the air, as if the tears of the many families that sat here blended to form the fragrance of a Galveston beach.

From behind, Delia cleared her throat, bringing De la Toure back to the reality of his mission. He wondered how long he'd stood entranced in front of this pair, their bodies interlocked, the terror in Raúl's eyes reflected in those of Lupe's. And then they turned to him. He held their gaze for only a moment before looking down. At their feet, the vivid pigments and the stylized design of the wool rug seemed inappropriate. Maybe it would have been best to leave the room with its linoleum floor and vinyl-upholstered furniture. Before, there was no misrepresentation.

De la Toure moved between the two wing chairs positioned at the carpet's perimeter and sat on the front edge of the one closest to Raúl. De la Toure leaned forward, cupping his hands on Raúl's knee, and looked straight into the desperate eyes.

"Raúl—."

"Mi preciosa, she is dead?"

"No. Lourdes isn't dead."

"Gracias a Dios."

"Gracias a la Virgen," Lupe said.

"Sí, tomorrow is her special day," Raúl explained to De la Toure and Delia. "The feast of the Immaculate Conception. The

Inmaculada will protect my innocent one." Lupe put her arm around Raúl and they both cried.

De la Toure waited for them to regain composure. He still had bad news to deliver. He cleared his throat to gain their attention.

"But she is critical. I do not know if she will survive."

"What happened to my little girl? You told me not to worry."

De la Toure felt Delia's reassuring hand on his shoulder. Her scent sparked a wave of memories. He recalled the way she rejuvenated him at this point in his life—the time when children leave home and husbands look at wives and feel old, used, wasted. His Susan was everything he wanted in a wife and mother, but Delia was everything he wanted in a woman and lover. Even now, she made him feel invincible. He could handle this.

"Raúl, any time in cardiovascular surgery—."

"But you said she had a good heart. Just a little hole inside, and you would fix it."

"Yes, and I did, but when we tried taking her off the bypass machine, she began to have difficulty."

"I do not understand."

Delia gently massaged the surgeon's shoulder, and he drew a deep breath. How could he explain a procedure that took years to learn? Moreover, how could he explain a complication that he himself didn't understand? Here was another patient with unexpected, unrelenting V-tach. How many had there been this last month? Too many.

"Raúl, it is very complicated. Lourdes developed a dangerous heart rhythm—."

"She will live, no?"

"I don't know. She is requiring a large amount of support: pacemaker, ventilator, and an excessive amount of vasopressive drugs."

Raúl nodded, but De la Toure wondered if this simple man understood the precarious nature of his daughter's condition.

"So, she's just like my wife was." A wave of hopelessness flooded Raúl's face. "Only the machines keep her alive?"

"In a manner, Raúl."

CHAPTER TWO

FIVE DAYS LATER, DECEMBER 12, THE LATINO community celebrated the feast of Our Lady of Guadalupe. Joe wanted to join his mother at church, but first he needed to check on Lourdes.

Hours before sunrise, he entered the rear stairwell of the Houston Heart Institute and climbed the pockmarked concrete steps to the second-floor landing. Soggy, pungent air filled his lungs. Drops of condensation spotted the surface of the industrial door that opened into the ICU. He reached for the metal handle and recoiled at the gritty sensation that shot through his palm and bolted up his arm. He returned his hand to the stainless-steel ball, worn from years of use, twisted the knob, and shoved the heavy door open.

Inside, like Dorothy in the Land of Oz, Joe found a new world—bright, modern, immaculate. Leaving behind the cold, humid, Houston air, he encountered the unnaturally clean and odorless atmosphere of the ICU.

In these predawn hours of the graveyard shift, the back patient bay of the ICU, the section for "long-termers" was quiet. Except for the patients, the space was deserted. He saw a bald-headed male in scrubs at the secretary's desk and assumed he was the nurse for this section. He probably had briefly stepped away, but it irritated Joe that no one was watching Lourdes. These patients were all stable, here for the long haul, on autopilot, but they—including Lourdes—needed attention. Lourdes deserved the best of care. She wasn't just another deadhead going nowhere. She was . . . she was special.

Joe moved to Lourdes's bed, alone with her except for the five other patients in this open ward, all on ventilators, oblivious to the world around them. Not even their individual curtains had been drawn to offer the illusion of privacy. At each bed, air flowed in and out of the respirators. Like a scene from the movie Coma with bodies suspended in animation. Cold, calm, motionless.

He could have been in the morgue except for the discordant beeping from the monitors, like back-up warnings from nine dump trucks, all headed for him, ready to roll over his body. He wanted to shout at them, "Stop!"

Joe looked down at his cousin, his friend. The word friend seemed so inadequate to describe their relationship. No one else in the world understood his origins. No one else appreciated his need to reinvent himself. When he'd chosen an Anglo wife, she negotiated for him with his mother. He married in the Church but absent the mariachis and the lasso ceremony. She accepted not only who he was, but also who he wanted to become. Unlike his mother, she didn't feel rejected as he attempted to move up in society.

"I'm here, Lourdes," he whispered. "We're all praying for you." Yet he wasn't. He didn't believe in the power of prayer. How simple if the Virgin would appear next to them, and he could ask her to save his cousin, but she wouldn't and he couldn't. He relied on science. Unfortunately, Lourdes hadn't fared well under his guidance.

Joe kissed her forehead, but Lourdes lay motionless, the distinction between life and death obscured. Vercuronium, a paralyzing medication, prevented her from fighting the ventilator. An endotracheal tube in her windpipe was securely taped to her mouth. Its flexible hose connected the clear plastic tube to the breathing machine. Bottles of intravenous fluid were connected to her arms via a number of thin plastic lines. Cables came from everywhere. Wires and tubing tangled like spaghetti. Lourdes's face had swollen to the size of a basketball. It was not the face of the former princess of the festival of Bellas Artes.

Then, she walked down the staircase in a long, black-velvet gown with a rhinestone tiara that held her hair back to frame exquisite features. His little cousin had matured into a young lady. She took Joe's breath away when she smiled and looked at him with those deep, dark eyes.

Now her eyelids were taped closed for protection. She couldn't even blink on her own. Her arms were marred by bruises, the work of needles with which nurses had jabbed her during the last five days. The glistening skin covering her swollen hands and feet stretched taut with blisters starting to form. Their color, a marbleized purple and blue.

Every six seconds, the girl's chest moved, thanks to the ventilator. On the monitor a sharp spike preceded each electrocardiogram complex, thanks to the pacemaker. Underneath the EKG readout, the arterial tracing indicated her blood pressure to be normal, thanks to the medications dripping into her veins.

This semblance of life was a grotesque tribute to modern technology. Lourdes looked like her mother did when she lay in the ICU suffering from gallstone pancreatitis. Raúl wanted every possible intervention and the surgeons had operated on her seven different times. In the end, her mother's body bloated beyond recognition. At

Lourdes's insistence, Raúl agreed to give the do-not-resuscitate order. But his wife didn't die until after many more days of torture. Now, Raúl had agreed to the DNR status for his daughter. And again, the patient hadn't cooperated. This semblance of life would not yield.

* * *

TWO MILES AWAY, JOE pulled into the driveway that circled in front of St. Anne's, the mission-style church and school that commanded the corner of Shepherd Street and Westheimer Boulevard. To the west stretched River Oaks, a bastion of the rich. To the east, an eclectic neighborhood with a number of Latinos, many here without documents. This dichotomy typified Houston, a city that both prospered and suffered from the effects of unbridled growth without zoning limitations. Ten-million-dollar mansions and adult bookstores stood within a few blocks of each other.

Inside this sanctuary, Houston's wealthiest worshipped side-by-side with those whose only assets were determination and desire. His mother had worked nights at the school in lieu of paying his tuition, and each day she taught him a new word from the S.A.T. prep list, words she could neither define nor pronounce, but Joe could memorize every one.

In the outside courtyard, hundreds gathered for las mañanitas, the predawn celebration of the feast day of Our Lady of Guadalupe. They sang to the Virgencita. In the cold, wet, December air, their words were made visible by the light from the candles they each cupped in their hands.

Zipping up his windbreaker to hide his scrub top with its Heart Institute logo, Joe waded through the crowd. His mother's height measured less than five feet but thanks to a father he'd never met, he stood almost six feet tall and he towered over the mass of short, dark-skinned people—men in denim and work boots, women in servant uniforms, and children of every age darting in and out. The familiar smell of working people pervaded the crisp, morning air. The mellow tones of their voices comforted the many babies wrapped in bright-colored blankets, snuggled against their mothers' breasts.

At the entrance to the building, Joe struggled to open the heavy rustic door. He stepped over the threshold onto the hard Saltillo-tile floor of the vestibule and let the door close behind him.

Blackness enveloped him. Blindly, he moved forward, and his outstretched fingertips found the lead grouting of the stained glass inset into the doors leading inside. His fingers read from left to right until they reached the wooden frame, and then they moved down to the brass door handle.

Inside, exit signs provided soft red light that extended only to the first stone columns supporting the vaulted roof. Along the walls, arched voids in the stucco replaced the multicolored windows, obscured by darkness. At the end of the center aisle, a single candle burned in the sanctuary lamp. The amber flame danced with its reflection in the gilded tabernacle.

Joe stopped at the third pew from the rear, genuflected, and thoughtlessly made the sign of the cross, bringing his right thumb to his lips, a substitution for kissing the crucifix of a rosary he no longer carried. He knelt next to a middle-aged woman with a brown complexion and prominent bone structure visible beneath plump cheeks. She wore a freshly ironed, sky-blue uniform, the skirt stretched at the waist by her generous hips. He imagined her mind was filled with thoughts of gratitude to the Virgin Mary and with petitions for assistance.

Joe leaned down, placed his arm around the woman's shoulder, and kissed her cheek. "Buenos días, Mamá."

She turned to him. "Thank you for coming, mi corazón," she whispered.

"Mamá, I got to first assist Dr. Carlisle on a heart."

"That's nice, José," she said softly.

"It was great. The cardiac surgery fellowship with De la Toure is as good as—."

"Shhh," she said, bringing her index finger to her pursed lips.

"Mamá—."

"Shhh," she repeated. "You tell me after Mass."

Joe sat back in the pew. As his eyes grew accustomed to the darkness, he could perceive the baldacchino, four, twenty-foot-tall pillars that supported an intricately carved marble canopy over the tabernacle, and he could see the outlines of a framed image hanging from the two rear columns.

Joe shivered as a gust of cold wind swept by, accompanying other early arrivals who were escaping from the elements. To make space, Joe and Lupe scooted down the well-worn wooden pew.

Joe watched as Lupe returned to her prayers. He doubted he believed in the Roman Catholic Church anymore, doubted he believed in anything. After all, he graduated from Rice University, founded by an atheist when being an atheist wasn't fashionable. Having majored in biochemistry, he understood the theories of evolution and the origin of the universe. There was no need to bring God into the picture. Yet here he knelt, surrounded by a group of poor, uneducated Latinos who gathered to celebrate the feast day of Our Lady of Guadalupe, the dark-skinned Virgin Mary, their protectress. In Joe's mind, the emphasis was on "their." He felt little community with these people.

Joe's thoughts were interrupted by the arrival of Raúl Sanchez. The short, stocky man, like Joe's mother, also came dressed in hospital garb. It seemed to Joe that Latinos cleaned the whole city. He glanced at his own surgical scrubs. How many times had he been misidentified as an orderly?

Joe looked toward Raúl for an acknowledgment but found only a vacant face with swollen eyelids barely open.

Raúl knelt and bowed low, burying his face in his open palms, muffling faint sobs. "Mi preciosa . . . ¡Qué horror! . . . that face. O, Dios mío. Dios mío. Por favor. . . ." His mutterings continued, indistinct amid his tears.

Joe tried not to listen, not wanting to share in such immense grief. Yet the frost of the damp, dark morning penetrated to his core and sadness covered him like a shroud. Joe felt the bone-cold air from outside as the doors were opened wide for the procession of worshippers to assemble inside. Fortunately, the wave of chill dissipated with the arrival of the crowd. The familiar sounds of Spanish hymns now filled the cavernous space, and the golden glow of candlelight illuminated the rear of the church. The smell of burning wax mixed with that of incense and rose to the ceiling. His mother believed that prayers rise with the smoke to heaven. Joe turned to view the gathering crowd. Down the pew, Raúl raised his head from his hands and looked toward the altar.

"O Virgencita, mi Virgencita," Raúl pleaded.

Suddenly, Raúl stood. He kicked up the kneeler but it bounced off the wooden stop and clanked on the tile floor.

"I can't stay here," he said to no one in particular as he moved into the aisle, jerking his head from side to side, a series of staccato no's. "Basta! Enough." Pushing his way past the celebrants waiting to start the worship service, he exited the church.

Lupe slowly shook her head as Raúl left and then returned her focus to the altar. Joe knew she prayed for both Lourdes and Raúl. As a young adult, his mother had been the beneficiary of new technology. De la Toure had closed a congenital heart defect, enabling her to lead a normal life. Now, Raúl's daughter seemed to be just beyond the reach of technology's ever-expanding scope, languishing in the ICU.

Mass began. From the rear of the church, a legion of priests and altar servers led the crowd of believers, the decorated appliqué of the priests' garments contrasting with the simple black-and-white dress of the altar servers. Each member of the procession carried a large votive candle to place in the sanctuary. Their luminaries covered the altar and overflowed onto the marble floor.

The entire apse glowed, revealing a large portrait of Our Lady of Guadalupe as she appeared to the Aztec Juan Diego in the hills outside modern-day Mexico City. Juan pleaded with her to cure his uncle. The Lady answered Juan in his native language: "Do not worry, my little child. Put it in your heart."

She instructed him to gather roses from a frost-covered mountain top and she arranged them in his tilma, a cactus-fiber poncho, to take to Bishop Zumárraga. As Juan stood in front of the cleric, the flowers fell to the floor revealing the miraculous image of the Virgin imprinted on the fabric of his cloak.

Joe stared at the sacred figure hanging from the two rear columns of the baldacchino, a reproduction of the image magically imprinted on the coarse material that had cloaked a poor peasant. The Aztec Virgin, clothed by the sun, looked down on her children. Without thinking, Joe joined his mother and the rest of the congregation in a prayer from his childhood.

"Santa María, Madre de Dios . . ."

His mother taught him that English was the language of science and education. To be successful, you became proficient in English, but when you prayed, you prayed in Spanish, the language of love.

Like the hundreds of other Latinos gathered in St. Anne's and the millions who kneeled in churches throughout the Americas, Joe prayed to Mary. He just wasn't sure why.

CHAPTER THREE

THE RINGING OF THE TELEPHONE SHATTERED THE early morning silence. With reflexes not yet dulled by his sixty-two years, Jacques De la Toure turned in his bed and grabbed the receiver from its cradle before it finished its first ring. His wife, Susan, rolled over, pulling her pillow over her head, a response conditioned by the perpetual intrusion of these middle-of-the-night calls. As De la Toure brought the receiver to his ear, he glanced at the digital clock. The phosphorescent numbers read 5:30. Good news never arrived at this hour.

"Hello." He sat upright in his bed, trying to mask the sleepy tone of his voice.

"Dr. De la Toure? This is Dr. Keith, Matt Keith."

"I know who you are, Matt. What is it?"

"Well, sir, I had to call you. I mean, Dr. Masters told me, she said to let you know this morning. You would have to—."

"What is going on?"

The phone was silent. De la Toure wasn't sure he was still connected to the ICU resident, but finally, Matt began. "The monsignor, well, after his bypass surgery . . ."

The short minute of pause seemed to stretch without limit.

"Get on with it," De la Toure said, but he didn't really want to hear the news about Father Francis. His friend, the Very Reverend Sean Francis O'Malley, had been on the fast track to bishop. He'd been dispatched to Rome where he'd earned a licentiate in canon law and upon his return to Houston he'd been appointed chancellor of the archdiocese and made monsignor. Fr. Francis moved in the best circles and was widely sought after for elite dinner parties and galas. But he loved all people. And it'd been no surprise, to De la Toure at least, when he left the chancery to launch Casa de Niños, ministering to undocumented families.

"I said 'continue.' "

"Yes, sir. The monsignor came out about four this afternoon. As you know, he was having a lot of irregular heart rhythms, a bunch of ventricular ectopy, and some short runs of V-tach. . . ."

Another pause. De la Toure wanted to prod the resident again, but his better judgment convinced him to wait. The kid was having enough trouble getting his words out, and the words like a vise gripped De la Toure's chest.

Matt continued his speech like he was reading from cue cards. "He started doing it again last night. I put him on everything. I mean, I contacted the faculty associate on call, Dr. Masters, and the cardiologist, Dr. Sufi. I did exactly what they said, but he kept having more ectopy. I . . . I mean, they had him on lidocaine, procainamide, and Amiodarone, but he kept with the PVCs, then V-tach. Like bam, no blood pressure."

De la Toure breathed deeply into the phone. His body sagged. The vise tightened, squeezing the air from his chest.

"I cardioverted him twenty, maybe fifty times. He came out of it with each shock, but then, he just went right back. I checked all his labs, but I couldn't keep him out of V-tach."

As the resident rambled, De la Toure replayed the case in his mind. Yesterday, Father Francis had been admitted with a heart attack and Sufi, the cardiologist, had pushed De la Toure to operate emergently. De la Toure should have known it would've been better to wait a few days. Unfortunately, he'd followed Suif's advice. Then, during surgery, the patient displayed every possible malignant rhythm, a virtual smorgasbord of deadly ventricular ectopy. Lately, all his patients seemed caught in this V-tach twilight zone. Unbelievable, yet all too real.

Matt continued talking as De la Toure struggled to listen to the words.

"Then, his arterial line went flat and I started CPR. Finally, even with chest compression, I couldn't produce any pulse, and he passed on."

"Excuse me?" De la Toure asked.

"He expired." Matt's voice was nearly inaudible.

"Are you telling me he's dead?"

"Yes, sir."

Monday morning, the week had not yet begun, but it had already delivered its first death.

As De la Toure put down the phone, a now-familiar discomfort settled in his left side. He opened the top drawer of the bachelor's chest next to his bed and took out a vial of pills. He placed one under his tongue, and the tightness began to subside.

* * *

JOE STOOD IN A SECOND-FLOOR hallway of the Houston Heart Institute, his hand poised over the metal disc that opened the electric doors leading into the ICU.

The ubiquitous Gulf Coast fog had rolled in and over him. More than two weeks had passed since Lourdes's death on the feast day of Our Lady of Guadalupe. And Joe wanted to leave the sadness, but a relentless undertow held him in the depths of despair. Christmas came and went with little joy. Not even the time spent with his wife and son offered reprieve from the grief and guilt. As through osmosis, an overwhelming melancholy seeped in through the pores of his skin and filled his body. He couldn't get past the sense of impending doom.

Lourdes was dead and he couldn't change that. He had to move forward. He owed it to his wife and child. Joaquín had his whole life in front of him, and it would be glorious. Joe would succeed in medicine, provide his wife with all the luxury she deserved, and from his prominent position on society's ladder, he would propel his son to the highest rung. It was his duty.

Joe shook his body like an animal emerging from a sudden thunderstorm, having been unexpectedly caught without shelter. He swallowed hard and smacked the metal plate. After the doors opened, he stepped up to the front desk of the ICU.

"Morning, Lakisha," he said to the night-shift administrative assistant. "You feeling better?" He flashed a toothy smile. If he didn't feel happy, he could act.

"Yeah. Just a little bit of the sniffles left."

Joe leaned over the counter. "Well, you look really fine."

Lakisha's grin stretched from ear to ear, and dimples appeared in her rounded cheeks. Joe imagined she didn't hear compliments often, and he tried to be nicest to those who needed it the most, especially when there wasn't any benefit to him.

"And where's young Dr. Keith this morning?" Joe asked, inquiring about his former college roommate.

"Back in the unit," she said. Lakisha looked away.

"Did he have a rough night?"

She slowly turned her head back to Joe and leaned forward in conspiratorial fashion. "You got to help him, Dr. Morales. He's at the edge." Abruptly, Lakisha turned from Joe. "Good morning, Dr. Masters."

Joe turned to see De la Toure's other senior associate approach. Her long, russet hair was pulled back, framing a plain but attractive face—green eyes, freckled cheeks, and thin, salmon-pink lips. Her open lab coat revealed a gingham blouse and a mid-calf denim skirt that topped red, loose-fitting boots.

"Howdy, Lakisha. Joe, your son is sure getting big."

"Thanks. But when did you see him?"

"Yesterday. Your wife brought him. Elizabeth and I needed to talk about her getting back to work, so I told her to bring Joaquín along."

"I don't think she's ready to go back. Not yet."

"We'll see. I'm getting ready to send off the cardioplegia grant proposal, and I need her help." Masters turned back to the front desk. "Lakisha, where's Dr. Keith?"

"In the back. Want me to page him?"

"No, I'll find him," she said as she walked away.

He hoped she wouldn't be too hard on his friend.

As the electronic doors leading from the operating suites opened, the crisp cadence of leather-soled shoes announced Dr. Carlisle's entrance. Joe turned to see De la Toure's favored assistant, a virile doctor straight from the set of General Hospital. He wore a navy, pinstriped suit, cut to accentuate his broad shoulders and narrow waist. The sporty scent of cologne preceded him. Joe stood up straight, consciously sucked in his gut, and expanded his chest against his buttoned lab coat. He looked at Carlisle, ready for any instruction.

"Good morning, Joe, Lakisha. Where's Keith?"

"He's in the unit with Dr. Masters," Lakisha said.

"Good. Joe, I need you for a moment."

Without waiting for a response, Carlisle spun around and headed back toward the surgical suites. Joe knew he had to follow. The doors closed, separating the men from Lakisha and the unit. Carlisle and Joe were alone in the front hall outside the operating rooms.

"Joe, Dr. De la Toure has decided to assign you to the ICU. In fact, you start tomorrow."

"What about Matt's other month?"

"He had another month but Dr. De la Toure is moving him to surgical pathology."

Poor Matt, he'll be devastated, Joe thought. "But tomorrow's New Year's Eve and I wasn't supposed to start the unit until April. Our baby's only two months old, and Matt is a good resident."

"Joe, I know you want the cardiac fellowship position. And when Dr. De la Toure makes a decision . . ."

Joe had no choice. "Yes, sir. I'll tell my wife."

"Good. You may take today off to get ready."

"Thanks, but I'm down to first assist Dr. De la Toure. I've been looking forward to it."

"Do what you want, but be ready in the morning." Carlisle headed down the corridor to the men's lockers.

The unit was a 24/7 assignment necessitating living inside the ICU. It was the one rotation that put the resident front and center. Joe knew that De la Toure based his cardiac fellow selection on a resident's ICU performance. Surgical skill was important, but patient care was paramount.

Joe turned back toward the unit, wondering whether anyone had told Matt about his banishment to pathology. Joe sure didn't want to be the messenger. Matt was Joe's friend, but if he had screwed up,

R. B. O'GORMAN

Joe had to step up to the plate. Only one resident each year would get the cardiovascular spot with the old man. If it wasn't to be Matt, it had to be Joe.

* * *

AS THE DOORS OPENED again, Joe found Matt at the front of the unit, his unkempt hair transformed into that of a Rastafarian, his trademark mustache and soul patch lost in an overgrowth of facial hair, his lab coat stained with coffee and God-knows-what, his upright posture maintained only by the support of the desk. It would be compassionate to end this misery.

"You look like hell," Joe said in what he hoped was a lighthearted tone. "Worse than after our all-nighter studying for the biochemistry final."

"Yo, man, you're looking good, too."

"Seriously, Matt. Are you all right?"

"Yeah, fine. I was up with the monsignor until three. Then, he died and Masters said for me to call De la Toure. Isn't that a piece of crap? Anyway, I spent the next two hours thinking of some way to break the news to the old man, and still sounded like a total fool."

"Hey, I'm sorry. But there isn't any easy way to tell him one of the VIPs croaked. It's not like you killed him."

"Come on, Joe. You know that everything that happens in this unit is my responsibility."

"Matt, every unit resident has his deaths. It's expected. This is heart surgery."

"No one has had problems like I've had this month. For patients coming out of the OR, there's been an epidemic of V-tach. Remember your friend Lourdes? She stabilized from the V-tach, but then she couldn't hold on."

"Yeah. Thanks for the memory."

"Sorry. I didn't mean . . . but there's been a bunch like her; they've been dropping like flies. Delia did a quality assurance audit, and she told De la Toure that I was responsible for the deaths."

Joe hadn't appreciated the magnitude of the problem, but as Matt talked, he realized there had been an excess of complications on Matt's watch. As surgeons, you grew used to death. It was unavoidable despite your best efforts. Sometimes, the deaths grouped together, but they still weren't anyone's fault. Yet Delia found that errors had been made and that Matt had made them.

Mistakes couldn't be tolerated. For the first time since Lourdes's death, Joe wondered if it had been Matt's screw-up. Had his friend's incompetence caused her demise? If so, maybe he deserved to be fired. Although Lourdes almost died on the OR table and was critically ill coming out of surgery, she'd been rock stable for four days. She would have recovered if Matt had been watching. The resident can't leave everything to the nurses. He has to be checking the labs, looking at the x-rays, examining the patient.

If only Joe had been taking care of her, she might have survived. He should have been watching more closely. She'd trusted him, and he'd failed her.

"Joe, you hear me? There's been an epidemic of V-tach."

Joe mumbled a response, not agreeing with Matt, but at least indicating he was listening. Matt continued.

"Something is seriously wrong in this unit, and contrary to popular opinion, it's not me. Someone's trying to sabotage me. Or maybe it's like that nurse who was killing patients for the rush."

"Come on, Matt."

"Joe, I mean it. It's not paranoia when they are out to get you. Everyone blames me—De la Toure, the faculty, the nurses, and even our fine, fellow residents. If I'm out, there's less competition for the cardiac spot." Matt laid a heavy hand on Joe's shoulder. "At least I can count on you."

Joe coughed into his fist. "What happened with the monsignor?"

"I don't know. He came out in trouble and stayed that way. I did everything possible, by the book. At least he died with good blood gases and normal labs. What more could I do? I'm only the resident."

Dr. Mohamed Sufi and Dr. Katrina Masters approached from the ICU patient area, their conversation animated. The stilted English of the educated, Middle Easterner (a distant member of the Saudi royal family) clashed with the slow drawl of the unpretentious Texan. They turned the corner and approached the front desk. Sufi's impeccable continental attire contrasted with Masters's pea-shucking dress. As the attending physicians neared, Joe and Matt stood still and silent.

"These deaths jeopardize my referrals," Sufi said to Masters. "And the prince will be here next week. I can't allow, I mean we shouldn't have any complications. Maybe it's time for De la Toure to retire."

"Look, Mo, you better dance with the one that brung you."

"What is your meaning?"

"You wouldn't have any referrals if it weren't for the old man."

The mechanical sound of the automatic doors terminated all conversation. De la Toure entered, his six-foot frame covered by a long, blazingly white lab coat over pressed scrubs. His mere presence commanded undivided attention. De la Toure looked straight ahead.

"Where is the cardinal?"

Joe looked at the floor. Poor Matt. He had to lead the old man to talk with the cardinal; to tell him his protégé, the beloved monsignor, was dead.

CHAPTER FOUR

ON THE STRETCHER OUTSIDE OR 19, JOE FOUND A rotund man with a shock of snow-white hair.

"Mr. Duffey?" Joe picked up the OR check list and verified the patient name and procedure. "Mr. Thomas Duffey?"

"Yes, son. But you call me 'Pops.' Everyone calls me Pops." He smiled widely, but quickly brought his right hand to cover his toothless grin, probably embarrassed to be seen without his dentures.

"OK, Pops," Joe said with a chuckle, amused by the nickname. "Let me just check your wrist band." Joe pulled back the sheet to examine the hospital ID bracelet. He found Pop's left arm cradling a teddy bear, clothed in a pure white tunic with openings cut in the back to free the wings, and hanging by a ribbon from the neck, a homemade card. A couple of dozen crayon signatures accompanied the greeting, "Get well, Pops."

"Let me put this with your other belongings." Joe gently retrieved the angel from the patient. "I'll have him for you when you wake up."

As the nurses moved Pops inside, Joe went to the stainless steel sink to start the surgical scrub.

Perfect. He'd be assisting Dr. Jacques De la Toure.

Joe reached inside his shirt pocket and grasped a pill. The beta-blocker slowed his heart rate, but more importantly, it eliminated the intention tremor that plagued him. It was an old trick some surgeons used. It bothered him that he couldn't control his nerves without pharmacological assistance, yet he was happy he had a way to deal with them. He knew he had to be an expert technician like Carlisle, whose movements were as measured as a fine jeweler. When Carlisle sutured, the closure looked as precise as the work of a sewing machine. Even De la Toure, in his sixties, didn't shake as much as Joe. The old man knew how to steady his elbow on the patient, how to use myriad crutches to make up for advancing age. Joe knew he had to be as technically gifted as he was brilliant, and long ago, he'd decided to do whatever was necessary.

He popped the medicine in his mouth. Then, he selected a head covering from the variety of boxes on the shelf above the sink. Usually, women wore the bouffant style and most men used the classic cap, but Joe grabbed one of the disposable surgical hoods. Marie Coleman had warned him more than once that the regular cap didn't adequately cover his hair. He pulled on the blue paper helmet. The front came down over his forehead. The sides completely covered his ears. He brought the two straps under his chin, and wrapped them around his neck in a crisscross. Before he tied them, he pushed back some of the thick curly hair that cascaded over his ears. Now he had completely hidden his uncooperative mane. He knew he needed a haircut.

Next, Joe selected a surgical mask from the four choices. He preferred the style with a thin strip of adhesive that secured the mask to the nose, preventing the required protective glasses from fogging. Joe looked at his reflection in the stainless-steel front of the paper towel dispenser. Only his prized, deep-blue eyes roofed by thick eyebrows could be seen. Marie would probably tell him to trim his eyebrows next. She was a perfectionist. That's why De la Toure valued her. She served as his quality control when he was absent.

Satisfied, Joe slipped on plastic goggles and started the surgical scrub. With his left knee, he hit the plate marked WATER. Spray spewed from the spigot like an open fire hydrant, splashing against the walls of the sink and soaking the front of his shirt. He was such a klutz. Joe adjusted the flow. While he waited for the water to heat, he popped open the covering for one of the antibiotic scrub brushes.

As he washed his hands, he thought about all that needed to be done. He had to memorize the intensive care protocols, go over his heart rhythms, and review his drugs. He had only one day's notice to prepare for the most important assignment of his life thus far, but did he really have to study? He was the best resident in his group, at least second best. He'd be ready.

Yet there was no way around Elizabeth. She was going to be major ticked off, home with the baby for two months while he stayed every night in the hospital. He couldn't blame her, but she would have to understand.

Joe felt the heat coming up from the sink and looked down to see the steam. He adjusted the temperature control and began the five-minute ritual of the surgical scrub. Meticulously, he cleaned his fingernails and scrubbed his hands with the brush. The not-so-soft plastic bristles generated a pink glow even through his dark complexion. He scrubbed even harder.

"Howdy, Joe," Eric Cunningham, a fellow resident, said before Joe realized he was there, requiring Joe's attention. "Helping the old man today?"

"You got it."

Joe looked back down to the sink, ignoring the interruption, wanting it to go away. Eric was a frat-boy jock with natural good looks, athletic ability, intellect, and charm. His curly blond locks and bronzed skin reminded Joe of some Roman god. Indeed, Eric had always acquired everything he wanted, everything Joe wanted. Joe may have been smarter, but he was actually too intelligent, almost nerdy. Eric was perfect.

"Joe, you always get the sweet assignments. The rumor mill has it that you're starting in the ICU tomorrow."

"That's right."

"What is it with the unit residents, some kind of affirmative action program?"

"Very funny." Joe never understood why someone so naturally blessed had to put down others to feel good.

"Hey, lighten up. You had the second highest score on the in-service training exam, and now you'll be the guy who bails out the ICU after Matt Keith screwed it up. You'll have the cardiovascular spot for sure. I'll be lucky if the old man lets me red shirt a year and start after you."

Joe had always hoped he and Matt would earn back-to-back positions and then work together when they finished. Now, Matt had blown it. And Joe didn't relish the thought of a cardiovascular fellowship that consisted of working side-by-side with Eric.

"Look, I'd like to chat, but I have to get inside." Joe banged his knee against the metal sink, shutting off the water. He headed toward the operating suite, hands raised, dripping on the floor. At the OR door, he turned and used his backside to push it. With it halfway open, he paused and looked back at Eric, the rich, pretty-boy.

"For the record, you're the golden kid, the one who's protected. I wish my father-in-law was Dallas McClintock."

* * *

"CUT."

"Cut," De la Toure repeated.

Startled, Joe grabbed the Mayo scissors and prepared to cut the suture that De la Toure held outstretched. Joe had been so intent on watching the master that he'd forgotten his role as first assistant.

As Joe moved his hand toward the fine thread, he noticed that the tips of the scissors were shaking.

"Dr. Morales, can you help me without leaving the room?"

"Yes, sir. I was—." Joe used his left hand to steady his right and quickly cut the string.

"Marie, are we ready?" De la Toure asked.

"Yes, sir," his scrub tech answered.

"Good. Begin cardiopulmonary bypass."

"Up to flow," Chiu said from behind the heart-lung machine.

Allgood leaned over the drapes. "Everything's cool up here, Chief."

Joe watched as the blue, venous blood drained out of Pops. The heart-lung machine removed the carbon dioxide, added oxygen, and pumped the now-red, oxygen-rich blood back to the patient.

"Now Dr. Morales, what's the next step of the procedure?"

"Cardioplegia," Joe answered.

"Cardioplegia catheter," De la Toure said. Marie had the tube ready. As in each step of the operation, the exchange between nurse and surgeon was seamless. Joe admired the teamwork.

"What's the purpose of the cardioplegia?" De la Toure asked.

Joe waited a moment to compose his answer. "We have to stop the blood flow to the heart in order to work on the arteries, to by-pass the blockages, but that makes the heart ischemic. It exacerbates the problem we're here to fix. So, you've developed—."

"Dr. Morales, no surgeon operates in a vacuum. I have contributed extensively to the science of cardioplegia, but I didn't invent it. All physicians depend on the totality of acquired medical knowledge, beginning with Hippocrates."

"Yes, sir."

"Continue."

"The cardioplegia is a solution high in potassium, which stops the heart. That enables you to work on the arteries more easily. The solution is cold, which reduces the metabolic activity, and it contains oxygen to help the muscle. Thus, we minimize the damage of cutting off blood flow until we can get the grafts open to provide a new oxygen supply."

De la Toure didn't comment.

From behind his mask, Joe smiled. Even the old man couldn't improve on his answer.

De la Toure held out his hand and Marie placed the appropriate instrument in his open palm with a slight slap.

The operation proceeded. No music. No lawyer jokes. No hospital gossip. De la Toure limited conversation to necessary communication about the patient and the occasional quizzing of the residents.

De la Toure didn't tolerate an assistant who hadn't studied the procedure, because the surgeon wasn't simply a technician. The surgeon had to understand everything that occurred in his OR. The patient's life depended on it. Pops depended on it.

Joe thought of the signatures on the get-well card. The huge family waited outside, praying that this simple man would live. Hopefully, he wouldn't follow the path of Lourdes and the monsignor.

Joe watched as the cardioplegia infused and waited for the heart to still. But instead of peaceful quiet, a chaotic storm overwhelmed the heart muscle.

Poor Pops.

CHAPTER FIVE

JOE WAS EXHAUSTED AFTER THE EIGHT-HOUR HEART surgery, but at least Matt would have the evening to stabilize Pops before Joe started in the ICU the next morning. Joe jumped into the front seat of his wife's five-year-old, navy-and-Bondo Ford Taurus, a college graduation present from her practical father. The Fortune 500-CEO could easily have given her a Lexus.

Joe felt invigorated by the car's warmth, trapped from the sun. Adrenaline surged through his veins. Joe had catapulted to the top of De la Toure's list, a position that had eluded him.

Throughout high school, Joe had been at the head of his class, but when he joined Matt at Rice University, he'd slipped to the "we try harder" position. Joe recalled rushing back from the mailbox brandishing his early-acceptance letter from Baylor Medical School only to discover Matt had one hidden in a drawer for days. Matt was hoping that they could celebrate together. That's what best friends do. Yet someone always had to be first, and it was always Matt.

When Joe scored in the 90th percentile during his intern year, Matt landed a 93%, and last year, when Joe earned a 95%, Matt came through with a 97%. There'd been no stopping him. At least, they had the two highest scores among all thirty residents. Actually, Joe had hoped that Matt would get the CV spot, and that then, the old man would let Joe redshirt a year and follow Matt in the program. Now, though, Matt's snafu created an opening for Joe. He had to take advantage of this opportunity, but he couldn't deny the guilt that tugged at his conscience.

Leaving the medical center, Joe turned onto Main Street and circled around the Mecom fountain in front of Hotel Za Za. This philanthropic gesture of Stanley Mecom had placed his family's name prominently in front of their own property. Effective.

As he turned onto Montrose Boulevard, Joe pondered the culturally and ethnically diverse section of Houston that was his home. Some of the inhabitants were a little strange, but there were also regular folks, like Joe—students at Rice or at one of the medical schools or other yuppies. They just weren't upwardly mobile, yet.

Pulling into his apartment parking lot, Joe made plans for the evening. First, he'd take Elizabeth and Joaquín to IHOP for supper. Then, they'd head to the Galleria. Christmas decorations would still be in place, and Joaquín would enjoy the lights. After Joaquín went down for the night, Joe would read the ICU protocols that had been passed down from resident to resident through the years. The roughly ten typed pages contained the totality of information necessary to survive De la Toure's cardiac unit rotation.

Joe, though, would do more than survive. He would triumph.

He climbed out of his car, jogged to the entrance of his home, and swung open the door. There, he was met with an unusual silence.

He walked inside the small apartment. It didn't take long to ascertain that Elizabeth and Joaquín were gone. The front room served as living room, dining room, and kitchen. Joe had to take only a few steps into this room to scan the adjoining bedroom and see that it, too, was empty.

Although Elizabeth kept it immaculate, the apartment was small and old. A helpful arsonist could end its misery. Fortunately, Elizabeth's father didn't repossess all her belongings when she married a Latino. So, although they began life broke, they started their marriage with nice furniture and a reliable automobile. The furniture had fared better than the car, but Joe never claimed to be a great driver.

The mahogany bed that had belonged to Elizabeth's mother overwhelmed the bedroom. Each post of the bed's richly grained wood was exquisitely carved with a shell motif. Elizabeth stored the matching nightstands, with their delicate, inlaid wood surfaces, in the closet to make space for Joaquín's bed. Lourdes wanted Joe's son to rest in the crib her father had made. Raúl had carved each individual spindle and assembled the structure without the use of a single nail. The sides were decorated with bright colors—red, blue, green, and yellow—and finished with a heavy lacquer coat that glistened.

Thin gauze hung over the crib, forming a cloud of protection. It looked decidedly Mexican. There was nothing elegant or expensive about the structure, but it meant so much to Lourdes, and now Joe was glad that he'd accepted the gift.

Joe moved to Joaquín's bed and pushed the diaphanous material aside. He stared at the indentation his boy's body had left in the mattress. Elizabeth probably had taken the baby to the neighborhood grocery store, Richwood Food Market. She liked to visit with rainbow momma or the poet-physicist among others there that she found delightfully eccentric. Joe kidded her about the place's nickname, Freaky Foods. He expected she'd be back soon.

Joe fixed a bowl of Cheerios and sat down at the table with the Houston Chronicle for a leisurely examination of international events. Although he didn't care a lot about Syria or Crimea, successful doctors knew how to solve the world's problems, and Joe tried to stay abreast of current conservative thought. He resented the inference of others that he would be a Democrat based on his skin color.

When he was finished, Joe folded the paper and tossed it on the table. He tilted his cereal bowl to pool the liquid at the bottom and salvaged a last spoonful of milk spotted with a few Cheerios. He liked the sugar-saturated sweetness of these final drops. Then, he pushed the bowl away, and it clinked against the vase in the center of the table, filled with a spring bouquet from the market.

The flowers seemed out of place in December, but Elizabeth loved plants. Even when there weren't blooms in her patio garden, and although they couldn't afford the ten dollars, she insisted on fresh flowers. Someday, he'd toss ten dollars to the pencil man down the street, the bum that sat at the busy corner and begged for money, but who offered yellow, wooden pencils in exchange, as if that legitimized his activity. Someday, Elizabeth could have arrangements delivered daily from River Oaks Florist, but now they didn't have ten dollars—and definitely not to waste on luxuries.

Joe recalled the time he didn't make the fifth-grade field trip to the Texas capital, because of ten dollars he couldn't spare. He'd saved for the excursion; a quarter at a time, but his mother needed the money more. He heard her crying one night, because she couldn't afford her heart medicines. When the day came for the bus trip to Austin, he pretended to be ill, and from that day forward, Joe never wasted money again. Instead, he morphed into junior entrepreneur, selling his food at lunch and charging for homework help. Then, he'd slip the dollar bills, one or two at a time, into his mother's purse.

Now, Joe was determined that Joaquín would never want for anything. Never.

Where were they? It was almost 6:00, a little late to have Joaquín out. After all, it was December, and even in Houston it grew cold when the sun went down.

Joe decided to ride over to Freaky Foods. As he walked outside, he spotted his wife, wearing a shrimp-colored, cashmere sweater over tailored winter-white slacks. The top accentuated her new-mother body. Her short, straight, highlighted hair swung back and forth as she walked, pushing Joaquín in front of her. She wasn't carrying any packages and none hung from the handles of the stroller. As Elizabeth approached, she called out to him, her voice too loud, as always.

"Hi, sweetheart, I'm glad you're home early. We have to—."

"I've been here for more than an hour. I was worried."

"What?" Elizabeth signed as she spoke, tracing her right forefinger down her left palm. "Speak slowly. Did you say 'worried'?"

Joe moved closer, his face inches away from hers. He repeated his words slowly, enunciating clearly. "Where have you been? You didn't leave a note and I was worried." He moved his hands deliberately as he signed the words. When he made the sign for worry, he accentuated the feeling with facial expression.

"I took Joaquín to the doctor, and then, we went to Mass."

"You did what?" Joe stopped. It wasn't Elizabeth's fault that he resented the church, the symbol of a culture that he wanted to flee. He forced himself to relax the muscles in his arms that had signed the words so violently. He started again, slowly. "I mean, I wouldn't have guessed you would go to Mass."

"I want—."

She stopped in mid-sentence and leaned over the stroller. She tucked the blanket in around Joaquín's bottom and under his feet. He was cocooned to the point that only small eye slits were visible. Joe waited patiently. He knew she had something to say, but like always, he had to wait on her. When she was ready, she'd make eye contact again. Finally she looked up.

"I want to join the Church when we have Joaquín's baptism."

"Elizabeth, we haven't set a date for baptizing Joaquín. I can't believe you would consider becoming a Catholic without telling me."

"I married in the Catholic Church for you."

"For my mother."

"Same thing. I let you decide on the church."

"That's not fair. Your father wasn't coming to the wedding."

"My father was concerned about our different backgrounds."

"Concerned? He was furious that I'm Mexican, but maybe my mother had reservations about having a deaf daughter-in-law."

"Joe!" Elizabeth's face went completely blank, as if all feeling had been instantly sapped from her. For a moment she stood staring at him, immobilized by his words.

Why did he say something so cruel? He admired how much she'd accomplished despite her physical challenge, a Ph.D. in biochemistry at twenty-three. More importantly, he idolized her, and his mother loved Elizabeth like the daughter she never had. He would never want to hurt her feelings, but why would she join the Church?

Elizabeth maneuvered the stroller around him and moved rapidly to the door. Joe hesitated a second and then ran to catch up with her. He grabbed her shoulders and turned her around to face him. Her sparse mascara was smudged and black rivulets rained down from the corners of her eyes.

"I'm sorry," he said as he signed the word. "No llores, mi corazón. Please, don't cry. I don't know why I said that. You know my mother adores you. It's just the Church stuff gets me going, but if you want to become a Catholic, I guess it's no big deal."

Joe embraced his wife and gazed at his child below. "I guess one of us ought to be," he said, but only Joaquín could have heard him.

* * *

DE LA TOURE STOOD ALONE in the dimly lit, glass-and-stainless-steel reception area of the Lutheran Hospital administration offices. It was past 6:00, and the administrative assistants had all deserted.

A beam of light covered him, and then was extinguished by a man's shadow in the open doorway into the CEO's office. De la Toure looked to find Evan Hackett, impeccably dressed in a Brooks Brothers suit, standing as if at attention.

"Jacques, it was kind of you to make time for me. Please, come in," Hackett said.

Despite Hackett's hospitable tone, De la Toure felt as if he'd responded to a summons, an order from an inferior who failed to recognize the department chair's rank. Still, De la Toure followed the hospital president into the office.

"What do you want to discuss? Some more cost-cutting initiatives?"

Hackett didn't answer. He waited until De la Toure took a seat in one of the Louis XIV chairs flanking the desk. Then, he slowly walked behind the elegant Napoleonic writing table. The executive office was decorated in total discordance with the starkly modern, public areas of the hospital. Hackett pulled out the diminutive, wooden desk chair, and sat, his movement rigid and perpendicular. De la Toure waited with as much impatience as he could communicate through body language and audible breathing. He regretted his part in recruiting this pompous administrator with his Boston-educated arrogance.

Hackett leaned forward. "I want to discuss tonight's meeting with HealthTex."

De la Toure sat back, pushing his body into the elegant upholstery and gripping both chair arms. "What is there to discuss?" He braced for Hackett's rapid speech with its affected accent, intentionally dropping his r's and mimicking a Kennedy as much as possible.

"You know McClintock plans to launch an Accountable Care Organization that would integrate the insurance carrier, the hospital, and the physicians."

"Evan, stop right there. I know what an ACO is and I'm aware that HealthTex Insurance is working with Medicare to launch a demonstration project."

"Good. Then, we can count on your support."

"Absolutely not. I plan to attend the meeting tonight. I'm indebted to Dallas McClintock, but I will oppose any insurance plan that removes traditional fee-for-service."

"Wouldn't it be prudent to listen to the proposal with an open mind? Why are you so adamantly opposed?"

"If we're paid a fixed fee, like a salary, then there's no incentive to provide advanced care for our patients."

"Jacques, the hospital is in financial trouble."

"You're always complaining about finances, but we're having our busiest year ever."

"You may be having a good year. But we, Lutheran Hospital, lose money on every Medicare patient on whom you operate."

Hackett took off his designer glasses and tossed them on the desk. He may have thought it was his turn to demonstrate anger and frustration, but De la Toure wasn't impressed.

"That's not my problem," De la Toure said.

"Yes, it is. We can't continue to waste our resources on these hopeless cases. They don't do well—you're destroying our statistics—and they aren't cost-productive. As president of this institution, I have a fiscal responsibility—."

"And as a physician, I have a moral responsibility to my patients. I, and only I, will determine the care they receive."

"Excellent," Hackett said sarcastically. "You do that, Jacques. And I'll communicate to the rest of the medical staff that you're unwilling to work with the hospital, that you're sabotaging a lucrative contract. You may find that even the great Jacques De la Toure depends upon referrals."

De la Toure stood abruptly, pushing his chair back. Its rear legs caught on the plush carpet and fell backward. He stopped and stared at the overturned French antique, but then left.

He would not let this pencil pusher or some insurance executive destroy his institution.

CHAPTER SIX

JOE LOOKED AT THE RAINBOW OF BOYSENBERRY, strawberry, and maple syrup that remained on his plate. With his fork, he pushed around remnants of pancake as he searched for words to tell Elizabeth about the unit. Sometimes, she could be difficult, and he sensed this would be one of those times. How could he blame her?

Across the table, Elizabeth picked at a half-eaten Spanish omelet. Beside her, Joaquín slept soundly. She put her fork down and placed her hand gently on top of Joaquín.

"Joe, I took Joaquín to the pediatrician today."

"OK," he mumbled, marginally aware of what she'd said.

"She heard a murmur, and they did an ultrasound."

"What?" Joe put down his fork and sliced his right forefinger across his left hand. He looked straight at his wife. She could lip-read and her speech impediment was barely noticeable. Elizabeth had compensated for her hearing deficit. But when it was important, Joe spoke slowly, exaggerating the movements of his mouth and he signed the words whenever he could.

"What?" Joe said as he repeated the action with his hands that represented the word.

"Joaquín has a small hole between the pumping chambers of the heart."

Joe sat upright and placed both hands on the table. "A VSD?" he said out loud. Then he slowly, deliberately, used his right hand to finger spell. As he formed the middle letter, all his fingers squeezed tight against his palm, the clenched hand representing the letter S.

Elizabeth retreated into the vinyl-cushioned dining booth.

Joe pulled back. He hadn't intended the gesture to be aggressive. He signed the three letters again, this time keeping the fist S close to his body, the transition between each letter swift and smooth, almost a secret communication.

"Yes, a VSD. She said it isn't serious. It will probably close on its own. But—." Elizabeth choked on her words and had to stop talking. Gently, she stroked their son's cheek.

Joe felt his own emotions seesaw from anger to pity. He was irritated that some pediatrician had made a big deal out of a trivial murmur and had talked to Elizabeth without calling him first. He was a surgeon. And he knew a hell of a lot more about heart disease than some baby doctor. Yet here was Elizabeth's meltdown. Obviously, she was scared.

"Elizabeth, don't worry. These small VSDs always close." Joe feigned confidence and hoped his face didn't reveal his true concern. After all, his mother required heart surgery to repair her VSD, and Lourdes . . .

As Elizabeth fought to regain her composure, Joe patted her hand. Her eyes pleaded with him to make her worries disappear.

"I promise, Elizabeth." In fact, it probably was nothing serious, but Joe would call the pediatrician in the morning and arrange for his son to see a cardiologist, an expert.

"I pray you're right." She leaned over and kissed their baby.

Joe waited. Despite the problem with Joaquín, he had to tell her about the unit. Finally, she looked up and their eyes locked. "Elizabeth, I have some news, too."

"Did something happen? I'm sorry. I didn't know."

"No, it's not super bad. At least, not for me. In fact, I had a great day. I got to first-assist De la Toure."

"I guess all those practice knots tied to the chairs paid off." Her joke lightened the atmosphere and her sadness dissipated with the laughter.

"Yes. Technically I was OK, except I shook a little. But I totally nailed his cardioplegia question. I think the old man was impressed."

Elizabeth picked up her fork and started to take a small bite of egg laden with picante sauce, but Joe wasn't finished. He reached out and grabbed her hand, accidently knocking her fork onto the plate, splattering salsa. Elizabeth jumped, startled.

"I'm sorry," he said. "I have to tell you something else."

"Go ahead." She focused intently on his face, his lips.

He hesitated, but there was no choice except to blurt it out. "I start in the unit tomorrow."

"What did you say? You start in what unit?"

"The unit, the cardiac ICU. Matt's really screwed up and De la Toure is pulling him out, sending him to surgical pathology." Joe had to fingerspell pathology. He didn't know the sign.

He wasn't sure if Elizabeth could appreciate the seriousness of Matt's situation, but Joe had plenty to deal with on his own.

"Poor Matt," she said.

"Yes, he's devastated. But it's no picnic for me, either. I'm starting the ICU without any time to prepare."

"I guess this means no New Year's Eve party tomorrow night?"

"I'm afraid so. In fact, I'm stuck in the hospital for the next couple of months."

"What about our vacation?"

"We'll have to cancel it."

"Just like that?"

"Yes." He could read the disappointment in her eyes. "I'm sorry too, but what am I supposed to do? Tell De la Toure that I won't be starting his ICU rotation because we have to make an important trip to Cancun, a trip we really can't afford."

"Exactly. Tell him you have to spend a few days with your wife, your wife who loves and adores you, your wife who has supported you for the last four years."

"I wouldn't say your six-hundred-a-month research stipend has kept us in the lap of luxury, and your father sure hasn't helped."

Joe watched her start to boil, but then regain control. He could almost hear her counting to ten. Then, he knew she would speak to him in that familiar tone of superiority. She could manage her emotions, and he would have to agree with whatever she said. It would be so logical.

"Joe, I need the break. Dr. Masters has been generous with this maternity leave, but I can't ask her for more time off when you finally get your vacation. Or should I say *if* you get a vacation?"

"Masters thinks you're going back to the lab soon."

"She's asked me. I told her I'd think about it. We're at a critical point in the cardioplegia research."

"But you agreed to stay home with the baby, at least for three months, maybe even longer."

"And you promised me a vacation, the two of us alone. I don't care where we go."

"Come on. You know it's totally out of my control."

"I know."

There was nothing more to say, so they sat unmoving, unmoved, like cars entering the Gulf Freeway on a summer Friday afternoon.

There was no place to drive forward, and no way to go back. They each had only a huge desire to arrive at the destination.

Elizabeth picked at the eggs for another five minutes but didn't take a bite. Finally, she laid her fork down. Joe took her hand in his and gazed into her hazel eyes. He could almost see his reflection, like the image of Juan Diego said to be mirrored in the eyes of the Virgin imprinted on the sacred fabric.

"Amada mía," he said.

"I love you," she said. She turned to gaze on Joaquín, sleeping, oblivious to worldly concerns.

"I love you, too," he said to himself. In the end, she always yielded to his needs. She was truly without fault. He was so lucky.

She was brilliant with a career of her own, and she also supported him unfailingly. But, could she survive the next two months? Could they survive?

* * *

DE LA TOURE CLOSED HIS eyes and longed for a distant time when he lay on the beach with Susan as their children built sand castles. He was protector and provider. Invincible.

Her fingers would wrap around his and she'd gaze into his eyes. "Thank you," she'd told him a million times.

"Thank you," a female said. It wasn't his wife.

De la Toure opened his eyes to look at Cassatt's painted children playing on the seashore. Beneath the artwork sat Pops's family; Mrs. Duffey sandwiched by two of her six children, each son in Duffey uniform—grey slacks, navy blazer and Notre Dame tie.

"What?" De la Toure asked.

One of the daughters sitting in one of the wingback chairs turned to face him. "Mom said 'Thank you.' She wants you to know how much we appreciate your efforts. You operated all day on Pops, and you're still here late tonight. It's just that . . ." Her words faded into sobs.

"Eleanor, it's all right," Mrs. Duffey said. "Dr. De la Toure, we don't want Pops to suffer any longer."

"He's not."

"I know, but your nurse, Bo, told us they've shocked him more than twenty times. That's enough. We want you to give the DNR order. You can continue your medicines, leave him on the ventilator and that balloon pump device, but no more heroics." She looked around the room, pausing to make eye contact with each of her six children. "We've decided."

They all nodded in agreement. "It's final."

* * *

AFTER THE FAMILY LEFT the ICU, De la Toure waited for the electronic doors to close, leaving Delia alone with him in front of the ICU control desk.

"Dr. De la Toure? Are you OK?"

"I'm fine."

"You want me to put in the DNR order?" she asked.

"Yes. It's the family's decision, but he seems to be stabilizing. Continue all of the anti-arrhythmic medications. If we can get him through the night, he could still survive."

"I'll ask Dr. Sufi to stick around for a bit. And I'm going to stay all night. I don't trust Dr. Keith. I think he's out of his league. You have Dr. Morales starting in the morning. He should be an improvement."

"Thank you, Delia. I must attend a meeting tonight with Evan Hackett and Dallas McClintock."

"Of course, Jacques. My pleasure." She ran her free hand down his side, stopping to play with the cuff of his starched white coat sleeve. Then, she slipped her hand inside his.

He couldn't deny the spark her touch elicited, but he wasn't going to jeopardize his family. He grabbed her wrist and squeezed until she stopped. "Please, you know I decided, we decided, this can't continue. Don't call me Jacques anymore." He released her arm.

"Of course, Dr. De la Toure." Her fingers remained in contact with his clothing, barely touching him, testing him to see if he could feel her groomed nails running down his arm.

He searched for words to diffuse her desires and anger, yet maintain a working relationship. "You're a good friend."

"A friend? Is that what I am?"

"Delia, please. We've discussed this. Can you still work with me? I very much value you. I need you."

"Dr. De la Toure, I'm a professional."

"Good. We've got to get your unit under control."

"My unit?" She pulled back. Her head jerked up, tossing her thick black hair behind her, and her eyes widened. Her hands came up in front of her, the highly buffed nails extending toward him. This lioness would protect her cub.

"Yes. I'm disturbed about the deaths you've had in the ICU this last month."

"You mean the deaths you and your residents have had?"

"Delia, I am not trying to assign blame here."

"I know exactly what you're trying to do. And listen, Dr. Jacques De la Toure, you're not going to succeed. I've worked hard. My reputation, my life is tied up in this ICU."

"Delia, please. Truly, all I want to do is find solutions and we must be ready for the Saudi prince next week. The world's eyes will be focused on the Houston Heart Institute."

His words worked. She visibly calmed. "I understand, Jacques, Dr. De la Toure. I do. There's no question Dr. Keith is incompetent, but I have higher hopes for Dr. Morales."

"I agree," De la Toure said.

"Now with respect to the nursing staff," she said, "we meet every quality benchmark. We've adopted care plans specifically for the coronary bypass patients. I have total confidence in my staff, their training, and their dedication to patient care."

"Excellent. So, you'll keep tabs on Dr. Morales for me?"

* * *

JOE WOKE FOR THE FIFTH or sixth time. He'd lost count. Although it was still dark, it wouldn't be long until dawn. D-day, his day of destiny.

Joe slipped from under the covers, dressed quietly, and tiptoed to the crib in the corner next to the window. Joe gently lifted his boy and then sat in the rocking chair. The baby woke but didn't cry, content in his father's arms.

As they rocked, Joe admired his child. Fortunately, Joe was taller and lighter-skinned than his mother, and thanks to Elizabeth's Northern European contribution, Joaquín would pass for Anglo, except for his name that Lupe begged them to use. And Joaquín could hear. A series of ear infections, not genetics, had caused Elizabeth's deafness. And Joe wanted his boy to be perfect.

Joe had a theory about the order of things. Lupe, a widow with little money, had propelled him up society's ladder. She never expected anything less of him than success.

Joe took pride in his personal accomplishments, but he had even higher expectations for Joaquín. His son would go to St. John's, the exclusive Episcopal prep school in River Oaks. Then, Joaquín could attend the Ivy League school of his choice. Joe was convinced Joaquín could do anything or be anyone, and he knew that one day, Joaquín would be rich and prominent.

Joe leaned over, placing his ear over Joaquín's chest. If his child had a murmur, he couldn't hear it. Last night he listened with his stethoscope. Nothing. Doctors were always over testing.

Joaquín was perfect and would always be perfect.

He hoped.

As he returned his son to the crib, Elizabeth scrambled out of bed and moved to his side. Joe reached down and placed his right hand on the top of the boy's sleeping head. He started to trace a cross with his thumb. Many times he'd seen Lupe bless his son, but he stopped. It was a meaningless gesture.

"Don't forget me, Joaquín." Joe turned and gave Elizabeth a quick kiss on the cheek. "I'll send you an e-mail tonight."

Outside, Joe loaded his belongings: a two-week supply of clean scrubs and underwear, three boxes of reference materials, and a present from Elizabeth, a cardboard tube with a poster. She'd stayed up late getting his belongings ready while he studied the ICU protocols.

As he drove toward the Institute, a hint of sunrise penetrated the early morning darkness. Despite the hour, he felt great. The ultimate irony was that he felt best when driving to the hospital, refreshed after twelve hours at home with his wife and child.

Now he faced, they faced, the two-month, 24/7 survival test. Technically, he couldn't work more than eighty hours per week, and he was guaranteed one full day off out of every seven. So, at least on the books, he was allowed to take night-call from home, and he was off on the weekends. Yet from a practical standpoint, he would never leave the unit. No resident did. His performance would determine his future.

Joe took a detour through River Oaks, driving past magnificent homes set far back from the thoroughfare: Italian villas, French châteaux, and Georgian manors fronted by expansive manicured lawns and formal gardens. Joe marked the seasons by the changing floral selections, from tulips to daffodils, and then, from caladiums to chrysanthemums. Joe knew each residence required a crew of servants—maids, cooks, nannies, chauffeurs, and gardeners—many working without the benefit of legal documents. Dallas McClintock's mansion sat on a corner. According to the Chronicle, it took three caretakers to maintain the gardens and his godfather, Raúl, worked there part time supervising the roses in exchange for the use of the garage apartment. One day, Joe would own one of these homes. All the important people—except De la Toure—lived in River Oaks.

As he turned onto Rice Boulevard, he wondered why the old man remained in the neighborhood next to Joe's alma mater. The West University area was nice: stately yet modest two-story, ivy-covered colonials. It was a neighborhood extracted from a Northeastern college town, but it wasn't River Oaks. Your neighbors weren't senators or governors. You didn't live side-by-side with royalty and international socialites.

On the radio, the comic duo of Dan-the-Man and Jenna Jane told lawyer jokes. They paused for a commercial break and a good old boy drawled from the speaker in the dashboard.

"HealthTex, Texas's own health insurance organization. Texans helping Texans. Last year alone, under the leadership of Dallas McClintock, HealthTex saved over ten million dollars by helping fellow Texans avoid unnecessary, potentially dangerous surgery, a savings we've passed on to you in lower premiums. And now we're working with President Obama's Affordable Care Act to develop a demonstration project that will provide even better care for less money."

"Sure," Joe said sarcastically and pushed the search button. The next station played Tejano music. After the song, the deejay launched into a mix of English and Spanish.

Joe turned off the babble. Almost there, he was eager for the clarity and certainty that only science could offer.

CHAPTER SEVEN

JOE STOOD IN FRONT OF McCLINTOCK FOUNTAIN AT the entrance to the Houston Heart Institute, the white stone structure rising above the cascading water. At multiple levels, steel-and-glass corridors connected the institute to the patient tower of Lutheran Hospital. All around, buildings rose into the dense fog. It was a magnificent collection of hospitals, research labs, offices, and professional schools of every variety, the world-renowned Texas Medical Center. This creation, a new Zion, stood as a living monument to people such as Jacques De la Toure and Michael E. DeBakey.

Joe hesitated before entering the building. He felt the way he had on his first day of high school and before his first date. He recalled standing outside Raúl and Lourdes's apartment. She had arranged for him to escort her best friend to Bellas Artes on the night of Lourdes's presentation as princess. He'd known both of them all his life, but still, he was nervous.

Ridiculous. After the unit rotation, the cardiovascular surgery fellowship would be offered to Dr. Joe Morales, the brightest resident De la Toure ever had. One day, he would join the ranks of the great heart surgeons of the Texas Medical Center.

Joe approached the front entrance and scaled the marble steps two at a time. He charged through the glass doors and headed across the atrium. Administration had remodeled this facade to give the illusion of modernity and the three-story entrance looked like the reception area of a contemporary, five-star hotel. Around the perimeter, ivy draped the balconies. Geometric patterns of emerald and ruby marble marked conversation areas on the travertine floor, each one furnished with two Scandinavian love seats and four matching chairs. In the center of each pit, a block of steel served as the coffee table.

Joe walked around the waterfall that cascaded down the wall behind the front information desk and headed for the stairwell. He never took the elevator. It was a matter of discipline. Next to the time clock, an assembly of hospital employees waited in line. The staff could not clock in more than four minutes early without supervisor approval, Hackett's initiative to reduce overtime expenses.

Raúl waved to him from the group. "Buenos días, José."

"Good morning, Raúl," Joe said as he hurried away. Each time he saw Lourdes's father, he recalled the image of her rotting away. He stepped inside the stairwell and pushed the door back, fighting the hydraulic mechanism that slowed its closure. Raúl had been like a grandfather. He felt guilty running away, but he had to go to work. And first, he had to talk with Matt, even more difficult than facing Raúl. More guilt. He guessed it was part of his Catholic legacy. Yet he was not to blame, not for Lourdes's death and not for Matt's failure.

* * *

ON THE TOP FLOOR of the Houston Heart Institute, Jacques De la Toure sat alone in his private enclave. He leaned back in his executive chair, the plush leather cradling his head, and looked out the two walls of floor-to-ceiling windows. Rather, he attempted to look. The humidity was so thick that it seemed as if the whole building was shrouded in a heavy mist. Outside, lights from surrounding buildings diffused through the haze, refusing to be hid, fighting to come forth. Truth will always out itself.

But what was truth? Why had the art of surgery become so difficult?

It had been a terrible weekend that wouldn't stop. Saturday, he'd met with Masters, Sufi, Allgood, and Delia discussing ways to improve ICU care. Then, all day Sunday, he operated on his friend, Fr. Francis, and the monsignor died the next morning. Monday, Thomas Duffey turned out to be a worse case than he'd anticipated and then last night, after finally getting Duffey's rhythm under control, De la Toure had to meet with Hackett and McClintock to argue about money.

Surgery used to be fun. What happened?

De la Toure sat forward and swiveled his chair toward the opposite wall of photos, diplomas, and awards, the culmination of a distinguished career. Now it seemed as if everything could disintegrate, could evaporate under the glow of the morning sun.

But a new year had begun and he had a new resident for the ICU, a fresh start. It could work. All around Houston, people were talking about Fr. Francis's death, but after he repaired the prince's heart valve, his reputation would be restored, an international reputation.

Masters stepped into the doorway that opened in the middle of the wall, parting the expanse of De la Toure's personal tributes.

Allgood and Chiu followed behind her like children waiting for their mother to engage their father first. Instantly, he wished he'd closed the door.

"Uh, sir?" Masters spoke in a soft tone, unusual for her.

"Yes?" he said.

"Good morning," she responded, and Allgood and Chiu echoed as Masters led them inside. "We want to talk with you before we send off this grant application."

"Of course," he said. He took the manila folder from her. "The renewal for the NIH cardioplegia study? I'll be happy to review it for you."

"Katrina," Allgood said, his right shoulder pulsating. "Tell him."

Chiu took two baby steps back.

De la Toure wondered if it was some kind of ambush. Of course, he didn't have much to worry about from this crew. They were excellent doctors, highly valued members of his team, but they were utility players, not stars.

"Yes. Tell me, Katrina. What is this?"

"Well sir, it's not the renewal. We're still working on that application. Kim and John have finished their sections, and I've almost completed the summary, but . . . this isn't the renewal. It's a new application."

"For what?"

"It's a proposal we've developed to study immune response to narcotic anesthesia and the heart-lung machine."

"Katrina, we've discussed this innumerable times. We cannot diversify our research efforts. At least, not at this point in time."

"Why not?" She placed her hands on her hips.

De la Toure stood and walked from behind his desk. "Kim, John, thank you for coming, but I need to speak privately with Dr. Masters."

"Yes, sir," Chiu said, and she scurried out the door.

"No problem, Chief," Allgood said. He followed, seemingly eager to escape. De la Toure closed the door behind them.

"Jacques," Masters said before the latch clicked in place. "I need this and so do Chiu and Allgood. They need building up."

"Katrina, let me point out the obvious. Chiu has to accept that she will never perform surgery in the United States, and Dr. Allgood doesn't need any extra exposure to narcotics. As far as you're concerned, you already have a position as the director of cardioplegia research. You don't need another project."

"But you knew I planned to work on immune response to surgery. You were aware of my interests when you hired me."

"You're young. Your career is in its embryonic stage. Later, there will be ample time for tangents."

Masters gestured to the papers in his hand. "This isn't a tangent." She spoke slowly and emphatically. Freckles, now red blotches of anger, dotted her cheeks like sparks exploding from a Fourth of July pyrotechnics display.

"Katrina, for your own good . . ." He tossed the grant proposal into the trashcan behind his desk and sat again.

She glared at him with arms crossed over her chest. "Jacques, I spent weeks on that application."

"Now listen. You have to trust me. Tenure will be coming up soon, and if you're successful, you'll be the first female professor of cardiovascular surgery in the history of this medical school. The cardioplegia research is important to your future but even more so to our patients."

"Immune research has value. If I didn't have so many clinical responsibilities, I'd have more time in the lab. I could research both."

"You're correct. You do have extensive duties, but surgical procedures provide nearly 95% of the income for this department. That pays your salary and subsidizes the lab."

"Yes, it provides the money, but I do the work. No one acknowledges the extra hours I spend with the residents and working in the lab. I wrote, I mean, I worked with you on the last two grant proposals. Carlisle is no help."

"On the contrary. Victor is our largest producer."

"Yeah, he goes for volume so he can keep his place in River Oaks and drive a Ferrari to work."

"Katrina——." He started to talk but a python wrapped around his chest, cutting off his words.

She continued. "I have a Ph.D. I was inducted into the AOA Honor Medical Society, I'm a member of the Society for University Surgeons, and yet that Neanderthal looks down on me because I don't want to operate like some mindless drone on an assembly line."

"That's enough," he managed to squeeze out. He could feel the warmth in his own face that matched what he saw in his junior associate. The tightness in his chest moved up into his jaw. He closed his eyes and took a series of slow, deep breaths, waiting for the pain to subside.

"Jacques, you OK?"

He looked at Masters. "You will continue working on the current lab projects and you'll be in the OR every day and take your share of the ICU faculty call. Is that understood?"

"Yes, sir. Perfectly understood."

Masters spun around on one heel and bolted for the door, only to confront Victor Carlisle head on.

* * *

ON THE SECOND FLOOR, Joe walked down the ICU front corridor to the resident's quarters, an eight-by-ten-foot cubicle furnished with a bed and metal desk that were appropriate for a military barracks or a prison cell. In one corner, a porcelain sink was mounted on the wall with an industrial mirror hung over it. Bare, white walls and a gray linoleum floor greeted him. It was an unadorned, colorless box, one of those rooms in which, after the door closed, there appeared to be no exit.

Joe found Matt stretched out on a thin, stripped mattress, stained from a series of residents, each serving their two-month sentence. Matt's fingers interlocked behind his head, and his eyes fixed on the asbestos-tile ceiling, like a prisoner in a B movie. Matt glanced at him and then returned his focus to the ceiling. Joe pulled out the solitary desk chair and sat.

"Matt?"

Slowly, Matt sat up and placed his feet on the floor. "Dr. Morales," he said, his eyes glazed.

"What's this 'Dr. Morales'? You OK?"

"Do you care?" Matt spoke in a mournful monotone.

"Of course." He did care. Besides Lourdes, Matt was his best friend; the only man he'd ever talked to about his hopes and dreams.

"Then why did you blindside me? I thought we were family. Is the cardiac spot that important to you?"

"Matt, you know I had no involvement in any of this. I'm just a peon like you."

"Then, why didn't you tell me yesterday? I'm your best friend. At least I thought I was."

"You still are, Matt. I hope."

"Dammit, Joe. I cried when De la Toure yanked me out of the unit. Go directly to pathology. Do not pass go. Do not collect a cardiac fellowship."

"At least you can joke about it."

"Joe, I cried. Do you understand? You didn't even have the decency—."

"I'm sorry. Honest. I would've told you, but I couldn't. I tried to take up for you with Carlisle."

"For real?" Matt fell back on the bed.

"Matt?"

Matt turned away from Joe and stared at the blank wall. Even Joe didn't believe his own words.

Joe sat looking at the back of Matt's head. Finally, he spoke. "Hey, why don't you tell me about the patients and then get out of here? It's New Year's Eve. You need a party."

Matt sat up again. Through glassy eyes, he looked at the pile of belongings next to the door. "Who am I going to celebrate with? My wife suggested I find another place to live. Can you imagine? A month in this hole. Christmas in this cell. And now, I'm walking out that door and going God-knows-where."

"It can't be that bad."

"What do you mean, 'It can't be that bad'? You've heard about the last month here in the unit. The nurses have been calling me Dr. Death, and De la Toure thinks I'm a total incompetent. I know I'll be cut from the program. What's left?"

Joe faced Matt head on, their eyes locked, and he felt drawn to his friend. They'd been buddies since their days at Rice. Some might find them an odd couple, but each one appreciated the other's uniqueness. Wealthy, erudite, jock meets poor but sophisticated, Mexican up-and-comer. Joe placed his hand on Matt's shoulder. Matt had royally screwed up. Now, Matt would have to regroup and try to regain his confidence and self-respect.

"Matt, this may not be the time, but it'll be all right. You're a good person, and you have friends."

"Sure. Like you?"

"Matt—."

"Bro, I didn't mean that."

"It's OK. Hey, why don't you go by our apartment and hang with Elizabeth and Joaquín? She could use a little distraction, too."

CHAPTER EIGHT

"VICTOR, COME IN. KATRINA, PLEASE STAY. I WANT TO discuss the resident situation."

Carlisle took a seat in front of De la Toure's desk.

"What did you think of Hackett and McClintock's meeting last night?" Carlisle asked.

"It was interesting," De la Toure said, "but I would hate to see us enter into McClintock's ACO. It's not in the patients' best interests."

"That depends on how you look at it, Jacques," Masters said as she moved behind the second chair facing De la Toure, next to the chair Carlisle occupied.

"Katrina," De la Toure said. "Please take a seat."

"Katrina, aren't we looking professional?" Carlisle said.

"Very funny, but I don't need to walk around in my scrubs all day to prove I'm a surgeon," she said as she sat.

"Right. Your lab coat looks like it barely survived Hiroshima. And underneath, is that a granny dress?"

"Victor, I'm here working on New Year's Eve."

"Just kidding," Carlisle said.

De la Toure, however, noted that Masters wasn't laughing. It was the aspect of Carlisle's personality De la Toure found most distasteful: launching a sarcastic barrage and then retreating under the cover of so-called humor, making the victim feel like he was overly sensitive for taking Carlisle seriously.

"What did you mean by your comment, Katrina?" De la Toure asked.

"Integration of the hospital, physicians and other providers is a good idea. And financial incentives don't require us to care for our patients differently, but even if we do, that's not necessarily bad."

"Insurance propaganda. I didn't know you worked for them," Carlisle said.

"Victor, don't be impertinent," De la Toure said.

"Thank you, Jacques—."

"But he has a point, Katrina," De la Toure said. "With an ACO, the hospital receives an up-front flat fee and they get to decide how to divide it. They're going to reward the doctors who cut corners."

"Yes," Masters said. "But physicians are still bound to do what's right for each patient, and who says our current system is better with its incentive to do more testing, more surgery?"

"Katrina, are you serious? Our patients understand that the more procedures we perform, the more we earn, traditional fee-for-service. Do you think they'll understand a system where we make more money by not operating, not ordering tests, not admitting them to the hospital for treatment?"

"Jacques—."

"No, let me finish. The hospitals employ every cost-cutting maneuver they can invent. Generic drugs. Off-brand sutures. Reduced length of stay. Less nursing staff. I could go on."

"Jacques, this is the twenty-first century."

"Exactly. Full of Orwellian double-speak. The hospital has the Resource Management Committee to make sure we buy the cheapest equipment possible. The Quality Assurance Committee monitors how long our patients are in the hospital, because it would be a real quality issue if our eighty-year-old heart patients stayed an extra day to regain their strength. And the Pharmacy and Therapeutics Committee determines which drugs I must substitute with cheaper medications and which ones I can't use at all."

"And your point?" Masters said with undisguised sarcasm.

"My point? I miss the days when the doctor and the hospital shared a common goal. Both made money by helping the most people. Today, we're at war. We doctors are the only ones whose interest is to provide the best care for each individual. Now, you want us to join forces with the hospital. This time our goal would be to collect our allotment and maximize their profit."

"You tell her, sir," Carlisle said.

"Victor, this isn't a joke," De la Toure said. He drew several deep breaths and held each one as long as possible. "Katrina, Victor, I got off point. Let me change topics. I really called you two here to discuss the residents."

"What's the problem, Jacques?" Masters asked.

"I want you to keep an eye on Dr. Morales. This month was a disaster with Dr. Keith. Not only did he manage to let some of the immediate post-ops die, he succeeded in watching the demise of some of our stable, chronic patients who were on the way to recovery."

Masters mumbled, "Yup, to an eternal nursing home."

"Katrina!" De la Toure chastised.

"I'm sorry, Jacques."

"Anyway, we can't repeat the experience," De la Toure said.

"Absolutely," Carlisle said. "We'll never get our statistics up to par, results that will stand out when we go online."

"Victor," De la Toure said. "This isn't the time."

"I'm not sure what happened to Matt," Masters said. "He and Joe are two of our brightest. They both received superior grades on my teaching rotation, they've both completed research projects in the cardioplegia laboratory, and both scored above the 95% mark on the in-service training exam."

"Yes," De la Toure squeezed in. "But remember, five of our six second-year residents scored above 90% last year."

"Yes, everyone except Eric Cunningham, who failed the exam again, and you gave him a new contract."

"Katrina, we have a bright group of residents, and I will see how Dr. Morales performs in the ICU. But as for Dr. Keith . . ." De la Toure paused. "In good conscience, I cannot let him finish our general surgery program."

"What?" Masters sprang to her feet, her face flushed. She drew a deep breath, like a cantor preparing for a seven-measure "Alleluia."

De la Toure braced for the hurricane.

"Jacques, I wish you had consulted me before you pulled Matt from the ICU. Remember, you appointed me the resident director."

"Katrina, be reasonable."

"Don't patronize me. This isn't my first rodeo."

"All right, then. Say what you have to say."

"Matt had problems, but he's bright and conscientious. Top-notch, blue ribbon. Yet I guess if he didn't survive your barbaric rotation, then he's not suited for our program."

"Well stated," De la Toure said. "You do realize, however, that I've trained thirty heart surgeons during my tenure as head of the Institute. Cardiovascular surgery requires attention to detail. Error during an appendectomy may produce an unfortunate complication, but error during heart surgery can result in death."

Masters pushed her hand at him, her palm a stop sign. "Precisely why the medical education board mandated the eighty-hour work week. Overworked residents bungle their jobs. I don't know if I can continue to ignore your blatant violation of the rules. You've set up the ICU call room, which enables the residents to stay in the hospital during their off time when they should be at home."

"Katrina, my trainees may not love me, but at the end of this program they represent the best in surgery, and I can tell you they respect me. You may not approve of my techniques, but then again, you didn't have the benefit of my training program."

Masters pivoted, turning her back to the two men, and left.

Carlisle let out a low whistle. "There's nothing worse than a woman in science."

"Victor, please."

"Excitable, you have to admit."

"Katrina has a passion for her teaching, her research, and her patients. I admire it."

"Watch out for the passionate."

De la Toure leaned back in his chair and crossed his arms. "Tell me. Did I overreact with Dr. Keith?"

"Of course not. You had no other choice."

"No other choice," De la Toure repeated faintly, but maybe Keith hadn't been the problem. Perhaps his age was the problem.

"Absolutely," Carlisle said emphatically. "Keith committed numerous errors. He's responsible for the deaths we've had. It's good you got rid of him before the prince comes next week."

"Yes!" Maybe Carlisle was right. The resident was responsible. "I agree. Now, what do you think of Dr. Morales?"

"As Katrina said, he's one of our brightest, but did you consider putting Cunningham in the ICU?"

"Sure. I know he's disappointed and I know I'll hear from Dallas. But I chose Morales for Eric's own good. He's talented technically, but he's not prepared for that degree of responsibility."

"I don't have to tell you of the damage if we don't offer Eric the cardiovascular fellowship spot."

"Yes. Dallas expects him to study with me. In fact, he expects he'll be an associate when he finishes."

"A natural," Carlisle said.

"Maybe. I feel sorry for Eric. Dallas makes a demanding father-in-law."

* * *

SHOWTIME. JOE HAD SPENT his whole life preparing for this moment. The office door from behind the administrative assistant's desk opened, and Delia Jackson stepped out. Joe put her age at about forty, but she still had it going. She was a study in contrasts: coal-black hair, blood-red lips, bright emerald eyes, Fake Bake tan. When she smiled, and she was smiling now, she commanded veneration.

She extended her right hand, gold rings adorning most of the fingers. "On behalf of the nursing staff, welcome."

He took her hand, and she responded with a firm squeeze.

"Thanks, but I'm not exactly a stranger," he said.

Without relinquishing her grip, she reached up with her left hand and held onto his shoulder. "True, but now you're the unit chief resident, the lead dog here. At least until you screw up."

Instinctively, Joe pulled back. He knew it was a joke, and he tried to laugh, but he felt disloyal to Matt.

"Did you get oriented?" she asked.

"Yes. Matt gave me the clipboard and—."

"Hit the door running."

She chuckled but Joe couldn't laugh about Matt's problems.

"Let me give you a few additional pointers," she said.

"Thanks. I'll take all the help I can get." Joe knew Delia was much more than the head nurse. She was in charge of Lutheran's Quality Care Initiative, and she'd traveled throughout the United States, helping hospitals set up their ICUs.

"Good. Matt didn't want help, and he definitely needed it."

That was a mistake on Matt's part, Joe thought. "Delia, all I want is a smooth, two-month tour of duty. I don't care who drives the car."

"All right, buckle up. The road may be a little bumpy, but you'll enjoy the ride." Delia started toward the first section of beds. As they walked, she offered advice. "Memorize the protocols and make sure your unit diagram is accurate."

"Got it. Can't tell the players without a program." Joe checked his clipboard. The first patient was Carlisle's heart patient from the day before.

Delia walked to the end of the row. She stopped at the first bed and picked up a paper. "You know about the flow sheets?"

"Yeah." Joe looked at the hospital form. The grid provided a row for each type of test: hematocrit, potassium, and others, and each column represented the more recent set of values. The nurses used point-of-care computer charting, but De la Toure preferred an old-fashioned paper chart for all the heart patients.

"Keep the results current and circle any abnormals in red." As she spoke, she stood close enough to Joe's left shoulder to touch him. She pointed to the first column. "Like this post-op potassium."

As usual, the potassium was high. "From the cardioplegia?"

"Naturally. The faculty will assume if you circled the abnormality, then you treated it. You want to end up with all normal labs." She moved her finger to the last column of boxes, each containing a normal value.

"Euboxic," Joe said. A lot of meaning in one word.

"Right. Not hyper- or hypo- anything. All normals."

Delia moved to the head of the bed. "Mr. Smythe, I think you're ready to move upstairs." She gestured to Joe. "This is Dr. Morales. He's taking Dr. Keith's place."

Joe summoned her with a jerk of his head and pointed to the computer screen where nurses had documented his vital signs and fluid status. "Smythe can't move out. Too much drainage from the chest tube." With his index finger, he directed Delia to the recorded output.

She leaned in, her hair brushing against his, and turned off the computer screen. Then, she wrapped her hand around the side of his head, and drew his ear to her lips. Her hot breath warmed him, and he breathed in her scent. He struggled to focus.

"Dr. Carlisle usually pulls it anyway. He likes to see his patients transferred upstairs."

"Yeah," Joe said. "Get them out of the expensive care unit and make the statistics look good."

Delia didn't laugh. "Joe, we monitor many quality indicators besides mortality. Time in the OR, hours until extubation, days in the ICU, length of stay in the hospital. They're all important."

"Uh, yes, ma'am. I didn't mean—."

"Good, but don't call me ma'am. It's Delia."

Delia turned to Mr. Smythe. "After Dr. Morales gets that tube out of your chest, I'll help you shave."

Delia continued with the tour of the unit and Joe made notes on his clipboard. Saving the sickest for last, she moved to the third patient bay. Delia stopped in front of bed 27 and Joe stood at her side. This bed had been Lourdes's. His body ached, and he couldn't pay attention.

He didn't have to listen to know that the patient, an old man, was critically ill—on the ventilator, face swollen, skin mottled, and his body connected by tubing to the intra-aortic balloon pump. With each heartbeat, the machine inflated a balloon inside the aorta to augment the blood flow, trying to compensate for the patient's failing heart.

Delia touched his arm. "Joe?"

"Sorry. You were saying?"

"Mr. Duffey has an order for do-not-resuscitate—"

Then Joe saw it. The teddy bear angel sitting on the window ledge. The card's "Get well, Pops!" The signatures, ranging from crayon scribbles to the flowery pen of teenage granddaughters. They'd made Pops DNR and moved him to the back bay.

"Mark your rounds list," Delia said.

"What? Oh yes, thanks." Joe jotted "DNR" in capital letters on his unit diagram.

* * *

THE MORNING WAS UNEVENTFUL. Joe had camped out with Pops. He was DNR and there was only so much Joe could do, but Joe carefully adjusted the medications and the heart rhythm remained stable.

"Do you think we should wean the ventilator?" Delia asked.

"No, let's let him chill today. His rhythm seems to be straightening out. I don't want to rock the boat. Besides, he's still paralyzed. He needs the ventilator for now. If he can ride out the next day or two, I think he'll make it."

"Dr. Morales, bed 3," Anita, Lakisha's daytime equivalent, called over the intercom in a distinctive, English-as-a-second-language accent. Like his mother, she didn't have much formal education, but she had learned enough to land the job of receptionist, a step up from the cleaning staff.

Joe looked at his list. There wasn't a patient in bed 3.

"That's Dr. Carlisle's case," Delia said. "We put his patients up front and transfer them out the next day. Are you ready?"

Joe didn't answer. He'd already started for the front bay. He first heard and then saw the approaching stretcher, its arrival heralded by the signature clomp of John Allgood's clogs. Allgood provided ventilation with an ambu bag, squeezing the blue plastic, egg shape, pushing 100% oxygen into the lungs, while he was entertained by music blaring out of headphones attached to an mp3 player clipped to his scrub pants.

Under his breath, Allgood sang along. It was something about cocaine and Casey Jones.

Meanwhile, Chiu pushed the foot of the bed, watching the patient's EKG, blood pressure, and oxygen saturation on a monitor the size of an iPad.

As the OR personnel parked the bed, three nurses descended on the patient. Soon, all the tracings were transferred to the overhead screen and Chiu and Allgood left. A short, plump, old-style registered nurse, complete with starched white cap bobby-pinned to her head, leaned over the patient, and listened with her stethoscope. She called out her findings.

"Lungs are clear. Heart sounds are a little distant."

Joe considered the nurse a dinosaur. The monitor told him what was going on inside the heart and lungs. With advances in technology, there was little need to actually touch the body.

Fifteen minutes after the arrival of the patient, Eric Cunningham sauntered to the bedside, covered with attitude. When Joe was assigned to the OR, he always accompanied the patients to the ICU along with the anesthesiologist and perfusionist. Fashionably late, Eric moved with a cowboy sway to make sure you didn't miss the imported Italian boots, the glossy luster of the rich leather reflecting the fluorescent lighting. Eric's footgear cost more than a month of Joe's salary.

As Eric passed by the head nurse, he spoke. "Howdy, Delia. You're looking fine. Hotter than an August day at the ranch."

"Thanks, Eric. How's your wife?"

"Don't be like that, sugar." Eric moved toward Joe, this time with a little more pep in his stride.

"Howdy, Joe. This is Mr. Jimenez." He pronounced the name GEE-MEN-EZ. It sounded ridiculous. "All the way from taco town. Like there's no heart surgery in San Antonio?"

Joe ignored the comments. "Good case?"

"Routine. Carlisle's fast. Four grafts before 10:30."

"Any problems?"

"Nope. This guy should fly, but he was a little wet."

As they spoke, Eric's focus shifted to a student nurse at the end of the section. Slowly, he moved in her direction, like a wolf inching up on a wounded caribou. Joe had observed this predator in action before. Always out for bigger game, as if his sense of self was measured by his latest conquest.

"OK, Chico. Later," Eric said, finished with Joe.

"Don't call me——." Joe started but stopped. Forget it. He turned to the rotund figure in the stiff white uniform standing next to the reservoir collecting the shed blood.

"How much out from the chest tube?" Joe asked the nurse.

"250 cc's."

Joe pulled the sheet down to examine the drainage tube. Not too much blood. "Go ahead and check his clotting studies."

"Dr. Morales, bed 27. Stat," Anita called overhead.

Joe jumped back, knocking the bedside table across the aisle where it collided with another and careened into an IV pole. He turned to rescue the pole from crashing into the neighboring patient. He started to say something, but instead, ran toward the emergency.

As he approached the entrance to the back section, he slowed. Bed 27 had been Lourdes's bed. Now, it was Pops. And Pops was DNR.

Joe stopped in mid stride at the entrance to the last patient bay. "Who paged me stat?" he said with hands on hips.

A hulking male nurse stood near the bed. "Sorry, Dr. Morales."

Earlier, Joe had noticed this guy, some kind of body builder. His glossy, shaved head topped a square face, bull neck, and V-shaped torso, bulging with muscles straight out of the gym, not from manual labor. He'd been in this same section the morning Lourdes died. Right after Joe had returned from St. Anne's and the celebration for Our Lady of Guadalupe.

Joe walked up to the nurse and checked for his name. A red, new-employee ribbon dangled from his I.D. card. "Bo, do you understand the meaning of 'DNR'?"

"Of course."

"Then, why did you page me stat?" Joe pointed to the monitor. He watched as the wide, rapid V-tach flattened into a straight line. "Pops is DNR. There's nothing I can do. The family already decided."

"It's just that I came back from break and he was in slap V-tach. Like all of a sudden. He'd been stable, so I guess I panicked."

"No excuses. You have to know your patients."

From out of nowhere, Delia stepped between them. "Bo, it's understandable." She patted one of his barbell shoulders and ran her hand down to the large biceps with swollen veins visible under the smooth depilated skin, the bulging upper arm muscles delineated by a ring of tattooed barb wire.

"No problem," she said. Then, she turned to Joe. "Dr. Morales, you have to fill out the death certificate." She picked up the patient's chart and headed toward the front desk.

Joe had to follow.

CHAPTER NINE

BY 2:00, MR. JIMENEZ'S BLEEDING HAD SLOWED, AND HE looked great. He was already off the ventilator. In fact, he was sitting up with a dinner tray in front of him.

Carlisle rounded the corner and strode into the first patient bay, commanding the attention of every female nurse and technician in the unit. "Good afternoon, Joe. It looks like you're getting settled in."

"Yes, sir. Thank you."

Carlisle looked immaculate. It seemed as if he wore a new white lab coat each day. Carlisle didn't have his name printed on his coat, as did De la Toure or the others. Over Carlisle's chest pocket were the simple block initials V.D.C. He wore his jet-black hair slicked back, and he used one of the paper hoods to avoid the imprint left by the traditional surgeon's cap. He exuded the self-confidence of a Wall Street executive or a Mafia don. Carlisle moved to the patient's bedside.

"Mr. Jiminez looks good," Joe said. "I think he'll be ready to transfer in the morning."

"Excellente." Carlisle didn't check Joe's notes or the nurses' computer entries. He didn't look at the lab work, or the chest x-ray, or even examine the patient's incisions. Instead, he went straight to the head of the bed.

Joe was overwhelmed. Had he already earned that degree of trust? Spectacular.

"Mr. Jimenez, you're doing great. Absolutamente perfecto." Carlisle spoke with an accent straight from the second ward, but Joe imagined he wouldn't drive through that neighborhood, not even in daylight.

The patient mumbled a response, his mouth full of red Jell-O.

"And we'll get you some real food," Carlisle said, walking back to Joe's side. He seemed to be waiting for something.

"Want to make some rounds?" Joe asked.

"Exactly."

Stupid question, Joe thought. He led Carlisle to bed 1.

"Mr. Smythe underwent coronary artery bypass yesterday."

"Good. I like to see the chest tube out on the first day."

Joe smiled. Thanks to Delia, he thought. She was awesome. She gave perfect advice about Smythe's chest tubes and Jiminez's bleeding; and then, she even offered to call De la Toure about Pops. Spectacular assist.

Carlisle left the first patient bay and entered the second with Joe following. When Carlisle abruptly stopped, Joe almost ran over him.

"Where's Mr. Herbst?"

"Oh, I—we moved him to the third bay."

"You did what?"

"The nurses asked. He's been here for three weeks and we haven't even started planning placement. They said—."

"Did you make him DNR?" Carlisle's lip stretched taut and his brow furrowed. His steel-blue eyes fixed on Joe, waiting for a response.

"No, sir." Thank God. Joe had thought about it. Bo had suggested it, but at least he hadn't made that mistake.

As Carlisle started walking again, Joe moved in front so he could get to the patient first, but when he walked into the back section he stopped.

This time Carlisle ran up on his back. "Joe, what are you doing?"

"Sir—." Joe didn't know how to answer. Immediately in front of him, Bo stood at the foot of bed 28, on which lay Dr. Verney, an elderly veterinarian, her white sheet pulled up over her head. Taped on the wall behind her, an array of animal-themed cards and photos of grateful owners with their rescue dogs. There were no IV infusion pumps, the monitor was disconnected, and the ventilator was pushed back.

Dr. Verney was dead.

Joe swirled around, bringing both palms up defensively, hoping to deflect Carlisle's anger. "This isn't your patient. She's Dr. De la Toure's. Dr. Verney was DNR. Mr. Herbst is in bed 30. Let me show you."

Joe started, but Carlisle pushed past him to Mr. Herbst's bedside computer. He checked through the vital signs, the x-rays, and the nurse's notes. Then he picked up the paper chart to look at the lab flow and Joe's handwritten notes. He read every single word. As he did, he kept muttering Sufi's name, and he didn't sound happy.

Joe tried to slow down his breathing. He had to concentrate. He could not sound like a fool even though he felt like one.

Carlisle turned back to Joe. "Don't you ever make one of my patient's DNR."

"Yes, sir. No, sir, I mean, I didn't, but just because they're DNR doesn't mean I won't take care of them. I'm paying attention to all of these patients. It's just that if they arrest, we're not going to resuscitate them."

"I don't need you to explain DNR to me. Now, do you under-stand my instructions?"

"Yes, sir."

"And next week, Mr. Herbst will be one month out. You can start placement plans then. He better leave here alive."

Joe understood completely. Then, the patient would pass the thirty-day period and be counted as a survivor no matter what hap-pened after the hospital stay.

In Joe's mind, there were only two options. Next week, Mr. Herbst would leave for a nursing home or Joe would leave to join Matt in pathology.

* * *

"VICTOR, THANK YOU FOR letting me know," De la Toure said. "Tell the nurses I'll be down to talk with Dr. Verney's family."

He dropped the receiver into place and picked up the small vial of pills from the middle drawer. As he fumbled to open the top, the nitroglycerin tablets spilled on the desk and onto the floor. He picked up one and placed it under his tongue. His body rapidly absorbed and transported the life-saving drug to his coronary arteries. The vessels responded, dilating, allowing more oxygen into the musculature. The heart released its hold on the body, and the pain subsided.

* * *

JOE LEANED BACK ON the rear legs of his chair with his feet propped by the desk. He surveyed the area. After rounding with Carlisle, he'd unpacked his belongings and tried to humanize his environs.

Joe emptied one of the boxes and lined up books along the back of the desk. He put out several frames with photos and cards, and above his desk, he put up a poster of the expansive Houston skyline, the land of opportunity. On the bed, he spread out a blanket that his grandmother made when he was born. He'd only been to visit Mexico one time and his grandparents had never been to Houston. His mamá said the trip was too difficult.

Joe slid two large plastic crates under the bed, one for scrubs, and the other for socks and underwear. He hung two clean lab coats from a hook on the wall next to his desk, then picked up his clipboard.

His first day, and already he had two deaths in the ICU: Pops and Dr. Verney. At least, they were DNRs from the back bay. He couldn't believe that Bo hadn't told him about Dr. Verney's death before he walked in with Carlisle, even if she was a DNR.

Who knows what Carlisle would tell De la Toure?

Joe assessed his diagram. The front two sections were fairly empty. He was going to transfer out Mr. Jiminez along with some of the other faculty's cases from Friday. There were a few left in both areas that had to stay because of chest tubes, but they were all pretty stable. In the rear section, all that remained were four of De la Toure's and one each for Masters and Carlisle. It would help if he could keep them alive for the next two months; even better, get some of them transferred to long-term care facilities.

Joe made a note at the top of his page: "PLACEMENT!"

With his clipboard in his hand, he headed back to the unit to check on his patients one more time.

CHAPTER TEN

LATE IN THE AFTERNOON JOE WENT BACK TO HIS ROOM for supper. He realized he'd been wandering through the ICU without accomplishing anything. The unit was under control. He'd examined each of the twenty patients, gone over their charts, and checked the lab forms. He'd even reread the ten typed pages of residents' instructions, and he'd sent two e-mails to Elizabeth.

He hoped the evening would be quiet. Joe needed a chance to get his head together.

A faint rap at the door preceded a creamy, Southern voice.

"Dr. Morales?" The honey tone and exaggerated syllables sounded more Georgian than Texan.

"Come in," he said and Delia entered.

"Just checking in. I thought I'd stop by and see if I can help in any way."

"Thanks." He righted his chair and tucked in his scrub top.

"You don't mind if we call you Joe?"

"No, of course not."

"It gets pretty familiar. At night, most of the nurses will walk back here with any questions they have, unless you want us to page the night-float resident."

"Absolutely not. I'll handle everything. Tell them to come on in. I don't sleep in the nude or anything."

"Oh? That would be interesting. Anyway, we're family. If you and your wife want some privacy, make sure to tell the administrative assistant out front. You know the door doesn't lock?"

"Don't worry. Elizabeth and I have a two-month-old. I doubt we'll be working on a sibling for Joaquín."

Delia sat on the bed and picked up a photo from the adjacent desk. "He's a good-looking boy, like his dad."

Joe felt his skin flush. He'd always had a baby face that mothers loved: smooth, caramel skin and round, blue eyes. He was cute, cuddly, lovable, but never handsome, macho, virile.

Delia stood and put her arm around his shoulder. "We're going to have a great two months." She gave him a friendly hug and started to leave. "I'll check on you in the morning."

"Thanks," he said as Delia left. This rotation wouldn't be bad. At least Carlisle had called the old man about Dr. Verney, Masters would be on Joe's side for sure, and Delia couldn't be friendlier.

Joe took out the cardboard tube Elizabeth gave to him, a good-luck present. Expecting a poster, he pulled out an acrylic painting of a window with four panes. Through the glass, he viewed a beach with the sun setting on the horizon. It resembled the pristine sand of Pie de la Cuesta, where his mother's family lived.

Joe smiled. Elizabeth was aghast there would be no window in his quarters. It was a simple enough solution: She made him one. He opened the desk drawer, pulled out some pushpins stored there, and attached the painting to the wall opposite the head of his bed. Satisfied, he lay back and looked out his "window."

Joe slid his hands under the pillow he brought from home and pulled it up against the back of his neck, cradling his head in the plush, fragrant cloud. The scent of spring flowers reminded him of the bed he shared with Elizabeth. As his head fell back, his hands felt some plastic. He retrieved the cellophane-wrapped square and examined it.

A condom. What in the world? Surely, Matt hadn't left it behind. Probably Eric's idea of a joke.

Joe turned over, tossed the neon package onto his desk, and picked up the poem in a red plastic frame. At the bottom were prints of Joaquín's infant hands. Fancy calligraphy proclaimed the title: "M.D." It began, "M.D. stands for my daddy." Elizabeth wanted to remind him that his most important roles were husband and father. Joe agreed and the best thing he could do for his family was to succeed beyond all expectations. Wealth begets wealth. If he could become a prominent heart surgeon, he could offer Elizabeth and Joaquín every possible advantage.

He missed Elizabeth and his boy.

Joe placed the homemade card on his desk, sat up, and grabbed his laptop. He clicked on the mail in-box. Still no message from Elizabeth.

He slammed the laptop closed. He really needed his family.

The day hadn't been too bad. He admitted eight fresh post-ops to the ICU, four of them hearts, but only one for De la Toure, Ms. Patricia Paragone. Unfortunately, this was the one patient who was having some PVCs. The good news was that her rhythm settled down quickly and she was able to have visitors.

There were at least fifty that wanted to see her. She had no children but Miss Pat, as they called her, had seemingly taught every ballerina in the city. And the dancers swarmed into the ICU when visiting hours started. All sizes and shapes—from little girls dressed in their costumes to statuesque beauties of the Houston Ballet and plain-old soccer moms who loved her from their childhood.

There were so many that the nurses rounded them up and made them leave. Then, Joe had to talk with them. They begged him to save their Miss Pat. He reassured them that she was doing well, and that a few—meaning not more than four—could visit at the appointed times.

With the unit chilled and the last onslaught of families ushered out for the evening, Joe thought it would be an opportune time to get to know the nurses better.

"Hi, Dr. Morales," they greeted him as he entered the lounge. One added, "Join our New Year's Eve party."

"This looks great," he said as he walked to the oblong table covered with food and grabbed a cold drink from the cooler. "How did you guys find Tab? They've almost quit making it."

"Delia heard you liked it," an attractive young nurse said. "She had to go to five stores to find some."

"We sure are glad to have you this month," one RN said.

"Gives the guys in the morgue a break," another whispered.

Joe surmised that Matt Keith didn't fare well with the nurses, and a warm wave covered him, the feeling of being wanted, desired, chosen.

"Thanks to you guys I'm off to a good start." He moved to the ICU nurse trainee standing at the door. Time to be magnanimous. Joe had to work with this guy for the next two months, and he realized he'd humiliated Bo in front of his peers. It was hard enough for male nurses to garner respect, and it looked as if this guy had seriously overcompensated. "Hey, Bo. I'm sorry I came down on you so hard."

"No problem. It was my bad, but after you called me out about the stat page on the first DNR dude, Mr. Duffey, I thought I'd just let you know about Dr. Verney's death when you came around. I didn't think about the faculty coming in."

Joe wasn't sure if it was intentional, a little passive-aggressive action, or maybe Bo was just that dense. Either way, he had to get along with the man. "No big deal, but next time, just give me a heads up."

The powerhouse left the lounge like a pet that had just received a newspaper across the nose.

Joe sampled the food, but he mostly concentrated on introducing himself and trying to learn names. He knew they were sizing him up just as he was evaluating them, looking for the ones who were both smart and trustworthy.

"Dr. Morales, bed 22," Lakisha called out from overhead.

Joe reflexively rushed from the lounge.

"He has those new-resident-in-the-ICU jitters," Delia said.

Joe started to turn around and set her straight, but he was in a hurry, and maybe she was right.

He checked the clipboard: Bed 22 was Patricia Paragone, De la Toure's post-op. Joe's own heart rhythm quickened. As he reached the section, he spotted Bo's beaming bald head, a beacon for trouble, but Joe found comfort in the lack of activity. He stopped and counted to ten before walking slowly to the bedside. If he reacted the same way to every overhead page, it would be a long two months.

"What's up, Bo?" he said, as friendly as possible. Even if the guy was a bonehead, it never helped to make an enemy.

"Ms. Paragone is wide awake, ready to extubate, but she's been having some PVCs." Bo handed Joe the EKG strips.

"Not bad. A few wide beats. No runs of V-tach?"

"No way." Next, Bo gave him the blood gas analysis.

"Great gases. Let's pull the tube."

"Thanks," the patient mumbled after Bo pulled the plastic hose from her mouth.

"Ms. Paragone, you're doing great," Joe said.

"Please, will you call me Miss Pat?" Her voice was horse from the breathing tube. And before Joe could affirm her request, she followed with another. "When do I get to see my girls again?"

"Well, Ms. Paragone, Miss Pat I mean, it's 10:30, at night. I think it'll be best if we wait until the morning."

"Please, just for a moment?"

"I tell you what, wait just a bit and when things settle down, Bo will check, and if they're some still here he'll let the older ones visit. OK?"

Joe headed back to his quarters. There, he texted Elizabeth again and again. He checked his email for the umpteenth time. Where was Elizabeth? What could she be doing so late? And who was watching the baby?

Joe decided to call his mamá. He didn't need this kind of worry. Not tonight.

* * *

JUST BEFORE MIDNIGHT, DELIA Jackson entered unannounced. In her right hand she carried a can of soda, small pieces of ice melting on the top. In her left hand, a wide assortment of food competed for king of the mountain on a Styrofoam plate.

"The food was going fast, so I fixed you a plate. And here's a Tab. The Coke machine doesn't sell it, so I have a stash for you in the nurses' lounge."

"Thanks," Joe said as he stood. "Answering my every need."

"Watch out, big boy."

Joe reached out for the food and drink, but Delia placed them on the desk, pushing the condom to the side.

"Look." She pointed to his clock; the phosphorescent numbers read 12:01. "Happy New Year," she said, taking his hand in hers. She pulled him close.

"Uh, Happy New Year," he stammered.

She gave him a quick kiss on his cheek, catching him off guard. Almost as suddenly, she released him and started to leave, but stopped at the door. "Get some rest. I'll try to screen any questions the nurses have. You sleep tight."

It took Joe a moment to find his voice. "Wait. Are you here tonight? This is New Year's Eve."

"When you're in charge, you have to work all hours. This unit is my baby, and I'm way past some teenage notion of champagne flutes and a roaring fireplace. Actually, I'm training Bo to be the night supervisor."

"Not Bo. He's a new graduate."

"What made you think that?"

"He has the red ribbon."

"He's just new to Lutheran. He's had a bunch of ICU experience."

"Boy, do I feel like a fool."

"Yes, but a good-looking fool." Delia walked away, her hips swaying to the beat of an internal samba.

* * *

ONLY CRUMBS REMAINED ON the plate on his desk. Joe glanced at his travel alarm clock. It was 1:00 in the morning. He should be asleep, but there was still no word from Elizabeth. She hadn't answered his e-mails or the text messages he'd sent. Her phone vibrated an alert when she got messages, but she hadn't responded. Finally, he'd called and talked with his mother. Elizabeth was out with Matt. His mother reminded him that January 1 was a holy day, the Solemnity of Mary, mother of God, as if that meant something.

Joe rose, pulled off his scrub top, and lay on the bed, not bothering to pull back the blanket or sheet. As he reached to turn off the desk lamp, he tipped over a small plastic statue of the Virgin of Guadalupe, the dark-skinned Madonna draped in stars, crushing the stone moon god, conquering the feathered serpent. Obviously, his mother had come by that afternoon when he was in the patient area.

As a child, his mother told him the story of Juan Diego. He remembered believing, admiring the poor Aztec who encountered the Virgin in the hills of Tepeyac, outside the capital of Mexico. How brave he was to go to the powerful European bishop and demand that the Spanish construct a church in honor of the Virgin with Native American features. Her very image was a testimony to the value of the indigenous population. Joe had only visited his relatives one time and he'd never met his dad's family. They sure didn't seem to value him.

Joe opened the desk drawer, dropped the Virgin inside, and lay back on the bed. A sliver of light seeped under the door, softly illuminating Elizabeth's acrylic, the window his room had needed. Elizabeth was the eternal optimist. She loved life and all it brought her, and she never dwelt on any shortcomings. If Elizabeth was in a sinking lifeboat, she'd say it was a great day for a swim.

Joe looked out his window. Time for sleep and dreams. He hoped he would find guidance in his dreams, like his namesake from the Bible. The story of Joseph and his multicolored coat fascinated him. It was a classic tale of triumph over adversity, victory for the underdog, but what he liked best about the allegory was Joseph's ability to interpret dreams and predict the future. As a child, Joe would pray to God to send him messages in his sleep.

He wanted to know about his father, the man responsible for his 5-foot-11-inch stature, deep blue eyes, and light-colored skin. Joe no longer had faith in God, but he still had a fascination with dreams. At Rice, he studied Freud and came to believe that through dreams, we communicate with the subconscious.

Through his window, Joe viewed the spectacular sunset at Pie de la Cuesta, a remote location twenty miles north of Acapulco. He recalled the clean smell of the sea air and the unblemished sand.

Sleep came quickly.

A crystal-white blanket of sand stretches in front of me forever. On the horizon, the last rays of daylight fight their way through low-lying clouds, shooting bursts of orange and yellow and brown.

I run on the carpet of soft sand, kicking a multicolored ball, pretending I'm on the soccer field, playing for Mexico. I'm alone with the blue-green waves crashing on the shore next to me, the sound so loud I can no longer hear my cousins behind me. I smell and taste the salt in the air. It feels like home.

I turn back to view where my cousins are surfing, using their bodies as boards to ride the gigantic waves. On the shore, Mamita sits with her sisters. Bright colors—the reds, greens, yellows, and blues of their dresses—decorate the ivory surface, small and brilliant in the distance.

I never get to swim with my cousins, even though I'm five years old and I know how, because Mamita says the tide is too strong and the surf is too rough.

"Please, Mamita," I beg in my sure-fire, never-fail, sweetest voice. "My cousins swim here every day. Please. . . ."

"José, mi corazón," Mamita answers. "They're los indígenas. This is their home and they know these waters. The Pacific is

treacherous and eager to claim a little gringo like you."

It's not fair. It makes me feel small and foreign, but I'm Mexican, too. I'll show them when I play in the World Cup. I prepare to launch my soccer ball the length of the field for the winning goal. I'm Pelé as I cock my leg to make the play.

A wave as tall as Mamita crashes next to me. Droplets of water rain over me. I jump into the spray like I play in the yard sprinkler, and I launch my attack. My leg springs forward as I land back on the sand. It's an awesome move! My foot, though, finds only air. The surf's fingers have reached up and kidnapped my ball, so I slip and hit the ground. I jump up quickly to check that no one saw me flub the play and lose the game.

I turn to the water. My ball is being carried into the ocean. I'll have to hurry before it gets away.

Maybe I shouldn't. My cousins talk about the Americans who have drowned here. But, my ball! It'll be lost.

Slowly, I step down the steep slope from the shore into the water, making sure I don't lose my balance again. I know the sand under my feet can disappear with a single wave, and I've seen even my cousins fall down. So I move down the bank, one careful step after another.

This is not so hard. The water covers only my ankles now, but with each wave, the spray splashes up to my chest. I gaze back over my shoulder. Mamita isn't watching, and my cousins don't care. I get closer to my ball, but with each wave, it is carried into deeper water, moving back and forth like a yo-yo.

I watch the toy as a cat stalks a mouse, ready to pounce. If I can sneak up on my ball, I can snatch it back from the sea. With the next incoming wave, I dive under the water and come up to the surface beneath the brightly colored globe. I clutch it with both hands and stand up as the wave returns to the sea. I am the victor.

I hold the ball over my head like Pelé raising the golden cup that proclaims his team champion of the world.

Applause erupts. The surf slams against the sand. The whole world shouts its approval.

Without warning, another wave crashes over my head. I feel the sand sliding away from my feet as it runs off with the white foam. I dig my toes into the coarse sand. It feels rough, like broken glass. I fight to hold onto my position despite the pain, but the sea is winning. My feet and my legs are pulled toward the deep of the ocean.

I scream out in Spanish, "Ayúdame. Ayúdame." But my words are lost in the roar of the surf.

There's no one to help me. Mamita, my cousins, they can't see me. The tide drags me down to the floor of the ocean. I try to breathe, but water fills my lungs.

I know I'm going to die.

CHAPTER ELEVEN

JOE WOKE TO A LOUD, REPETITIVE, BUZZING SOUND.
Mercifully, it soon stopped.

Perspiration dripped from his forehead as he struggled for
orientation. He sat bolt upright in bed and looked out his window:
the beach at Pie de la Cuesta. As a child, he visited this beach once.
He played in the pounding surf, and he almost drowned.

The obnoxious noise returned like an alarm clock whose snooze
button had been pushed one too many times.

Joe glanced around his quarters: the small desk with its solitary
chair and on top of the desk, in front of the books, sat a stack of
hospital charts awaiting dictation, a picture of Elizabeth and Joaquín,
and the "M.D." poem with his baby's tiny handprints.

Again, the rude sound spewed from the speaker mounted in the
ceiling.

An announcement followed: "Code blue. Code blue, bed 22."
Lakisha's high-pitched voice screamed urgency. "Dr. Morales, bed 22,
STAT."

Joe felt the surge of excitement mixed with fear. He pulled
on a scrub top, slipped his feet into his shoes, grabbed his

clipboard, and headed out. He hurried down the hallway, past the front desk, through the first bay and into the second. Already, four nurses and John Allgood were gathered around the patient's bedside.

He wondered what Allgood was doing here in the middle of the night.

"Dr. Morales," Bo said. Even before the nurse spoke, it was apparent Bo was agitated. His eyes bounced inside their sockets, pinballs jostled by lighted rubberized posts.

"Ms. Paragone just went into V-tach. You knew she was having some wicked premature beats ever since surgery, but no runs. Then, all of a sudden, V-tach."

"All right, Bo. It's OK." Joe spoke in as calm a voice as he could summon. He admired Carlisle's composure under pressure, and he tried to emulate his superior, but it was all an act. He could feel his own heart pounding inside his chest.

He looked to the HP monitors. He didn't have to know how to interpret the EKG, because the computer inside did all the thinking. To the right of the tracing on the screen, under the heart rate, beeping and flashing, the lighted message in all caps, read VENTRICULAR TACHYCARDIA. If he couldn't stop the malignant rhythm, the patient would die.

Out of the corner of one eye, Joe noticed Delia poised at the bedside, standing on a small step stool, both arms extended over the patient's chest, ready to start CPR.

"No, Delia!" Joe shouted, louder than he anticipated.

"Joe, she's been in V-tach for three minutes," Allgood said as his right shoulder twitched. "She's losing her blood pressure, Dude. Delia, do it to her."

"Wait just a minute." Turning, Joe said, "Bo, give her two hundred milligrams of lidocaine."

Bo hesitated. The usual dosage was fifty milligrams, maybe a hundred. "Dr. Morales, do you think—."

"Now!" Joe said. "Do it."

From the crash cart, Bo opened two boxes of lidocaine. His hands shook as he administered both dosages.

The tachycardia instantly broke.

"Yo, look. Sinus rhythm," Allgood said. "Sinus rhythm."

"Great," Joe said as a collective sigh escaped from the group. He spoke to Allgood. "Go ahead and place her on a non-rebreather mask with 100% oxygen."

Allgood looked puzzled. "Man, her oxygen saturation is already 96%. It don't get much better."

"I know, but oxygen never hurt anyone."

"Whatever," Allgood said with obvious disagreement.

Joe placed his hands on his hips and turned slowly in a circle, making eye contact with each person. "You guys, I may be young, but I know what I'm doing. Someone has to be in charge." He drew himself up, trying to affect the stance of authority, which he doubted as much as anyone gathered.

Allgood placed the non-rebreather that looked like a 1950s aviator mask over the patient's face. As he pushed it into place, he spoke to Ms. Paragone. "Here's the oxygen your surgeon wants." And then, he turned to Joe. "Yo, man. Because you're so knowledgeable, I'm out of here. Good luck." As he walked away he muttered, "You'll need it."

Joe didn't say another word as Allgood left the unit. Although the best, he was only an anesthesiologist, and Joe didn't even call for anesthesia to help. No matter what happened, Joe would be blamed. He controlled his own destiny.

The adrenaline rush started to subside. He'd handled the emergency with ease. The patient's rhythm remained regular.

Then, the tone of Bo's voice shattered his calm. "Dr. Morales, we got some wicked wide beats again. PVCs for real."

"Did you start the lidocaine drip?" Joe asked.

"You didn't tell me—."

"Bo, it's basic ICU." He was sorry for lashing out, and he didn't expect an answer, but it was the truth. "Delia, give another bolus and start a drip."

Again, the lidocaine worked instantly, but this time, Joe felt no sense of relief, only of foreboding. Within a few short minutes, the ectopic beats returned. The HP monitor counted them with each minute. The screen flashed "ALARM—PVC>6."

Ms. Paragone was throwing six PVCs per minute, even on the lidocaine. Joe saw short runs of V-tach; bullies grouped together, three and four beats in a row, waiting to charge.

He wiped the perspiration from his brow and fought to stay calm. "Bo, did you page the cardiologist?"

"No, Dr. Morales," Bo answered. "Like, you were here, and it's been wicked crazy."

"That's no excuse." Joe instantly realized he was losing control. "Hey, I'm sorry. I didn't mean that." He turned to the head nurse. "Delia, call Sufi now. And page Dr. Carlisle. He's on for De la Toure. And I want to give this lady some procainamide."

"Do you think her pressure will tolerate it?"

"We have to do something. Otherwise she'll arrest."

"Bo, go to pharmacy and bring us a procainamide drip along with a fifty milligram bolus," Delia instructed.

Joe approached the head of the patient's bed. He chose his words carefully. "Ms. Paragone, you're OK. You had a little irregular rhythm. Relax."

She wasn't oblivious to the carnival atmosphere around her and her eyes filled with tears as she reached up to move the plastic cup covering her mouth. "Call me Miss Pat," she whispered.

Joe pushed her hand away. "OK, Miss Pat, but don't talk. You have to wear the oxygen." Joe returned the mask to its original position. He adjusted the elastic that pulled the plastic cup tight against the patient's face, and the rubber bands popped against her cheeks. She looked at him, terror-struck. "My girls, I have to say good bye."

"You'll be all right," Joe whispered. "I promise. Trust me. And we'll let you see them as soon as we can." He spoke with purposeful confidence. The same way he'd reassured Lourdes.

Bo hurried back. Fumbling with the IV line, the nurse kept looking back to the monitor. Joe hoped Bo felt guilty for this fiasco. Helpless, Joe watched short runs of PVCs, three and four ectopic beats in a row, gang up on his patient. Soon, the terrorist army would rally: V tach, and Joe couldn't stop it.

"Dr. Morales," Lakisha called from the speaker overhead, "Dr. Sufi on line three." Joe rushed to the phone.

"Dr. Sufi, I have a problem. You remember Ms. Paragone?"

"Yes, I know her. She is having trouble like the others?" At the end of each sentence, Sufi's inflection typically rose, whether he asked a question or not.

"Yes, sir, she's been in V-tach."

"Joe, you should have called me sooner."

"I thought she was OK. She was having a few PVCs, but no runs. This morning, though, she went into a sustained V-tach."

"V-tach, another patient?"

"Yes, sir. The V-tach broke with lidocaine, but came right back. Her potassium was only three, but I treated it. Oxygen is OK. I'm checking the magnesium and calcium. They're not back."

"You should have notified me earlier, but given that you didn't, you can try procainamide now."

"Yes, I thought the same thing. They're hanging the drip."

"Dr. Morales," the speaker sounded. "Line one."

"Joe, I should come in?" Sufi asked.

"No, sir, I can handle it."

"All right. You will call back if you have problems?"

"Yes, sir," but he'd try hard not to. He recalled the residents' prime directive: Never hesitate to call, but to call is a sign of weakness.

"Dr. Morales. Dr. Morales," Lakisha's voice repeated. "Line one." Joe punched the lit red button.

"This is Dr. Morales."

"Joe," Carlisle said, "don't ever page me at night. You pick up the phone and call me at home, and if I call in, don't keep me on hold. Now what do you want?"

"You know Ms. Paragone—."

"No, I do not know Ms. Paragone."

"She's a patient of Dr. De la Toure. She had a coronary artery bypass today, and tonight, she kind of went into V-tach."

"What do you mean 'kind of went into V-tach'?"

"She was having a lot of PVCs. Then, suddenly she went into V-tach. I've given her lidocaine and—."

"Joe, this is just your first night. Do you need the night-float resident to help you or are you going to be able to function in our unit?"

"Sir?"

"Can you perform? Are you capable of taking care of post-operative heart patients?"

"Yes, sir."

"Then do it. Call Sufi if you need medical advice, if you don't know what to do, but don't call me unless someone needs to go to the OR. Do you understand?"

"Yes, sir."

The disconnect clicked in Joe's ear, followed by the ominous tone of an open line. He returned the phone to the hook and stared, his hand still clutching the receiver, unable to release it. He was alone. Only he could salvage Miss Pat's life.

"Joe," Delia called. "Come over here."

"What's the problem?"

"The blood pressure is way down, systolic around eighty."

Joe looked at the monitor. The pressure was falling, but at least the PVCs were gone. There were only two choices: stop the infusion and wait for the V-tach or continue the drug while watching her blood pressure hit bottom. He could knock her off either way. Choose the poison: hypotension or V-tach.

"My girls! Please, help me," Miss Pat said clearly despite the mask.

Joe looked at the terror in her eyes. Somehow, he had to find an answer.

Maybe there was a third option. "Delia, go ahead and stop the bolus, but start the routine drip."

"What? I told you the BP was eighty. You want another death?"

"Begin the routine infusion. That's at a real slow rate. Hopefully, her blood pressure will be OK with the procainamide at the slow rate."

"If that's what you want to do." She adjusted the infusion pump, but her tone and rigid movement telegraphed disapproval.

Joe waited.

The blood pressure dropped to seventy-five. He could see his future being torn from him, pulled out to sea. But worse than ending his career, Miss Pat's girls would be devastated.

"Here we go again," one of the nurses whispered to Bo. "Like last month. The return of Dr. Death."

Slowly, though, minute-by-minute, step-by-step, Miss Pat seemed to improve.

An hour later, life returned to her face. Her heart resumed a normal rhythm, regular, no ectopic beats. Her blood pressure steadily rose above the one hundred level. Maybe . . .

"When you get time," Joe said, "let's move Ms. Paragone to the first bay. Her rhythm should be fine on the procainamide, but I'll feel better if she's up front. And I apologize if I chewed on anyone. Bo, I'm sorry. For real."

"It's all good," Bo said.

"Thanks, everybody, I'm going to bed."

As Joe rounded the corner into the front hall, Delia caught up to him from behind. Her hand brushed against his scrub pants, pushing the cotton fabric against his moist skin, making him aware that his whole body was covered with sweat.

"I wanted to tell you that you did a great job out there. I was worried about that drug with her blood pressure, but I guess we were lucky." Delia stroked his shoulder.

"Lucky, hell. We were good," Joe said.

"You were good. You are good." She squeezed his deltoid.

Joe beamed. No woman ever admired him for his body. "Yes, thanks," he stammered. He'd won the endorsement of the ICU head nurse, arguably the most important opinion in the unit, maybe in the hospital. Everyone knew she had De la Toure's ear, not to mention the attention of the administration.

"One thing about a code: It gets the juices pumping," she said. "It takes me a while for the stimulation to subside."

"What?"

"Aren't you aroused, juiced up on adrenaline?"

"Are you serious?"

"Yes, the thrill of saving someone's life. We're kind of gods. Ms. Paragone is alive because of us. We saved her. We could've just as easily let her go."

"I guess you're right, but she didn't really code. We didn't pump on her chest."

"That was a code, Joe. And you were awesome."

They arrived at Joe's door. A perfect ending to a perfect day, his first night in the ICU, and he'd triumphed. Suddenly, he felt awkward, as if he should kiss Delia good night. He suppressed a chuckle at his sophomoric thoughts.

"Need me to tuck you in?" Delia asked jokingly.

"No, I guess I'll be all right."

"OK, sleep tight, and don't let the bed bugs bite."

As Delia started to close the door, Joe moved next to his bed. He pulled the scrub top over his head. At the apex, he paused, flexing his shoulder and back muscles, stretching the material. It felt good. "Awesome" she called him. He grinned like the Cheshire Cat.

As he tossed the shirt onto the back of his desk chair, he noticed Delia watching through the slit between the door and its jamb. She smiled at him and nodded.

"Good night," he said.

She pointed to the desk next to his bed. "Did the tooth fairy leave you something?"

"What?" Perplexed, he turned. The psychedelic square of plastic clamored for acknowledgment. Joe was mortified. "Oh, it's something I found," he stammered, but Delia had already left and closed the door.

* * *

JOE LAY ON HIS BED. Only half asleep, but eyes wide open. Joe thought about Delia. Did she want him? He'd never felt so desired and it felt good.

Startled awake, he glanced at the clock. Six o'clock. It was New Year's Day, but Carlisle might still come through early. He grabbed his clipboard and hurried out of the room.

As he walked, he examined the diagram for De la Toure's patients. Hurrying through the first patient bay, he headed for the second group of beds. Joe, however, stopped in mid stride. Last night, he'd told them to move Miss Pat to the front bay, and he hadn't updated his diagram. To no one in particular, Joe called out, "Who has Ms. Paragone?"

"Over here, Dr. Morales," Bo said.

Joe went to bed 9. "How's she doing?"

"Slap stable."

Joe grabbed the lab flow. The morning results had been recorded, a column of normal values. No red circles. Euboxic.

"Thanks for filling in the lab results."

"Don't thank me," Bo said. "Delia did it. She said you'd crashed and burned, so she filled out all the heart patient forms."

"Nice."

"Can you talk with Ms. Paragone?" Bo said.

Even though he had to check on other patients, he recalled the terror in Miss Pat's eyes the night before. He leaned over and squeezed her shoulder.

"You're going to be just fine, Miss Pat."

She managed a weak smile.

"You're in great hands and visitation starts in an hour. All the little girls will be here to cheer you up."

Now, he had to roll. There were over a dozen patients that had to be checked before Carlisle showed for rounds.

As Joe tried to leave, Bo stopped him.

"Be sure to come back. She's had a smooth night, gravy since the code, but she's spooked and needs some reassurance."

Joe started to correct him. It wasn't a code. They didn't perform CPR, but he didn't have time to teach this goofball nurse. As Joe left the bedside, Bo continued talking like a kid trying to hold on to an older brother, wanting to be an equal.

"You want to come down on the procainamide drip? She hasn't had any more of those wicked rhythms. All sinus. Smooth."

"No. Leave it for Sufi. I don't have time. I'll be back."

Joe jogged through the unit. Only one patient in the whole ICU had a lab abnormality, hypocalcemia, and Delia had already written a verbal order. Finished with his superficial inspection, he was sure nothing catastrophic had transpired in the last two hours. Had it been only two hours since he'd gone to bed? He'd take a nap after morning rounds. He knew the danger of starting a rotation sleep deprived. The resident had to remain alert.

People's lives depended on him.

CHAPTER TWELVE

"DR. MORALES, DR. MORALES," ANITA CALLED FROM the overhead speaker. Reflexively, Joe looked around the back patient bay. Then, he realized Anita was calling from the front. Carlisle was there for rounds.

He hurried through the ICU to the information desk. As he walked, he reviewed the names on his clipboard, the location of each person, the procedures they'd undergone. He planned how he would start the presentation of the first patient. Joe left the front bay and headed towards the entrance.

De la Toure waited, arms crossed, jaw clenched. Anita's focus remained fixed on the computer screen.

"Happy New Year," Joe said. "I didn't think you would be making rounds."

"Dr. Morales, are you ready to start?"

"Yes, sir. I was just——."

De la Toure had started walking without waiting for an answer, passing Joe before he could turn around. Joe pivoted and headed into the ICU on De la Toure's heels, trying to catch up. Residents' law: Always lead the old man.

"Dr. De la Toure," Joe said. The old man stopped. "Did Dr. Carlisle let you know that . . . the DNR—." He glanced at his clipboard, but he'd marked out the name. Now he couldn't read the patient label, and even to save his job, he couldn't remember Dr. Verney's name. "Did he tell you the heart in bed 28 died?"

How could he be so stupid?

"Yes, Dr. Morales. I am aware Dr. Danielle Verney died yesterday afternoon. I met with her family." He stressed the name for dramatic effect, and Joe felt appropriately shamed. "Now can we make rounds?"

"Yes, sir. And did Dr. Carlisle tell you about last night?"

De la Toure didn't answer. He'd already passed through the first bay and entered the second patient area.

"Bed 9," Joe said, almost shouting. De la Toure stopped, turned, and glared at him. Joe gestured to the right side. "You have a patient here."

De la Toure retraced his steps to the front section. "Dr. Morales, I realize you may not know any of the patients' names, but you don't even know where they're located. Have you seen anyone this morning?"

Joe didn't respond. How could he? He walked to the foot of bed 9, where Miss Pat now lay. At the portable stand for the computer, he moved the mouse to select the tab for the patient's vital signs. Then, with fluid motion, he moved random papers covering the bedside flow sheet and opened the patient's chart to the most recent page of doctor's progress notes.

Joe peered over De la Toure's shoulder. He was taken aback by the date of the last note, 12/31. Yesterday. Why hadn't he written any notes this morning? He might as well walk out the door and down the stairs to the parking lot and aim his Ford Taurus for the Mexican border.

No! He could pull this off. "Ms. Paragone is one day status post coronary artery bypass times four. She was doing well until last night, when she developed some ventricular arrhythmia, one period of actual V-tach. I gave her lidocaine according to the residents' protocol, but she went back into V-tach, and I started her on procainamide."

De la Toure didn't say a word.

Well done, Joe thought. Articulate, concise. He'd handled the emergency with aplomb.

Joe stepped aside for the old man to advance to the head of Miss Pat's bed, but De la Toure didn't move. Instead, for five interminable minutes, the old man examined the bedside flow sheet, his index finger pointing to the arterial pressure measurements, blood gases, potassium, magnesium, every lab result.

De la Toure turned to the computer stand and opened up the summary page where nurses typed their notes. To Joe's dismay, De la Toure began to read, screen after screen, moving the mouse down. Click. Click. Click.

No one read the nurses' notes. Document skin care. Document IV sites. Record vital signs and medication administration. Not much information.

De la Toure, though, read every one. Then, he pushed the cart away and returned to the chart, reading and rereading the progress notes. As he read, he mumbled, "Another patient with V-tach, and every lab is normal. I do not understand."

In the background, Joe heard Carlisle enter the unit with a friendly greeting for Anita. Carlisle turned the corner into the front bay, but he headed for the opposite side to examine his own patient. He offered no reprieve for Joe. Finally, De la Toure closed the chart and moved to the head of the patient's bed. After checking the pulse, he held Miss Pat's right hand.

"Good morning, Ms. Paragone. How are you feeling?"

"Exhausted. Like I was up all night sewing costumes and painting sets."

"That's understandable. You had a little problem with your heart rhythm. We'll have Dr. Sufi examine you this morning. He's the rhythm specialist."

De la Toure gave her hand a little squeeze. Releasing his grip, the old man turned, walked out of the patient area, and headed back toward the front desk. Joe followed, confused. What about the other patients?

At the entrance to the ICU, De la Toure stopped abruptly and Joe almost ran over him.

The old man turned and glared. With extended index finger, he poked Joe's breastbone three times, driving an invisible stake into his heart.

"What are you doing?" De la Toure asked.

Joe stood still, dumbfounded.

"Are you trying to kill my patients?"

"No, sir. I don't know—."

"I cannot allow incompetence, Dr. Morales. You wrote your progress note yesterday afternoon. The patient was having frequent ectopy. Did you talk with my associates, Dr. Carlisle or Dr. Masters? Did you call the cardiologist, Dr. Sufi?"

"Not right then, but—."

"Then last night, when Ms. Paragone coded?"

"She didn't actually code. She just had some V-tach."

"Do not contradict me. Ever."

"Yes, sir."

"In the point-of-care, there is a code form filled out by Bo Getty. Ms. Paragone was hypotensive, and yet, you started procainamide."

"But the patient responded, it worked, and I thought—."

"Dr. Morales, let's get one thing clear. I do not care what you think. Do you understand?"

"Yes, sir."

"You are here to be my eyes and ears. We have an abundance of highly trained specialists working in this hospital, and you have Delia here to guide you. They will do the thinking. You aren't an expert on anything. You're here to obtain your surgical education, and if this behavior is repeated, you'll be looking elsewhere for your training. Probably without much success." As De la Toure left the unit, Carlisle and Delia appeared from the patient area and followed De la Toure out of the ICU.

When the doors closed, Joe realized he was shaking. He was at the front of the ICU, out of view of patients and nurses, but still, he thought everyone was watching. Everyone witnessed his humiliation. He wanted to race to the restroom and empty his stomach, drain his body of this feeling of inadequacy.

His only hope was that Carlisle and Delia would come to his rescue. Last night, he had talked with both Carlisle and Sufi. Somehow, De la Toure would understand.

Only five minutes passed, but it felt like fifty before Carlisle reappeared through the electric doors.

"Are you all right, Joe?"

"I'm not sure."

"I wouldn't worry too much. Sometimes, Dr. De la Toure gets a little carried away. Delia is trying to calm him down. I explained how well you handled the situation last night. Now, why don't we go ahead and make some rounds? Dr. De la Toure asked me to see the rest of his patients."

"Yes, sir. Thank you, sir."

* * *

DE LA TOURE LOOKED up from the list of December's cases that lay on his desktop. Masters stood directly in front of him.

"Katrina, are you here for tomorrow's schedule?"

"No, sir. I wanted to talk about my proposal."

"Stop. I don't have the time or energy to discuss the lab."

Masters spun around and moved toward the door, only to meet Carlisle head on.

"You guys decide on our schedule?" Carlisle asked.

"No." Masters took a side step to pass by Carlisle.

"We were just getting to that," De la Toure said. "Katrina, wait a minute."

Carlisle pulled a rounds list from his lab coat. Masters stopped and faced them, but she didn't move closer. She stood behind Carlisle next to the exit.

"How many cases?" De la Toure asked.

Carlisle read from the patient list. "We have three hearts. Mr. Ottis, the redo. Mr. Kubecka, you know. He's a week out from his heart attack, the farmer with the daughters. I think he's ready. And Mrs. Wendt. Also, an aneurysm and a lung."

"Heaping full schedule for the day after New Year's," Masters said.

"It's all right, but not great," Carlisle said. "I've wanted to discuss our volume with the two of you. On the 15th, HealthTex is set to announce the makeup of its demonstration project, McClintock's Accountable Care Organization. If he picks us, it will be like winning the lotto."

Masters squeezed her arms that were already crossed in front of her chest. "Victor, I can't work anymore than I do now. I'm here on New Year's Day just to find some lab time."

"That's part of the problem, your misplaced priorities."

"Look, Victor. You can take this job and shove it."

"Don't give me some country-music cliché."

"Victor, Katrina, enough," De la Toure said. "Let's settle on our schedule and get out of here. It's New Year's Day." De la Toure picked up the surgery schedule and took a sharpened pencil from the brass holder on his desk.

Carlisle spoke first. "Put me down for Wendt. She's from New Braunfels, and I went to medical school with her primary doc."

"Sure. Do you want the aneurysm or the lung resection?"

"I'll do them both. No problem."

"All right," De la Toure said and jotted the initials VDC next to the appropriate patients.

"Jacques, I told the OR that you'd do Kubecka," Carlisle said. "He had a small heart attack, but he'll do well. He's only fifty-two."

"Sure, but I performed Mr. Ottis's first operation."

"I'm sure Masters won't mind doing him. Then, you take Kubecka and I'll take Ottis. Is that acceptable to you, Katrina?"

"Whatever."

"Fine," De la Toure said, eager for the unpleasantness to leave. "I'll see you both tomorrow."

Carlisle started for the door but stopped. "Katrina, want to join me for some breakfast?"

"No, I'm needed in the lab. You know our boss doesn't make allowances for my research responsibilities. He's happy for me to pursue them in my free time."

"Katrina, I'm sitting right here, and that is neither accurate nor appropriate," De la Toure said.

Carlisle said, "You have to admit that it doesn't produce income."

"Look, I don't have the time for this," Masters said as she bolted for the door.

"I'm out of here, too," Carlisle said. "I'd like to get home before the games start."

With a mixture of jealously and awe, De la Toure watched Carlisle leave. He was young, handsome, a gifted surgeon. Carlisle knew exactly what he wanted and how to get it. De la Toure used to feel that way.

After they left, he grabbed a stack of mail. On top, the announcement for the monthly QA meeting. It wouldn't be pleasant. Then, there were three other committee notices. He stared at them, but tossed them on his desk. Why did physicians let so many outside influences dictate the practice of medicine? De la Toure pushed the unopened envelopes to the side. They could wait. He walked out the door after his two associates, his two children. They liked to bicker, but they were the best. Masters had a fantastic mind. Carlisle had incredible hands.

At the elevator Carlisle pushed the arrow pointing down.

Masters stood at the intercom outside the research labs. She pushed the red button beneath the speaker.

"Yes," a deep voice said.

She looked up at the security monitor. "This is Dr. Masters. Can you open the door?" With a buzz the electronic lock opened. Masters grasped the door, and pulled it toward her. She paused. "Victor, want to join me? There's a stack of reports you could review."

"No, thank you. I'm assigned research duty in April, and that's too soon for me."

* * *

THERE WERE NO O.R. CASES on New Year's Day, so for seven hours, Joe circled the unit, stopping at each bed. Every third patient he'd go back to Miss Pat, checking her monitor, looking for any PVCs plotting an attack. Inside the break area, a group of nurses watched a bowl game on TV. He didn't know who was playing, but wherever the game was located, it was getting dark, and he assumed that night approached outside in the real world. For the next two months, Houston might as well be as far away as Los Angeles or New York.

Joe carried out all of Carlisle's instructions. Sufi came through and seemed happy. In fact, everyone was pleased with his performance except De la Toure. Unfortunately, De la Toure's was the only opinion that mattered.

Delia approached him from the hallway leading from his quarters.

"Are you back?" Joe asked.

"Yes. I have to regain control of my unit. Your friend Matt screwed up things, and unfortunately, you doctors try to pin the blame on the nursing staff. I won't let that happen."

Joe decided it was best to ignore her remarks. Matt was his friend, and in a way, it was "us against them." Residents had to band together against the nurses and the attendings, even though all the residents were competing for the same cardiac spot with the old man.

"Anyway," Delia continued, "I thought that because there wasn't any surgery, I'd work the night shift again and help Bo get acclimated."

"You said he's had a lot of experience."

"He came from Amarillo Heart."

"So, why would he leave their program? It's huge."

"I don't know. Maybe he wanted a change."

"You checked on him, right? He doesn't seem to be that knowledgeable, and he's as jerky as a Mexican jumping bean."

"Joe, you know nurses are at a premium. Sometimes we have to take what we can get."

"But not for the charge nurse position."

"I'm keeping a close eye on him. And on you." She chuckled with her final words. "Rough day?" she asked.

Joe wondered if he looked as bad as he felt. "Not really. Just the fiasco this morning. De la Toure was totally unreasonable, but the rest of the day has been smooth."

"Don't worry about Jacques. That's the way he deals with complications. Dr. Carlisle and I straightened him out."

"Thanks for the help this morning with the labs."

"Oh, it was nothing."

Joe yawned. "I think I'll go lie down for a minute." He went back to his quarters, slipped off his shoes, and lay down on the bed. He closed his eyes and tried to sleep. He needed Elizabeth

* * *

HIS WIFE'S TYPICALLY LOUD knocking signaled her approach. Joe sat on the side of the bed as she entered. Her red wool dress conformed to a shape that belied her new-mother status; she'd lost the baby weight instantly. The outfit exuded class with its simple, straight lines, except for Elizabeth's natural curves.

"Elizabeth, you came."

"Of course, mi corazón." She liked to use his mother's term of endearment. "Your mother is watching Joaquín."

She walked over and gave him a hug. A wave of smells splashed over him: the clean scents of Ivory soap and baby powder. Joe remained seated, his stocking feet barely touching the cold linoleum floor.

"Are you all right?" she asked as she sat.

Joe leaned back on the bed with his head propped by pillows lined against the wall. "I guess."

"You don't seem too sure," she said, her expression full of concern. The deaf knew how to display a wide spectrum of emotion across their faces.

"It's just I've had a difficult start."

"You want to tell me about it?"

"I had a tough night, a code—well, a sort-of code—followed by some rather unpleasant rounds, or should I say, round."

"What?" She signed the word forcefully, obviously confused.

"De la Toure saw only one patient, accused me of trying to kill the lady, and left."

She made the sign for "kill," and then finger spelled K-I-L-L.

"That was his word."

"Pretty mean," she signed.

"Not really as bad as it sounds." Joe sat up straight, moved forward, and placed his feet into the tennis shoes on the floor in front of him. "It was a case of the old man not wanting to hear about a complication. You know us surgeons. Because we do perfect work, we expect perfect results."

"Yes, and you typically shoot the messenger who points out the imperfections."

"Exactly." Joe smiled. "I actually handled the code well. My only error was in presentation this morning. I should have told him about the complication at the same time as the death."

Again, she seemed incredulous. She furrowed her brow as she signed, "You've already had a death?"

"Just a DNR, two actually, but I should have told the old man about the almost-code before we arrived at the patient's bedside. Hey, let's not talk shop." As Joe moved down the bed to be closer to Elizabeth, he spotted the condom on his desk. He thought he'd thrown it away. He jumped in front of her, gently pushed her chair back from the desk, opened the drawer and tossed the offending package inside.

Joe's eyes caught Elizabeth's. Did she see it?

"I wrote you a card to read later," she said. She reopened the drawer to put the envelope inside, but her hand came out holding the neon orange plastic square. "What's this?"

"Eric's idea of a joke," Joe said. He grabbed the condom and tossed it in the trash. "Now, tell me. Where did you and Matt go for New Year's Eve? I talked with Mamá at midnight, and I sent you three texts and two e-mails." He hoped she would let him change the subject.

"Yes, Lupe told me, but I thought I'd come in person."

"So, how was your date?" She couldn't hear the tone of his voice, but he hoped she understood that he was annoyed.

"Dinner was nice, but I guess we stayed out a little late. Matt took me to Brennan's. Can you imagine? I haven't been there since . . ."

Since we married, Joe thought. Elizabeth gave up a huge amount when she picked him instead of another trust-fund kid. Her father cut her off, and Joe knew she had to miss the life she'd left behind.

"Pretty fancy," Joe said, "but you shouldn't have let him."

"He has the money."

"I know, but still."

"I'm glad you encouraged him to stop by our house. I told him he could stay with us for a couple of days. Until he can find a place."

"Elizabeth, I don't think it's a good idea."

"Why?"

"I'm here. You're there."

"Joe, I know you're not jealous of Matt."

"No, I'm not, but how's it going to look?"

"When did we start worrying about what other people think?"

"You know what I mean."

"Sure, Joe, but it will be only for a couple of days."

"He could stay with Eric."

"You're joking, I hope."

Elizabeth looked away, finished with that conversation.

Joe searched for a neutral subject. He touched her arm and pointed to the acrylic poster pinned to the wall. "Thanks for the window. You totally captured the sunset at Pie de la Cuesta." He was only five when he'd visited, but in his wallet, he kept the photo of his cousins and him playing. He was sure that if he was blindfolded and dropped on the beach, he'd recognize it immediately.

"It was nothing much, but this was so sudden, and maybe I was unreasonable."

Elizabeth moved closer as she spoke. She took his hand, and as he stood, she pulled him to her and hugged him.

Sometimes it helped that she couldn't hear, because he didn't know how to put his feelings into words, anyway.

He realized how lucky he was. Even when he was totally exasperated, Elizabeth knew what to say and how to say it. She was always the first to make up. He responded to her embrace, hugging her tightly. Then, he ran his hands gently down her back, trying to communicate his deep love. He could feel moisture on his neck and knew it was from her tears.

He opened his eyes to find Delia standing at the door.

"Excuse me," Delia said.

"No problem. Come in. This is my wife, Elizabeth." He turned Elizabeth around and signed to her as he spoke. "Elizabeth, this is Delia Jackson, head honcho of the ICU."

Elizabeth held out her hand. "Nice to meet you, Delia."

Joe winced slightly. Elizabeth was good at lip-reading, but her speech pattern lacked variation of pitch and volume. He recalled his own shock when he discovered she was deaf.

He'd arrived late for the biochemistry tutorial session with one of the grad students. Elizabeth, statuesque with short straight hair, stood at the blackboard. Her tailored slacks and silk blouse seemed out of place with the T-shirt-and-jeans crowd. When she turned to face the group, he saw the pearl necklace that confirmed his initial impression: that she was a rich, sophisticated beauty. Then, she talked and Joe realized she wasn't quite perfect. Something wasn't quite right.

Delia stuttered for a moment, and then spoke as she took Elizabeth's hand. "You're even prettier than your picture. We sure appreciate your sharing Joe with us these two months. He's a sweetie." Delia spoke slowly and loudly, but it didn't help because as she talked, she moved over to Joe, breaking the line of sight between her lips and Elizabeth's eyes.

"Yes" was all that Elizabeth said.

An awkward silence followed. Joe looked from his wife to Delia and back to his wife. He guessed Delia was taken aback by his wife's deafness, and he could tell from Elizabeth's stance that she knew about the head nurse's reputation.

Finally, Delia put her arm around his shoulder. "Joe, I need you to check on some patients. Sorry, Elizabeth, but I have to steal your husband."

Elizabeth didn't speak. Maybe she didn't understand.

Joe said, "Delia, I'll be right there."

Delia released him and started to leave but stopped at the door and turned to face Joe. Grinning, she summoned him with her right forefinger.

Joe explained to his wife, signing as he spoke. "Sorry." He tried to effect the facial expression of a Shakespearean actor. "But I have to get back to work."

Only when Joe started to move did Delia leave them and head

back to the ICU. Following, Joe escorted Elizabeth down the hall. Delia waited for him at the front desk. She took his elbow and directed him toward the first patient bay.

"Good night, Joe," Elizabeth called out.

He looked over his shoulder to say goodbye, but Delia gave him a tug, and he didn't speak. Instead, he had to follow Delia, leaving his wife behind.

CHAPTER THIRTEEN

DE LA TOURE CLOSED HIS EYES AND LEANED HIS FACE into the pulsating water. It was the day after New Year's. It would be the first operating day of 2014.

He stepped out of the steam-filled shower onto the polished marble floor, slipped into a luxurious Egyptian-cotton robe and headed across the expansive bath to his mirror. There, he critically evaluated his changing facial features. He thought he resembled a Shar-Pei: Thinning hair topped deep furrows over sagging eyelids, the sadness of his face reflecting an inner disquiet. He wasn't vain, but he had to confront the effects of his advancing age. His back ached after a long day leaning over the operating table, his eyes strained to examine the intricate sutures, and he'd developed a fine tremor that he had to mask by supporting his arm against the patient's body.

He thought of the young surgeons under his tutelage, their lack of experience and knowledge compensated by strength and energy. The weight of the recent ICU deaths hung on his shoulders like a lead coat.

De la Toure didn't want to be forced into retirement, but he was approaching his sixty-third birthday. He wondered how much longer he could operate, and whom could he trust to tell him when it was time to quit.

At least this morning he'd be operating on Mr. Kubecka; it'd be a simple straightforward procedure. But first he had the QA meeting, less fun than a root canal.

"Good morning, Jacques," Susan said sleepily as she moved behind him. Her smiled beamed from the vision reflected by the mirror. Glistening, snow-white hair framed an exquisite unlined face. As his aging accelerated, hers seemed to slow. The ten-year gap between them now seemed like twenty.

She always said age was just a number. He loved her for that. And Delia hadn't found him too old, but whom was he kidding? Fortunately, he came to his senses before Susan knew, before he'd gone too far astray. He hoped.

"You're up early." She moved behind him and wrapped her arm around his waist. She looked into his eyes in the mirror.

"Remember our first New Year's Eve?"

"Yes, I do."

His cheeks filled with a deep rose color. December 31, 1982. He hosted a business party at the Cohen House on the Rice campus, and he asked his then-nurse Susan to serve as hostess. At midnight, a display of sparklers in the garden dazzled his guests. As they watched from the terrace, he asked Susan to become his wife.

Now, thirty years and six children later, he loved her immensely. Despite his mistake with Delia, or maybe because of it, he cherished her more than ever. He thanked God he hadn't destroyed his marriage. He promised himself it would never happen again.

"How about tonight? Dinner at seven?"

"It sounds wonderful."

He was proud of their children: a lawyer, a teacher, a computer programmer, a nurse, a biology student, and a seminarian. If he retired now, what would be the effect? Susan would love him regardless, but how would they finish educating their youngest three?

* * *

JOE STAYED UP ALL NIGHT trying to keep Miss Pat in a regular rhythm, his head never hitting the pillow. Her students deserved this effort, but he was exhausted. He felt like he'd been cast in a reality video, "V-tach Gone Wild," patients performing for the rolling cameras in order to secure their fifteen minutes of fame. Too bad it wasn't funny.

Each death was driving another nail into his coffin. No matter how sick they were, he had to keep them alive.

Joe went back to his room to shave and brush his teeth, hoping a splash of cold water would refresh him.

Eric thumped on the door, pushing it open with each bop of his knuckles. He stood in the doorway with his trademark smirk.

"Do you ever wait?" Joe said. He tried to mask his annoyance with a little laugh. But it was already seven o'clock, and Joe only had a few minutes of quiet before the newly arriving nurses would start in with questions on the thirty-odd patients under his care. He'd just sat down on his bed. "What you need?"

"I came by to say howdy and give you today's OR schedule. Sorry I didn't get it by last night, but it was New Year's. Right? I'm glad to see you're getting some rest."

Joe started to say something. Eric had little to do this month and he was still trying to slide by every chance he got.

As Joe stood up to take the list from Eric, he noticed a huge bruise on the back of Eric's neck. "Man, you get another hickey like that and you'll need stitches."

"Very funny, Chico." Eric grabbed the front of his white, lab coat and pulled it down, hiking up the rear collar, hiding last night's trophy.

"Eric, what does your wife say when you come home with those wounds?"

"Look, Joe. You think you know me. You think it's all a vacation living at the McClintock's. Well, screw you."

"Hey, sorry. It probably isn't cool living with the in-laws." Joe imagined how bad it would be to live with Elizabeth's dad. "But if living in River Oaks is torture, chain me to the wall."

"Here's the OR list," Eric said.

Joe took the typed sheet from Eric's outstretched hand and quickly perused the columns of names and associated procedures. "Only three hearts?" Joe asked.

"Yup. One each for the old man, Masters, and Carlisle." Eric lay down on Joe's bed and patted the mattress, feigning a comfort Joe knew didn't exist. "Not too bad, Chico. You spend your days stretched out here, while I'm working my butt off."

"For real? Let's swap. I wish I was in the OR this month," Joe said. "My first assist with De la Toure was awesome. Now you can scrub the old man anytime you want."

"Wrong. I'm going to hang with Carlisle as much as possible."

"I thought you wanted the cardiovascular spot. No better chance to show the old man what you've got."

"Double wrong. I know you operated with De la Toure last month, but that's a no-win. You can't impress him, and you can definitely screw up. I'll stick with Carlisle. He's fast, makes me look good, and I get out early to boot."

"I thought you were asking Masters about a research project. That's a huge time commitment. I ought to know."

Eric sat upright. "I'm planning to. I'll probably start in March."

"After the cardiac fellowship is announced?"

"I guess."

"But then you wouldn't need to do the research project."

Eric grinned back at him. He was caught, but he showed no remorse.

"You do what you have to do, Chico."

"You think you have it all figured?"

"Yep. Eric's law. It's how you play the game that determines who wins and who loses."

* * *

"GOOD MORNING, DOCTORS," Sufi said to begin the Quality Assurance meeting in the Lutheran boardroom.

"Good morning," echoed the assembled members: Hackett and the hospital lawyer; Masters, Allgood, Chiu and assorted other physicians; Delia and her crew of QA nurses, professionals who'd been trained to scour the charts for any variance from established benchmarks.

De la Toure shook his head when he thought of the number of nurses the hospital employed for quality assurance, the constant struggle to satisfy various government agencies and insurance companies. Sometimes he wondered if they assured any quality of patient care.

"We have a lot to cover," Sufi said. "So, let's get started."

De la Toure thumbed through the handout until he came to the surgery statistics. He pored over the numbers. From two seats away, Hackett glanced at De la Toure's agenda and opened his copy to the same page. Like overeager students, both men read ahead, oblivious to Sufi's discourse.

"Our first item is a review of blood use." Sufi continued with various housekeeping functions. No subjects aroused any special interest. Then, he came to the final item.

Sufi paused. "Before we review these statistics, I want to remind everyone of the confidentiality of this committee."

The assembled members exchanged questioning looks. Usually such a warning indicated a delicate topic was upcoming, a physician with an addiction or perhaps a particularly unfortunate complication, such as amputation of the wrong leg.

Sufi continued. "Nothing is to be discussed outside of this venue, and all of the materials are to be left here."

The committee members exchanged muffled comments.

Then, Sufi started. "I asked Delia to assemble the mortality statistics for the cardiovascular surgery service. If you'll turn to page fourteen." There was a rustle of pages. "Delia, please elaborate."

"Yes. If you'll look at the bar chart, I've compiled our results, and for comparison, I've included the mortality rates at the four similar hospitals that HealthTex provided us when they performed our cost analysis along with the national average."

"Delia, it looks as if our rates fall barely within the national standard," Sufi said.

"Yes, sir. From an overall standpoint, our statistics put us in the expected range, although at the upper end."

Katrina Masters raised her hand. "What worries me more is that the deaths are steadily rising. And these rates are over the top. Mine can't be this high."

"Yes. If you'll turn to page sixteen, I've separated the deaths by doctor. Of course, all the results are blinded."

De la Toure looked at the page. The mortality rates were listed in columns for surgeons A through E, but it didn't take a forensic accountant to figure out which was his column. It stood out like an out-of-tune violin in a string quartet.

"Delia," Sufi said, reclaiming the group's attention. "Did you determine the acuity level of the patients, the coexisting conditions that would affect the outcome, such as age, heart failure, emphysema, or renal failure?"

"I tried, but I didn't have that kind of data."

Masters raised her hand again. "Exactly, Mo. These stats don't mean diddly squat. Without knowing specifics, we can't compare small variances between individual surgeons."

"But these differences are dramatic," Hackett said. "One surgeon has three times the mortality rate of the other four."

"No, we can't really draw that conclusion," Sufi said.

"But Evan's right," Masters said. "Overall, we're at the upper end. We have to lower our mortality rate."

"You're right, Dr. Masters," Hackett said. "We have to be concerned with our statistics. Not only the business sector, but even Medicare is searching for health care bargains. They want competitive prices and good results. Many hospitals are putting their statistics on the Internet. We've been approached by BestHospitals.com, and HealthTex will be announcing with which hospital it will partner for their ACO demonstration project."

"Evan," De la Toure said. "This is neither the time nor the place for this sort of scare tactic."

"Don't interrupt me," Hackett said.

"Gentlemen," Sufi said. "Be reasonable."

The group silenced. Sufi recognized Dr. Allgood, who wanted to speak.

"All of us here are concerned with quality." The group mumbled its affirmation. "Right, Chief?" he asked De la Toure.

De la Toure nodded slightly, giving his permission for Allgood to continue.

"But we can't base decisions on bogus data. Why don't we pick some docs and nurses to examine the outcomes? They can evaluate the surgeons and the residents, and also examine anesthesia, cardiology, perfusion services and the nursing care in the ICU."

De la Toure thought the assembled group was waiting for his response. "I think that's an excellent suggestion. I move we appoint Dr. Allgood as the chair of the subcommittee."

"Second," Masters said.

"Any opposed?" Sufi asked. No response. "Good. Dr. Allgood, I'll help you, and I know Dr. Masters will, too."

"You betcha," Masters said.

"If there's no other business, this meeting is adjourned."

As the group began to leave, De la Toure approached Hackett. "Your comments were entirely inappropriate. As a representative of the administration, you're here as an observer."

"Right, Jacques, but it's our charge to monitor the results of our medical staff when they fall below standard." He moved to the door, denying De la Toure the opportunity for rebuttal.

Delia tapped De la Toure on the shoulder, and then took his hand to turn him around. "Jacques, I have to tell you something."

He turned to face her. "Delia, I've asked you not to—."

She moved in close.

De la Toure stepped back. "What do you want?" He spoke with intentional harshness, wanting his words to push her away.

"Excuse me, but I was trying to warn you," she said.

"Of what?"

She spoke in a whisper. "I'm missing a copy of the agenda with the CV stats, your mortality rates."

Someone wanted to tell the world about the old, incompetent heart surgeon. They wanted to remove him from the equation so that the hospital could claim to be the best. What was he to do?

He had to consider Susan and his children, all the sacrifices they'd made: the family vacations without him; the soccer games, school plays, and award ceremonies he hadn't attended; the bedtime stories he didn't read; all the hugs and love that had been missed.

But his first priority always had been his patients. If they took them away, he wouldn't have any purpose.

* * *

JOE DECIDED TO PUT MISS PAT back on the ventilator. That way he could keep her sedated but still well-oxygenated. And it seemed like it made it easier to get her rhythm under control. He needed to have her stabilized before the new hearts started coming out from the OR.

Then he went back to his room. Time to focus, to try and retain control. Fortunately, the faculty QA meeting meant a late start for the OR. Joe closed his eyes and waited. . . .

"Dr. Morales, bed 5," Anita called.

The first heart was on its way, with two more to follow. Joe sat up and let his feet dangle on the side of the bed. He pulled out the resident instruction sheets and read about fresh post-ops for the umpteenth time. He played out the steps in his head. He could do this. First, put the patient on 100% oxygen until the blood gas result comes back. Second, examine the chest x-ray. Third, check the labs. Keep the hematocrit above twenty-four, use bicarb and Lasix to bring down the potassium from the cardioplegia, and treat the calcium and magnesium. Fourth, if the patient is bleeding, check the coagulation studies.

Yes. He could do this.

* * *

LATE THAT AFTERNOON, JOE sat staring at a plate of cold mystery meat and vegetable surprise immobilized in congealed grease. He was hungry but he didn't have the energy to eat.

De la Toure's patient, Steve Kubecka, had arrived in unrelenting V-tach. Joe shocked him at least ten times. Now, he had every imaginable drug dripping into his veins. Joe had given him potassium and magnesium. He put him on 100% oxygen.

At least he'd stabilized enough for visitors. A widower, the former minor league shortstop had four daughters. So, he'd supplemented his farming income by coaching softball at the Wharton County high school. All of the girls were there to see him—his own and those from various teams—maintaining a vigil for Coach Steve. Like Miss Pat's ballerinas, they pleaded with him to save Coach Steve's life. As if Joe had control, like an emperor turning his thumb up to save the life of a gladiator. He wished he had a fraction of that power.

He'd sat at Kubecka's bed for hours, but finally decided he needed to try to eat something. He was exhausted and needed the change in scenery, if only it was his resident cell.

"José?" his mother called from the doorway.

Joe rose from his dining table, the small surface on wheels that functioned as an all-purpose table for patients. "Mamá, what are you doing here?"

"I came to see my little one." Lupe embraced her son, and kissed his forehead.

"You working tonight?" Joe asked.

"I'm cleaning the labs, and I saw your Dr. Masters. A nice lady, but she needs a husband and a baby. All she does is work."

"Mamá, she's a professional."

"She told me you have problems. Is everything OK?"

"Yeah, Mamá, I'm fine."

"Mi corazón. My heart cries for you. This work is hard on you and on Elizabeth, too. Why don't you talk with Dr. Carlisle? You always admired him. He will help."

"Mamá, por favor! This is my job. I can handle it."

"Mi corazón, I will pray for you. All of us are praying."

Joe knew she meant Latinos when she said "us," and he wanted to scream that he wasn't part of "us."

"Thanks, Mamá. You pray, but right now, I'm eating lunch."

"Lunch?" Lupe looked at her watch. "Mi pobrecito." Lupe took a silver chain with a medallion and placed the charm around his neck. "Remember, the Virgin told Juan Diego to put it in his heart." Lupe blessed her son. Then, she took the medal and brought it to his lips.

After kissing the Virgin, he took his mother's hand that held the image and placed it over his left chest. Since his youth, his mother had taught him to give his worries to the Virgin. He went through the motions, but he didn't believe the Guadalupana could help him.

"Thanks. I have to go now," he said as he hid the medal under his T-shirt. He loved his mother and didn't want to hurt her feelings, but he wasn't going to wear a religious medal for everyone to see.

"I'll come back."

"OK, but please, only after ten."

"Why so late? Are you ashamed of your mamá?"

To be honest, he was embarrassed. He wanted to explain, but it was complicated.

"Because I clean the floors?"

She couldn't understand. "No, Mamá, you know. . . ."

"Cuidado, corazón," Lupe said.

I'll be careful, he thought.

* * *

THAT EVENING, JOE STOOD guard at Kubecka's bed. Coach Steve had arrived in unrelenting V-tach. His daughters and his players, current and prior, had set up camp in the waiting room. At least Miss Pat had stabilized after he'd put her back on the ventilator. He'd moved her to bed 32 in the back patient bay. Everyone was tucked in, except for Coach Steve. Joe couldn't let him die.

Somehow, if he stood here and stayed alert, it wouldn't happen. It couldn't happen.

Not again.

CHAPTER FOURTEEN

ENTERING FROM THE PATIENT SECTION, RAUL MET
Joe at the front desk. "José, we're proud of you. If my Lourdes
were here . . ."

We? Joe moved a few steps away. When he was young, his
mother told him to stay away from neighborhood thugs. She said if
you ran with wolves, you learned how to howl. He loved Raúl, but
Joe had escaped the barrio, and he didn't want anyone—Raúl, Anita,
his mother—pulling him back inside.

With a ding the elevator doors opened to reveal an oversized,
silver-haired man in a tan, western-cut jacket. He wore the face of a
common workingman, leathery and lined from too many years in
the sun.

"Buenos tardes, Señor Dallas," Raúl said.

"Buenos tardes, Viejito," McClintock responded.

They both chuckled at the reference to Raúl as an old man. Like-
wise, Joe grinned, amused that this insurance giant would be so
friendly to a gardener who lived over the garage.

"Mr. McClintock," Joe said, moving back to Raúl's side. "I'm Dr.
Morales, Joe Morales. May I help you?"

"I'm looking for Dr. De la Toure. Is he out of surgery?"

"Yes, sir. He's probably upstairs in his office."

"I was just there. If he comes back through, tell him Mr. Hackett and I are waiting for him in the administration offices." McClintock pushed the elevator button and turned back to the desk. "Joe, my son-in-law speaks highly of you."

"Thanks. Eric's a great guy."

"Yup. Of course, he's disappointed you beat him out of this ICU rotation, but I say competition's good. Next time, he'll work harder."

Joe didn't know how to respond, so he smiled. McClintock returned the gesture with a big grin of his own. The elevator doors opened. McClintock hesitated. With his hand, he prevented them from closing.

"Raúl, I can't believe we've still got some rose blooms even now in January. You're a miracle worker."

Joe thought of Juan Diego and the roses he'd picked on a frosty mountain top for the Virgencita.

"Dr. Morales, Dr. Morales," the overhead speaker screamed as the elevator doors closed. "Bed 32, stat."

The elevator doors closed and Joe raced to Miss Pat's bed.

* * *

AS DE LA TOURE APPROACHED Hackett's office, a heated discussion from within startled him, so he waited outside the door and listened.

"Don't worry about Jacques," McClintock said. "He knows you're bright, but frankly, he doesn't want new ideas. You're upsetting the apple cart."

Hackett said, "Sir, in my defense—."

"Evan, hold your horses. I don't give a rat's ass what Jacques De la Toure thinks of your work. And neither does the rest of the board. Jacques resides in a different decade. He thinks we're still living in the time of cost-plus billing. Hell, any idiot could have made money in those days."

"That's true," Hackett confirmed.

"Yup. The bureaucrats talk about the exploding cost of medical care, but they created the monster, a sector of the economy in which the greater the money spent, the greater the profit. What did they expect? The incentive was for more and more. Never say die."

"So now that the government is tightening its belt, we have to drag these doctors into the era of cost containment."

"Kicking and screaming all the way."

De la Toure opened the door and entered.

"Jacques," McClintock said. "We were talking about you."

"I heard," De la Toure said.

"Good," McClintock said. "You know I don't mind speaking my piece."

"And what would you have us do, Dallas?" De la Toure asked. "Let patients die?"

"Look, here's a prime example." McClintock picked up a two-inch-thick computer printout and handed it to De la Toure. "This customer of HealthTex was admitted with a fatal heart attack. In the old days, he would have received some IV nitroglycerin and a little morphine. There was a greater than 90% chance he would have died in a day or two, but thanks to decades of uncontrolled technological advances, he received this dad-blasted clot-busting medicine."

"You mean, TPA," De la Toure said. "Tissue plasminogen activase."

"You got it. He gets the clot-busting stuff, then about twenty thousand dollars' worth of ICU bull, and is he cured? Nope. He keeps having chest pain, so he gets a heart catheterization, which to no one's surprise shows blocked heart arteries. The next step is open-heart surgery and a balloon pump."

"What was the outcome?" Hackett asked as if on cue.

"He survived surgery in order to spend his last days above ground on a ventilator. Overall expenses topped two hundred thousand. Thank goodness he didn't last another week or two. At least he died on the third day after surgery."

"Pardon me, Dallas," De la Toure said. "I'm not sure what you're leading up to. What would you have us do?"

"The point is this, Jacques. Every day, I get these printouts of outliers, patients whose expenses exceed the normal range. We call the doctors and harass them, but once the horse is out of the barn, what you gonna do? What we need is to get you cowboys to stop before you start. You know which of these patients is going to be a long haul for a short gain."

"Dallas, I'm tired of trying to explain to some insurance clerk on the telephone why I, the patient's doctor, have decided to operate."

"But what you don't realize is that medicine has to work like a business. You cut your losses."

"I'm sorry, but you can't apply the same principles to the hospital that you would to running a McDonald's."

"You joke about McDonald's, but how long would they be in business if they were selling hamburgers at a loss?"

"All right. Enough. What do you want? Specifically."

Hackett leaned forward in his chair. "We want your support for the joint venture with HealthTex."

"Get on with it."

"Lutheran Hospital and the Houston Heart Institute are widely respected," Hackett said. "If we join together to form an Accountable Care Organization, we'll corner the Medicare market. Dallas has enough influence on the hospital board to get it approved—that is, with your support. If you fight us, it could get bloody. I'd have to let the rest of the medical staff know you're blocking them from a very profitable contract."

"Are you threatening me, Evan?"

"Jacques," McClintock said, "Evan didn't mean any threat, but if we play on the same team, we're gonna score a lot more touchdowns, and no one will get hurt. Now listen, the Affordable Care Act offers a lot of opportunity. Obama wants demonstration projects just like the one we're proposing. We'll get a fixed amount of money and if we spend it wisely we'll make a bundle. It's like a bird's nest on the ground."

"Explain," De la Toure said.

"If we control our expenses and cut utilization, we can make a real profit. With my company's reputation, Lutheran as our platinum-level hospital, and the Heart Institute as our cardiac provider, we can capture the Medicare market for this area. Every bozo and redneck in the state will sign up with us."

"But if we lose money on Medicare patients, as you say, then how do we operate on even less money?"

"We have to be more efficient," Hackett said.

"You mean selective. Limit services, avoid spending the money on the high-risk patients." De la Toure said. "Your profit comes at their expense."

"Jacques," Hackett said, "you can twist this any way you want, but we can't continue to waste money on hopeless cases. We have to be more . . . selective, if you want to use that word."

"And it wouldn't hurt your stats either," McClintock said.

"What?"

"I'm trying to make Lutheran our platinum-level hospital, the highest quality designation HealthTex can assign, and Dr. Carlisle has talked with the board about participation in the BestHospitals.com project. Masters and Carlisle's results are the finest in the nation, and the rest of the staff is excellent. Now you have to lower your complication rate."

"How would you know about my QA statistics?"

"I mean only that if you avoid some of these high-risk patients, you'll save money plus improve your results."

"Dallas, Evan, my bottom line:" De la Toure stood. "I support Lutheran in every possible way. I do not object to the hospital forming an alliance with HealthTex. Yet—."

"Here it comes," Hackett said.

"I will not, and my doctors will not, participate in a plan in which the goal is to provide less care. It won't happen while I'm chief of surgery."

"Maybe we need a new chief," McClintock said.

CHAPTER FIFTEEN

JOE FINISHED FILLING OUT THE DEATH CERTIFICATE for Miss Pat. He had a hard time getting all her dancers out of his mind.

When he returned to his quarters, lunch had been removed. In its place sat a dinner tray. Joe tossed Miss Pat's chart with the others waiting on his desk. He'd dictate the death summaries later. Instead, he pulled the stainless-steel lid off the plate to find cold enchiladas made with processed cheese. He hesitated, but sat down and tried to eat.

"Howdy, Joe," Eric said.

Joe wasn't eager for company. "Did you finish the pre-ops?"

"Almost. I have the interns working. So, I thought I'd come by and check out the scenery. Here's the surgery schedule for tomorrow. Five hearts. You'll be busy."

"Thanks." Joe took the typed sheet.

"One pre-op is here in the unit," Eric said.

Joe glanced down at the paper. "Hank Simpson. I thought they'd put him on for the morning."

"Yup. Hey, I still have a bunch of work left upstairs. I'll come back later and get him set up, unless you want to. I mean, because you already know his history."

"All right. I'll take care of him. No sweat."

"Thanks, partner. See you tomorrow." Eric stopped at the door and turned to face Joe. "By the way, what you think of the new night charge nurse?"

"Bo? He's OK. Why do you ask?"

"No reason, but I heard Amarillo Heart got rid of him after a bunch of suspicious deaths."

"What? Who told you that wild story?"

Eric's pager began to beep. "Sorry, Joe. Got to run."

* * *

AT THE FRONT DESK, Joe found Raúl visiting with the night clerk. "Evening, Lakisha, Raúl."

"Buenas noches, José."

"Raúl, did you prep Mr. Simpson?"

"Sí. I washed him with the iodine soap and shaved him. I thought it was the wrong patient, at first. Mr. Hank, he is so young and strong. I think he is too healthy for heart surgery."

"You're right. Mr. Simpson doesn't smoke. He exercises regularly, gets a check-up every six months, and never lets an egg touch his lips. Only one problem."

"What is the problem?"

"Genetics. He can't find a way to change parents."

"His family is the problem?"

"Yes. His history is one for the textbooks. His father died at forty-two from a heart attack. His grandfather popped a stroke. Not one male in his family has lived past fifty."

"¡Qué lastima!"

"Yes, Raúl. It is a shame."

* * *

JOE PULLED OPEN THE curtain enclosing bed 17 to find the construction worker stretched out on his hospital bed. With a muscular physique and slick, tanned skin, he looked more like a male model for a Calvin Klein ad than a patient shaved for heart surgery.

"Mr. Simpson?" Joe said.

"Yes."

Joe moved to the head of the bed. Pinned to his pillow, a large silver disc imprinted with an image of the Virgin of Guadalupe reflected the overhead lighting. Rays shot out from the sun that surrounded the Mother of God.

"What's this?" Joe asked without thinking. This guy was a total redneck. What was he doing with a Latino sacramental?

Hank gazed at the medal. "The orderly Raúl gave it to me. I know your people pray to her."

"Not all of us, Mr. Simpson. Just because my mother's family is from Mexico, it doesn't mean I believe in some miraculous Virgin."

"I'm sorry, Dr. Morales. I didn't mean anything."

Joe felt bad. He wasn't trying to give Hank a hard time.

"No problem. I don't know why this stuff bothers me, but put your faith in doctors, not superstition."

"Deal."

"Okay, I'm here to get you ready for surgery tomorrow. Real scientific treatment. I'm sure Dr. De la Toure has reviewed your catheterization with you."

"You mean the heart drawing? Yeah, he showed me."

"Good. And I know he explained everything to you. You have extensive, atherosclerotic, occlusive, coronary artery disease, and in this situation, he recommends complete revascularization."

Hank Simpson seemed perplexed.

"Heart surgery," Joe said.

"Just like that?"

"Yep. Just like that."

"I've been reading the information booklet, and I'm a little scared. I didn't know about all the complications. I could have a stroke?"

"Don't worry. You're in the best place to have an operation. Dr. De la Toure is constantly adopting new techniques and developing new heart solutions in order to minimize the chance of complications."

"You mean the surgery's experimental? You want to experiment on me?"

"No, sir. You're in good hands. The best, in fact. Dr. De la Toure is the finest surgeon in the world." Exactly what he'd told Lourdes.

"I'm sorry. I didn't mean anything."

"Don't apologize, Mr. Simpson. It's natural to be nervous."

"Would you please call me Hank? And can I call you Joe?"

"Okay. Now, do you have any other questions?"

"No, Joe."

"Then, I'll see you in the morning." Joe wanted to escape this conversation.

"Joe?" Hank said.

He stopped and turned back to the patient. "Yes?"

"I'm sorry if I insulted you. I truly am. But I'm scared. I want you to like me. You know, kind of like a friend. You don't really know me, but I figure you'll try harder if you like me. I'm really not a bad guy."

"Mr. Simpson, Hank, we're going to take care of you like we would one of our own. I promise."

"Thanks, but I'm afraid. I think I'm going to die."

"No, Hank. Nobody's dying tomorrow."

* * *

FRIDAY MORNING, BEFORE HEADING downstairs for surgery, De la Toure sat alone at his desk, the office as silent as when the early morning fog moved in. He turned on the brass, hook-arm lamp Susan gave him, and examined the case lists for the last week of December and the first week of January.

They were very disappointing. He had hoped that, with a new ICU resident, his problems would dissipate. That's how it had always been. There were rough periods: a run of complications and deaths. He'd always kept operating, and the problems abated. He must move forward, but the first days of the New Year brought more deaths. The prince was due to arrive on Monday; his surgery was scheduled for Tuesday. De la Toure had to get the ICU under control.

So, for today's case he selected Hank Simpson, a young, healthy man. He'd always disdained surgeons who cherry-picked patients, selecting those that would provide the best results and favorable statistics. But if he had to be honest with himself, that's what he'd done. Hank was young, healthy with excellent myocardial muscle function. He'd only sustained a small heart attack. The anticipated mortality was as close to zero as you could come.

De la Toure leaned forward with his head propped up by his hands. Medicine had always been a challenge. It was never easy to lose a patient. Deaths called into question your technical skill and judgment, and then there was the threat of lawsuits, but why was it even worse now?

During the last decade, the issue of quality assessment reared its ugly head, giving the illusion that excellence could be measured like the temperature, and now physicians were reporting their statistics in the lay press and on the Internet, advertising their superior outcomes. Insurance companies talked about blue-ribbon hospitals and first-tier hospitals, but they failed to disclose that economics determined the designations.

For the first time in his career, De la Toure questioned his own medical judgment and even his surgical ability. It seemed his doubts were racing to an intersection, and he feared the convergence would result in an explosion. Sometimes, it felt as if the inside of his chest was ready to split wide open.

"Dr. De la Toure?"

He looked up. "Victor, please come in. Take a seat. I want to speak with you about the residents."

"Did Masters complain that I've been too hard on them? She's such a Nazi about this eighty-hour work week."

"Oh no, not at all, but I am concerned, and I want an objective opinion. Matt Keith was a disaster. Now Joe Morales is off to a bad start. Masters thinks he's the best resident in our program, but he's done research for her and his wife works in the lab. I don't think she's capable of evaluating him objectively."

"I see, and I'm the tough guy of the department?"

"To be honest, yes."

Carlisle straightened in his chair.

"This is not a party to which we've invited the residents," De la Toure said. "I feel personally responsible for the education of these young people, but, more important, I am ultimately responsible for all of the lives they will touch when they leave. I will not allow one surgeon out of my program unless I have total faith in him or her, unless I would let the doctor take care of me or my family."

"And you're worried about Morales?" Carlisle asked.

"Yes. He seems overwhelmed by the job and the prince will be here Monday. What's your impression so far?"

"He's bright, but he seems to lack self-confidence."

"I see. Do you think we should pull him before there are more problems? I made a mistake in leaving Keith there too long."

"I don't know. Morales may be treading water right now, but I'd give him a little time. He has a lot of potential."

"As we discussed before, we could move Eric to the unit, and there would be positive PR with McClintock."

"Eric would be good, but why don't I have a talk with Morales? If I think he can't handle it, I'll let you know."

"Thanks, Victor. I appreciate your assistance. We've had a lot of trouble in the ICU. Last month was bad, but this month is off to even a worse start. I want to make sure things run smoothly."

"I'll help you in any way I can. We have to watch out for administration—especially given that Sufi launched that special committee with Allgood to evaluate our statistics."

* * *

JOE EVALUATED THE GRITS on his plate. Even with heavy doses of butter and cheese, they still tasted like crushed cardboard.

He picked up the OR schedule lying next to his breakfast tray. TGIF. If he could get through the day, he'd have the weekend to get everyone settled in and mellowed out. Hank would be a slam-dunk: young guy, big coronaries, good heart. And Carlisle and Masters had four more hearts on the schedule. They all seemed straightforward, but still there'd be five patients to care for. Joe frowned.

He pushed the food aside. Maybe lunch would be decent. He walked over to his bed, lay down, and peered out his window. He valued the two hours of peace before the real day began.

* * *

DR. DE LA TOURE STOOD next to Hank Simpson's stretcher outside OR 19. The patient was nervous, and he tried to bring some calm by placing his hand on Simpson's shoulder. Silently, he prayed, but not for the patient. He always prayed for his patients when he washed his hands at the OR sink. This morning, though, he prayed for their surgeon. For himself. He couldn't face another death. In his whole career, there'd never been such a series of disasters, as if a plague had descended on him.

It couldn't really be his fault. He wasn't that old. And a study from the Annals of Surgery concluded that surgeon age was a weak predictor of operative mortality.

Actually, it was the patients who were older and sicker. He had to expect more complications if he continued to take on the most difficult cases, and that's why he told Carlisle he wanted to operate on Hank today. The young construction worker was healthy, as strong as an ox. He had no other medical illness, no diabetes or hypertension. A near-zero percent chance of mortality.

Allgood approached, a stethoscope draped nonchalantly around his neck. De la Toure noticed that Hank's attention was drawn to the long hair, pulled back and constrained by a rubber band, and to the silver cross dangling from Allgood's left ear lobe. Allgood was the best anesthesiologist in the hospital, but De la Toure could only imagine what Hank Simpson was thinking.

"Morning, Chief. Mr. Simpson, my name's Johnny Allgood. I'll be passing the gas this morning."

"Uh, great," Hank said.

"Dr. Allgood, I'll leave you two." He knew that Allgood was a gifted physician, but it was truly painful to listen to this conversation. Sometimes Allgood sounded like the washed-out addict he used to be, but at least he did as he was told, which was more than he could say about most anesthesiologists. "I'll be in the lounge. You may proceed." It would take a minimum of twenty minutes before the operation would begin.

"Super," Allgood said. "We can get cooking," he said to Hank Simpson. "I have a few more questions. Then, I'm going to start a small IV. Next, we'll move into the operating suite and put you to sleep. After all that, Dr. De la Toure will fix your heart."

"Sounds great," Hank said.

De la Toure wished he shared some of his unbridled optimism.

CHAPTER SIXTEEN

"IS EVERYONE READY? START THE CARDIOPLEGIA." DE la Toure surveyed the set up before opening the first artery for bypass. The pump with its roller head turning, squeezing the blood through the tubing, was invented eighty years before by a young medical student, Michael E. DeBakey, who had the rare combination of academic genius and technical skill.

From the heart-lung machine, the blood was pumped back into the aorta, the largest artery of the body, immediately above the cross clamp he'd applied. The clamp prevented any blood flow into the arteries of the heart. That's where the cardioplegia came in, protection for the cardiac muscle.

Satisfied that all was working properly, De la Toure turned to his scrub tech. "Marie," he said with his most seductive French accent.

Marie Coleman blushed underneath her mask, even through her dark complexion. He knew she liked the mild flirtation.

"Marie, let me see the vein."

With fluid motion, Marie took a white towel from the scrub table, and laid it in front of him. "There's one bad spot near the end," she said. She directed his attention to a branch of the vein that wasn't adequately tied.

He spoke to her as he repaired the defect on the vein that Eric had harvested. "Marie, you are a treasure."

He valued her. How many times had this scrub technician, her formal education concluded with a high school diploma, kept him from serious complications?

While he examined the vein, De la Toure spoke to Eric. "You see. This is why I have Ms. Coleman. To keep an eye on you. Your mistake could have killed this patient. Will you ever learn attention to detail?" He watched Eric fidget in silence. He'd been a little harsh on the kid, but he knew he had to start working with the boy if he was going to develop into a real heart surgeon.

"One liter of cardioplegia," Chiu said. "But we still have no arrest."

Routinely, the EKG would be completely flat after half that volume. Today, the EKG showed a ragged, coarse V-tach, even after a whole liter of the high potassium solution. De la Toure wondered if it was caused by electrical interference. He inspected the heart. No, there was a coarse quiver of the muscle. De la Toure understood what it meant at the cellular level. ATP molecules were giving up their energy to fuel the frantic motion of the cardiac muscle. He lifted the heart, checking the placement of the cannula administering the cardioplegia.

"The cannula is in good position. Let's go ahead and start. Continue the cardioplegia slowly. It may take a while to get good arrest."

De la Toure went to work. After selecting a site on the heart for bypass, he stuck the artery with a pointed knife and extended the opening with fine, curved scissors. Without speaking, he and Eric each held out a hand, and the appropriate instruments appeared, courtesy of Marie. De la Toure began attaching the vein to the opening in the artery using a 7-O Prolene, the suture invisible as it passed through the air.

The work proceeded with well-rehearsed movements, the occasional remarks limited to questions for the resident to answer. De la Toure began with a simple toss-up for Eric.

"What classification of suture is this?"

De la Toure waited patiently for the answer that should have been instantaneous, even from a new intern, much less a third-year resident.

"It's a synthetic, sir. . . . A non-absorbable," Eric said with hesitation. "And a monofilament fiber," he added as if an afterthought.

At least it was the correct answer. The operation proceeded without De la Toure asking Eric anything more. He could barely tolerate the boy's mediocrity. Finally, he finished the last suture.

"Nicely done, Dr. De la Toure," Eric said.

De la Toure ignored the obsequious remark.

"We never got arrest of the heart," Chiu said. "I give three liters of cardioplegia. That's very much."

"What is his potassium?" De la Toure asked.

"It's OK, Chief," Allgood said.

"Good, let's see if we can get him out of here."

De la Toure removed the cross clamp. Blood filled the aorta, the new grafts, the native arteries, and the whole heart. The fine fibrillation became more vigorous. Hank Simpson was experiencing coarse V-tach.

"Paddles," De la Toure said.

Marie Coleman moved swiftly behind De la Toure and retrieved the internal defibrillator. She handed the cord over the drapes to the anesthesiologist to connect to the power source. She placed the long paddles in De la Toure's hands.

"How high you want 'em, Chief?" Allgood asked.

"Let's start with twenty joules." Careful not to hurt the newly constructed bypass grafts, De la Toure slid the two paddles into the chest.

"Clear? Fire."

The patient jerked slightly as the electric current passed from one paddle through the heart to the second paddle, and then dissipated by releasing its current into the body. The fine quiver stopped. The muscle stilled.

"Turn the pacer on," he instructed the anesthesiologist.

"Rate of eighty, demand pacing," Allgood said.

The irregular heart movement returned.

"Watch out," Allgood said. "He's back in V-tach. Pacer off."

"Give him another hundred milligrams of lidocaine," De la Toure ordered.

"A vicious cycle," Allgood said. "The V-tach makes the heart ischemic and that causes more V-tach. The dog's chasing his tail, and we can't get it to stop."

"Let the lidocaine circulate for a minute or two. What were his last blood gases?" De la Toure asked.

"They fine," Chiu answered. "Normal pH, oxygen was four hundred, bicarb was within limit."

"How about the magnesium, calcium, and potassium?" De la Toure asked.

"Mag was a little low, but I treat it. His calcium fine. K was low. I treat it, too."

"His potassium was low?"

"Yes, sir. I recheck it first and then I give the bolus."

"Good. If you've fixed his electrolytes, shock him again," De la Toure said. "Forty joules this time."

"Charged," Allgood said.

"Fire." The heart stilled and then started to contract. De la Toure waited patiently. Slowly, the muscular pump squeezed harder and harder. "Thank God, this guy is young. The heart is contracting nicely, now. Let's let him eject a little."

Chiu went into motion. She allowed the heart to fill with blood. The arterial tracing on the monitor now showed a noticeable blip.

"That's good," De la Toure said.

"I come down," Chiu said.

"Stop. Hold your volume," De la Toure ordered.

"We're starting to see some nasty beats, Chief," Allgood said.

As De la Toure watched each beat of the heart, a nagging question repeated in his mind. What could be causing so much V-tach? Fortunately, the heart slowly improved.

"Dr. De la Toure," Chiu said. "We ready to start working off pump."

"Go ahead, but come down slowly this time."

Chiu weaned the patient from bypass. "We off."

The heart steadily improved and De la Toure started the process of closing.

Satisfied, he stepped back from the table. Crossing his arms and grasping his gown from each side, he tore the paper garment from his body with a sharp snap. He wadded the gown with his discarded gloves and tossed them into the trash container.

"Thanks, everyone," De la Toure said. As he exited, he pulled off his surgical cap and wiped the sweat from his brow.

"Thank you, Dr. De la Toure. I'm glad I was able to help," Eric said.

CHAPTER SEVENTEEN

THAT AFTERNOON, JOE SAT ON A STOOL IN FRONT OF bed 6 with his forehead supported by open palms, his elbows resting on his knees.

"José?" his mother said.

He looked up.

"Are you all right, mi corazón? Anita told me you're having so much problem. We're watching out for you, even if you don't know. We all want to help you."

Joe shook his head from side to side. What was she doing here? Did she have any idea how embarrassed she made him feel?

"Mamá, basta! Enough."

"José, you know we're so proud—."

"Mamá, right now, I can use some solitude. Do you understand? Please, leave me alone."

He buried his face in his hands, willing her to go away.

"Joe?"

"Mamá, I asked you—." Joe stopped in mid-sentence as he looked up to find Masters standing in front of him where his mother had been.

"Oh, I'm sorry, Dr. Masters. Hello."

"Howdy, Joe. I came by to check on you before afternoon rounds with De la Toure. Any problems?"

He wanted to howl with maniacal laughter. "In a word? Yes. There's plenty. Where do you want me to begin?"

"What?"

"All hell's broken loose. The ICU was full of disaster patients when I came, and it's getting worse."

"Joe, we always have a bunch of sick folks. This is the cardiovascular surgery rotation with Dr. Jacques De la Toure."

"Fine. You think it's normal. Then, let me enumerate. Mr. Duffey and Dr. Verney died Tuesday and Pat Paragone yesterday. They were sick, DNR's, but they were rock stable. I've been working on Mr. Kubecka's rhythm all day. I haven't even told Dr. De la Toure, yet."

He pointed to the plasma screen over the bed. The monitor read "PVC—8/min." V-tach waited around the corner.

"I'll be coding him tonight."

"You haven't told Dr. De la Toure about Mr. Kubecka?" she asked, her voice rising with each word, demanding an explanation.

"No. I tried to grab Dr. De la Toure when he talked with Hank Simpson's family, but as you can see, I couldn't leave."

"I understand."

"No, Dr. Masters, I don't think you do. I've hardly slept in three days. I'm barely hanging on." He felt near tears.

Masters lowered her voice. "Why don't we step into the conference room and go through the patient list?"

Masters walked briskly behind the administrative assistant's desk and Joe followed. After he entered the room, she locked the door, turned, and glared.

"Joe, let me offer you some advice. I like you. You're bright and an excellent researcher and technically, you're pretty good, but this is a difficult rotation. Sometimes, Dr. De la Toure tackles more than he can handle, taking on very ill patients. And Dr. Carlisle's a machine. He believes in volume. The end result's a lot of work for you, a lot of patients, and some are pretty sick." She paused, relaxed the corners of her mouth that had pulled her lips into a taut line, and smiled. "Now you've got to get it together. I'll tell Dr. De la Toure I've made afternoon rounds and I'll let him know about the problems you're having with Mr. Kubecka."

"Thank you, Dr. Masters."

"Don't thank me, Joe. Just cowboy up."

* * *

AFTER A SHOWER AND SHAVE, Joe felt more awake and alert. The problems that seemed insurmountable just a couple hours before weren't that bad. Three deaths had lumped together. The number was unusual, but not unheard of.

Joe placed both hands on the Formica counter and leaned into the front desk of the ICU. Like an exhausted marathon runner, he stretched his aching calf muscles one at a time. Caring for five routine hearts was a challenge for any ICU resident. And these weren't routine. Eric told him De la Toure's case, Hank Simpson, had a rough time coming off bypass—runs of V-tach—but at least, after arrival in the ICU, he stabilized. Fortunately, Coach Steve had settled down also. Joe decided to take advantage of the lull in the action.

"Lakisha, I'm going to lie down. I have to have an hour or two of rest. Ask the night float if it's an easy question, but call me if you need me. I hope you guys can give me some time."

Delia emerged from the patient area. "Go ahead, Dr. Morales. It's been a rough one, but things have settled down. De la Toure's gone, along with Masters and Carlisle. If you want to take a nap, I'll wake you in a little while."

"Thanks, Delia."

Joe plodded down the hallway. Before entering his quarters, he turned back to Delia, who had followed him into the corridor. "Come get me at nine."

"For sure, Joe. I'll keep it quiet for you."

By seven o'clock, Eric had already come through the unit with Monday's OR schedule. Eric wanted to exchange war stories and check the body count, but Joe wasn't in the mood.

Then, Matt came by. He said, "Now you have your own deaths." Not much of a friend.

He faced a difficult night with Hank and four other fresh hearts to watch over, not to mention Kubecka and the two sick-as-hell DNRs left in the back bay.

Joe slipped his scrub top over his head and tossed it on the chair. He lay down flat, face up, on the firm bed, his hands folded on his chest. It seemed as if all four walls were moving toward him, the room imploding on him.

He wanted to scream like a torture victim does immediately before unconsciousness, but he wouldn't. He couldn't. He had to focus. He had to relax for a few minutes or an hour. A night of vigilance awaited him. Internally, he repeated a familiar mantra: No more deaths. No more deaths. No more deaths.

Joe considered his space. Plain, barren, the only color provided by the Houston skyline poster and Elizabeth's seascape. It did look like Pie de la Cuesta, the foot of the mountain. As a five-year-old, he had visited the remote beach. He recalled the unblemished sand and the clear, emerald waves crashing on the shoreline. At sunset, there was a surrealistic orange sky. From all around the world, people came to that stretch of beach north of Acapulco to watch the day find its end, each time creating a masterpiece.

Man, what a day. Joe drifted off to sleep.

I sit on the edge of the shore as the sun works its way down to the sea.

The sand feels hot, full of the energy it absorbed throughout the day. Even at dusk, the unrelenting rays burn my skin, my noticeable pigment still inadequate protection for the intense radiation, inadequate compared to the dark color of Mamá's native people. My father must have imbued me with a considerable dose of European genes.

I sit alone at the top of a sharp decline, the steep slope down to the sea created by the ravage of towering waves, and I wiggle my toes into the coarse sand, fascinated by the contrasts of texture and color: the coarse, white crystals against my soft, olive skin covered with thick, jet-black hair.

A wave slams in front of me, erupting like a volcano with water spurting up and raining down lava on my feet. I hear the happy voices of children interspersed with the roar of crashing waves, and I turn to find the source.

A group of dark-skinned boys frolic in the surf, engaged in a tribal dance of youthful joy. Closer to me, a preschool-aged boy runs up the beach, kicking a vinyl ball decorated in primary colors. He weaves in and out with exaggerated zigs and zags, dodging invisible defenders, heading for the goal.

The child jumps into the air and retracts his leg, preparing for one final boom that will send the pretend soccer ball streaking past the goalie.

He moves with the agility of a martial arts expert, but before he can complete his play, the sea reaches up and captures his toy. When he propels his leg forward, it fails to meet the ball and the vacuum left behind sucks his foot into the sand.

I chuckle, not laughing at his inadequacy, but sharing his innocence. I relish the joy of simple play: a boy, a beach, a ball.

I stop laughing when I realize that the boy's crying. He watches the sphere bounce on top of the foam. The ocean taunts him, dares him to retrieve his property, holding it a few feet in front of him, just beyond his reach.

The child starts down the sharp decline of sand and eases into the shallow water. It rises only to his knees, even with the incoming waves, but the surf crashes less than a yard in front of him, forming an impenetrable wall of water, a force field guarding the prized beach ball.

Suddenly, the boy dives into the next incoming wave and disappears from sight. I'm worried that he has fallen into the drop-off near the shoreline, but he resurfaces, preceded by the multicolored globe that he holds high over his head.

His arms rise toward the sky, victorious, tightly holding the championship prize. His undeveloped chest swells, and he thrusts the ball upward. The world recognizes his manly accomplishment.

I clap my hands in agreement.

The child's face is familiar. He reminds me of myself. In fact, he could be my son.

From nowhere, a tower of water rolls toward him. The boy doesn't see the attack that's ready to blindside him. Blue and green surf together with the white foam of a mad dog race toward him, ready to devour him.

CHAPTER EIGHTEEN

"JOE?"

Joe heard someone call, but he didn't want to leave the beach. He rolled over and buried his face in the mattress. His muscles tensed.

The boy. It was his little boy.

"Cuidado, Joaquín!" Joe yelled.

"What did you say?" the voice asked.

"Cuidado. Watch out!"

Someone shook him. "Joe, you're dreaming."

"What?" Joe raised his head and peered over his shoulder toward the source of the kind voice.

"You're having a nightmare," she said. Velvet hands gently massaged his bare shoulders. "Are you OK?"

Her caressing warmth filled him. It was balmy and aromatic. "Yeah. Thanks. I had a dream about my boy."

The massage resumed, and she continued speaking in a calm, melodious voice. He didn't listen to the words so much as embrace the feelings, her tone, her warmth, her fragrance.

"That feels good," he said from the twilight zone between sleep and awakening.

He closed his eyes as his head fell into the pillow. Slowly, her hands moved down his body. She worked her fists into his lower back.

He turned over to face his visitor. She leaned toward him. Her tan contrasted with the white lace bra visible under her V-neck scrub top. He could also see on her chest a tattoo of a viper. He closed his eyes as she squeezed his pectoral muscles rhythmically. He wanted to return to sleep, to dream pleasant dreams.

Suddenly, he was awake. "Delia?" He looked up at a creature unlike any that had ever been attracted to him. Her hands stopped moving, but held their position.

"Yes, Joe," she said with her Georgian accent that caressed like a soft summer breeze. The fragrance of jasmine wafted toward him. Time almost stopped.

"Delia, I'm married."

"I know that, Joe. I know." She continued the forceful massage of his chest. "I'm looking at forty. I'm not some little student nurse in search of a doctor husband. Been there, done that, got the divorce papers to prove it."

"But Delia—."

"Shhhh," she whispered and her hands resumed.

A loud pounding on the door caused him to completely awaken.

"Joe?" Elizabeth called from outside the door.

Joe leaped from the bed, leaving Delia sitting, her position almost unchanged. On the way to the door, he grabbed the scrub top. "Wait a minute," he said reflexively, knowing his wife couldn't hear him, but hoping through some miracle that it wasn't her.

She opened the door while he was pulling the shirt over his head. "What's going on here?" As she spoke, she signed the words with forceful movements.

"Delia was waking me."

157

"Excuse me?" A flash of incredulity filled Elizabeth's face.

"I had a rough day and I took a nap. I asked Delia to wake me, so I could check on the post-ops."

"That's right, Elizabeth. I came in to get Joe out of bed. He was having some kind of nightmare, so I sat with him until he fully woke."

Joe signed bad dream to make sure Elizabeth understood what she'd read from Delia's lips.

"Nightmare?" Elizabeth asked.

"Yes," Joe said.

"This is incredible, Joe."

"Why didn't you tell me you were coming? I e-mailed you that today was busy. I thought you were coming tomorrow. Are you checking up on me?"

"You know better than that. I brought Joaquín to see the doctor, and I saw your mother here at the hospital. She said she'd keep Joaquín so I could come visit you."

"It's just that you took me by surprise," he said.

"Obviously." Elizabeth placed her hands on her hips and let out a slow sigh. She stared past Joe to the ICU nurse. "Delia, would you mind?"

"No, of course not," Delia said. Deliberately, Delia rose and strolled from the room. At the door, she stopped and turned back to them. She spoke slowly, enunciating her words clearly. "I'll try to keep it quiet so you lovebirds can have some privacy."

"Tell her I'm deaf, not stupid," Elizabeth said to Joe in a stage whisper.

Joe grimaced. Fortunately, Delia let it drop and left.

Before the door closed, Elizabeth began. "Joe, what were you two doing?" She spoke loudly and her arms flew through the air as she emphatically signed her words.

"What are you talking about? With Delia? Don't be ridiculous. Do you think I'd do something right here in the unit?"

"You are so naive. Can't you see that woman is putting the moves on you? She knows you're vulnerable, and she's moving in for the kill. Wives talk. There isn't one of us who hasn't heard about Delia Jackson."

"Elizabeth, I know all of the stories, but honestly, there's nothing between us. She's been really good to me."

"I bet."

"Yes. She's saved me more than once already. She told the old man I handled Pat Paragone flawlessly even though she died. And De la Toure didn't blame me. It was a miracle."

"Yes, Saint Delia."

"Elizabeth, you have no idea what kind of day I've had."

"Mine was no picnic, either. Joaquín isn't feeling well."

"How can you compare taking care of a baby with trying to keep these thirty patients alive?"

"Dr. Morales, bed 17," intoned the overhead speaker.

"Elizabeth, I have to go."

"You want me to wait?"

"Honestly? No. I have a lot to do, and it's already late."

Elizabeth pulled an envelope out of her purse. Joe recognized one of her trademark, brightly colored designs decorating the cover that would enclose a page of flowery prose. Elizabeth had always been self-conscious about her voice and thus had mastered the forgotten talent of letter writing.

As Joe spoke, Elizabeth walked over to his desk and pulled open the drawer to drop off her note.

Joe looked down and saw a cellophane-wrapped neon square, but he knew he'd thrown it away. He grabbed the letter from her hand. "Thanks," he said as he dropped the envelope and then closed the drawer. Enough with that joke. "I'll read it tonight. Right now, I have to round on the patients, check labs, write progress notes—."

"Joe, we have to talk."

"Dr. Morales, bed 17." Lakisha's voice called again.

"Elizabeth, I have to go."

"It's OK," Elizabeth said. "I know you're busy. I'll come back tomorrow."

Joe followed her down the hallway to the entrance of the ICU. Before she could exit, he tapped her arm and she turned back to face him. "Anyway, what was wrong with Joaquín?" For a moment he recalled his nightmare. This time, the boy in the surf was his son.

"He's been running a little fever. Because of the VSD, I want to be extra careful. We saw the resident who staffed the clinic, and he said it was a mild upper respiratory infection. He gave him some penicillin."

"So, nothing really."

"Dr. Morales, bed 17. Now." Lakisha's voice was emphatic.

"I have to go," Joe said.

Elizabeth grabbed him by both shoulders. The suddenness of her action startled him. "Joe, I love you a bunch, and we're going to get through this, but you watch out for that woman."

"Elizabeth, really."

Elizabeth started to kiss him, but his attention was drawn to Delia, standing in the entry to the first patient bay, motioning for him to come. As Elizabeth brought her lips toward his cheek, he turned his head and her kiss landed on the hair hanging over his ear.

"Joe, we really need you. Sorry, Elizabeth," Delia said.

Joe wondered if Elizabeth understood Delia. He turned to his wife. "I have to go. Really," he said, and headed quickly for the patient area.

CHAPTER NINETEEN

AS JOE ARRIVED AT DELIA'S SIDE, SHE TOOK HIS ELBOW with her hand and guided him to Hank's bed in the middle bay.

Bo started talking when Joe was still yards away. "His cardiac output has gone down steadily since coming out of the OR. Man, I'm really worried about him, Dr. Morales."

"Bo, why didn't you tell me sooner?" Joe asked, not expecting an answer.

Ms. Paragone was already in the freezer. Now, this would be a second one for the icebox today. And this was Hank. A young, easy heart. He couldn't let it happen. He had to concentrate.

Assess the patient, step by step. Oxygen saturation was 95%. Good. Blood pressure was ninety over sixty, adequate, but the EKG showed lots of ectopy and some short runs of V-tach. Bad sign. And the cardiac output was plummeting. Very bad sign.

"Why is it always the nice guys?" Joe asked himself.

"Dr. Morales," Delia asked, "did you say something?"

"What?"

She summoned him with a glance, and he moved to her side. She leaned in close and lowered her voice, offering counsel while letting him maintain the illusion that he was in charge. "Do you want me to call the perfusionist and get ready for an intra-aortic balloon pump?"

"Uh . . . yes. Exactly." She was so smart. Matt was stupid not to follow her direction. Emboldened by her wise suggestion, he barked the orders. "Call the perfusionist. We're going to put in a balloon." Joe glanced at the monitor, ticking off each PVC. "Tell them it's stat, and get me a femoral line." He looked to Delia and she returned his gaze with positive assurance.

"I'll put in the arterial line now, and then the balloon will go in quickly when they get here."

The whistle blew. Delia directed the troops.

Nurses went in every direction. One went to page the perfusionist. One went to the OR to get the balloon accoutrements. One moved to get the femoral line paraphernalia. And one moved to get a permit from the next of kin.

"Delia, get Dr.—. No, never mind. I'm going to call Carlisle myself. Hand me the bedside flow sheet and the chart." Armed with data, Joe walked to the end of the patient bay. Time to take his licks. He lifted the receiver and punched in the number of the answering service.

"Hello. This is Dr. Morales. Would you page Dr. Carlisle for me? And go ahead and make it a stat page. No, don't make it stat, but can you type in urgent? Wait, try his home first."

"Are you sure, Dr. Morales?" the operator asked.

"Yes, I am. Call his home."

"I'll ring Dr. Carlisle."

As Joe waited, he couldn't help but think of the delicate balance that determined his future. He knew he stood on the verge of losing everything, and he needed the cardiovascular surgery fellowship. But what of Hank's future? Joe had promised Hank. He couldn't let him die.

The operator was talking. Carlisle wasn't at home, and she asked if she should page him.

"Yes, thank you. I guess you'll have to. Can I hold? And when Dr. Carlisle calls, you can patch him through."

As the operator went to work, Joe walked as far as the phone cord would stretch. He couldn't read the numbers from the monitor screen over Hank's bed, but he could see the tracings. He watched the once sharp curve of the arterial pressure dampen, the proud peak flattening into a small mound. Hank was barely hanging on.

Come on, Hank, for both our sakes.

The operator's voice returned his attention to the phone. "Dr. Morales?"

"Yes."

"I'll connect you."

Joe could barely hear Carlisle, but he knew by the volume of ambient noise that the phone connection had been made. "Dr. Carlisle, I'm sorry to bother you, but we're having a problem with De la Toure's patient, Hank Simpson."

"Get on with it."

"Well, he's the young guy. De la Toure let him cool off in the ICU before surgery."

"Joe, cut to the chase. I'm busy. Have you spoken with the attending cardiologist, Dr. Sufi?"

"No, sir. Hank's looking weak here, and I think he needs a balloon pump. I thought I should call you."

"All right," Carlisle said. "Get everything set. I'll be there in a little while, and I'll put the balloon in for you if he needs it."

Joe could hear Carlisle speaking to his companion. "Order me Tony's apple tart and a decaf coffee." Returning to his trainee, Carlisle said, "You understand, Joe?"

"Yes, sir, but—."

"Good."

Joe found himself listening to the dial tone as he watched the activity swirl around him, but even though hospital personnel clogged the aisle, he stood alone, completely and utterly alone.

"Get it together," Joe told himself.

Dr. Masters walked into the middle patient bay. She surveyed the activity at Hank's bed, and then she turned toward Joe as he hung up the phone.

"Got some action, Joe?" she asked.

"Dr. Masters. Boy, I'm glad you're here. This is De la Toure's heart from today. He's looking bad, and I think he needs a balloon pump. I just got off the phone with Dr. Carlisle."

"Actually, I'm in the middle of an experiment upstairs and I don't start unit call until tomorrow. I'm sure Victor will be here soon. You might want to get Sufi's input, also, but I have to go. Sorry."

Joe watched as she walked from the patient area. Some friend. He took several deep breaths while rethinking his options. Then, he walked back to Hank's bed.

Joe outlined his plan to the nurses. "I'm going to put in a femoral arterial line now. Then, when Dr. Carlisle gets here, it'll be quick to insert the balloon into position over a guide wire."

"Good idea, Joe," Delia said.

Joe slipped on a pair of gloves, and painted the groin with an iodine solution. He then laid out sterile towels, draping off a small rectangle around the right groin. "You may feel a stick," he said to Hank.

Intubated, eyes closed, the patient made no response, no movement.

"Don't you want some local anesthetic?" Bo asked.

"No," Joe said.

"You don't think that sharp needle is going to hurt?"

"The stimulation will do him some good. He should be so lucky that he remembers me sticking him."

"Dude, you're cold," Bo said.

Joe decided to ignore the remark. He pressed on the groin crease with his left index finger. He felt nothing. He pushed harder and felt a thready pulsation, barely discernable. He took the long catheter in his right hand and aimed underneath his finger. The needle popped through the skin.

There was no response from Hank. That wasn't good.

The plunger was shaking and Joe realized it was his tremor. He stabilized his right hand with his left and slid the catheter slowly inside. A squirt of blood erupted from the end. Joe pulled the needle out from the center channel and guided the plastic tubing farther into the artery. With each heartbeat, blood spurted from the end.

Pressure coming up. Better.

"Great. Give me the femoral arterial line," he said.

"Yes, sir," Kim Chiu said.

Joe looked at her and she smiled in response. Straight black hair fell around the edges of her round face. A few strands of gray offered the only hint of her age. He wondered how old she was, and he couldn't believe she called him "sir."

"I'm glad you're here, Kim, but what were you doing in the OR? The hearts finished hours ago."

"Paperwork. I heard all excitement. So, I thought you need help."

She handed him the appropriate clear, plastic tubing.

Joe connected the arterial line and checked the pattern on the monitor. "Let's see what we can do while we wait for Dr. Carlisle."

"Good," Chiu said. "I have all materials you need."

Joe took the two bundles from the OR and opened them, forming a sterile field with the necessary equipment out on top. He removed the intra-aortic balloon from its packaging and readied it for insertion. After covering the setup with sterile towels, Joe pulled off his gloves and took a seat on a stool. He watched and waited.

Hank's condition remained precarious. He was hanging on by a thread. After a few minutes, Joe rolled the stool over to a corner and leaned his head back against the wall.

"Joe, if you want to lie down for a minute, we'll holler when Dr. Carlisle comes in," Delia said.

"No. Thank you, though. I'll just close my eyes here."

Time passed. Joe wished it would stop. He had to have a chance to recoup.

"Joe," Delia said.

He opened his eyes, slowly, reluctantly.

"Joe, V-tach!"

Her words splashed over him like cold water. "Get the paddles," he said, unaware that the nurses had already brought the crash cart to the patient's bedside and had the defibrillator ready.

"Charged," Delia said.

Joe rushed to Hank's bedside. The fast, wide rhythm filled the monitor screen. The arterial pressure line was flat. Not diminished, not dampened. It was a flat line.

Joe took the paddles from Delia's outstretched hands, and placed them on the patient's chest.

"Clear." Joe punched the button discharging the electric current into the patient. "Fire." Hank's body jerked. The EKG resumed a regular pattern, and the arterial line showed a minimal pressure blip with each beat.

"Back in sinus," Joe said. "Great. Now back off on the epinephrine."

"But his pressure?" Bo said. "We can't turn the epi down."

"I said 'back off on the epi.' It's making his heart go too fast. And I'm putting in the balloon now."

"Shouldn't we wait for Dr. Carlisle?" Delia asked. She moved next to Joe. "Don't forget you're only the resident." She spoke in a soft voice that only he could hear.

"I'm putting in the balloon. Now."

Joe pulled new sterile gloves onto each hand. Quickly, he disconnected the pressure tubing and threaded a guide wire down the femoral line. He then removed the catheter, leaving the wire in place. Over the wire, he passed the intra-aortic balloon, and connected the device to the console.

"Turn it on," he said.

"Yes, sir," Chiu said. "Balloon is on. We have one to one. Augmentation good. Pressure good. Patient good."

"Turn the epi down some more," Joe said to Bo. "Leave it at twenty-five. That's plenty. Continue with the other drips."

Joe took his bows. He'd never been known for his surgical skill before. He was a bit clumsy and his tremor was a problem. But tonight, he'd inserted a balloon in less than three minutes. The nurses and technicians were clearly impressed, and they should be.

Hank's condition slowly improved. The arterial line now resembled a normal pressure curve. The cardiac output was inching up. A sense of relief was palpable in the crowd.

Joe squared his shoulders and stood erect.

¡Qué hombre! He was the man.

"Wicked," Bo said with approval.

"The patient be much better," Chiu said. "I go now."

"Good job, Joe," Delia said.

He was very good. What did Carlisle say? It's not conceit if you really are the best, and Joe agreed. No one wants humility in his heart surgeon.

Delia walked over to Joe and squeezed both of his shoulders. "You saved this man's life. What a rush."

Joe shrugged. He moved away from her, suddenly self-conscious of her attention, her admiration in front of the other nurses. He returned to his stool, his sentry post.

With time, Hank's color improved. The arms and legs, mottled from the high dose of the epinephrine, started to pink up.

Pink up: It wasn't a scientific term, but it was accurate. Hank was getting better. For sure, he was improving. His skin was now toasty and full of color. Relief flowed through Joe's system. Finally, he could let down his guard, and even though he sat on a rolling stainless-steel disk, he relaxed, almost to the point of sleep.

"Joe?" Carlisle thundered, shattering Joe's peaceful state.

"Yes, sir." Joe jumped up a little too quickly, upending the stool and then tripping himself in an unsuccessful attempt to prevent the noisy crash. Joe looked up to see who'd walked into the second patient bay. "Sorry, Dr. Carlisle," Joe said getting up off the floor.

"How's Dr. De la Toure's patient?"

"I had to put in the balloon, but he's better now."

Carlisle performed a cursory examination of the nurse's flow on the computer screen and the paper chart. "I agree he's better, but do you think he really needed the intra-aortic balloon?"

"He was looking bad. Masters saw him. She knows."

"Don't worry about Dr. Masters. It was your call, Joe. No problem from my standpoint. You were here and you made the decision."

Carlisle trusted my judgment, Joe thought. Awesome.

CHAPTER TWENTY

SATURDAY MORNING, JOE ENTERED THE LUTHERAN Hospital auditorium for M&Ms, the monthly morbidity and mortality conference. Its official purpose was to determine errors and thus introduce changes in the care of future patients, but it mainly served to scorch the residents. They would learn from mistakes in judgment by the exposition of their real or presumed errors. There was nothing like a public flogging to generate humility.

Joe plumped in a cushioned chair in the back row. Faculty members stretched across the front row, but the residents sat as far back from the chopping block as possible.

Eric turned to him. "Glad you could make it."

Joe didn't appreciate the snarky remark. Joe was late for conference, but Coach Kubecka had arrested just after shift change, and he couldn't get him back. Horrible night, first Hank and then Coach Steve. He didn't blame himself for Thomas Duffey or Dr. Verney's deaths. They were DNR when he started the ICU, but Joe knew somehow he'd failed Miss Pat and Coach Steve. They had died from unrelenting V-tach, a totally preventable post-op complication.

Fortunately, Masters rounded early and she didn't seem that upset about Kubecka or Simpson.

Joe glanced at Matt, seated in the row below with Eric at his side, fellow travelers commiserating about the deplorable highway conditions.

Eric smiled, obviously bemused by something. In a low voice he sang the refrain of Queen's "Another One Bites the Dust."

"All right, folks. Let's get this show on the road," Masters said to start the program.

"We'll begin with cardiovascular surgery," Carlisle said.

Matt had to present the last month's complications and deaths. It pained Joe to see Matt Keith stand up to take his punishment.

As Matt walked down front, Eric licked his lips like an eight-year-old in front of a banana split.

"Dr. Keith," De la Toure said. "Please explain the need to take Mr. Martinez back to the OR for postoperative hemorrhage."

"Mr. Martinez is a sixty-four year old gentleman, status post coronary artery bypass in 1975 and in 1990. He presented with unstable angina and underwent evaluation, including cardiac catheterization. He was felt to be a suitable candidate for surgical intervention, and Dr. De la Toure performed third time redo-coronary artery bypass times five. After surgery, he had an increased chest tube output, 500 cc's over the first hour."

"What was your differential diagnosis?" De la Toure asked.

"Given his previous operative procedures, I thought he might have a coagulopathy."

"Dr. Keith, don't you realize the most common cause of surgical bleeding is technical?" De la Toure asked.

"Yes, sir, but I was sure that he'd improve with blood product replacement."

"Obviously, you were in error," De la Toure said. "What did his clotting studies show?"

"Well, . . ." Matt stammered, breaking the first rule of M&Ms: Never hesitate to lie, but if you lie, don't hesitate. Matt probably didn't know the exact lab results off the top of his head, and he'd missed his chance to improvise.

Joe hated to see his friend on the chopping block. Matt didn't need this humiliation, not after the month he'd just been through. He had to help him.

"Dr. De la Toure," Joe called out. He found himself standing up. De la Toure turned in his chair and glared at him. What was he doing? You never initiated conversation during M&Ms. Was it worth the risk to save Matt? And Joe was in enough trouble already.

"Yes, Dr. Morales," De la Toure said.

"I brought Mr. Martinez out from surgery." Joe stepped into the aisle before continuing. "As Dr. Keith said, he was a little wet, and I told one of the interns to watch him and start some Amikar. I thought with his previous surgery and fibrinolysis, the drip would control his bleeding."

"I see," De la Toure began. "Then, because of your extensive personal experience, you were comfortable treating this patient medically, not following the residents' protocol."

"Yes, I mean, no, sir. I suppose I didn't follow procedure exactly, but it wasn't necessary. So, I told the intern——."

"You took a patient undergoing his third surgery, a patient in whom one might expect increased bleeding, and you turned him over to an intern, the most junior member on your team."

Joe didn't know what to say. All he could come up with was "Yes, sir."

"I don't think I've ever seen such a disregard for protocol. If this is indicative of your judgment, we may have to rethink your position as our ICU resident."

"Joe, you got Dr. De la Toure's point?" Masters asked.

"Yes, ma'am."

"Good. I know you won't repeat that mistake. Right? Matt, continue."

Joe plunked back into his seat.

Eric leaned backward. "Masters to the rescue. I thought you were dead meat."

Joe didn't respond, because Eric was right. As Matt finished his presentation, Joe noticed that Eric pulled out his beeper and worked its buttons.

When Matt sat down, Masters spoke to Eric. "Dr. Cunningham, are you ready to talk about your complication?"

Joe leaned forward as Masters spoke and whispered into Eric's ear, "All right, smart ass. Your turn."

"Yes, ma'am." Eric stood and moved to the front of the room, but before he started talking, his pager began its shrill call.

"Sorry," he said.

* * *

JOE COLLAPSED ON HIS BED. He was thinking life couldn't get much worse when the phone rang.

"Dr. Morales," Anita whispered.

"Yes."

"Dr. De la Toure is here."

"What?" Joe said, but he didn't wait for an answer. He'd already rounded with Masters, but now De la Toure was here. He tried to stuff his bare feet into his tennis shoes, but ended up walking on the heels as he struggled to slip on a scrub top. He rounded the corner, trying to stuff in his shirt.

"Good morning, Dr. De la Toure." As he spoke, he realized he didn't have his clipboard, but there was no turning back.

He hesitated only a moment, and then started walking. He passed through the first section of healthy post-op patients, none of which belonged to De la Toure. He hoped Masters had told him about Kubecka's death and he made the decision not to bring it up. Then, he led the old man into the second bay.

"Bed 17, Mr. Hank Simpson," he said. "He underwent coronary artery bypass times five yesterday. He was unstable coming out."

De la Toure glared.

Bad start.

"But, he was doing pretty well. Then, as the day went on, his cardiac output started falling. I, I mean we started him on Inocor and went up on the epinephrine, but he worsened. At about ten last night, we put in an intra-aortic balloon. I think he's looking better this morning."

"I'll determine that, Dr. Morales." De la Toure terminated the presentation. Joe knew when to shut his mouth. There was no way to know what Carlisle told him about last night or what Masters reported to him about her morning rounds.

De la Toure approached the bedside and began his examination of the patient record. Closing the chart, he spoke to Joe. "With whom did you discuss the intra-aortic balloon?"

"Dr. Masters came through, but Dr. Carlisle was on call—."

"Who put in the balloon? Your note doesn't say."

"I got everything set up, and called Dr. Carlisle. Unfortunately, Hank, I mean, Mr. Simpson, started having increased ectopy. Actually, he went into V-tach and we had to shock him. I didn't think there was time to wait."

"You didn't think? Exactly. We don't manage rhythm irregularities with an intra-aortic balloon pump. You are obviously unaware, but there are a plethora of antiarrhythmic medications. Why didn't you call Dr. Sufi?"

"It wasn't just his rhythm, sir. I mean . . ." Joe looked down for a minute. He gathered his thoughts before continuing. "He was also dropping his blood pressure and cardiac output. I decided—."

"Dr. Morales, you are not my associate, thank God, and you are not the cardiologist or the anesthesiologist. You are a student. A resident in training in general surgery. I know you have aspirations to cardiovascular surgery, but if you plan to obtain a fellowship position—. Let me just say, you better get your act together, if you plan to finish this month, much less finish my program."

"Yes, sir," Joe said, his head bowed.

CHAPTER TWENTY-ONE

THE NEXT MORNING, JOE WAITED IN FRONT OF THE secretary's desk at the entrance to the unit. He buttoned his lab coat to cover his scrubs, but he noticed that the wrinkles and multiple stains extended to his outer garment as well. He used his fingers to comb the thick hair off his forehead. He felt the two-day-old stubble on his face. At least, he'd taken a quick gargle of mouthwash. He didn't want to lay Masters out with one good dragon breath.

Joe glanced at the clock. Masters was running late.

"Shoot, here comes the old man," Joe said to himself. He couldn't believe the old man was back to round on a Sunday morning.

"Good morning, Dr. De la Toure," Joe said as his chief entered.

De la Toure didn't respond, but continued to the patient area. Joe quickly passed him and led the way. He was going to say "good morning" every day. He didn't care what De la Toure did.

"The first patient is Mr. Hank Simpson." Joe moved to the patient's bedside. "He is two days status post coronary artery bypass surgery and insertion of an intra-aortic balloon counter pulsation device. He remains intubated on high doses of pressors."

"How much epinephrine?"

"50 cc's per hour. I made it double strength, but his cardiac output is still marginal. He's had no urine output for the last four hours, and his extremities are becoming mottled."

De la Toure advanced to the bedside. He didn't bother with the flow sheet or the hospital chart, but quickly scanned the monitor and examined the drips. Joe had Hank on the maximum dose of five different intravenous medications. It looked bad for the home team.

"Mr. Simpson?" De la Tour called. Hank made no response. Hank's eyelids were so puffy they couldn't be opened, even forcibly. De la Toure bowed his head. He placed his hand on Hank's shoulder.

For a moment, Joe thought he might be praying.

"He hasn't been responsive this morning," Joe said.

De la Toure yanked the sheet back exposing the lower extremities. From the waist down, the patient's skin color was white with purple splotches, like that of a corpse. De la Toure took the back of his hand and ran it down the right leg with the intra-aortic balloon taped to the thigh where it exited the groin. Joe had examined Hank earlier. He knew the whole leg was cool, and from the knee down, it felt like ice.

"Did you bother to check his pulses?" De la Toure asked. "Let me see the Doppler."

"Yes, sir. He has both pedal pulses by Doppler ultrasound. It's not only the effect of the balloon. He's totally clamped down. The right foot is about as cold as the left."

Delia scurried over with the ultrasound stethoscope. As De la Toure positioned the earpieces, she applied K-Y jelly liberally to the appropriate locations on both feet.

De la Toure listened and Joe waited.

De la Toure pulled the stethoscope from his ears and tossed it onto the bed. "I guess you were right, but if he doesn't get the balloon out, he'll still lose that leg."

Joe looked up as Masters entered the middle patient bay. She nodded in their direction but moved to the other end of the bay without speaking.

As abruptly as De la Toure had entered, he walked away from Hank's bed and out the door of the unit without examining another patient.

After De la Toure left, Joe walked over to the faculty associate. "Good morning, Dr. Masters."

"Morning, Joe. How ya doing? Surviving?"

"Yes, ma'am, but barely."

"I don't think I've ever seen a rougher week, much less your first one in the unit. I'm proud of you for hanging tough."

Joe straightened, ever so slightly. "Thank you. I appreciate your saying that."

"Good, let's make some rounds."

The two worked their way through the three patient bays, twenty-two patients in all. Masters saw all the faculty's patients. Most were doing fairly well, except poor Hank, straddling the line between this world and the next. Masters decided she had to get Hank's balloon out. The right foot was barely viable. They returned to the front, and Joe escorted Masters to the elevator.

"I have to speak with Dr. De la Toure," she said. "Then, I'll come back and we'll take out that balloon."

"Yes, ma'am. I'll have everything ready."

* * *

DE LA TOURE SAT WITH Masters at the small, round mahogany table at one end of his private office on the twelfth floor. He leaned back in an upholstered chair, his hands tented in front of him. As Masters went through the rounds list, she took gulps of black coffee from her souvenir Texas Longhorn mug. His associate did her best to paint each patient in a favorable light, minimizing the complications, optimizing the prognosis for each. No sugarcoating, however, could mask the bitter taste. Too many sick patients were doing poorly, and Simpson's balloon had to come out, even though his chance of survival without the device was marginal at best.

Finished, Masters laid the typed list on the table and set her mug on a paper napkin that was protecting the burled wood surface. She turned in her chair to face De la Toure.

"Okey dokey, here goes."

"What?"

"Jacques, I don't know any easy way to say this, but it's time to hang 'em up. Time for you to stop operating."

Her words struck him squarely between the eyes, and he wanted to fight back, but he realized she didn't mean it as a personal attack. It was even something he'd considered.

"I'm not ready, Katrina. I understand your concern, and I've given it consideration. Lately, with all the deaths, I've thought about it. I may cut back, but I plan to operate for another year or two. Then, I may stay on as chairman and devote my time to cardioplegia research."

Masters didn't respond. So, De la Toure continued. "Now I know you want to move up the academic ladder, and——."

"No, Jacques, my aspirations are not the issue here."

"And what is?"

"You. Your age, your results. Look, I understand, at least, I think I understand your feelings. We base so much of our identity on our work, but there comes a time. Yours has arrived. I've reviewed the deaths from the last two months with Allgood. Your mortality rate is astronomical."

"I don't have to tell you how sick the patients have been."

"Jacques, no excuses. Your last death, Coach Kubecka, was a healthy, elective heart. Zero percent mortality. Hank Simpson is another example. He should have been a slam-dunk. It really is time. I want you to think seriously about giving up your operating privileges. At least why don't you let me perform the valve replacement on the prince."

"Enough, Katrina. I'm not ready, but I'll consider what you've said. I'll take tomorrow off. OK?"

"That's not enough."

"OK. I'll consider letting you or Victor perform the prince's surgery. Satisfied?"

She didn't look satisfied but at least she left the office. And she had no idea of the sacrifice he'd just made. He'd never, not in fifty years, halted operating because he was sick or tired. He couldn't just quit overnight.

CHAPTER TWENTY-TWO

SUNDAY EVENING, JOE STRETCHED OUT ON HIS BED. All in all, it hadn't been a bad day. It was a Sunday, so, there were no new cases from the OR. Hank's leg stabilized with the balloon out, and Joe thought Hank might survive. Joe would keep his promise. He hadn't been able to save Miss Pat or Coach Steve, but he was getting Hank out of the hospital. Otherwise, there were a few long-termers left in the back bay, but they were on autopilot. Elizabeth had come for a visit, and it was great to see Joaquín.

He needed to catch up on some sleep. He even thought about asking the float resident to cover for him. But he couldn't trust his future to anyone.

Still, he had to get some rest. Looking out his window, he remembered his only visit to his mother's home. He closed his eyes.

"Pleeeeeeease, Mamita," I beg. "Please, Mamita. Let me go swimming."

"No, José." "I've explained to you many times, but look what I have for you." She pulls a multicolored vinyl ball from behind her back.

"Oh, Mamita. Un globo." I take the beach ball from her hands and turn it over and over, looking at all the sections' bright colors: red and blue, yellow and green. "Muchas gracias, Mamita."

"Now you can play here in the sand, while I talk with your aunts, but you do not go near the water. Right?"

"Yes, Mamita. Thank you, Mamita."

Joe opened his eyes and tried to orient himself. He wasn't at the beach. He was in the resident's cell in the ICU. He stared at the clock for several minutes before deciding the time was six in the morning, not the evening. Monday morning. He'd slept uninterrupted for over eight hours. Unbelievable.

He quickly dressed and started his own morning rounds, checking labs, pulling tubes, and writing notes. He'd learned to finish before the nurses came out of morning report where they'd meet to discuss their patients. At 7:00, they would gather in the conference room, leaving a skeleton crew at the patients' bedsides.

Joe returned to check on Hank one more time. Then, he headed back to his quarters for a quick breakfast. Entering his room, he turned to the bedside table to drop off the clipboard, but it wasn't in his hand, he'd left it behind. Again. With a quick about-face, he retraced his steps to the second bay, bed 17.

As he passed the front desk, Lakisha spoke. "Dr. Carlisle was just looking for you. He said he'd talk with you after his case."

"Thanks," Joe said and continued to the second patient bay.

Rounding the corner, Joe spotted Raúl standing next to Hank's ventilator, both hands on the machine, as if he'd pushed the piece of equipment back in place after cleaning under the large box on wheels.

"Good morning, Raúl. Are you still here?"

There was no equivalent of report for the cleaning staff. They functioned like members of a relay team. One shift came on duty as the other left.

Raúl held his mop and pushed a bucket toward the front of the unit. "I was leaving. Adios, José."

Some force drew Joe's attention to the monitor over bed 17. Hank was in V-tach. The rapid, wide complexes on the EKG corresponded to an ineffective squeezing of the heart muscle. The blood pressure tracing was almost flat: 45/35. The oxygen saturation was only 55%, incompatible with life.

Damn! Joe looked around. There were no technicians, no respiratory therapists, no physical therapists, no clerks, no nurses except Bo at the opposite end of the bay. While everyone was in report, Bo had stayed to watch this section.

Joe looked back at the monitor. It couldn't be. Hank was doing well, improving since the balloon came out.

What happened?

Joe hollered at Bo, "Call a code, bed 17."

Joe could not let Hank die. He'd promised.

* * *

FIRST, HE HAD TO GET that oxygenation up. Joe reached for an ambu bag. Removing the ventilator connection, he connected the plastic tubing to the oxygen coming directly from the wall.

"Code blue, bed 17." From the overhead speaker, Anita's agitated voice broke the silence.

Silence? There'd been silence. What happened to the alarms? Joe's eyes moved to the monitor mounted over Hank Simpson's bed. The flashing yellow letters read ALARMS SUSPENDED. Nurses came pouring into the second patient bay like seagulls descending on a returning shrimp boat. Bo pushed the red crash cart to the patient's bedside.

"Give me a hundred milligrams of lidocaine and an amp of bicarb," Joe said. "And get ready to defibrillate."

"Lidocaine in. Bicarb in," Bo said.

"What's our oxygen saturation?" Joe asked.

"90% and coming up."

"Are the paddles charged?" he asked.

"They're ready, two hundred joules. Wait, he converted."

Joe looked up. The patient's rhythm was now a regular sinus. Blood pressure was eighty-five over sixty and rising.

Joe leaned over the patient. "Hank, you're doing fine. You may have felt a little faint, but everything's all right."

Joe turned to Delia. "At least he's fine now. I don't know why his oxygen saturation was so low," Joe said. "But when I bagged him, it came right up. Maybe he had a mucous plug."

"Dr. Morales, we're up to 100% now. Can we put him back on the ventilator?" the pulmonary technician asked.

"OK."

"What the—" the pulmonary technician said.

"What's wrong?" Joe asked.

"This ventilator was turned off. The vent record says he's supposed to be on 90% oxygen. And he was on vercuronium. Paralyzed. He hadn't been breathing any on his own."

A wave of understanding swept over Joe.

CHAPTER TWENTY-THREE

UPSTAIRS, DE LA TOURE REMAINED AT HIS DESK, immobilized, staring at the patient list. He'd told Masters he'd take the day off, but he couldn't stay at home. He wanted to check on Hank Simpson. And he would in a little while, after the rest of the faculty was in the OR.

Was it time to retire? Was this the end? Surely, he had more to contribute, and who could replace him? Carlisle was the best surgeon, the best hands. He was aggressive and he could maintain control in the department, but was he too cold? Masters was maybe the brightest and definitely the residents' favorite instructor, but she was young and idealistic.

He couldn't leave the department without direction, a ship without a rudder. So much was changing in medicine, but although De la Toure understood that the surgery department had to be part of it, he wondered what role should the surgeons play, and who would be their director?

De la Toure looked up at Allgood standing next to Sufi in the open doorway from the outer office. "Gentlemen, what do you need?"

"We need to talk with you, Chief," Allgood said as he stepped into the room.

"You have time?" Sufi asked.

"Actually, I was about to leave." De la Toure stood and started for the door. He had no desire to launch an extended conversation about any hospital matter. "And John, you should be getting to the OR yourself."

"Just give us a sec. You got to hear this." As he finished the last sentence, his shoulder jerked.

"This is critically important, Jacques," Sufi added.

"All right. All right. But keep it brief. What do you have?"

"Let us sit?" Sufi motioned to the round mahogany table.

"I guess."

As Sufi and De la Toure sat, Allgood slowly closed the door until the latch secured and then he placed a manila file on the table and seated himself in front of it.

Opening the folder, Allgood began. "Chief, we've got a serious problem with the mortality rate in the heart program. You're aware the Joint Commission on Accreditation requires the hospital to monitor the bypass surgery statistics, and you know from the QA meeting and Delia's study, they're running wicked high."

"I know we've been having some increased complications, but I hope our new resident will help us improve care. Part of the problem is we're seeing sicker patients these days. The cardiologists steal all the simple cases. He gestured to Sufi. They get ballooned, laser angioplasty, some of the new stents, or the rotoblader."

Allgood raised a hand, wanting to speak. It jerked upward in time with the tic of his shoulder. "Look, Chief, we're here as friends." He turned the page to the four-color graphic, the blue column towering above the others. "It wasn't all the docs that fell out in the statistics. It was just you." Allgood pointed to the figure with vivid confirmation of De la Toure's skyrocketing deaths. "Your mortality rate last year was double everyone else's. Now, we're looking at the December numbers and your death rate tripled. Plus, you're off to a wicked bad start for this month. As a friend, I'm telling you to avoid the high-risk cases. Give them to Carlisle or Masters."

"Dr. Allgood is right, Jacques. You should leave the difficult procedures for Dr. Carlisle or Dr. Masters. And please, let one of them perform the prince's valve surgery. Acceptable?"

"I will look into the situation," De la Toure said.

"Think about it, Chief. We're not the enemy." Allgood rose and headed toward the door. Sufi followed.

De la Toure reached them as Allgood's hand grasped the knob. "John, Mo, I appreciate your coming by, but you both know that what we do is complicated. You can't reduce it to some simple, computer-generated analysis."

After Allgood and Sufi left, De la Toure pushed the door closed with both hands, leaning into the smooth mahogany. He couldn't argue with the numbers. The same cases in the same ORs with the same anesthesiologists, perfusionists, nurses, and residents, but only his patients were dying. It was his fault.

He had to stop operating.

De la Toure ran down the stairs to the ICU. He paused at the bottom. The exercise had caught up with him. What in hell was he doing, running the stairs like some adolescent with his feelings hurt? A tight sensation began in the left of his chest, and the discomfort moved down his left arm. He sat down on the bottom stair to keep from falling over.

Relax. Slow, deep breaths. Again. And again. It was working; the pain was subsiding.

He made a mental note to carry some nitroglycerin tablets in his coat. Before, he'd resisted the idea. He didn't want anyone to spy them, but now he realized he needed them. He would place them in an aspirin bottle.

Relieved of the chest discomfort, De la Toure rose, opened the door into the ICU, and stepped inside, only to confront the announcement blaring from the overhead speaker.

"Code blue cleared, bed 17. All clear."

Anita looked up at him and surprise filled her face, but she didn't speak. Instead, she pressed the button again that activated the paging system.

"Dr. Morales." Anita's voice summoned from the speaker overhead. "Dr. Morales, front desk."

Joe raced to the front, where De la Toure waited.

"Dr. De la Toure, I must speak with you privately."

"I heard the code overhead. Bed 17. Isn't that Mr. Simpson?"

"Yes, sir. That's what I have to speak with you about."

"What is going on here, Dr. Morales?" Without waiting for an answer, De la Toure started for the patient area.

"Dr. De la Toure," Joe said as he grabbed his chief by the arm. "I must insist we speak in private."

Taken aback, De la Toure accompanied Joe into the conference room where Joe told an incredible story about what Joe had just witnessed: Raúl pulling the plug on Hank's ventilator.

* * *

DE LA TOURE HALTED AT the reception desk in the Lutheran administration offices.

"I'm sorry, Dr. De la Toure, but Mr. Hackett has someone with him," the perky young lady said.

"Heather, I just called and you told me he didn't have any

appointments."

"I know. My bad. Mr. Hackett was free when I told him you were walking over, but then Mr. McClintock came, and you know, he doesn't wait for anybody. I mean, Mr. McClintock said he needed only a second. He'll be out soon."

"Then, I guess I have to wait."

"Want a cup of coffee? You probably need decaf."

"No." De la Toure walked over to the large aerial photograph of the Texas Medical Center. He exhaled slowly. The discovery of Raúl's actions filled his thoughts. He would tell Hackett and there would be an investigation. It would explain the run of deaths. The Quality Assurance Committee was quick to condemn him personally. Now he would be exonerated.

A pang of guilt came with his self-focus. What about the patients who'd died? He did care about the individuals whom Raúl killed, but he couldn't deny that he was also concerned about the stature of the Institute and his reputation.

"Jacques, good morning," McClintock said, exiting the president's office, Hackett in tow. "Sorry if I cut in line, but I had to bend Evan's ear for a minute. Hope we didn't keep you waiting." McClintock stopped in front of De la Toure and took his hand. He squeezed it so tightly that De la Toure's entire arm shook, the coarse leathery skin cutting into the surgeon's silky palm.

De la Toure used his left hand to extricate his right one. "Actually, Dallas, I do have to get back to the OR. Evan, can we step inside?" McClintock made no movement, and Hackett remained behind the insurance executive as if attached. "Dallas, if you'll excuse us."

"OK. Two's company. I'll get out of your hair."

De la Toure didn't wait for McClintock to leave before charging into Hackett's office.

In the waiting area, McClintock leaned over to Hackett's ear. Although he whispered, De la Toure caught a few of the words. "warning . . . don't want . . . get legal."

"Evan," De la Toure called from the C.E.O.'s office. "I'm waiting."

Hackett shook McClintock's hand and returned to De la Toure's side. As he entered his office he looked back. "Heather, hold my calls."

"You may want to close that door," De la Toure said.

Hackett complied and walked behind his desk. Deliberately, he pulled out his chair and sat. He motioned for De la Toure to do the same. "What is it you have to discuss?"

De la Toure remained standing, towering over the hospital administrator. "This morning, I discovered that one of your hospital orderlies, Raúl Sanchez, was turning off the ventilators for our sickest patients, resulting in their deaths."

Hackett moved his chair forward and placed both hands on the polished, slick leather top of the desk. "Now, Jacques—."

"Did you hear me? I said he's been killing my patients in the ICU."

"Yes, I've already been briefed on the events of the morning. I understand your resident, Dr. Morales, thinks an orderly might have disconnected a ventilator. Accidents occur all the time."

"Thinks? Evan, this is serious. I wouldn't come to you with a supposition. I am convinced Raúl has been killing my—our patients. He's responsible for the rising mortality rate. I want—no, I demand an immediate investigation, and you will notify all the members of the Quality Assurance Committee of this discovery and its obvious ramifications, including exoneration of my work."

"Jacques, I will take appropriate action, but we must proceed with caution. You know just as well as I do that there are serious medical-legal issues here, not to mention the negative publicity. We have no evidence other than this one resident's suspicions. Now I will suspend Mr. Sanchez with pay while we investigate, but you do realize we must keep this quiet."

"You can't keep this quiet."

Hackett rose from his chair and walked around to the front of his desk. "Jacques," he said, stretching out his hand.

Reluctantly, De la Toure offered his own. Hackett's hand closed around his long fingers, a vise tightening, but De la Toure fought back, gripping the younger man's hand firmly. What was it this morning? First McClintock and now Hackett engaged in this juvenile demonstration of power.

De la Toure looked squarely into Hackett's steel-gray eyes. It was a standoff.

Without letting go, Hackett spoke. "I know you'll be circumspect in your conversations. For my part, I assure you that I will personally supervise a full investigation of the deaths in the ICU, and I will communicate the findings to the Quality Assurance Committee. Fair?"

It was anything but fair.

CHAPTER TWENTY-FOUR

JOE LEANED BACK IN HIS CHAIR AND PROPPED HIS feet on the desk. After the commotion of the morning, the day went smoothly. De la Toure didn't do a heart; Masters and Carlisle's cases each came out rock stable. Joe couldn't remember a better day. He even enjoyed the dinner tray.

He glanced over at the charts that needed death summaries dictated. So far, there hadn't been time to take care of them. What a pile. How many were Raúl's fault? They could wait. Some people speculated that Raúl flipped when Lourdes became so sick, that he couldn't watch her endure such agony, so he helped her die, and then he helped others.

Raúl could turn off a hopeless patient's ventilator and let nature do its thing. Then, he could turn the machine on again along with the alarm. The nurses would come to find a dead patient, not unexpected for one of the long-termers.

At least, he caught Raúl before he'd sent Hank to the morgue. Joe closed his eyes.

"José?"

He looked up to find his mother standing at the door.

"Mamá. ¿Qué pasa?" Joe said as he sat upright.

"¡Niño, mío!" Lupe ran to Joe and hugged him. "I heard about Raúl. It can't be true. It can't!" She looked devastated.

"It was incredible, Mamá, but I saw him with my own eyes."

Lupe sat on the bed, facing him. Her body trembled. "His Lourdes. I guess he could not stand to see his beautiful daughter so sick. Maybe he decided to help her. Then, the others. I do not think he is a bad man. ¡Qué pobrecito! We must pray for him."

"Pray for him? Mamá, he killed people, and he let me take the fall. He almost cost me my fellowship position."

"José, mi corazón. There is much you do not know. You do not understand."

"Really? Well, I understand that our so-called friend may have killed his own daughter and then decided to play God here in my unit."

"I don't know if this is true, but I do know that Raúl saved my life. He saved your life, too."

"What do you mean?"

"I never wanted you to know—."

A flood of sobs interrupted his mother's words, tears cascading down her cheeks. He'd never seen this tough woman cry so unabashedly.

Lupe leaned toward him and pulled his head into her breast. "I never wanted you to know my disgrace."

"What?" He pushed her away, back onto the bed facing him. "Tell me, Mamá," he commanded.

"Your father was only a boy. I don't blame him, and he was so handsome and wealthy."

"What are you talking about?" Joe felt betrayed, confused. "My father was a migrant worker. You met him when you came to Texas. He died before I was born."

"No, José. I told you that, but it is not true. Your father was—is—Esteban Castillo de Guzman. That's where you get your blue eyes. I worked for Esteban's father, your grandfather."

Joe was stunned. "You mean the family with the pink villa?" Joe recalled the Castillo de Guzman estate that towered over Acapulco bay. It rose in steps up the side of a steep cliff. At each level, luscious green vines hung from the balconies. His cousins told him there were swimming pools on each of the levels. The rich patrón could swim right to the edge of the cliff and look down on the poor indígenas below.

"Sí, mi hijo." She took her sleeve and wiped her eyes, struggling to regain composure. "Your father, Esteban, was . . ."

As she said his name, a smile stretched across his mother's face. She paused, lost in the memory.

Joe couldn't smile, though. He had to know all. "Tell me the truth," he said.

"He was only seventeen. Not a bad person, but he thought he could have anything he wanted, including me."

"He raped you?"

"No, José. I loved him, and he loved me, too, but his father, Don Castillo de Guzman, could not have a servant for a daughter-in-law. They gave me five hundred dollars. That was a lot of money."

"What about my father? What did he say?"

"José, he was only a boy. He couldn't—."

"You mean he just walked away. He had his fun and he was done?"

"No, it was not that way. Honestly. He went with me to the clinic, to the Castillo de Guzman doctor. That is the first time I learned about my heart. The doctor said the hole would get bigger with the baby growing inside me, that my baby, that you, would kill me before you could be born."

Shock immobilized Joe. He imagined a peasant girl, pregnant with the boss's child and trying to decide whether to terminate the fetus that threatened her life and her dignity. He wanted to move to his mother's side, to comfort her, but he couldn't. How could she have kept his heritage from him? He was a Castillo de Guzman, one of the most influential families in all of Mexico.

"The doctor and Esteban . . . everyone wanted me to have the abortion, and then, they hoped I would not tell anyone my sin, but I could not, José. Your godfather, my cousin Raúl, rescued us and brought us here to Houston. After you were born, I wrote Esteban that you died. It was easier that way."

"What? How could you make that decision? It was easier for you. What about me?"

* * *

IT WAS ALMOST MIDNIGHT.

As Joe brushed his teeth and washed his face at the small sink mounted in the corner of his room, he looked into the industrial mirror hanging on the wall, the reflective surface dulled from years of service. His skin had a suggestion of brown and his cheekbones jutted out. He could not deny his mother's Aztec heritage, but even through the blemished glass, piercing blue, European eyes looked back at him. His birth father boasted a pure, unsullied Castilian background.

Joe thought about his father's family and their history that everyone in Acapulco knew. King Carlos had appointed his ancestor to rule the North American continent and he established a brutal reign. But later, Bishop Zumárraga who had led a campaign to evangelize the indigenous population interceded on their behalf and excommunicated Beltran de Guzman. Unfortunately, Bloody

Guzman merely moved his conquest westward until he reached the Pacific. Joe's father traced his family back to the first president of the New World.

What would his father say if Joe showed up at the entrance to the family's Acapulco villa? Joe told himself that he might just do it: appear at the Castillo de Guzman villa. After all, he wasn't some poor peasant hitting up the rich relatives. He was a heart surgeon, almost.

Finished with his nighttime ritual, Joe stretched out on top of the bed. All the patients were tucked in. No problems. The discovery of Raúl explained the deaths. Now, calm water lay ahead. His life would be as serene as Elizabeth's painting.

Joe smiled as he closed his eyes to sleep.

I hop into a pink jeep and head down the oyster-shell road that winds along the cliffs connecting the villa to Playa Condessa, Acapulco's adult playground, a beach far removed from Pie de la Cuesta of my childhood. I pull into my reserved spot in front of Club de Playa and head for the saltwater tide pool sculpted from a volcanic rock formation.

As I stroll around the deck, heads turn, and I suck in my gut. I don't have a six-pack, but I'm trim and handsome, not to mention the fact that the Castillo de Guzman family is one of the wealthiest in Mexico. Everyone knows I'm the missing heir, welcomed home with a series of grand fiestas. What they don't know is why I was lost for twenty-six years, only to return as the new manifestation of my father. Like Cortés, I return to Acapulco unchallenged as if I'm the light-skinned reincarnation of Quetzalcoatl.

I come to a royal blue–striped cabana fully prepared for my arrival. The canvas pavilion anchors the far corner of the flagstone terrace and is situated to provide a view of the public area or the beach or the lush tropical grounds, depending on which side curtain is retracted. When the situation dictates, the tent also offers complete privacy for intimate relations amid the crowd. For now, the canvas curtains facing the pool are held back with gold cords.

I enter my private sanctuary. At each side of the entrance stands an ebony-skinned young man dressed in starched white linen pants and guayabera, the front of their shirts decorated with two rows of ten pleats sewn closely together, crisp and straight.

I inspect the table of fruits and cheeses, but decline. Instead, I choose the chaise lounge and stretch out. One of the boys immediately brings a Baccarat champagne flute filled with Dom Perignon, the golden fluid bubbling up the deep vertical cuts in the glass to the surface before exploding with effervescence.

An American goddess materializes in front of me. She has obsidian hair, satin skin, and ruby lips. She is voluptuous, sensuous. As her gaze fixes on my body, I hope that I pass inspection. An affirmative smile stretches across her face. She shoos the young men from the tent and unties the golden cords, allowing the front curtains to close, but the interior still glows from the sun pouring through the striped canvas.

She moves to my side and leans forward, her near-naked body ready to cover mine.

I can see a viper tattoo on her chest, camouflaged by her tan. The snake flashes its emerald eyes, ready to strike, to immobilize its prey and then consume him.

Joe heard a door open and then, softly close. He sensed movement, but he didn't open his eyes. He wanted to pretend, as in a dream, as if he had no control, no power to stop the inevitable.

"Joe?" the female voice whispered.

He felt her sit on the edge of his bed. Her thick, luscious fragrance permeated the air. With eyes still shut, he felt her closeness as she bent low toward him, enveloping him. Her hair brushed his skin. She brought her lips to his.

When Joe opened his eyes, Delia placed a finger on his lips. "Don't speak. Don't ruin this moment." She began to kiss his neck, his shoulders, and his chest.

"Delia, I shouldn't."

"Joe, we're here in the trenches. Supporting each other. It's all right."

Wait! His hands grasped hers. He couldn't do this. Deep inside, he knew it wasn't right. He could not betray Elizabeth.

"I told you, it's OK." She spoke quietly but firmly.

"No. Stop!"

Joe sat up. The suddenness of his movement surprised Delia, pushing her off the bed. With the loss of balance, she struggled to keep from falling on the floor.

"I'm sorry, Delia," he offered her a hand to steady her, "but we can't do this."

Recovered, she returned to her seat at his side. She placed her arm around his shoulder. "Joe, settle down. I know you're committed to your wife. That's admirable, but this is a rough two months. You need some comforting."

"Thanks, Delia. Honest. But I can't."

"I understand." She eased closer to him, reached around his back, and started to rub both of his shoulders. "But you have to loosen up. If you stay this tight, you won't make it through the rotation."

"You've been a big help, Delia. I appreciate what you've done for me with De la Toure, but I'm married. Remember?"

Delia continued the slow motion. "Joe, I'm not interested in a long-term relationship." She moved her hands down to his shoulder blades, and then to the small of his back, working her fist rhythmically, forcefully. She leaned her face close to his. Her breath was hot and moist; her fragrance, intoxicating. "This is like being off at war. No one will blame you."

Joe stood up.

"I can't. I just can't."

"Joe," she said, stretching the word into two syllables. Her full lips pushed forward in a pout. "I know you want to."

"No, Delia. This is not happening. You have to leave." As he started to open the door, she approached him, and her arms encircled his waist.

He turned and shoved her away. She stumbled, surprised at the force of his action.

"Dammit, Delia. You can't have everything you want. Don't you understand the meaning of the word 'no'?"

She regained her balance and stiffened her back.

"I understand, Dr. Morales, but maybe you don't understand all it's implications."

CHAPTER TWENTY-FIVE

"DR. MORALES, YOU LOOK LIKE YOU FLOATIN'," Bo said, standing next to Carlisle's post-op heart from the morning.

Delia had moved Bo to the 7 a.m. shift. Joe figured she had him working days for some remedial training. At least Bo wouldn't be taking care of the prince.

"Sorry if I was humming." Joe felt great, relieved that he'd discovered Raúl and that explained the deaths.

The unit had chilled. Hank was better. And today, there'd be three routine hearts. Masters and Carlisle's cases were already out. Totally stable. No PVCs. Next would be the prince. Maximum profile. But he was young and healthy undergoing an elective aortic valve. Piece of cake. Not to mention that Sufi and the prince's two private physicians would be glued to his bedside.

Joe felt like Atlas after he'd tricked Hercules into taking the big ball off his shoulders. It was hard to admit error, but he'd been wrong about Bo. Seeing Raúl took him totally off guard. Who would have guessed the deaths were intentional?

Joe drew a deep breath. "Bo?"

"Yeah."

"I screwed up the other day. I was a jerk."

"It's cool. You were pretty wound. I understand."

"Really?"

"It's all good, and with Raúl gone, clear sky's ahead. This lady looks perfect: blood pressure, rhythm, gases." Bo pointed to Carlisle's patient in bed 5, Ms. Beckett. "But, she's a little wet."

"Yeah," Joe said. "Carlisle doesn't waste a lot of time drying up. How much is in the tube?"

Bo leaned over and looked at the plastic container collecting the blood draining from the chest cavity.

"There's about 350 cc's."

Joe looked at the computer record. "Man, that's over two hundred in the last fifteen minutes. Let's check a coagulogram. And have the lab start thawing two units of fresh frozen plasma, but hold them until we see the clotting studies."

"Yes, sir."

"Just call me Joe."

"OK, Joe."

"Bo, I shouldn't have listened to the rumors about you. I'm truly sorry about the other day."

Delia approached them then.

Joe glanced at her.

She smiled warmly at Bo, and Joe hoped he was also the recipient of her good will. He tried to return the friendly gesture, flashing his best, say-cheese, toothy grin. His mother always said that amigos son mejores de enimigos, and he agreed. You couldn't have too many friends. And the last person that he wanted on his enemy list was Delia.

"Good morning, Dr. Morales," she said with her most seductive Southern accent.

"Good morning, Delia." Joe tried to read her. Was she angry, hurt, undaunted? He would have to play this hand carefully for the next month.

* * *

"DR. MORALES, BED 26," intoned the speaker.

The prince was coming out. The night before Joe had helped the nurses move out all the patients from the back section. De la Toure wanted total privacy for the Saudi royalty. Even in the ICU, there'd be a dozen in attendance, mostly security people. But he'd also brought two personal physicians, one from France, one from Saudi Arabia. And that didn't count Sufi, who was as nervous as a presidential candidate on election night. Sufi would become either the most respected doctor in the Arab world, or he might need to change his name.

Joe headed to the third patient bay. As he walked, he thought about Carlisle's patient who was bleeding. Carlisle was definitely fast, but was he good? De la Toure's patients were always the last out in the morning. As he approached De la Toure's patient, the corollary hit him: Was De la Toure bad because he was slow, or did his slowness reflect a desire for perfection?

Residents had little tolerance for slow surgeons. They say there are good surgeons, and there are fast surgeons. There are good, fast surgeons, but there are no good, slow surgeons. Was that right?

"How are we doing?" Joe said as he approached the bedside.

Allgood moved aside so that the respiratory therapist could connect the patient to the ventilator. Then he answered. "Not too good, man. The prince has been having some nasty ectopy, and he's already on every possible drip. He had a lot of trouble coming off the pump, kept having ectopy, some wicked V-tach. De la Toure shocked him, like, twenty times, or maybe more. His heart was big and he came in with some mild heart failure."

"Yes," Sufi said, "but he is young and otherwise healthy. He had normal coronary arteries, just the leaking valve."

"For sure, Mo. I didn't say he was dying material."

"Exactly. He will do well. Joe, you just need to stabilize him."

"He is V-tach now. No blood pressure," Chiu called out.

"Shock him, Joe," Sufi ordered, as if Joe didn't know basic cardiac resuscitation.

"Get the paddles," Joe said. He moved to the prince's chest and ripped off the dressing overlying the sternal incision. Chiu handed him two Vaseline-coated pads. He placed one on each side of the midline. The two paddles followed. Joe gripped the handles tightly and placed them on the greased pads.

"Charged," called Allgood. "All clear?"

"Fire," Joe said. Electricity traversed between the two pads and dissipated through the body of the chest, resetting the heart.

"What's his rhythm?" Joe asked.

"Still wide and irregular. V-tach," Sufi said.

"Crank up the juice," Joe said. "All the way." He waited as the charging signal began sub-audible and increased in frequency and volume until it resembled an alarm and then silenced, the machine ready to generate the shock.

"Clear," Joe said. "Fire." The prince's body levitated and the skin sizzled. The smell of scorched flesh assaulted Joe's senses. Joe just hoped he'd exorcised whatever evil had the patient trapped in the underworld of V-tach.

"We have a slow junctional," Allgood said. "Rate is 40."

"Turn the pacer on. Rate at eighty," Sufi said.

"Pacer on," Joe said. "It's capturing."

Joe looked to the monitor. Each second, the pacer fired, triggering the heart muscle to contract. The blood pressure looked good, 120/80.

"Turn up the lidocaine, and get a stat blood gas and electrolytes. What was his potassium in the back?"

"It was low," Chiu answered. "But I give him a bolus."

Joe looked down at the Foley bag. There was already more than a liter of urine output. With a low value to start and all that urine to boot, he would surely need some more potassium.

"Go ahead and give him forty more of potassium," Joe said.

"We should wait until we get the post-op lab results?" Sufi said, but his inflection made it sound like a question.

"He had a bunch of high-potassium cardioplegia," Allgood said, adding to the argument that Joe should wait.

"It will be too much potassium," Chiu said.

"No. If we don't watch it, he'll be back in V-tach," Joe said.

"Yo, man, you never listen to our advice. We're out of here," Allgood said.

Allgood and Chiu returned to the OR, leaving Joe in charge. The responsibility for the prince's life weighed heavily.

Initially, the rhythm improved with potassium infusion and the lab work showed the prince needed even more potassium.

For the next hour, Joe stood at attention at the bedside, having to listen to Sufi and the two other cardiologists. Lots of conversation; criticism, but not the least bit constructive.

He had to shock the prince two more times. He checked the oxygen at least ten times. He even had them bring in a new ventilator. Still, the V-tach could not be quelled.

Joe wondered what he was doing wrong. He felt his early-morning confidence slipping away. But with every minute, Joe hoped the prince was a little closer to stabilizing. He had a good ventricle, good muscle pump, if he could just get the rhythm under control.

CHAPTER TWENTY-SIX

"DR. MORALES?" JOE'S CONCENTRATION WAS BROKEN by Dr. Carlisle's voice. The attending didn't sound or look happy as he approached.

"Yes, sir."

"What's going on in this ICU?"

"The prince has been having some ectopy."

"Do you know what's happening with my patient?"

Joe glanced at his clipboard. "Bed 5, Ms. Beckett? Yes. She was a little wet when she first came out. I know you want us to hold on giving blood, so we're checking a coagulogram. I don't think it's back yet."

"You don't think? That's accurate. Do you have any idea what you're doing?"

"Sir?"

"What's the most common cause of postoperative bleeding?"

Catch twenty-two, Joe thought. The correct answer was surgical bleeding, tie off of a vein branch, or other operative maloccurrence. De la Toure had painfully reinforced that concept at M&Ms, but Carlisle wouldn't consider that he might have made a technical error.

"Well, sir, I thought she might have a little heparin left on board or maybe a coagulopathy."

"Joe, are you recalcitrant to learning? You'll never pass your board exams with answers like that. The most common cause of postoperative bleeding is technical."

Carlisle moved close to Joe, their faces inches apart. Joe stood his ground. He grew up in the barrio, and he didn't back away from anyone.

"Are you trying to kill another one of our patients?"

"No, sir. Of course not. But I was here with the prince."

Carlisle spoke, his voice deep, his rhythm slow. "Joe, we frequently have VIPs, but you must take care of all our patients. If you're overwhelmed, you need to ask for help. I know Eric has offered to help you several times. And Delia is always available, correct?"

"Yes, sir, she's been helpful, but—"

"We cannot tolerate a unit resident who is not paying attention to detail. If it weren't for Delia and Eric, Ms. Beckett would have bled to death."

"Delia and Eric?"

"Look, you'd better get with the program, and listen to Delia. When she tells you a patient should go back to the OR, you better respond. Understood?"

"But Delia didn't—."

"Do you understand what I'm saying, Joe?"

"Yes, sir."

Carlisle pivoted. As he walked out of the back patient bay, the soles of his Cole Haans clicked on the linoleum.

Joe glanced at the monitor over the prince's bed. The PVCs had decreased and the pacer was working perfectly. "Dr. Sufi, please watch the prince's rhythm. I'll be right back." He was just a resident and he couldn't really give orders to an attending but he had to find out what happened.

When he arrived in the first bay, his attention was drawn to the empty space formerly occupied by Carlisle's patient. There, Bo stood with hands in pockets like some muscle freak who'd missed his bus because he didn't know he had to buy a ticket.

"Bo, what happened?" Joe asked.

"First, Eric came by to check on the patient. He's helping Carlisle today. Then, Delia brought Carlisle, and he said he had to take the patient back to the OR."

"Didn't you carry out my instructions?"

Bo looked down. He stammered, "I did. Kind of. I ordered the coagulogram, but I'm still waiting on the lab. The patient only put out another 215 cc's, so it looked as if he was slowing down. I tried to tell Carlisle, but he asked where you were and I told him you were wicked busy with De la Toure's patient."

"Gee, thanks."

"Whoa, I guess that was the wrong thing to say, huh?" Bo finally looked up at Joe.

"What do you think, macho man?" Joe said with intentional sarcasm. This nurse could cost him his job.

Bo's jaw locked, and his small facial muscles twitched with increasing frenzy. Soon, his whole body tensed, biceps and triceps flexing, the barbed wire ready to cut up somebody.

"Dr. Morales," he said through clenched teeth. "I didn't front on you—."

"Look, Arnold, I don't need your 'roid rage.' " Joe had enough of this incompetent muscle head.

Suddenly, the mild-mannered dufus morphed into raging terminator. "I tell you what," Bo said. "Let's step into the stairwell."

Maybe Joe shouldn't have mentioned the steroids.

Joe wasn't a fool. He possessed the intellect to bury this cretin, but he knew better than to engage in a physical contest. He'd pushed Bo to the limit. It was time to retreat. Fortunately, Bo's position didn't block Joe's escape route from the patient section.

"I don't need this," Joe said. He turned to leave the section and almost ran over Delia.

She greeted him with a smile as sincere as the one an undertaker puts on a corpse. "Sorry, Dr. Morales. Is there anything I can do to you? I think the prince needs you."

Joe kept walking, unsure of a response.

"Dr. Morales, bed 26, stat." The announcement was followed by the all-too-familiar blare of the code blue alarm. "Code blue, bed 26. Dr. Morales, code blue, bed 26."

Joe hurried back to the third patient bay and initiated the CPR protocol with which he'd become too proficient. Fifty shocks later, after two hours of resuscitation, the prince expired in the ICU.

CHAPTER TWENTY-SEVEN

IN THE OFFICE OF THE HEAD OF THE HOUSTON HEART Institute, Dr. Jacques De la Toure sat alone, looking at a photo of his parents. He recalled how proud his father was of his success, the way his father beamed during the grand opening of the new surgical ICU and operating suites. From De la Toure's earliest memory, his father garnered his whole sense of worth from the accomplishments of his prodigious son. What would his father think now, as De la Toure's career crumbled?

De la Toure said a short prayer, "Eternal rest grant unto him and let perpetual light shine upon him." The prince was Muslim and De la Toure was Christian, but they were both men of faith. He finished with the sign of the cross, lowered his head into his hands and cried.

As much as he hated the decision, there was only one choice. In his whole career, he'd never intentionally jeopardized his patients. De la Toure blew his nose in some facial tissue. Then, he picked up the phone and dialed Masters' beeper. At the tone, he punched in his four-digit extension followed by the pound symbol. Within a minute, the phone rang in response.

"Katrina?"

"Yes, sir. You paged?"

"On tomorrow's schedule, don't put me down for a heart. I'll do the aneurysm or the carotid, but no more hearts for me. Ever."

"That's good, Jacques . . . but maybe you ought to take the day off completely, maybe take several days."

"No." He'd spoken too loudly, almost angrily, but it wasn't Katrina's fault. He began again, calmly. "I've thought about what you said. I'll stop doing hearts completely, but I have to keep operating. I must." Pain ripped through his chest almost cutting off the last words of his sentence. De la Toure suppressed a gasp.

"Are you all right?" she asked.

"I'm fine. Yes, I'm fine. I'll see you tomorrow."

"You don't sound well. Want me to come up?"

He thought about her offer. "No, but thank you. Good night."

De la Toure returned the phone to its cradle, opened the top desk drawer, and retrieved the small vial. He unscrewed the child-proof cap and placed one of the nitroglycerin pills under his tongue. After a moment, the pain began to subside. Then, he rose and walked to the windowed wall that overlooked the Texas Medical Center.

As the natural lighting began to dim, the finale of an orange sunset filtered through the windows. The impending darkness contrasted with the lights burning in every office on every floor in every building. The Texas Medical Center was a monument to the ultimate status medicine once enjoyed. Someday, would a future civilization be able to decipher the purpose of this collection of structures? Would the anthropologists understand that medicine once meant much more than dollars, that once upon a time, there were physicians, healers, whose only concern was the welfare of the individual patient at hand, who did their job unencumbered by the need for cost control?

The phone broke through De la Toure's thoughts. The answering service should have picked up, but it kept ringing. De la Toure looked down. The call was coming through on his private line. He lifted the receiver from its cradle.

"Hello," he said as he sat.

"Jacques, it's a quarter to seven," Susan said. "Dinner's almost ready. Chicken Kiev. Can you come home?"

"You know me so well. Dinner with you is exactly what I need. I'll be home in fifteen minutes."

"Thanks, sweetheart, I'll be waiting."

De la Toure replaced the phone. He envisioned the dining table, resplendent with fresh flowers, fine china, silver, and crystal. The Chicken Kiev would be worthy of the Russian Tea Room. Butter would pour forth when he cut into the exterior. It was the one dish for which he abandoned his diet without regrets.

How he loved Susan. She was his salvation.

There was a faint knocking at the door. "Jacques?"

With what seemed like Herculean effort, De la Toure pushed himself up from his chair. The visitor rapped more forcefully. De la Toure moved to the door, one step after another. The distance seemed to stretch farther in front of him with each step he took, but he was determined to make it. The stress of death and his decision and the pain in his chest and arm had taken their toll. As he arrived, the knock evolved into banging. It angered him. He would not be hurried to respond to some outsider's summons.

De la Toure acted with ever slowing movement, partly as a message of defiance, but mostly because it sapped all his energy to pull open the heavy mahogany door.

"Evan, what are you doing?" he asked Hackett, standing at the entrance to his private office.

"Jacques, I'm glad you're still here. May I come in?"

"It's almost 7:00."

"This is critically important."

"Then, have a seat. You're working late this evening."

Hackett sat at the small, round table, and De la Toure gingerly lowered himself into the opposite chair. Hackett cleared his throat and then began talking. "I've just come from a called QA meeting. It went on forever."

"There was a QA meeting, and I wasn't included?"

"Well, Dr. Masters came to represent the department."

"I spoke with Dr. Masters this evening, and she didn't mention a QA meeting. Oh, I think I understand." How could she have betrayed him? "Evan, you asked my junior faculty member to represent the department. When you meet concerning cardiovascular surgery, don't you think the chair should be there?"

"Actually, Jacques, the meeting wasn't about the department's problems. It was focused exclusively on you."

"I see. And?"

"It looks awful. We've seen more deaths in the last two months than in the previous year."

"But they were caused by that orderly, Raúl Sanchez. It's not my fault you don't want the city to know your employee was killing patients."

"Actually, we've identified only three deaths Raúl might have caused, and we can't even be certain of those."

"That can't be correct."

"We examined each death for the last two months and checked the shifts Raúl worked and the mechanism of death. You can't escape the fact that your results have plummeted. There have been an incredible number of patients with terrible complications, and the deaths are mounting. I don't know how we'll deal with the PR nightmare of the prince's death. It's been all over CNN and FOX."

"These were sick individuals, Evan." They weren't, though, he admitted to himself. Deep down inside, he knew who was responsible. He'd seen it happen too many times: surgeons past their prime but unwilling to retire.

"Jacques, don't make this difficult. The Quality Assurance Committee has asked me, as president of the hospital, to bring this report to the board. I don't want to give you a summary suspension, because I would have to report that action to the National Data Bank. Technically, any limitation of privileges must be reported. Maybe, if you would voluntarily stop operating, we could keep this in-house."

"Do what?" De la Toure threw his arms out to each side. His right hand caught the handle of a coffee cup, knocking it off its saucer. It tumbled across the mahogany top, black liquid running across the polished wood surface and dripping onto the Oriental rug.

Hackett grabbed some tissue and made a futile attempt to clean the mess.

"Leave it," De la Toure said as he rose from his chair. "I don't need your help with anything, and you don't tell me what I can or cannot do." De la Toure walked over to the door and grasped the handle. He jerked the door open, but Hackett kept his seat, turning to face the chief of surgery.

"Jacques, this isn't easy. If you force me, I will suspend you from the hospital. Please. Think about your illustrious career. What I'm asking is for you to voluntarily stop operating. Take a week off. We can talk again, review your options."

"Evan, I made this hospital. In fact, I gave you your job. How dare you come into my office making demands?"

Hackett rose slowly from his chair. As Hackett spoke, De la Toure took notice of the determination in the administrator's voice. "Jacques, I know you'll make the right choice. I have to tell you, though, that if you come to the OR tomorrow, I'll be there. I will summarily suspend your privileges and have security escort you from the building. Please, don't make me do that."

Hackett strode from the room without waiting for a reply. De la Toure listened as the hospital president moved through his administrative assistant's office and then out into the hall that lead back to the elevator.

The now-familiar tight sensation gripped the center of his breastbone. The dull pain swept through his left chest and ran down his arm. The proverbial elephant sat on top of him, and De la Toure found himself gasping for breath. His whole body shook.

He stumbled to his desk and sat there. Again, he pulled out the top drawer for some nitroglycerin and placed the medication under his tongue. The pain subsided.

De la Toure sighed. Life as he knew it was crumbling around him, like a sand castle being washed out to sea. He sat alone.

The sun had dropped, shrouding his office in darkness, heralding the coming of night. The requisite exit sign over the back door generated the only light. It softly illuminated a family portrait on the wall. The photograph was a true work of art. Susan and he sat on a wrought-iron bench in their yard, flanked by their extensive family, the backdrop awash with color provided by caladiums and impatiens.

Susan would be the center of whatever time was left him. He would see Mo Sufi tomorrow, he decided. His angina had worsened, and he would retire for medical reasons, with dignity.

De la Toure picked up the phone to tell Susan he was on his way, a little later than the fifteen minutes he'd promised, but she understood "doctor time."

A sudden sensation overwhelmed him, forcing him to drop the phone. This wasn't simple tightness. His body ached. The elephant crushed his chest. Its giant hoof ground into his jaw until excruciating pain ran the length of both arms. He felt the flush of his face, sure that he must look as red as an overripe tomato. Perspiration formed on his forehead and dropped down onto the desk.

De la Toure reopened the drawer, reaching again for the nitroglycerin. Suddenly, vomit erupted from his mouth. He needed help. Life slipped through his fingertips.

Again he picked up the receiver. "Susan!"

Just a dial tone—no one was there.

He touched the "O" on the telephone and tried to get the mouthpiece to his face, but it clunked down onto the wood of the desk. He leaned over the phone.

"Operator 13," the voice answered.

"Help," he tried to say, but a gurgling, rattling sound from his throat obscured the word.

"Excuse me?"

"Code blue," he said.

He slumped over his desk, laying in his own regurgitation; his respiration, shallow and erratic. The world-renowned cardiovascular surgeon, the victim of a heart attack, lay in his office at the Houston Heart Institute.

CHAPTER TWENTY-EIGHT

JOE SAT IN THE SMALL DICTATION AREA NEAR THE front of the ICU. His boss was headed for surgery in a couple of hours and Joe felt that he should finish all the paper work for the old man. A kind of closure.

Completion of medical records was everyone's least favorite job. And even here in the unit, the resident couldn't avoid them. At least, the only charts he was responsible for were the death summaries. Unfortunately, there seemed to be an abundance of them, and mostly they were for the old man's patients.

Joe launched the electronic medical records program and selected Msgr. O'Malley's admission. He actually died on Matt's watch, but Joe felt like he might as well dictate it also.

Joe opened the paper chart and examined the case, fairly routine until they came off pump. The monsignor developed a lot of ectopy. V-tach city. But he had stabilized in the ICU. Matt's last note said he was improving. Then, bam, he was dead. Unfortunately, he had left a DNR directive before he ever went into surgery. He didn't want heroic care. But he hadn't anticipated Raúl Sanchez.

Joe's mother didn't want to believe that Raúl could have killed anyone, not intentionally. But it wasn't that the ventilator was accidentally unplugged. Someone had changed the oxygen setting to room air, turned the respiratory rate to zero, and silenced all the alarms. Undeniably intentional.

Joe finished the dictation on the monsignor and picked up Thomas Duffey's chart. He spoke into the Dictaphone.

"The patient underwent routine CABG surgery but went in to V-tach upon arrival to the ICU." He moved the mouse to the results tab on the computer screen. "Potassium on arrival was 3.5, hematocrit 32%, oxygen saturation 99%." Joe smiled to himself. Euboxic. No one could blame the resident. When the patient arrested, all the labs were normal.

Joe noticed that Duffey had HealthTex insurance. He checked the other patient files, and they all had the same carrier, HealthTex—McClintock's company. And Raúl lived in McClintock's garage apartment. It seemed bizarre, and Joe wasn't a conspiracy theorist, but what if McClintock had somehow recruited Raúl to take out patients who were burning up too many resources?

Get real, Joe thought. That's too absurd.

Joe continued with the rest of his work. With each chart, he found himself thinking about the personhood of each patient. During his first year of training, he spoke of the gallbladder or the appendix, as if the disease process defined who they were. But today, he thought of Fr. Francis and the families at Casa de Niño, Thomas Duffey and his teddy bear angel, Dr. Verney and all the rescue animals, Miss Pat and her tiny ballerinas, Coach Steve and his girls, both his own and those from the softball teams. Raúl had done so much damage. How could he?

* * *

DE LA TOURE LAY NAKED beneath a thin hospital sheet. A shiver ran through his body. He wondered if this was the result of the ambient temperature, or was it the result of raw fear?

The activity outside OR 22 was frantic. It made the normal busy mornings seem positively calm. Heads of every department came: Mo Sufi checked his EKG, Kim Chiu prepared the pump, John Allgood started an IV.

The only calm soul was Marie Coleman. After opening the instruments, she came out and prayed with him. They shared a deep spirituality. Despite the stark contrast between their respective traditions—Roman Catholic for him and Primitive Baptist for her—they appreciated each other's commitment to faith.

Thank God for Marie Coleman.

Katrina Masters walked up to his stretcher. "You ready?"

"No," he said, chuckling. "Who could be ready? I'm about to relinquish control of my life to you and Victor. I trust you, but it's a horrible feeling. Take good care of me, will you, Katrina?"

"Yes, sir. I'll take care of you like you were my father, I mean, brother."

He laughed again. "Just do me one favor."

"You got it."

"No hillbilly music until I'm totally asleep."

"Deal." Masters turned to Allgood, "OK, guys, let's go, let's show, let's rodeo."

The orderly wheeled De la Toure into the OR.

* * *

FINISHED WITH ROUNDS IN the unit, Joe sat on his bed, waiting for the CABG to come out of the OR, the only case for the day. He was going to be taking care of Dr. Jacques De la Toure.

Joe wanted to be ready, so he pulled out the residents' notes for review one more time. He reread the remarks regarding post-op care following coronary artery bypass: "The potassium is always elevated, so when the patient arrives in the ICU, use bicarb and Lasix to lower it."

He recalled De la Toure quizzing him in the OR. Cold potassium cardioplegia stopped the heart and reduced the metabolic activity, protecting the muscle while the new bypasses were constructed.

Joe read the line again: "The potassium is always elevated."

He thought about the charts he'd dictated the night before. He recalled the patients, like Hank, who developed V-tach upon arrival in the ICU. They were euboxic. Their oxygen saturation, hemoglobin, potassium—all normal. Raúl may have ended their lives, but why were they so sick coming out of surgery. If all the labs were normal, what caused all the V-tach?

Suddenly, he had an idea. He felt like Isaac Newton sitting under the tree when the apple popped him on the head. He was brilliant.

Obviously, their hearts weren't protected adequately during surgery. Maybe they didn't get cardioplegia high in potassium in the OR, and that's why there was so much V-tach.

It was imperative that he go to the OR right away. Joe rose from his bed and headed out of the ICU in the direction of the operating suites.

"Where are you going?" asked Anita at the front desk.

"I'll be right back."

"Joe, you can't leave the unit."

"Cover for me. If you need me stat, call me in OR 22."

CHAPTER TWENTY-NINE

JOE DONNED A CAP AND MASK, AND SLIPPED INTO the operating room unnoticed. Kicker music blasted from the speakers and electricity filled the air. The normal crew during surgery numbered a half dozen. Today, twenty people bounced around the room in Brownian motion. Joe moved along the side of the OR and came up beside Allgood and Sufi, who stood behind the sterile drape hanging from two IV poles. This was the ideal vantage point from which to observe surgery.

Anesthesiologists liked to think they stood on the brain side of the blood-brain barrier. Joe peered over the surgical sheet. He recalled checking in on Lourdes's surgery. ¡Qué pobrecita! Now, he peered down on his hero, Dr. Jacques De la Toure. The old man looked so vulnerable with his chest split open, his heart exposed for all to see.

The cannulas were in place. Blue, unoxygenated, venous blood drained from the heart to the machine. Oxygen was added, and then the heart-lung machine pumped the red, oxygenated, arterial blood back to the body. The preparations were complete. It was time to start the actual bypasses.

"Show time," Masters said.

"Do it," Carlisle confirmed.

Masters took a large clamp and placed it on the aorta. "Start the cardioplegia. Give a liter," she commanded. "And crank up the volume. That's my song."

Joe watched the heart as Mary Chapin Carpenter sang about feeling lucky despite portents of doom.

Joe knew the normal progression of events. The high potassium solution would run through the veins, and potassium would make its way across the cell membranes, causing the muscle to relax. The heart would become flaccid, still. It would use the least amount of energy in this resting state.

As the cardioplegia solution entered De la Toure's body, an uncoordinated rapid movement replaced the regular pumping of his heart. Ventricular tachycardia. The muscle didn't still, but contracted violently, irregularly.

It was a bad sign. The heart should be as placid as the predawn Gulf waters that resemble an enormous lake. Instead, the frantic action increased like the violent surf that precedes a hurricane's landfall.

"Give another 500 cc's of cardioplegia," Masters ordered.

Additional cardioplegia didn't help. The heart dilated and the muscle hardened, while the rapid-fire, nonproductive quiver continued.

This was a very bad sign. De la Toure's muscle cells were dying as Joe watched. Joe knew he had to do something dramatic. He had to tell the attendings, the anesthesiologist, the perfusionist.

"It's the potassium," Joe said from his vantage point, speaking barely above a whisper.

"What did you say, Joe?" asked Sufi.

Peering over the green curtain, Masters spoke in surprise. "Joe, what are you doing here?"

Joe spoke louder. "It's the potassium, Dr. Masters. That's why his heart won't stop. There's not enough potassium in the cardioplegia."

Joe knew she didn't believe him, but he had to act, even if he seemed crazy. With sudden movement, Joe stepped back from the drape. He scanned the top of the anesthesia cart. He spied a vial of potassium, grabbed it, inserted a syringe, and drew up the whole volume. But as he started to inject it into the cardioplegia bag Allgood took the syringe away.

"Joe, you're crazy, man!" Allgood said, looking bewildered, his eyes more glazed than usual.

"Dr. Morales, what are you doing? You do not give that," Chiu yelled, standing up from her machine.

Carlisle turned to them. "What's happening back there?"

Joe realized they all thought he'd gone over the edge.

"Joe," Masters said. "Can you explain to us what in the Sam Hill is going on here?"

"Please, put some extra potassium in the cardioplegia solution." He had to make her understand. She was the cardioplegia guru. She could grasp the problem. "I don't think there's any in there, or not enough. That's why the patients have been coming out with so much ectopy. They're staying ischemic during surgery and the hearts are never still. They have no protection. That's why patients have died on the table. That's why we've seen all the V-tach in the ICU." Joe stopped the run of sentences long enough to draw a breath.

Both faculty members glared at him with total incredulity.

They have to believe me, Joe thought. "Raúl may have messed with the ventilators, but why were the patients having V-tach to begin with? He must have changed out the cardioplegia solutions."

After considering Joe's explanation, and looking at De la Toure's frantically active heart, Masters made her decision. "Dr. Allgood, add the syringe of potassium to the cardioplegia and Dr. Chiu, give another five hundred."

"You do not give that much cardioplegia for the operation," Chiu argued.

"It can't hurt," Carlisle said. "Chiu, do what Dr. Masters told you."

"Now, Joe, you get back to the ICU," Masters said.

"Yes, ma'am," Joe said, but he hesitated, waiting to see the effect of the additional potassium.

The solution infused, and the heart stilled. "Thanks be to God," Joe said before realizing he'd spoken out loud, giving the Creator some credit. But it was just a figure of speech.

Carlisle spoke. "I want the potassium checked in all of the cardioplegia bags for today's cases."

Yes. They will see, Joe thought.

"Dr. Carlisle, I know I use correct solution," Chiu said. "I know how to do my job."

"Chiu, send out all the bags to have them checked. Do you understand me?" Carlisle said.

"Victor is right, Kim. Let's check all the fluids," Masters said.

"If you say, I tell lab, but I know the solutions are right."

"That boy is wound a little too tight," Allgood muttered.

Joe started to comment on Allgood's perspective on messed-up physicians, but he decided to let it pass. He'd accomplished his mission, and when they checked the other cardioplegia bags, they would discover he was right. Then, he would be like the Lord and Redeemer. He had saved Dr. Jacques De la Toure's life.

CHAPTER THIRTY

JOE LEANED AGAINST THE FRONT DESK. THE UNIT was rock stable. There had been no deaths since De la Toure's heart attack, not even a code. Peace had arrived in the ICU, except for the commotion around De la Toure's surgery. The unit was already buzzing about Joe's heroic action. He'd shown genius to figure out the potassium problem and intervene for De la Toure.

Now he was about to care for his idol. There could be no greater honor than to care for the nation's preeminent cardiac surgeon.

This was the opportunity to secure everything he'd wanted. Joaquín's tree house in a River Oaks backyard was just around the corner.

As Joe waited for the patient, Dr. Victor Carlisle walked through the doors, chatting amiably with Delia Jackson. She looked up to the attending like an awestruck groupie.

Joe was furious that she and Eric had sabotaged him with Ms. Beckett's take-back, but he couldn't let it show. He had to play the game. Stay smart. He smiled widely at them both, flashing his pearly whites.

"How's Dr. De la Toure doing?" Joe asked.

"That's not your concern. Come with me to bed 5."

"Yes, sir." Joe could sense Carlisle was angry. He watched the Jekyll-Hyde transformation, from grinning pup flirting with Delia to junkyard dog ready to devour a piece of raw hamburger.

What now? He hadn't screwed up in days. Did Delia complain about something? At least, his OR intervention should outweigh any shortcomings.

Carlisle didn't wait for Joe. He charged ahead with Delia, walking toward the front patient bay.

Ms. Beckett was in bed 5, but she had done well after Carlisle took her back for bleeding, repairing a small vein branch that Eric had missed, but no one seemed to blame him for the technical error.

That morning, Delia said Carlisle wanted her extubated, and Joe wasn't about to argue. Unfortunately, she'd been a little too sleepy, and anesthesia put the tube back down.

It was no big deal. Joe followed the two. As he rounded the corner, he found Carlisle and Delia facing him, prosecutor and judge standing behind Ms. Beckett's bedside table.

Carlisle began the inquisition. "When did you put my patient back on the ventilator?"

"A couple hours ago. I knew you wanted us to try to extubate her, and she did OK for a bit, but then she kind of petered out. I didn't actually intubate her. Anesthesia put the tube back down. No problem."

"No problem? Are you stupid, or is it that you just don't care?" Carlisle didn't wait for a response. He continued the barrage. "Haven't you learned your lesson about paying attention to the postoperative patient? Where were you?"

"You know I went to the OR to check on Dr. De la Toure."

"Are you aware that the unit resident is never to leave the ICU unattended?"

"Yes, sir, but I was just next door in the OR. Dr. De la Toure needed me. Remember? I suggested adding potassium. I saved his life."

"Joe, I wouldn't bring up that fiasco. You acted like a lunatic. Dr. Masters checked all of the solutions, and they all contained the correct amount of potassium."

"What? They couldn't—."

"You are aware that the last time a resident abandoned the ICU, Dr. De la Toure removed him from the service."

"Yes, sir, but you have to understand. I had to go to the OR."

"I hate that you've forced me to do this, but you leave me no choice. You're out of here. Now go over the patients with Eric and report to pathology in the morning."

Joe couldn't speak. He turned away. For the first time, he noticed Eric Cunningham standing smug, a safe distance away, like a spectator at a public execution. Joe wished he could slap that smirk off his face.

As Carlisle exited the unit, Delia Jackson moved to Joe's side and patted him on the back. "Tough luck, kid."

* * *

JOE SLUMPED ON THE ICU resident bed, on what used to be his bed. Two hours ago he claimed the title of savior of the Houston Heart Institute. Now he was banished, turning over the reins to Eric Cunningham.

Somehow, he had to get up and pack his bag, but he couldn't move. Maybe it was all a bad nightmare.

"José, mi corazón," Lupe cried out as she ran into his room.

"Mamá?"

"O, mi pobrecito." She reached his side and wrapped her short arms around his neck, pulling him close. "Anita called me. I'm so sorry. We must pray. We put it in our heart. The Virgin will help us."

"No—"

"Oh, José." She drew him into her embrace. "God holds us tight, even when we cry out against him." As he tried to pull away, she squeezed harder. "The angry child screams and hollers, trying to break loose, but really he wants to be held, feeling the parent's love even while denying it." He still struggled against her embrace. "The child fights until he's exhausted, then collapses in His arms, swallowed up by His spirit."

Joe wanted to argue. He no more accepted his mother's ridiculous beliefs than he thought Carlisle would walk in with a contract for the cardiac fellowship. He wanted to shove her away, to strike out against the Virgin and her God.

He didn't have the energy, though.

Exhausted, he collapsed in his mother's arms and let himself be loved, let her absorb the desperate sobs of his devastation.

* * *

AS DARKNESS FELL OUTSIDE, Dr. Jacques De la Toure lay on a bed in his own ICU. Vercuronium, the paralyzing medication from surgery, hadn't worn off. Every few minutes, air flowed into his lungs, expanding his chest. He couldn't move his extremities, but he could feel the sheets covering his body and the tape pulling his eyelids closed. And he could hear the syncopated beat of cardiac monitors mixed with the background noise of conversation. He concentrated on the voices, trying to imagine their identities.

"No, he's not awake, yet," someone said.

"Did you hear what happened with Morales?"

"Made a fool of himself."

"Or maybe he saved De la Toure's life."

"No, they checked all of the cardioplegia solutions. I think Morales flipped."

CHAPTER THIRTY-ONE

JOE SLAMMED THE DOOR TO THE BEDROOM LEAVING Elizabeth and Joaquín behind. He didn't have the energy to deal with Elizabeth, with her need to dissect the situation and find a cure.

In the living room, he collapsed on the sofa. He heard Joaquín coughing and then start to cry, but he didn't go to his boy. He wanted to; he just couldn't. He felt totally inadequate, impotent. And he knew that Elizabeth would calm the baby.

Instead, Joe grabbed the remote control and turned on FOX News. For hours, he watched one segment after another, none of which remotely interested him.

The civilized world decried nuclear weapon development in North Korea and Iran, but none of the eight nuclear weapon-possessing states responded to Secretary General Ban Ki-moon's call to eliminate nuclear weapons.

The White House refused to budge on the Health and Human Services' mandate requiring Catholic Charities and other organizations to provide employees free abortion-inducing medications, sterilization, and birth control, but one observer pointed out that Catholic Charities and the Catholic Health

Association had been the strongest proponents of universal health care and Obama's attempt at reform.

Administration officials defended the use of remote-controlled drones while others decried the violation of the rights of American citizens. No one mentioned the deaths of non-Americans.

The stories began to repeat, shuffled and replayed in a new sequence, unending, like the drip of a leaking faucet.

Intermittently, Joaquín coughed and cried. Joe turned up the volume again and again to the point at which static obliterated the voices. Elizabeth wouldn't hear, and Joaquín couldn't complain. The baby had his mother; his father was useless.

Finally, it seemed that the baby had fallen back asleep. Elizabeth entered without speaking. Pushing Joe's feet aside, she sat next to him. She picked up the remote and hit the mute button, as if she could hear the sound. But she wanted his attention, and she decided when they talked and when they didn't.

"I understand you're disappointed, sweetheart," she said as she signed the words.

"You can't understand," he said. "This is my whole life that's destroyed."

"It's our life."

"Screw Carlisle. With one strike, he's ruined my future. I'll never get my fellowship." With the word never, he violently made the snakelike sign, vibrating his hand from side to side.

"But you admire Dr. Carlisle."

"It was Delia. She sabotaged me."

Elizabeth frowned.

"Maybe if you hadn't made such a scene," Joe said.

"Joe, I don't know what's happened. I don't even want to know. I'll always support you. Whether you're a surgeon or you work in a biochemistry lab, it doesn't matter, but I'm not responsible for this."

He knew she was right. Like the old joke, he was blaming the hangover on the olives. But dammit, he had to blame someone.

For at least an hour, they sat in silence. Neither spoke. The FOX anchor mouthed words without the accompanying output from the TV's speakers. Joaquín cooperated or perhaps joined as coconspirator. Joe felt like a suspect under interrogation, but he wouldn't give in. He wasn't going to explain himself or ask for forgiveness. He was the injured party.

A single tear journeyed down Elizabeth's cheek. She wiped it away with the back of her hand; leaned over; and placed the moist, creamy skin against his own, trying to share the sadness, to bond with him. The sweet fragrance of baby lotion filtered into his nostrils. He felt the contrast of her smoothness against the coarseness of his stubble.

He looked past her to the TV. A split screen: the Saudi prince's kind face next to the towering Houston Heart Institute. The enormity of disappointment and hopelessness overwhelmed Joe. No one, not Elizabeth, not his mother, not even the Virgin could comfort him.

All he could do was stare at the TV. He didn't make eye contact with his wife. He didn't want to talk any more. He didn't ever want to talk about what happened.

This was his catastrophe.

After several minutes, Elizabeth pulled her hand back. On cue, the baby started to cough again and then, to cry.

"Joaquín needs you," Joe said.

She slowly stood. "Joe, what can I do?" She looked down at him, her eyes pleading, longing for a reply, but when he didn't respond, she went to the bedroom.

He wanted to answer, to accept her condolence, but he couldn't. She didn't understand. He'd been emasculated. Delia, Carlisle, Masters, Eric, Bo, even his best friend Matt. It was their fault.

* * *

DE LA TOURE OPENED his eyes. According to the wall clock, it was 6:00. He assumed it was the morning after his surgery.

The paralyzing medication had worn off, but he couldn't move his hands or feet, because they were constrained by the lamb's wool restraints.

Eric Cunningham approached with Delia at his side. "Sir, are you ready to get that tube out?"

De la Toure nodded his assent. In fact, "ready" was truly an understatement.

While Delia untied the restraints, Eric removed the tape that secured the plastic cylinder to De la Toure's mouth.

"Take a deep breath," Eric said.

De la Toure breathed deeply as Eric pulled the garden hose from his windpipe. The stimulus made him cough and phlegm filled his mouth.

"Here" Delia offered him a tissue.

De la Toure wiped his mouth, coughed again, and blotted his face with the tissue, now soaked with his own secretions.

Delia chuckled. "Oh, Jacques." She took a moist washcloth and wiped his face. Like a sick child's mother, she held up a tissue to his nose and waited for him to blow. She tossed away the used tissue and tenderly began to clean him again.

"Thanks," De la Toure said. The hoarseness of his voice took him by surprise. "Please, pull the curtain."

"OK," she said, reaching up to pull the material hanging from the ceiling.

"Eric, what are you doing here?" De la Toure asked.

"Well, sir, it's kind of complicated."

Delia moved to Eric's side. "Let me explain, Dr. De la Toure. Dr. Morales became unstable. He was acting irrationally and even left the unit, abandoning one patient who sustained a respiratory arrest. Dr. Masters and Dr. Carlisle had to transfer Morales to pathology."

"I'm sorry to hear that, but it seems as if I knew that already. Did it happen before my surgery?"

"No, sir," Eric said. "It happened during your operation. Thank God, you weren't already in the unit. Who knows what Joe might have done?"

"I see. That's disappointing. I had high hopes for Dr. Morales, and I hope for the best for you too, Eric, of course. I'm glad to see you here. I know your father-in-law must be proud."

"Yes, sir. When I told him I'd be taking care of you, he just about popped his buttons, and as you know, he's a hard man to impress."

"But it still bothers me about Dr. Morales."

Exhaustion overcame him and he closed his eyes. It took work to breathe and to talk. He didn't have the energy to try to understand what had happened.

CHAPTER THIRTY-TWO

AS JOE AWOKE, HE REFLEXIVELY SHUT HIS EYELIDS tight, straining to prevent the intrusion of light that emanated from the lamp on Elizabeth's side of the bed. He felt the dampness of the sheet over his torso. The evaporation of his own sweat chilled him, but he repressed the desire to reach for the blanket.

Joe felt Elizabeth rise from the bed, and he listened as she showered, dressed, and then bundled up Joaquín to go outside. He imagined the multiple layers of clothing she put on the boy: a T-shirt and knit jump suit with feet, a flannel sack and stocking cap. Only Joaquín's baby-blue eyes would be visible. Even though they lived on the Gulf Coast, Elizabeth felt she couldn't protect too much against the cold. She was determined her child would never have an ear infection, and now, she had the VSD to worry her.

He heard the slap of her hand on the light switch as they left the bedroom, followed by the slam of the front door as they left the apartment.

Finally alone, he opened his eyes. Natural light streamed through the window. Without fail, the sun had risen, and he had to face another day.

* * *

SURGERY TRAINEES DUBBED the residents' pathology office, the reading room. It seemed to define the predominant activity of the rotation. Pathology residents spent hours researching the most bizarre explanations they could find for the most routine illnesses, but for the surgeons, the pathology rotation meant reading about anything except pathology.

In the center of the reading room stood a large, square table with an octopus of a microscope. Spokes connected the main eyepiece with teaching heads, accommodating five viewers at the same time. Around the room's perimeter, each resident had a private cubicle and a small individual microscope. Stacks of papers and slides cluttered most desks. Reference works lined the bookshelves above each desk.

"Yo, Joe," Matt called, leaning back in his chair, two cubicles away.

Joe leaned back also, establishing eye contact. "Morning, Matt."

"Don't act so glum, man. You'll get into this rotation, a real jelly roll."

"Thanks," Joe said. "But I wasn't looking for an easy exit."

"Yo, Bro. I was fired, too. Remember? And it may have been the best thing that ever happened."

"Yeah, that and your wife ditching you."

"Very funny."

"Sorry, Matt."

"You called it, man," Matt said. "I'm getting my life on track. My own life. I'm into this ER moonlighting. In fact, I'm going to apply for an emergency medicine residency position for next year. Let me tell you, it's the life."

"Great. Glad to hear that, but I have some slides to review."

Joe pulled his chair in close. He kept his head low, hoping he could pass the remainder of the morning undisturbed, free to wallow in self-pity. Yet he didn't examine any specimens. Instead, he focused his attention on a Michael Palmer novel about a doctor who risked his career to expose a fake medical cure.

After about fifty pages, he was transported to a different world and momentarily forgot his pitiful position.

"Dr. Morales?" The soft voice came from the white-haired pathologist standing in the doorway.

"Yes, sir," Joe said.

Weisenthal, the chairman of pathology, limped toward the central table. With each forward step, he pushed his weight off the floor using a carved wooden cane with an elaborate silver knob. He placed a cardboard folder containing ten prepared slides on top of the table and eased himself into the chair in front of the teaching microscope.

"Come over here and help me with these cardiac sections."

Joe rose from his desk. He slid his paperback under a pathology textbook and ambled over to where Weisenthal was already seated.

"I think you'll be interested in this case," Weisenthal said. "This patient died last week during coronary artery bypass surgery."

Joe groaned internally. What was this guy's problem? Surely, Weisenthal realized Joe was fired from the cardiovascular unit.

Weisenthal pulled off his wire-rimmed glasses and pushed back his overgrown, curly white hair as he leaned over the main head of the microscope. After adjusting the focus and moving the slide to select the best section, he raised his head and spoke.

"Joe, you've had extensive training in biochemistry. Plus, you've worked in the cardioplegia lab. You've examined more cardiac sections than any of the pathology residents. Tell me what you see."

Reluctantly, Joe leaned over, grasped an eyepiece with his right hand, and looked at the specimen. He adjusted the fine focus. More intent, he started moving the slide around, examining it in its entirety. Finished, he lifted his head.

"It's straightforward, acute myocardial infarction," Joe said. "The worst I've ever seen. Severe coagulation necrosis."

"I know. That slide was from the anterior surface of the heart. Now check this one. Same patient, inferior wall."

Joe took the bait. Now he was interested. He sat and looked through the eyepiece at the new slide. A few minutes later, Weisenthal repeated with a lateral wall specimen, and then another, and another.

"These are all alike," Joe said. "They can't be from different sections of the same heart."

"They are, Joe. I've never seen such a global event in all my years as a pathologist. We see perioperative infarcts, but they always involve only one part of the heart. In this case, the whole muscle died. A global infarction."

"Pretty unusual, for sure."

"What's remarkable is that I have four other cases like this one. I don't understand what could account for these findings."

"Show me the charts," Joe said. "I mean, please." At last, some-one else, someone in authority, realized there might be a serious problem with the cardiac surgery patients.

Joe grabbed the folders from Weisenthal's hands. He flipped through the pages of the first until he came to the lab flow sheet. The patient died euboxic. Every lab result was normal. He closed the chart, and picked up the next. It was the same, as was the third and the fourth. All had a low potassium during surgery. And every patient had HealthTex insurance. Joe peered through the eyepiece one last time.

"What are you thinking?" Weisenthal asked.

"These hearts were ischemic, globally. Obviously, they didn't get any protection during surgery. The potassium was normal at the end of the cross-clamp period. Therefore, you can only conclude that the cardioplegia didn't have enough potassium or maybe these patients didn't get cardioplegia."

"That's interesting, Joe. Tell me more."

Suddenly, something occurred to Joe. "Excuse me, Dr. Weisenthal. I have to go. I mean, can I please have an hour? I've got to run a quick errand."

Without waiting for a response, Joe jumped up.

"This really is important. I'll be right back." He gathered the four charts and headed for the door leading from the office. He started to exit, but stopped and turned back to face the pathology chief. "Is it OK? I promise I'll be right back. And I'll finish all my paperwork before I go home."

"Sure," Weisenthal answered with a look of complete perplexity.

* * *

JOE WAITED OUTSIDE of OR 22. He would tell Masters. She could understand the subtlety of the cardioplegia problem, and she had the power to do something.

When Masters walked out of the operating suite, Joe blocked her path. She had to stop.

"Joe, what are you doing here? We moved you to pathology."

We? Did Delia get to both Masters and Carlisle? It didn't matter. He still had to intervene. He had to make her understand that he'd been right.

"Dr. Masters, I have to talk with you. Please, just hear me out." Joe was insistent, and Masters looked annoyed.

"Okey doke. Don't blow your stack. Let's step in here where we can have some privacy."

Joe followed Masters inside a storeroom and closed the door securely. As he handed Masters the charts, he spoke. "These represent four deaths from last month. I reviewed the path slides of each heart's muscle with Dr. Weisenthal. In each case, the patient came off cardiopulmonary bypass with a bunch of ectopy."

"Yes, but that's not uncommon."

"What's strange is they all had a low potassium post-bypass."

"Yes. Ventricular ectopy is associated with low potassium. Joe, I really have to get back to surgery." She tried to leave.

Joe backed up against the closed door, preventing her exit. He couldn't let her leave yet

"Wait. Answer this question: Why would patients who received more than two liters of high potassium cardioplegia come off pump with a low serum potassium?"

"You tell me."

"Because they didn't receive a high potassium solution. Before I started the rotation, I read the resident instruction sheets at least twenty times. Everyone knows that with all the cardioplegia, the patients have a high potassium when they come into the ICU."

"Go on," Masters said.

"The cardioplegia had to be defective or they didn't get it. I don't know, but the hearts never had good arrest, like De la Toure last week."

As he waited for Masters to respond, he gazed around the utility room: the mops and buckets and cleaning fluids. Dust particles, illuminated by the fluorescent lighting, slowly drifted down. Some seemed suspended in midair. He felt as if he was caught up in a surrealistic nightmare, like the unsuspecting fool who found himself trapped in the twilight zone, recognizing the unreality but unable to extricate himself.

Joe started to laugh. He was standing in a storeroom with a member of the cardiovascular surgery faculty, discussing defective cardioplegia, and he couldn't stop laughing.

Masters stared at him intently, obviously considering his mental stability. Finally, she spoke. "Joe, you know there's a lot of variability in how different patients react, what their lab's do. You've helped me with the research. Cardioplegia is far from an exact science."

He would not be patronized. He bit his lip to feel the pain, to force his brain to return to reality. "Dr. Masters, I'm sorry, but listen to me. In the unit, all of your and Carlisle's patients' potassium values were off the wall. Then, De la Toure's patients each had a low potassium level, and his patients died. Today, in pathology, Dr. Weisenthal showed me the path specimens."

He pointed to the charts in her hand. "Each was a patient of De la Toure, and in each case, the myocardium was totally smashed, globally. I mean, the whole thing. It doesn't make sense unless the hearts weren't getting protected, and the only way that could happen was if the cardioplegia was messed up. Maybe the potassium we're using is bad, or . . . I don't know what. I had to tell you so you could protect the patients."

"Joe, after you busted into the OR, Chiu pulled all the solutions. The potassium values were all in the correct range. Every one. You're getting yourself worked up. It's not healthy."

She handed the charts back to him. "Relax. Enjoy pathology. Get these last weeks behind you and then regroup. Come talk with me and I'll help you plan a future."

"You mean find another program to finish my general surgery. Or maybe you don't think I can finish a surgery residency. Maybe I should do emergency medicine."

"Joe, it's going to be all right. I'm your friend, and I'm going to help you."

"Thanks for nothing," he said, as he left the utility closet.

Masters didn't believe him; she didn't even look at the charts. Instead, she was going to help him, help him out the door. But what about his future, Joaquín's future. And who would protect the patients?

CHAPTER THIRTY-THREE

JOE ROLLED OVER IN BED, TURNING HIS BACK TO Elizabeth and Joaquín, who lay between them. It had been a long night without rest, but if he was awake, how did he dream?

Joaquín hadn't slept either. He was coughing and crying. Elizabeth brought the baby to their bed so she'd know if he needed her.

She'd asked Joe to examine Joaquín or write a prescription for some antibiotics, but what did he know about kids' ears? He told her she should take Joaquín to the pediatrician.

She climbed out of bed and turned on the overhead light, but Joe pretended to sleep as he listened to her getting dressed. He had no desire for another confrontation. They said unpleasant things last evening, and he knew if they spoke now, it would be vitriolic. Better to continue the standoff in silence. As his mother taught him, you couldn't retrieve words once they were said.

Joe waited to hear his wife and child leave.

Once safe, he climbed out of bed and moved to the living room, his command post for the day. He didn't even bother calling in sick to pathology. They could figure it out. Besides, what could they do to him? There wasn't any worse service to move him to.

Outside, it was still dark, the night reluctant to give way to the dawn. Joe sank into the sofa as the radio blared from the bedroom. He leafed through yesterday's newspaper while out of one eye, he watched "FOX & Friends." Brian Kilmeade was fooling around, but Joe didn't find him the least bit funny this morning. Matt liked to refer to him as not-Steve Doocy and Matt refused to ever acknowledge the blond in the middle. Joe liked all of them, but this morning he just wasn't in the mood.

From the kitchen, he retrieved some bean dip, a large bag of chips, and a two-liter bottle of Diet Coke. No Tab. At least Delia kept Tab in stock. Maybe he made the wrong choice when he rejected Delia's offer. If he'd enjoyed Delia a little more and thought about Elizabeth a little less, his whole life might be different. He would still be caring for De la Tourc, cementing his position as the next cardiac fellow. But whom was he kidding? It wasn't Elizabeth's fault. And he would never cheat on Elizabeth. Not for any reward. She was the most important person in his life.

Hours passed. Elizabeth and Joaquín didn't return. For a few minutes, he entertained the thought of her leaving him. No way. She wouldn't. Would she?

Joe surveyed his surroundings, trash littering the coffee table. He'd tossed sections of the newspaper on the floor along with every magazine that had been on the end table next to him at the start of the day. The room was a mess.

Diagnosis: clinical depression, but he should be depressed.

Morning gave way to afternoon, and night couldn't be denied. Still, there were no Elizabeth and Joaquín. He was alone forever.

Sadness covered him. He realized he was viewing the same news clips shuffled and recycled, but he watched, immobilized.

The doorbell rang and the signal in the kitchen flashed, but he ignored them. They rang and flashed a second time, and a third.

Reluctantly, he rose and went to the entrance, but before he arrived, the loud clanging of the brass knocker began. It sounded like a linebacker throwing his weight against the solid wood. Without seeing, Joe could identify his visitor: Matt Keith.

He opened the door and Matt entered, uninvited.

"Matt, what are you doing here?"

"Well, you didn't show for work. I know it's Friday and pathology's pretty loose, but then, Elizabeth sent me a message. She didn't think you were coming in."

"Why did she—."

"Bro. How you doing?"

"What do you think?"

"You look like a pile of roach droppings."

"You got it, friend."

"Where are Elizabeth and Joaquín?"

"They couldn't stand me, either."

"Yo, it ain't that bad. Let's talk."

Matt walked across the living room. Reluctantly, Joe followed and sat down in his corner of the couch, reclaiming the crater his body had left. Matt took a seat in the overstuffed, matching chair and leaned forward, ready for dialog, but Joe kept his focus on the TV.

"Joe, it's gonna be all right."

"Yeah. Whatever you say." Joe tried to ignore his visitor, pretending to concentrate on the FOX news brief he'd already seen three times. He grabbed the remote and cranked up the speakers. The high volume of the television competed with the music from the bedroom radio, finally winning out over the sweet jazz. After watching a segment on some of the new demonstration projects that are part of Obamacare, Joe picked up the remote, muted the television, then turned and faced Matt.

"Matt, didn't you notice after Lourdes died that Raúl was killing people, turning off their ventilators?"

"Well, we had unexplained deaths even before she died. But Joe, you've got to let this go. Life's not that bad."

"What do you know about problems? You're a rich, smart, jock. You have everything. Now take me. I have nothing. I'm just some nerd who thought he could be the next Mike DeBakey. Man, I don't even know what I'm going to do next year."

"Listen, Joe. You're being ridiculous. I'm the one who should be envious. When I went to Rice, people thought of me as another dumb jock who was there on an athletic scholarship instead of my National Merit award. I was scared stiff, but you were different from the others."

Joe picked up the remote and increased the TV volume again.

Matt stood and moved to the sofa, clearing a space beside him. He took Joe's shoulders and turned him away from the television, forcing him to peer into his eyes. "Man," Matt said. "I would do anything to help you, but I can't fix this."

Matt squeezed both of Joe's biceps tightly. The thick hands hurt him, but Joe didn't yelp. Since their days as college roommates, he resisted acknowledging Matt as his superior at anything, even obvious overwhelming strength.

Matt continued. "Don't you understand? Nothing's broke. You're the guy with it all: a beautiful wife and child, and a wonderful life ahead if you'll live it."

"Yeah," Joe said. He shrugged his shoulders and Matt released his grip.

Matt laughed. "Man, I'm telling you, the ER life is great. You should try it."

Joe didn't respond. He couldn't.

Matt continued. "We could work together. Buddies, right? It'll be a hell of a lot more fun than spending another five years with the old man."

Joe turned back to the TV and cranked up the volume again.

"All right." Matt said. "I've said all I can say. But watch out Bro. You're going to jeopardize what's really important. You've got a wife and a healthy kid. What else could you want?"

Joe had Elizabeth and Joaquín. Matt was right; there was nothing more important in the entire world. But . . .

"All right. I'm out of here." Abruptly, Matt stood and left, pulling the door closed behind him.

Joe wanted to follow, to stop him, to make him understand. But he just watched from his seat near the window as Matt walked to his car. In the flowerbed next to the door, the final rose withered, dropping its petals as Joe watched.

He was caught in a Catch 22: He could fight the faculty and be unceremoniously fired, or he could acquiesce, bide his time in pathology, and slide out at the end of June. Either way, there'd be no cardiovascular surgery fellowship. Not anywhere. Not ever.

De la Toure had proved mortal. The faculty and Delia had turned on him. Other nurses disdained him. Fellow residents reveled in the loss of competition. Everyone of value had disappointed, failed, or turned against him—everyone except Elizabeth, his mother, and Matt. Even though he needed to blame them, he couldn't. They were totally faithful.

On the TV, FOX launched a review of the prior year's significant news events, most focused on war.

NORAD tracks a missile launch from North Korea.

Pope Francis decries the flow of weapons into war torn Syria as a moral evil. The pontiff is named Time Magazine's Person of the Year.

Suicide bombers hit targets in 18 countries including Israel, Russia, Turkey, Lebanon, Syria, Sri Lanka, Pakistan, Afghanistan, Iran, and Iraq

Military leaders complain about pending budget cuts and the financial difficulties of fighting wars on multiple fronts.

Enough of war. Joe grabbed the remote.

Westboro Baptist Church pickets a Methodist church for teaching what it believes to be the lie that God loves everyone.

Click.

Honey Boo Boo teaches her mother about mayonnaise.

Click.

Pope Francis confounds the press who can't decide if he's liberal or conservative. They don't realize that he's neither. He's Catholic.

Click.

The world celebrates the birth of Prince George and mourns the death of Nelson Mandela.

Click.

The weather channel presents a review of the prior year's destruction: tsunamis, earthquakes, hurricanes, tornadoes.

Click.

Ultimate fighters slug each other to see who can sling blood the farthest.

Click.

On EWTN, a bald-headed, bearded monk in brown hooded cassock with a Rosary cinched around his waist lectures on Thomas Merton, the famous Trappist, whose spiritual search led him to a hermitage on the monastery grounds. In Thoughts in Solitude Merton writes, "I have no idea where I am going. I do not see the road ahead of me. I cannot know for certain where it will end. . . . But I believe that the desire to please you does in fact please you. . . ." Joe tried to follow the lecture but he couldn't.

Click.

A local newscaster stands in front of the McClintock fountain at the Houston Heart Institute and reads a message from De la Toure's spokesperson. The medical icon expresses gratitude for the outpouring of concern, especially from his boys, his emissaries who've gone forth to share their training and knowledge, each famous in his own right like Houston's Dr. Victor Carlisle.

Elizabeth texted that she and Joaquín were spending the night with Joe's mother.

Joe hurled the remote at the old TV screen to shatter the glass and explode the picture tube inside, but instead, the plastic of the remote shattered into pieces and showered onto the hardwood floor.

He dragged himself from the trash heap he'd created and moved to the TV set that he had to turn off manually. Then, he went to the bedroom and silenced the radio.

He sat in silence on his bed, hoping the stillness would protect him. Somehow, he had to get past this or die trying. He lay down and squeezed his eyelids shut, begging God to guide him.

Maybe his mother was right. She would say, "put it in your heart."

The TV monk had talked about Merton's dark night of the soul. Well, here he sat in the abyss. Could he turn it over to God?

CHAPTER THIRTY-FOUR

SATURDAY MORNING, JOE STOOD ON THE PORCH outside the garage apartment behind Dallas McClintock's River Oaks residence. Matt's visit, a sleepless night, desperation, who knows what brought him here? Something caused a paradigm shift in his thinking. Perhaps it was as Thomas Merton described: You had to hit the absolute nadir of darkness and despair before you could search for the light. No matter, here he was. Ready to move on with his life or at least to try. He couldn't lose Elizabeth and Joaquín.

The door opened a crack and then swung fully back. "José, Qué sorpresa!" Raúl said.

"Good morning, Raúl. May I come in?"

"Of course. Is everything all right?"

"I don't know, mi padrino."

A smile stretched across Raúl's face and he moved to embrace Joe. It had been a long time since Joe had called Raúl "godfather."

"What can I do?" Raúl asked.

"I guess I want the truth. Or maybe I want the opportunity to apologize. I'm sorry for what I've said about you."

"What? You would never do anything to hurt me."

Joe felt the rush of guilt that had overwhelmed him the evening before. In his mind, he'd replayed the ICU events of the last few weeks and he had to admit his rush to judgment had been far too rash. And then Matt said that some of the suspicious deaths occurred before Lourdes died.

"Raúl, you didn't turn off Lourdes's ventilator did you?"

"Of course not. You think I could kill my Lourdes?"

"I'm sorry. It's just that you work for Mr. McClintock and most of the ICU patients who died so suddenly had HealthTex. Lourdes had been stable. And I saw you with Hank's ventilator. I just thought—"

Raúl held up a single hand, halting Joe's speech. "Come inside. Eat. I'll fix you some huevos con chorizo."

Joe complied. In the kitchen, he sat on a vinyl-seated metal chair at a linoleum-topped table and watched as his godfather made his breakfast.

When Raúl set the plate in front of him, Joe started talking again. "I just need—"

"No, José. Eat first. Then we talk. It's going to be OK."

Raúl sat opposite him and made the sign of the cross. He offered the traditional Catholic blessing but then added, "Gracias a Dios. Gracias a la Virgen por mi nietito."

Nietito means little grandson but Joe liked the endearment that Raúl had always used for him. How could he have had so little faith in this man?

Joe slugged some juice, washing down the spicy Mexican sausage and eggs. "I'm sorry, Raúl, but I saw you turning off Hank Simpson's ventilator. I was sure."

"No, José. I did not. I was just cleaning the floors that morning. But maybe by accident. I could have I guess."

Raúl was willing to confess to an action just because Joe thought it had happened. But—. "No, you couldn't have done it by accident. The alarms were turned off, too. Someone intentionally wanted to kill Hank Simpson."

"I'm sorry—."

"No, I'm the one to apologize. How could I have suspected you? You weren't responsible. I realize that now. And that means someone else is killing patients at the Houston Heart Institute."

It was easy to make amends with Raúl, who had welcomed him like the prodigal son. He just wished it could be so easy with Elizabeth.

Joe stood, walked over to his godfather and gave him a big hug. "I hope Elizabeth will forgive me too."

"She will, mi nietito. Take her some roses. And love her. Really love her. She will love you back."

* * *

WHEN JOE OPENED THE door to his apartment, he was pleased to find that Elizabeth and Joaquín had come home. He never really imagined she'd left him. But still . . .

"Mi corazón," Joe said as he approached Elizabeth, studying at the dining table. She didn't respond, because she hadn't heard him enter. That was unusual. Normally, Elizabeth would feel the movement of air when the door opened, or the pounding of Joe's feet on the wood floor, but this morning, she seemed intent on her work.

Joe touched her shoulder and she turned to face him.

"For you," he said, holding out a colored ceramic pot with one of Raúl's miniature rose bushes plunked inside.

"Oh, sweetheart." She stood and wrapped her arms around his shoulders with their caressing warmth and the smell of baby powder.

He buried his head in her scented hair. "Don't let go," he said. Although she couldn't hear his words, she complied. They stood still, their bodies intertwined, locked together. He wanted time to stop. Finally, he looked up and was surprised to see Joaquín's crib in the corner. The little boy seemed to be mesmerized by the mobile of angels circling above him under the filmy cloud of gauze.

Elizabeth pulled her head back to look at Joe's face. She noticed his focus. "I decided it was time to move Joaquín out of our bedroom. Is it tacky to have a crib out here?"

"No, not at all. I like it." He choked on his words. She was perfect. Absolutamente perfecto.

Joe walked over and picked up his boy. He gently tossed him in the air, careful to support the infant's head. "¿Qué pasa, Joaquín?"

The child dribbled his response on Joe's T-shirt. Joe grabbed a cloth diaper from the crib, placed it on his shoulder, and gently placed the boy's head into the position of comfort. Carrying Joaquín, he returned to the dining table and seated himself across from Elizabeth.

"What you working on?"

"I've been thinking about your problem at the hospital," she said.

"What?"

"You were right. The answer has to be in the cardioplegia."

Elizabeth pushed three medical tomes toward him, each with a dozen or more slips of paper marking appropriate sections.

Joe placed his right hand on top of the books. With his left, he cuddled his infant. He looked straight at Elizabeth, her face radiating love in return.

Sometime in his life, he must have been very good.

"You believe me?" he asked.

Elizabeth reached across the table and laid her hand on top of Joe's. "Yes, sweetheart, I always have, and together, we're going to get that cardiovascular surgery fellowship."

He loved Elizabeth and she knew a lot about cardioplegia, but how could they discover the truth?

CHAPTER THIRTY-FIVE

SUNDAY MORNING, DE LA TOURE LAY AWAKE, EAGER for the first rays of sunlight, but then he thought of the words of St. Gregory, "Dawn intimates that night is over, but it doesn't proclaim the full light of day." De la Toure wanted the full light of day; he needed the new beginning that just wouldn't come. From his hospital bed, he gazed out the window at the McClintock fountain below.

"Nice view," Susan said.

He didn't speak. Slowly, the sun rose, but he felt stuck in the dawn, still waiting for the full light.

"Do you want me to help you shower and shave?" Susan asked.

"Not now."

"Do you want me to wheel you down for Mass in the chapel?"

"No."

"Jacques, you've spent the last twenty-four hours in bed. You're not going to get out of here if you don't get a move on." She walked to his bed and lowered the rail. She started to pull the covers back like a mother urging a lingering teen.

"I said later." He grabbed the sheets and blanket and yanked them back up to his chin.

Susan stroked his forehead. "I don't have to tell you it's normal to have the blues after surgery, but don't let them devour you."

De la Toure jerked his head to the side, knocking her hand away like a cow shooing away a bothersome fly. He stared out the window.

"Jacques?"

"Yes."

"This isn't the end here. You'll get your strength back."

"That's not the issue."

She gently touched his cheek and returned his gaze to hers, forcing him to face her as she talked. "Then, tell me. Share with me. Please," she begged.

"I have to face the fact that my career is finished."

"Don't be ridiculous. You've performed thousands of heart surgeries. How many of your patients go back to work? Almost all."

"Susan, it's not that simple." He turned back to the window.

Please, God. Dear God, reach down and pull me up before I drown.

* * *

JOE WAS A THREE-TIMER Catholic. He'd been baptized and married by a priest, and he imagined that someday his family would attend his funeral at St. Anne's, but he didn't think he had any other needs that the church could fill. So, he rarely darkened the door, except for the occasions when he went with his mother.

He'd not taken his wife to church since their marriage. She'd never asked before, but today she had, and he couldn't deny her. So, here they stood, at the threshold to the sanctuary.

Inside, a kaleidoscope of color danced on the walls—the rich reds, blues, and greens from the stain-glassed windows, the stories of Jesus, Mary, and Joseph played out in Technicolor. Incense permeated the air, and a mariachi group practiced at the altar.

Joe stopped at the baptismal font. He reached his right hand into the water and with his moistened thumb formed the sign of the cross on his infant son. Warmth filled his body, fueled by the familiarity of his surroundings and the memories of his youth coupled with the love he felt for his wife and child.

"Joe," Elizabeth whispered. "I want to light a candle before Mass."

"All right." He led her into the side chapel, inhabited by a multitude of statues and icons.

"Joe, we must have faith. In our hearts, we must believe in the things we've asked for, despite what we see with our eyes."

"OK." He wasn't going to argue with her about anything. He was so lucky to have her.

Elizabeth knelt down in front of a portrait of Our Lady of Guadalupe. She placed a folded dollar into the offering box and lit a votive candle. Joe stood behind her, holding Joaquín as she bowed her head in prayer. He stared down at his child, the personification of innocence. Inmaculada.

He needed his wife and Joaquín so much that it hurt.

Elizabeth stood. "Can you feel the Virgin's eyes?"

Joe nodded. His mother said that in the real tilma, the peasant's coat hanging in the basilica in Mexico City, you could see Juan Diego reflected in the Virgin's eyes.

"I love this picture," she said. "Your mother says she is Queen of the Americas."

"Yes."

"Where did this image come from?"

Joe turned around. They were alone in the small side chapel, and Mass wouldn't start for ten minutes. He spoke softly. "It's a legend.

The Virgin appeared to a poor Mexican, Juan Diego, and spoke in Nahuatl, his native dialect. It was December, but she told him to pick roses from the top of a snow-capped mountain and take them to Bishop Zumárraga, who'd been named protector of the Indians. When Juan opened his mantle, the roses fell to the ground, leaving the Virgin's image imprinted on the coarse fabric. It was an image more beautiful than any human hand could create, an image of an Aztec princess with high cheekbones and dark skin. That bishop protected the indigenous population from Beltran de Guzman, the despot who'd murdered and enslaved thousands."

Joe thought about Bloody Guzman and his great-great-great-great-grandson, Joe's father, who'd taken advantage of his mother, the poor servant.

"It's a beautiful story."

Elizabeth's words brought him back to the present. "Let's sit down, OK?"

* * *

AFTER MASS, JOE AND Elizabeth left Joaquín with his mother and headed for the monumental stone building that housed the Texas Medical Center library. Inside, thick reference books and volumes of bound periodicals littered the tops of the many oak tables. In the bookshelves around them, every medical journal in every language awaited.

Joe went to the stacks and pulled the volumes from Elizabeth's list, while she scanned the articles, culling the also-rans. Cardioplegia research provided justification for tenure for many academics. When they'd finished going through the materials, they faced a mountain of journals with the most appropriate studies. Ironically, De la Toure authored a number of the classic articles, Masters joined him in the more recent papers, and Elizabeth's name was on two of them.

Joe sat. One by one, he began to examine the pieces, working backward from the most recent. Elizabeth stood behind him, reading over his shoulder.

Articles began to run together. Frustrated, Joe slammed closed a volume of the Journal of Thoracic and Cardiovascular Surgery. Too many facts. His head ached. He placed his head in his hands, and his thumbs bore into each of his temples.

Elizabeth gently massaged his shoulders. "It's all right," she whispered.

Thoughts percolated through his brain like the coffee his mother made in an old-fashioned pot on the stove, but no answers could be filtered out of the jumble. Of all the different formulas for cardioplegia, the main ingredient remained potassium. A lack of potassium could explain everything, but Masters and Carlisle had checked the solutions, and Masters said they were all normal. Unless the patient didn't get the cardioplegia, and how could Chiu and Allgood get away with that? Maybe Masters had lied.

"Joe," Elizabeth said, almost in a shout.

Joe turned around quickly, bringing his index finger to his lips. "Shhh, we're in the library."

"I'm sorry." She began again, this time in sign language. "We're going about this all wrong. You don't think all of the cardioplegia was faulty?"

"That's right," Joe signed. "Most patients behaved regularly."

"Then, let's use a scientific approach. Check for a pattern," she signed.

"Yeah, right," Joe said out loud.

He startled himself with his sarcasm. At least Elizabeth couldn't hear the tone of his voice, but maybe she read it in his expression. It didn't matter. Joe grabbed the next book from his pile and opened it.

Elizabeth squeezed his trapezius muscles, and Joe reflexively yelped. The book in his hands fell to the table with a dull thud, and he turned back to look at her.

"I'm serious. I think I know where to find our answers. Come on." Without waiting for him, she headed to the stairs leading outside. There was little Joe could do except follow.

* * *

JOE AND ELIZABETH TREKKED across the medical center to the Houston Heart Institute at Lutheran Hospital. In the elevator, Elizabeth selected the twelfth floor. They rode without further communication.

He followed her out of blind faith.

When the doors opened, she turned down the corridor that led to two steel security doors. To the right, De la Toure's offices filled one wing. To the left were the cardioplegia laboratories. As they approached the lab, Joe wondered if they would be admitted.

The security man didn't know what they were doing, what they were thinking. Hell, even Joe didn't know what Elizabeth was thinking, and they both had worked in the cardioplegia lab. Surely, he would let them inside.

Elizabeth pushed the red button on the intercom and then placed her open palm on the speaker.

"Yes, may I help you?" the voice responded.

Elizabeth felt the sound vibrations and waited for the guard to stop talking, a skill she'd learned at fast-food drive-thrus.

"This is Elizabeth Morales," she said. "Open the door to the cardioplegia lab, please."

She put her hand on the speaker again.

"Come on through," the guard said.

When the speaker silenced, Elizabeth looked up at the television surveillance camera and waved a thanks to the faceless voice in the remote location. Joe lowered his head as they entered.

Elizabeth used her master key to open the door to the room where the cardioplegia was made, and Joe entered behind her. The size of a large walk-in closet, it contained a small metal desk and a vinyl-seated chair. At the end of the lab, there was a ventilated hood over the counter where the sterile solutions were prepared. A stainless-steel cabinet held the bags containing the basic fluid. To these, a variety of substances were added, yielding the final cardioplegia solutions.

Elizabeth moved to the desk where the logbook was open. "As the solutions are sent to the OR, they're signed out here," she said.

Joe examined the log. For each case, there was a patient sticker, the surgeon's name, the serial number of the fluid bag, and a code for the cardioplegia solution it contained.

"What are these codes?"

"They let us pull charts of patients who received different solutions. Masters is always changing the components. Now she's experimenting with free-radical scavengers."

"There isn't a clue here. There are too many variables."

"Now wait a minute," she said. "Let's search for a pattern. For the last two months, all patients received solution M-19-54." Elizabeth ran her finger down the columns of the logbook. "Wait. Look at these serial numbers for the solution bags."

Joe's gaze followed her fingertip as it moved down the column of numbers.

"They're random," he said. "If you pull bags randomly from the shelf, their serial numbers are not going to be in numerical order."

"Yes, but they all begin with the same five numbers, except these." She used her index finger to show him the cases. "These bags came from a different lot. Why?"

"I don't know," Joe said. "But it has to mean something."

"Look at the surgeon column," Elizabeth said. "Each one of these bags from the different lot was signed out to a patient of De la Toure."

"Exactly. Here's Dr. Verney and Ms. Paragone, and I recognize these others. They all died shortly after surgery." He turned the page to find the solutions made for Lourdes and Pops Duffey. They were murdered, too. They received the same faulty cardioplegia. It wasn't Raúl or Matt's fault.

"Except this one," Elizabeth said. She pointed to the entry in the surgeon column. "This one is Masters' patient."

Joe took her finger and slid it sideways to the attached patient sticker: "Jacques De la Toure." Joe had been right to demand that they add the extra potassium. He'd saved the old man's life. He had to make De la Toure understand.

CHAPTER THIRTY-SIX

DE LA TOURE SAT UPRIGHT IN HIS HOSPITAL BED, A compromise he made with his wife. She wouldn't let him pass the day in slumber, but he refused to move to the recliner.

A mound of reading material covered the rolling table pushed up next to him. His wife had led him to the water, but she couldn't make him drink. She'd brought the latest Carolyn Haines and W.E.B. Griffin novels, some Rome travel guides, Weigel's biography of John Paul II, and several medical journals. She even brought an Enquirer.

Deep down, he knew she was right. He had to redirect his focus. He had to move forward, to reengage his brain.

The door to his room clanged open. De la Toure startled as his resident Joe Morales tried to keep the door from rebounding off the wall.

"Sorry," Joe said.

"What are you doing here?" De la Toure asked.

Susan De la Toure rose from the visitor's chair and moved toward the young resident. "Dr. Morales, please come in. Jacques, I know you're glad to have one of your boys visit. Exactly what the doctor ordered."

She didn't know. He hadn't regaled his wife with wild-resident-out-of-control stories.

"Thank you, Mrs. De la Toure." Joe strode across the room and stood next to the bed. "Dr. De la Toure, I have to talk with you for a minute. Please."

"Joe, I've already heard your story. Dr. Carlisle and Dr. Masters briefed me about your actions. Besides, I do not think this is an appropriate time to discuss your situation. When I'm better, I'll help you find a new spot."

"No!" Joe screamed, but then quickly said, "I'm sorry, I didn't mean to yell."

Susan De la Toure maneuvered behind Joe and headed toward the door. "I'll be right back, Jacques."

Joe turned to her. He held up both hands, a posture of innocence. "It's all right, Mrs. De la Toure. I'm not crazy or anything. I didn't mean to scare you, but this isn't only about me. Please stay. Please, hear me out."

"I will," she said. "But only if you remain calm, and you can talk for only a few minutes. Dr. De la Toure must get his rest."

"Yes, ma'am." He turned back to face his chief. "Dr. De la Toure, my wife, Elizabeth, and I went to the cardioplegia lab yesterday."

"You did what?" De la Toure asked.

"You know that Elizabeth does research with Dr. Masters, and she checked the cardioplegia solutions. You need to, also, before someone can cover it up. All of your patients for the last two months received a different solution than the other surgeons' patients. It's apparent in the serial numbers."

"Joe, slow down. What are you talking about?"

Joe moved to the head of De la Toure's bed. He'd been waving his hands erratically. Now Joe stuffed them inside his pockets. He appeared to be struggling to stay calm, but De la Toure didn't think Joe had succeeded.

Joe began again slowly. "We found they've been giving your patients a different cardioplegia, and I think they even tried to kill you."

"Joe, Dr. Masters and Dr. Carlisle told me all about your theories. They checked the cardioplegia."

"Don't you understand what I'm saying?"

"I think you should leave."

"Won't you listen? You have to."

De la Toure pushed the nurses' call button. A crackle from the speaker heralded the clerk's response from the nurses' station.

"Yes?"

"Call security," De la Toure said.

Within seconds, an army of hospital personnel burst into the room. One male nurse grabbed Joe by his arms, jerking them behind his back.

"I'm leaving," Joe said, wincing. "I'm sorry, but check it out for yourself. You'll see."

"Let him go," De la Toure said to the nurse. "Joe, just get out of here."

Gradually, the commotion settled down.

Security guards arrived and then returned three times in rapid succession, even though Joe was already gone.

Finally, De la Toure was left alone with his wife. He asked her to turn off the light so he could rest, but he couldn't sleep, even with a triple dose of sedative. Instead, his mind played, rewound, and replayed the scene he'd just witnessed.

Could Joe be correct? Maybe the horrendous results weren't his fault. Could someone have altered the cardioplegia solutions?

CHAPTER THIRTY-SEVEN

AT THE RESIDENT'S TABLE IN THE PATHOLOGY department, Joe sat fixed to the eyepiece of the teaching microscope. The strands of myocardium were globally infarcted. There simply wasn't enough blood supply, the arteries plugged from years of tobacco and cheeseburgers. Joe's mind raced from one idea to the next, searching for answers.

The cause of the deaths had to be faulty cardioplegia. The obvious defect would be a deficiency of potassium, but if that was true, why did all of the cardioplegia solutions test normal? Why did all of the problems occur only with De la Toure's patients? And why did his cardioplegia solutions have a different sequence of serial numbers?

Wasn't the real question whether someone had intentionally altered the cardioplegia used by De la Toure? Maybe McClintock took advantage of Raúl's grief to knock off some hopeless cases before they spent too much money, and then—No. Raúl told him he didn't do it and Joe believed his godfather. Plus, Raúl wouldn't know how to change the cardioplegia solutions. Why, though, alter the cardioplegia on elective, routine cases? Finally, more important, how could Joe prove it?

"Joe," Elizabeth called from the open door.

"Elizabeth, what are you doing here?"

Joe rose from the microscope and turned toward his wife. As she made it to his side, she collapsed in his arms.

"What's the matter?" he asked.

"It's Joaquín." Her voice cracked and she stopped, trying to glue it back together.

"What's wrong? What happened?" He pushed her away, so that she could see his face. He repeated the question. "What's wrong?"

"Joaquín, he's in the pediatric ICU."

"What do you mean?"

"I took him to see the doctor. You know he's had that little fever and cough the last couple weeks. So, like you suggested, I took him to see the pediatrician, and they say he has pneumonia—."

"He can't have pneumonia. I just saw him this morning—."

"And congestive heart failure." She started to cry. "The VSD must be bigger than they thought. The hole must be growing. What's going to happen?"

Joe felt he was in a free fall. "I'm sorry. Oh man, I am so sorry. I didn't recognize heart failure. I'm incompetent."

"No, Joe. It's not your fault. I'm not blaming you."

"But you should. Why didn't I think? I wanted him to be perfect—."

"Mi corazón, it's not your fault," Elizabeth said. "You said to have him checked. That's what was important. If you hadn't insisted, I don't know what would have happened." Her voice succumbed to sobs and she couldn't continue.

Joe hugged Elizabeth for minutes without speaking.

"I'm so scared," she finally said.

Joe took control. He untangled Elizabeth's arms from around him and took her hand. "Come on. Let's go see Joaquín now. I have to check on him myself. We'll get a cardiologist and a pulmonary specialist. I'll make sure he's OK."

When they entered the hallway leading from the residents' reading room, Joe stopped abruptly, turned, and firmly grasped both of Elizabeth's shoulders. He peered into her eyes, overwhelmed by the fear he saw there.

"Elizabeth, I love you."

"I love you, too, Joe."

"It's going to be all right; we're going to be all right."

CHAPTER THIRTY-EIGHT

IT WAS A LONG DAY FOR JOE AND ELIZABETH. Although the nurses normally bent the rules for doctors' families, Joaquín's nurse thought the child was too sick to have constant visitation. So, Joe and Elizabeth kept vigil in the waiting area, like so many other parents, working puzzles; reading out-of-date magazines; and watching TV without listening to a word that was said onscreen.

They also prayed. They prayed together for the first time ever.

Joe noticed the worried expressions on the faces surrounding him. Even given the gravity of his own crisis, he felt a strong empathy for these families facing the same or worse.

They were regular people, working people, the same as his mother. His father would never have invited them to his villa. Yet these people still had value. They had worth, without regard to their accumulation of materials.

As if they'd been summoned, the mass of parents and grand-parents rose and moved toward the double doors leading into the pediatric ICU. Like sheep, Joe and Elizabeth followed. Without checking, everyone assumed it was time for the evening visiting hours to begin. Standing with the crowd in front of the doors, Joe glanced at his watch. There was a minimum of another fifteen minutes to wait.

In a daze, he glanced around the crowd. The group slowly encroached upon his space. He moved closer to Elizabeth, placing his arm over her shoulder. There was no place to look through the mass of people, so Joe looked up.

Mounted in an upper corner of the hallway was a surveillance monitor like the one outside the cardioplegia lab. Joe recalled the lesson of grade-school class photographs. Teachers told the children that to be seen in the picture, the student must be able to see the camera's eye when the photo is taken.

Joe looked into the monitor, knowing that somewhere a security guard was staring back at him, and a sudden thought came to him: If McClintock or someone else had entered the cardioplegia lab, his entry was recorded.

* * *

JOE AND ELIZABETH STAYED in the waiting room all night, talking occasionally, never sleeping—not even a short nap. They each slumped low in a hard plastic chair. Joe's back ached. He was tired, hungry, and worried.

At 7:00, the pediatric pulmonologist came through on his morning rounds.

His words were brief. "No change."

What the hell does that mean?

Joaquín had to be either better or worse. How could there be no change? Joe didn't expect him to be well overnight, but why couldn't they tell them the child's going to be better in a day or two?

"I think he's arrogant."

"Last night, you told me he was the best pediatric lung specialist in the country. He spent the whole night with our child. You saw his eyes. He looks as bad as we do. How can you call him names?"

"All I said was that he was arrogant."

"Get out, Joe."

"What?"

"I said, 'get out.' I won't spend today waiting with you. Before I make a scene, get out."

Elizabeth began to cry. She was losing it, and Joe realized he'd been out of line. He reached out for her.

"I'm sorry—."

Elizabeth, however, pulled away and turned her back to him. She wouldn't listen.

Joe left the waiting area and walked down the corridor, unsure of what to do. After turning the corner, he stopped in the middle of another hallway. People passed him. Joe stood still, oblivious to the hospital activity.

Finally, he decided to return to the pathology department. It was where he was assigned.

Joe sat in his cubicle, leafing through a report he'd dictated, checking it for error, but his actions were perfunctory. He read the words, but they didn't register.

The neurons in his brain exploded with other information. Joaquín's echo showed that the VSD had enlarged, and that the size of the hole caused his child to go into heart failure. That's why the baby was coughing so much. There was fluid building up in his lungs, and his condition was complicated by the development of pneumonia. Joaquín could die from the heart defect, but he was young to have a definitive repair. He would do much better if he could wait a couple of years.

Joaquín was his little boy. What would happen to him? What would happen to all the plans he had for his son?

At least the pulmonologist had said he'd stabilized. If he worsened, Joe was going to call Father Wall. He still wasn't sure about the church stuff, but he wouldn't let his boy die without a baptism.

Joe picked up the next group of papers to review, the final autopsy report on one of De la Toure's patients. There was no escaping the conclusion that someone killed De la Toure's heart patients, and that the same person likely tried to kill De la Toure.

Joe stared at the video surveillance camera focused on the expensive microscopes in the center of the table. He recalled looking into the lens outside the pediatric ICU the night before. He picked up the phone and dialed housekeeping. When they answered, he asked for his mother.

Lupe came to the phone. "José, is Joaquín all right?"

"Yes, Mamá, no change."

"¡Gracias a Dios! I was scared to death when they said you were on the phone."

"Mamá, I need your help."

"Anything."

"Do you have any friends who work in security?"

Lupe chuckled. "Ricky Gutierrez works there. He's been trying to get me to go out with him for more than a year. What do you need?"

"Can you meet me there in five minutes?"

"Sí. Is everything all right?"

"It may be."

* * *

JOE WALKED OUT OF THE security area with a DVD, a copy of digital recordings Ricky Gutierrez made from the twelfth floor

271

surveillance camera. His mother's friend went out on a limb for him because he was Mexican. He was willing to risk his job to help Joe.

Armed with proof, he headed for the ICU and the operating suites. Entering the unit, Joe encountered Eric and Delia at the front desk. When she saw Joe, Delia moved in close to Eric.

"Hey, Eric, Delia," Joe greeted.

"Dr. Morales," Delia said as she placed an arm around Eric's shoulder, "are you here to get some advice from our unit resident?"

Joe tried hard to ignore her. He knew there was nothing to be gained from a direct confrontation. "Eric, has Dr. Masters come out from her first case?"

"No, Masters and Carlisle don't have cases. They haven't even been through for morning rounds."

"You've got to be kidding."

"Eric doesn't kid," Delia said. "He's our most serious and sincere resident ever."

Joe fought his instinct to lash back.

Eric said, "I guess you haven't heard."

"What?" Joe asked.

"Something big is happening here at the Institute. My father-in-law says it's going to shake the whole hospital."

"Why would Mr. McClintock and HealthTex be involved in the Institute's business?"

"Don't be naive, Joe. The insurance companies run the show now, and my father-in-law is pretty big here at Lutheran."

"So what does that have to do with Masters and Carlisle?"

"Tomorrow, there's a big meeting with all the muckity mucks. I guess the faculty has to explain all those deaths when you and Matt were here in the unit."

"You do remember?" Delia asked.

Eric continued. "Maybe they're locked in their offices, searching for answers. Who knows? I hope they don't throw you under the bus."

"That would be a shame," Delia said.

Joe felt so frustrated by this pair, but there was little he could do.

Eric took a step toward Joe. "By the way, Chico, I've heard you've been spreading rumors about me over in pathology."

"All I said was that your wife's pregnant and you're sleeping with Delia."

After Joe's words, Delia turned to Eric and slapped him, leaving a red impression of her hand on his left cheek.

"Your wife's pregnant?" she asked rhetorically. "I guess it's a miraculous conception, because you said you weren't having sex with her."

Then, she slapped him with her opposite hand, creating a mirror image of the first crimson mark, and she glared at Joe. "You doctors are all alike. You're a bunch of liars!"

Never before had Joe seen Delia lose control. He let her leave without any further remarks. He actually felt sorry for her.

Eric seemed to disappear under his lab coat, like a turtle retreating inside his shell.

As enjoyable as the scene had been, it hadn't helped. Joe felt guilty for making light of a terrible situation, and deep inside, he realized how unhappy Eric must be, trapped in a marriage in exchange for a dream.

The double doors into the unit opened, and Katrina Masters entered. She didn't seem happy either.

"Joe, what are you doing here?"

"I have to talk with you."

"Again? We've already spoken."

Masters took Joe's arm and led him out of the unit, leaving Eric behind. After the doors closed, she resumed her lecture.

"You're causing quite a ruckus. I don't know whom you talked to or what you said, but you've been running your mouth, and there are a bunch of upset people here at the hospital. Mr. Hackett is madder than a wet hen."

"Dr. Masters, I really believe someone killed De la Toure's patients. I thought Raúl was knocking them off in the unit for McClintock, but I realize now it was the cardioplegia."

"Stop right there. These are wild, crazy stories. Joe, do you know what you're saying? You've already been fired from the ICU. If you don't watch it, you're going to be out on the street, and don't think you'll be able to get another residency position. I won't be able to help you."

"Dr. Masters—."

"Listen to me. There's a Lutheran board meeting in the morning. And tomorrow is the day McClintock is going to announce which hospital will be asked to partner with HealthTex Insurance. Carlisle and I have been told to be available for questions. If the board members get wind of these ridiculous rumors, you might lose everything. If the hospital calls the state board, you'll lose your license to practice medicine. Period. Forever."

CHAPTER THIRTY-NINE

JOE SAT INCHES AWAY FROM THE HIGH-DEFINITION television screen in the hospital library. His mother's friend had pulled up the surveillance recordings from the eleven-to-seven shifts for each date prior to one of the suspicious surgeries. To his delight, each night a visitor approached the cardioplegia lab and buzzed security to obtain entrance.

The quality of the images, though, left much to be desired. Like the surveillance videos from the Oklahoma City bombings, they were of marginal use. He played the videos over and over again. Whoever it was didn't look up and wave when they asked for entrance.

The individual wore a long white lab coat, scrubs, and one of the paper hoods used in surgery. Carlisle wore the same head covering, but so did Joe, Eric, and Matt. What's more, Joe couldn't be sure someone like McClintock or Hackett hadn't dressed in scrubs. The visitor onscreen could be anyone, even a woman: Delia or Masters. Joe paused the DVD to examine the hand as it engaged the buzzer. He couldn't really tell if it had masculine or feminine features. Masters didn't wear polish, and Delia's nails, although highly buffed, weren't painted. He let the tape play. The visitor was asking for security to open the door. He could see the lips moving. If only he had audio to go with the video. But he didn't. There was no way to identify the person who entered the cardioplegia lab.

All Joe really knew was that someone altered the cardioplegia solutions and that the person was a regular in the hospital. Security had given entrance into the laboratory, even though it was late at night.

He wished he could take the DVD to some CSI lab. They could angulate, rotate, enhance, but he didn't know what was really possible and what was TV, and he could only imagine some cop's reaction if he walked in with his wild story.

An intrusive beep pierced the silence.

Startled, Joe retrieved his beeper from his hip. He hadn't received a page since he started on pathology. He pressed the small green button twice. The first press silenced the beeper. The second displayed the message from the paging system.

"Pediatric ICU—stat."

Joe stared at the screen for one millionth of a second. Then, he ran.

He ran down the corridors and up the stairs. His heart pounded in his chest. With each breath, the air burned inside his lungs.

He threw open the stairwell door to the waiting area, and raced to his wife's side. He examined her facial features, searching for the answer to his question.

"Joaquín's OK," she said.

"What do you mean OK?" Joe almost shouted.

"Don't start."

"I'm sorry. I'm sorry." Joe inhaled slowly, exhaled and began again. "What's happened?"

Tears cascaded down her cheeks. "They put the breathing tube in. My poor baby."

Joe hugged his wife. "It'll be OK. It will, mi corazón. I promise."

Elizabeth placed her head against Joe's chest and cried.

For hours, Joe sat with Elizabeth in the pediatric ICU waiting room, staring blankly ahead.

Elizabeth pulled out the rosary Lupe gave her at their wedding and asked him to teach her how to pray to the Virgin.

He taught as best he could.

They were allowed to visit at 2:00 p.m. and 5:00 p.m.

After six, the cardiologist and the pulmonologist came by on evening rounds. They spoke frankly. The specialists explained that Joaquín was extremely ill. In fact, he was critical. The VSD had enlarged, causing heart failure and pneumonia that were, maybe could be, fatal. Yet Joaquín was too sick to undergo heart surgery.

Laying the black crepe, that's what the residents called it. Joe understood. They thought his little boy was going to die, and his parents had to be ready. No one liked to have families falling down on the floor when a death was announced. So, smart doctors gave a little preview, the he's-not-doing-so-well speech. Joe wondered if Elizabeth knew. She probably didn't, and he wouldn't tell.

After the doctors left, Elizabeth started hyperventilating and then, coughing. She bolted for the restroom and Joe followed. Through the closed door, he heard her retching, dry heaving. He tried to open the door, but it was locked. Maybe she did know what the doctors were really telling them.

Later, she returned, composed, and they sat in silence, waiting for the 9:00 visitation, their last chance to see Joaquín for the night, maybe forever. At one point, Joe slipped away and called the rectory. Father Wall was out, but Joe left a message. He knew the kind priest would be available if Joaquín needed him.

Inside the ICU, they stood next to the bed. Elizabeth grasped Joaquín's right foot, the only extremity that didn't have an IV or an oxygen monitor or a blood pressure cuff. She held onto this remnant of normal and wouldn't let go. For fifteen minutes, Joe stood beside her, his arm pulling her to his side, their bodies melding. Gently, he stroked the top of her hand. He wanted to reassure her, but he had nothing positive to say.

Fortunately, Joe knew his baby's nurse from his pediatric rotation as a medical student. Amy was the ultimate new-graduate RN: cute, perky, and very bright. Although assigned to the night shift, she embraced her position and threw herself into the job.

As the clerk announced overhead that visitation was finished, Amy approached, her trademark ponytail swinging from side to side. With a simple smile, she communicated her concern and understanding. She touched Joe's shoulder.

"Dr. Morales, the unit is quiet. If you'll wait until the other families leave, you can stay at the bedside."

"Elizabeth?"

"Yes, you stay, Joe. I'm OK. I'll wait outside."

Amy motioned Joe to wait at the nurses' station as the families began to file out. She gave Elizabeth a consolatory squeeze. "I wish we could allow you to remain, Mrs. Morales," she said. "I'm sure you understand. If we did, the other families would all want to stay. We just can't."

"You're kind to let my husband. Thank you so much."

Joe heard her voice crack.

He wished with all his heart that he could tell her that he knew Joaquín would be all right.

CHAPTER FORTY

THROUGH THE NIGHT AND INTO THE EARLY morning, Joe sat on a stool beside his child. Although Joaquín was only ten weeks old, at fifteen pounds, he dwarfed the surrounding premature neonates in clear plastic incubators. He lay on an open stand with overhead warming lights. Joe recalled that as a medical student, he heard the pediatric residents call these devices hot dog stands. Somehow, as he looked upon his own son, that levity seemed grossly inappropriate.

An endotracheal tube passed through the child's mouth into his windpipe. It was connected via flexible plastic tubing to a respirator. Gone were the days of a bellows moving up and down. Now the flux of air went unnoticed, controlled by the mechanics of the machine contained in the large blue box.

Joaquín lay immobilized by the paralyzing agent. This allowed the machine to breathe for him, unencumbered by the struggles of the infant. Joaquín seemed peaceful.

The tape over his baby's eyes bothered Joe, though.

Because the medicine prevented a normal blink reflex, salve was applied, and his son's top lids were taped to his cheeks to protect his eyes, but still, it seemed horrific and Joe recalled Lourdes's eyelids taped closed. He knew Joaquín couldn't move because of the vercuronium, but what if his child was awake, locked inside, wanting to cry out?

He took Joaquín's little hand and wrapped it around his right index finger. "Joaquín, no llores mi hijo. Don't cry. Your papá is here. Ya estoy."

Joe felt moisture on his cheeks and tasted salt on his lips. He wiped his nose with his sleeve. Although embarrassed, he couldn't stop crying.

"I'm sorry. I am so sorry, Joaquín. If I'd paid attention, if I hadn't been so preoccupied. . . ."

He stared at the small child. Only Joaquín's chest moved, in rhythm with the ventilator.

He lowered his face, placing his forehead against Joaquín's little hand. Nothing else in the world mattered. Nothing mattered if he lost Joaquín or Elizabeth. His mother was so right: Good health was God's greatest blessing.

It wasn't important whether or not he was chosen for the cardiovascular surgery fellowship with De la Toure or finished general surgery. Even if he lost his medical license, he could still make a living for his family. If he had a family. They were what was important, and now this illness threatened to steal his child, this little boy he barely knew.

Joe prayed for the first time in many years.

"Please, forgive me, God. Perdóname, por favor."

As he looked up, his attention was drawn to a holy card Lupe had taped to the support for the warming lights. It was an image of Our Lady of Guadalupe. Her dark, Native American eyes met Joe's.

He prayed, "Virgencita, you intervened for Juan Diego's uncle, because Juan believed. I'm trying. Please, help my little boy."

He knew she heard him.

He pleaded, "Madre mía, Virgen de Guadalupe, ayúdame. Help me, please."

He could feel her presence.

A dark-skinned Latino woman entered the room, but his gaze remained focused on the holy card, the Virgin, his protectress. He knew his prayers would be answered.

He heard her gentle, sweet voice. "José, my little one, do not think your mother would ever leave you alone. Let nothing concern you. Put it in your heart."

He felt the warmth of a mother's embrace and looked up.

"Mamá, the Virgin—."

"Do not speak, my child. I know. She hears our prayers. She will protect our Joaquín."

* * *

THE BEEPING FROM THE infusion pump startled Joe, but Amy quickly silenced the alarm and turned off the IV. Joe looked where the line from the machine entered the vein in Joaquín's left hand. It was rapidly swelling to match the bloated right hand.

"Dr. Morales, we need to start a new IV," Amy said.

She left and returned with a cut-down tray, which she opened up, exposing the scalpel and other necessary instruments.

"I've paged the pediatric resident," she said. "I'm afraid we'll need to cut down to find an adequate vein."

"I understand," Joe said. They'd already used all the easy ones. Now, they'd have to look for something deeper. The day before he might have been disappointed or even angry, but not today. The Virgin had promised Joquin would recover. But for now the doctors needed a vein to administer fluid and antibiotics.

"I'm sorry, but I have to ask you to leave," she said. "This will only take a little while."

Outside the ICU, Joe sat with his wife and mother in the pediatric waiting area. He was at peace. His child would survive. He was sure. He loved his wife, and he was right with God.

Joe drifted to sleep, his head resting on Elizabeth's shoulder.

I sit in my cabana at the Acapulco Beach Club as my little boy plays in the sand in front of me. I am so proud of him. He is brilliant and handsome. Someday, he will grow into a man of power and influence.

"Be careful, Joaquín," I call out. He loves the beach ball I brought for him. It's a simple toy, an inexpensive vinyl globe filled with air, the exterior made of bright colors straight from the crayon box. He runs up and down in front of me, kicking the ball.

I warn him, "Not too near the water."

Joaquín moves away from the shore. He always obeys me.

I lean back in the cushioned chaise lounge and stretch my legs in front of me. From the table next to me, I retrieve my champagne and savor one of the fresh strawberries floating on top of the bubbles. This is the epitome of wealth. I have arrived.

I put the crystal flute down and lay my head back against a pillow. Above me, the royal-blue-striped, canvas fabric protects me from the blindingly bright sun. It's the perfect ending to the perfect day. I'm rich and successful, living the beautiful life with a perfect son.

I feel the air cool, and darkness starts to encroach upon my holiday. "Joaquín, time to go," I call before looking out. When I do, I realize he is too near the dangerous surf. "Joaquín, not so close to the water."

The tentacles of the deadly Pacific reach up to steal his ball.

The waves entreat him to enter their domain, to take those first steps into the lair, to be trapped forever.

The waves mask their ferocity. Only small thrusts come to bounce the multicolored globe on the top of the surf, just out of his reach, playfully teasing him.

Only I know the treachery that awaits, the real purpose and mission of this sea.

"Don't, Joaquín. Leave it. It's only a cheap toy. It's time to go home."

"I have to get my ball," Joaquín says. He starts down the steep slope leading into the ocean. Without caution or reason, he's moving toward his doom.

"No, Joaquín! No!"

I watch with horror as the hungry wave crashes over my little one's head. The noise is like a building imploding, collapsing onto this innocent child. Evil devours my son.

Yet as the water recedes, he remains standing. What a little man. Strong and brave. He holds the ball.

I am so proud of him.

But then, Joaquín cries out in agony from the broken pieces of oyster shells that cut into his skin. He is, after all, only a little boy, and I love him despite his weakness.

He stretches out his arms toward me.

"Papito. Please, help me. Please."

I jump up and race to the water's edge.

As I run, I watch the ocean claim its two prizes, the ball and my child. The tide sucks them down and they disappear in the surf.

When I reach the steep slope that runs into the ocean, I freeze. The surf is too rough here. I cannot enter.

My child is gone. A pure sacrifice I've made in exchange for success and wealth. He's been claimed by the Pacific Ocean.

Not my Joaquín. Not my boy.

I will save him.

But the undertow is too strong for a gringo.

Joaquín needs a Mexican, un indigena, to rescue him, and I feel inadequate.

I stare at the backs of my hands, at the copper-toned complexion of my own Aztec heritage, my mother's contribution to my character, the part of my being I try to deny.

I am Mexican. I am.

"I'm coming, Joaquín," I yell. I run down the steep slope. The ocean responds with an attack against me. A wave of water assaults me, trying to knock me off my feet. The undertow grabs both of my ankles and pulls them down into the sand, holding onto me, ready to add me to the evening's catch.

But I will not let that happen, and I will not let this ocean take my child.

As the next wave lands violently on the shore, I dive toward the ocean floor. I will battle even the devil for my son.

I grab Joaquín, still holding his precious toy, the cheap but irreplaceable gift I'd given him earlier.

I hold onto my son with strength exceeded only by that with which he clutches his toy. I push him up toward the sky. Even if the sea holds onto me, my son will be safe. He gasps for air. He breathes. He's alive.

I launch him toward the shallow beach. He lands and races up the hill of sand with his brightly colored globe.

I'm ready now to meet my death, knowing that I've saved my son. But without explanation, the surf calms.

Water runs away into the sea, leaving me standing, happy, tired. And proud of all that I am.

CHAPTER FORTY-ONE

JOE WOKE WITH ELIZABETH HOLDING HIM TIGHTLY. He listened to her soothing voice.

"You were dreaming," she said softly. "Are you all right?"

"Yes, I'm fine. Everything's fine." Joe laid his head back on Elizabeth's shoulder. "Perfectomundo."

* * *

"STOP. I'M GOING TO WALK inside," De la Toure said to his wife who was pushing his wheelchair. He clutched a red, heart-shaped pillow, courtesy of the Houston Heart Institute.

"Jacques, you have to conserve your energy."

"I let you push me over here, but I'll walk into the board meeting on my own two legs."

"All right." Susan moved around to the front of the wheelchair to help him disembark. "But I'm coming in with you."

"Only if you stay out of my way." De la Toure wobbled as he stood. He started to fall back, but he grabbed an arm of the wheel-chair until he stabilized. "I will say what I have to say."

He realized his career was finished. He would take his punishment like a man, as his father used to say, but he would not let McClintock and Hackett use his inadequacies to support their new plan for the hospital: a Houston Heart Institute in which money reigned.

Susan extended her hand. "I don't want to stop you, but let's not have another heart attack."

He grasped her hand and he was steady; Susan released him and moved to open the door to the boardroom. De la Toure pulled himself erect, handed Susan the pillow, and strode inside. He would not let anyone see the pain he felt, physical or emotional.

The scattered polite conversations stopped abruptly. The city's business executives and civic leaders put down their coffee cups and stared at him, the aging chairman of the cardiovascular surgery department.

What had they heard? De la Toure wondered.

"Jacques," the board chair said, hurrying around the table to great him. "It's good to see you up, but shouldn't you be resting?"

"Thank you, Barbara, but I'm fine. I understand your agenda pertains to the cardiovascular surgery department." He accepted her hand and shook it gently.

"Yes. Yes, it does." She moved in close and whispered, "Are you sure you want to be here for this discussion?"

"Yes, I'm quite sure, if you don't mind allowing me to sit in as a guest."

"Of course not." The chair returned to the head of the conference table.

"I see you have invited Dr. Carlisle and Mr. Hackett," De la Toure said as he sat slowly. He couldn't help but wince and he felt his sternum creak as he used his arms to lower himself into the plush leather chair. He wondered how he would get up without assistance.

The movement initiated a paroxysm of coughing. He wished he'd kept that pillow to squeeze against his chest. Instead, he clutched himself in a one-person bear hug.

* * *

JOE SAT WITH ELIZABETH and Lupe in the family lounge. The pulmonologist had come through.

No change.

Broken record, Joe thought. Yet it didn't anger him, not today. He knew his child would get better. He knew. The Virgin had promised.

The waiting room soon filled. Newly formed friends exchanged updates on the conditions of their loved ones. In the background, CNN played on the television. Lupe loved CNN. She loved Michaela Perciras multi-ethnicity, the daughter of a white Canadian and a black Jamaican. This morning they were discussing immigration and the wall being constructed along the Mexican border. Lupe wanted this distraction from her concern over Joaquín. She turned to Joe.

"Some people want that fence so much. You wouldn't be alive if Raúl hadn't brought me here illegally?"

"Yes, Mamá. I agree."

"I guess it's all right for the people already here, but who brought them to America?"

"Mamá, I agree with you. I understand."

"You do?" Lupe looked at him with total disbelief.

"I really do, Mamá. You were right about so many things."

"¡Qué milagro!"

A physician entered the waiting area to talk with other parents. Casually, he reached up to the television mounted overhead and pushed the "volume down" button until the TV was silent. Joe sensed Lupe was a little miffed. Why didn't the doctor have the courtesy to take the group to a conference room?

Joe gave Lupe a little nudge.

Lupe said, "Elizabeth, tell me what they're saying."

"Mamá, please," Joe said. Lip-reading wasn't some parlor trick.

"I don't mind, Joe. They're saying that the numbers of undocumented workers—."

Suddenly, Joe jumped up. "Elizabeth, we have to go."

"What do you mean? Why?" She sat unmoved, totally perplexed.

"I don't have time to explain." Joe leaned forward to kiss his wife, and pulled her up from her seat. "Trust me. Joaquín's improving. I know it, and now, we have to help Dr. De la Toure."

CHAPTER FORTY-TWO

JOE KNOCKED ON MASTERS' OFFICE DOOR. THERE WAS no response.

He knocked again. Louder.

"Joe, she's not here," Elizabeth said.

"She has to be." He banged on the door. "Dr. Masters, we have to talk with you."

Still, no answer.

He kicked the door with the toe of his shoe. "Dr. Masters? Open the door."

Finally, she opened the door. "Joe, what are you doing here? I've told you I can't deal with your problems right now.

"Dr. Masters, as a favor to me, won't you let us come in? Just for a moment," Elizabeth said.

"All right, Elizabeth. For you."

Joe and Elizabeth followed Masters into her office. She scooped up a number of manila, letter–sized envelopes from her desk. Joe noticed that they were addressed to major medical schools.

"Joe, we've already talked. There's nothing to be gained here. In fact, I probably won't be around by the end of the year anyway."

"What?" Elizabeth said. "I didn't understand what you said." She turned to Joe and signed, "What did Dr. Masters say? She won't be here at the end of the year?"

"Dr. Masters, I have to make you understand. Elizabeth and I have to make you understand."

"Joe, they're starting the Lutheran board meeting, and Dr. Carlisle is there to address the group. I think he's going to be named the new chair of the department, and he's already told me that he'll drastically reduce my research budget and increase my clinical responsibilities."

Joe signed as Masters spoke to make sure Elizabeth could follow the conversation. "Oh, no," Elizabeth cried. "That would be awful."

"Elizabeth, I think I can still give you a spot when you come back from maternity leave, but honestly, I'm looking for a new position myself." She motioned to the papers and mailing envelops cluttering her desk.

"You can't leave," Elizabeth said.

"I know that I complained about Dr. De la Toure, but he actually sought to balance academic surgery with clinical practice. I think Carlisle's goal is to shut down the labs completely. So, I'm working on my exit strategy."

"You may not need that," Joe said.

"Joe, don't start with that conspiracy stuff. If you're not careful, the administration is going to put you out on the street, and I'm not going to be able to help you at all."

"You have to take us to the board meeting. We have evidence now." Joe pulled out the DVD. "Just look." He moved behind her desk to the computer and inserted the disk.

* * *

DE LA TOURE LISTENED as Barbara Jorgen called the meeting to order. With booming oratory, she dispatched the mundane items on the agenda, one by one, until she came to new business. Then, she looked up from the list in front of her. She directed her words to McClintock.

"Now Dallas, you wanted to address the group."

McClintock stood. De la Toure noticed he appeared particularly imposing. He wore ostrich-skin boots, buffed to a luminous shine. He sucked in his gut, giving his torso a forceful shape. His barrel chest promised power. McClintock ran his hands through his wavy hair, pushing errant strands behind his ears, and he gazed down the table to Hackett, who offered an affirmative nod.

"Thank you, Madam Chairperson." He accentuated the second half of the compound noun to make sure Ms. Jorgen appreciated his attempt at political correctness. "I appreciate you putting me on the agenda."

Turning to the rest of the table, he continued.

"As I explained to our chairperson before the meeting, we have a difficult morning ahead. I know many of you have heard of the unfortunate occurrences these last two months at the Houston Heart Institute. We have to discuss them, and we have to resolve the problem, or should I say problems."

McClintock had their attention. "Lutheran Hospital is at a critical crossroads. Our hospital prospered during the cost-plus decades, but now the times are changing, and Lutheran is about to go under."

"How can you say something so preposterous?" interrupted the CEO of First Houston Bank. "During the last five years, this hospital has had its most productive period ever, far superior to that of either Methodist or St. Luke's."

"Exactly, but this year, Lutheran's running a twenty-million-dollar deficit."

"What's the point then?"

McClintock smiled broadly. Then, he began again, more slowly, his Texas drawl pronounced. "We have to make some hard choices. We can hang on by a thread until the government cuts it, or we can be proactive. Y'all know HealthTex is the preeminent insurance entity in the state of Texas. I want to see Lutheran become our flagship. And today we'll announce which hospital will be selected for our first ACO demonstration project."

"And if we decide to follow along with you?" the CEO asked.

"First, we replace Dr. De la Toure as our chief of surgery." He turned to De la Toure. "Sorry, Jacques." He continued talking to the group. "Y'all know about Dr. De la Toure's operation. What you may not be aware of is the abysmal results we were having with our coronary patients before his illness."

"You can't make unsubstantiated accusations," the bank CEO said.

McClintock smiled with all his country-boy charm. "That's why I gave y'all a copy of the Quality Assurance report. Check the statistics in your folder."

He paused while the members flipped through the agenda to the appropriate page. Over the towering blue column for surgeon A, McClintock had written "DLT" in large block letters.

Everyone stared at the numbers in black and white.

McClintock turned to the bank executive. "Now, you tell me if you find anything unsubstantiated."

Each member of the board examined the numbers.

Finally, the bank CEO gazed directly at De la Toure. "Jacques, I'm sorry, but these figures are horrendous."

De la Toure struggled to keep his head upright, his gaze focused straight ahead. At the opposite end of the table he thought Barbara Jorgen might cry.

McClintock cleared his throat. "And if you'll notice the red column for surgeon B, that's Dr. Carlisle's data."

"Incredible," several at the table muttered. The mortality rate was less than 0.5%.

"Continue, Dallas," Ms. Jorgen said.

De la Toure thought she wanted to end the agony. It was best to rip the dressing off the wound.

Dallas had total control of the meeting. "I've asked Evan Hackett and Dr. Carlisle to give y'all a short presentation. Listen to what they say."

Hackett stood as McClintock sat. He opened his briefcase and passed out a thirty-page prospectus for the new entity HealthTex Medicare.

Hackett turned on the PowerPoint presentation on his laptop.

A pie chart filled the screen. "Here is Lutheran's market share in comparison to that of our competitors. The drop in the last five years has been dramatic."

A second pie chart showed income changes. The third demonstrated the percentage of managed care, which was short of the national average or even local average. The Medicare percentages were up. Private insurance reimbursement was way down.

Hackett impressed the businessmen. They followed his presentation. They didn't know about MRIs or PET scanners, but they knew where Hackett was coming from. They understood dollars.

With the financial presentation completed, Hackett introduced Dr. Carlisle.

Carlisle stood and nodded towards his chief. De la Toure couldn't read him, but instinctively he knew that ambition guided his junior associate.

"We have to market not only the most cost-effective care but also the highest quality, the best results." Carlisle reiterated the devastating cardiac statistics and the lack of attention paid to cost containment and quality control. He advocated a plan of quality assurance that included economic credentialing. Physicians whose expenses exceeded the average would simply be excluded. Offending physicians would be removed from the staff, fired.

"We have to begin with Dr. De la Toure," McClintock interjected. "He's been raping the hospital, running up overwhelming expenses for chronic patients, and he threatens our reputation as a heart center with his terrible mortality rate. I propose we replace Jacques with Dr. Victor Carlisle, and with the support of our president, Mr. Hackett, they can begin the institution of a new system of total quality management."

The board murmured their affirmation. These two spoke their language.

"Can I have your proposal in the form of a motion?" Jorgen asked.

De la Toure lowered his head into the guillotine and waited for the blade to fall.

CHAPTER FORTY-THREE

JOE HELD OPEN THE DOOR AND THEN FOLLOWED DR. Masters and Elizabeth into the dark-paneled Lutheran boardroom. In the center, a dozen or more people sat in leather chairs around a massive conference table, anchored by Barbara Jorgen at one end and De la Toure at the opposite.

McClintock stood in front of his chair. His cowboy boots added several inches to his six-foot-plus frame. He began his decree: "Ms. Jorgen, I move that the board permanently rescind Dr. De la Toure's operating privileges, and that we appoint Dr. Victor Carlisle to be the new chief of surgery and medical director of HealthTex/Lutheran."

"That's quite a mouthful, Dallas," Masters said.

McClintock turned and glared at the trio standing near the door. "Dr. Masters, this is a closed meeting. Your presence is neither required nor desired. You can leave and take your guests with you, and don't let the door hit you on your way out."

"Oh, I don't agree," Masters said. "Ms. Jorgen, may I address the committee? I have something to add to the discussion."

"This is highly irregular, Dr. Masters," Jorgen said.

"I know, but you have Mr. Hackett here and Dr. Carlisle. They aren't members of the board." Masters moved toward De la Toure as she spoke. "Jacques, make them listen."

"Why, Katrina?"

"Because I have important information."

"OK. Barbara, friends, you've known me a long time. I hope you will let my associate speak."

"Dr. Masters, I assume this must be of grave importance," Jorgen said.

"Madame Chairperson," McClintock interrupted. "Let's not let the self-serving interests of a couple of doctors prevent us from pursuing our destiny." His right hand fanned across the color graphic on the table in front of him. "This is our future. Now Ms. Jorgen, I believe there's a motion on the table."

"Yes, Dallas, but as you frequently tell me, hold your horses. The chair will recognize Dr. Masters, but only for discussion with regard to Mr. McClintock's motion. Dr. Masters, you may continue."

McClintock sat back down.

"Thank you, Ms. Jorgen." Masters scanned the table, making eye contact with each member, trying to ensure that every person would not only hear, but also listen to her words. "Madam Chair, members of the board, friends, a lot has happened these last two months, and I'm only now beginning to understand, in no small part due to the efforts of this young man and his wife." Masters gestured to her companions. Joe and Elizabeth moved forward a few inches.

"Dr. Joe Morales is a surgery resident here. You are aware there's been an unusual number of deaths in the cardiovascular ICU. Unfortunately, an employee, Raúl Sanchez, was accused of unplugging ventilators, leading to these deaths."

"Katrina, why do you say unfortunately?" De la Toure asked. "Dr. Morales saw him disconnect a patient from the ventilator. He was involved in the ICU deaths, but Mr. Hackett won't admit that. And I think Mr. McClintock was connected."

"Jacques, you're losing it, old man. Don't make 'em all think you're crazy to boot," McClintock said.

"Dallas, I saw you in Hackett's office on the morning we discovered that Raúl had unplugged Hank Simpson's ventilator. I heard you threaten Evan Hackett."

"Dr. De la Toure," Masters said, patting him on the shoulder, "I don't think Raúl had any part in this mess."

"We need to replace this old man," McClintock said. "He's incompetent and crazy as a hoot owl."

"Dallas, I'm not finished." She looked to the head of the table. "Ms. Jorgen, may I?"

"Continue, Dr. Masters."

"Thanks. Mr. McClintock wants to replace our surgery chairman. All of you know that Dr. De la Toure has presided over this hospital since it was little more than an ER in the middle of a cow pasture out in Katy. He brought the hospital here to the Texas Medical Center and established the Houston Heart Institute. Maybe he's out of step with the new economics that Mr. Hackett and Mr. McClintock envision. I don't know, but this isn't the way to replace him. Recently, Dr. De la Toure's professional reputation has been grossly maligned. I'm sorry to say I participated in this attack. I personally made him quit."

She stopped and looked at De la Toure.

"Sorry, Jacques," she said softly.

De la Toure nodded in affirmation.

Masters continued. "But I was wrong. Dr. Morales here is responsible for discovering the truth, and I want to let him tell you what's happened in our little hospital."

Victor Carlisle and Evan Hackett sat motionless during Masters' tirade against McClintock and her impassioned plea on behalf of De la Toure. Carlisle now picked up a pencil from the desk. He slowly tapped the handout that sat in front of him, Evan's color graphic, a pronouncement of the greatness Lutheran Hospital would reach under their direction.

Joe took one step forward and Carlisle glared at him.

"Ms. Jorgen," Joe said. He paused, shifting his weight from side to side. He placed both of his hands in the large front pockets of his white coat.

"Go ahead, Dr. Morales. You're among friends here."

"Yes, thank you. What I want to tell you . . . I mean . . . let me start at the beginning. Last month in the ICU, the other resident, Matt Keith . . . he's a good doctor, but he was having a terrible time. I came in, and it became worse. The patients were dropping like flies. Excuse me. I mean no disrespect."

There was a small amount of nervous laughter.

"Go on, Dr. Morales," Ms. Jorgen said.

"Well, when I caught Raúl, at least I believed I did, I thought it would be easy sailing—no more deaths—but it got worse. I assumed, like everyone, that it was Dr. De la Toure's fault, you know, his age and all. But I noticed a lab abnormality, or really a lack of abnormality. Actually, it's too complicated to explain here, but I discovered someone was messing with the cardioplegia solutions. I know I'm getting technical again."

"Slow down, Joe. Breathe," Masters said.

Joe continued, a little more slowly. "Let's just say, someone was changing one of the drugs from pharmacy, substituting it with something else, and the result was that the hearts weren't protected during bypass surgery. All of De la Toure's patients were getting the bad stuff and having massive heart attacks. Someone did this on purpose, trying to make De la Toure look bad or worse than bad. It made him look awful—."

Carlisle interrupted. "Joe, this is preposterous. You couldn't possibly have any proof. We checked the potassium. Ms. Jorgen, let me explain."

"By all means, Dr. Carlisle. Explain it to us. I know I'm totally confused."

"Joe developed this crazy theory." He gestured to everyone at the table, making sure everyone was aware of this incompetent resident. "He barged in on Dr. De la Toure's surgery, acting in a totally unprofessional manner. Not only was he wrong, but also we checked the solution in each bag and found the potassium present in the correct dosage. He abandoned his watch in the ICU to come to the OR. A patient almost died and we had to fire him from the service."

Joe wanted to retreat into the wall. He couldn't take on Carlisle. He was outmatched.

Masters raised her hand. The whole group gave her their attention.

"Actually, Victor, I think Joe is right," she said slowly and forcefully. "We can let the board examine this in detail later, but I want you all to understand that I believe Dr. Morales. Someone did change the cardioplegia solutions for Dr. De la Toure's patients. Joe discovered that the numbering system on every one of Dr. De la Toure's patients for the last two months was out of sequence. We checked other surgeons' cardioplegia. They weren't altered."

"How convenient," Carlisle said.

De la Toure cleared his throat. Everyone took notice.

"Dr. Carlisle, have you been working in the cardioplegia laboratory?" Masters asked.

"Of course not. I haven't been there in months."

"Liar," Joe said. He called out the man he once admired.

Carlisle pivoted in his chair and scowled at Joe. "Joe, you'll never practice medicine again."

Joe pulled a DVD from his pocket. "Dr. Carlisle," he said, waving the disc in his hand. "I have a video of you entering the lab the night before Dr. De la Toure's surgery."

"Victor." De la Toure spoke his associates name with a deep sadness in his voice.

Joe imagined how betrayed he must feel. Joe looked at Carlisle's face, absent any emotion, as cool as a player in a Texas Hold 'Em tournament. He would not return De la Toure's gaze.

All the people remained fixed in their seats. No one even lifted a coffee cup for a drink. In fact, no one moved a muscle, as if the first to stir would be shot.

Joe advanced to the front of the group, placed the disc into the video machine and pushed the play button. The image projected onto a sixty-inch flat screen mounted on the wall behind Ms. Jorgen. The security video showed a surgeon in scrubs, wearing a long white coat, his head covered with a paper hood. In his left hand, he carried a plain briefcase.

"You can't tell who that person is," Carlisle said.

"Watch the video," Masters ordered.

The figure turned toward the intercom with head lowered so that you could only see the lips moving as he pushed the button.

"Joe, explain," Masters said.

"This is my wife, Elizabeth, and she can lip-read. She's examined this recording and six others, each taken the night before one of the suspicious cases."

Elizabeth moved to Joe's side. She signed as she spoke. "The surgeon is saying, 'This is Dr. Carlisle; open the lab door.'"

"Ridiculous," Carlisle said. "This is no proof."

"Ms. Jorgen," the bank executive said. "I've seen enough. I move that we issue a statement of board support for Dr. De la Toure. While he recovers, we should appoint Dr. Katrina Masters the acting chief of surgery. Furthermore, I suggest you establish an ad hoc committee, headed by Dr. Masters, to examine these issues and the involvement of Dallas McClintock, Evan Hackett, and Dr. Carlisle. Raúl Sanchez's name must be cleared and we must inform the police and the state authorities."

Frenzied conversations filled the air. The orderly meeting descended into civilized chaos.

Joe touched Masters' shoulder, and she turned to face him.

"Do you mind if we leave now?" Joe asked.

"Go ahead. Joe, Elizabeth, thank you."

"Dr. Morales, thank you," Susan De la Toure said before erupting into tears of joy. She moved to her husband's side and embraced him.

"Thank you, Joe," De la Toure said.

Joe pointed to his wife. "Elizabeth figured it all out."

De la Toure said, "Dr. Masters, maybe we should give Elizabeth her own lab."

As the room laughed, Elizabeth signed to Joe, "Let's go see Joaquín."

"Absolutely, but first, I should check in with pathology and tell them where I'll be."

"Joe!" As they started out the door, Carlisle grabbed his arm with a force that would leave behind his fingers' imprint. "You'll regret this day."

"No, I don't think so, Dr. Carlisle."

"Trust me. I'll make you sorry you ever came to this meeting."

CHAPTER FORTY-FOUR

JOE STOPPED BY THE PATHOLOGY DEPARTMENT AND asked Dr. Weisenthal for the remainder of the day off. All he needed to do was sign out a few charts. Then, he and Elizabeth headed for the pediatric ICU.

Great. Joe had convinced the board of a murderous plot to harm De la Toure and he hoped Carlisle would go to jail. With CSI-style technology, they could prove Carlisle had altered the cardioplegia bags and the post-op labs proved that the patients didn't get the correct solutions. However, Joe also knew that with enough money, many obvious murderers walked, but that wasn't most important.

His son Joaquín was better. His hero Dr. De la Toure had been vindicated. And his wife Elizabeth would stand by him until the end of time.

Perfectomundo!

* * *

THEY ARRIVED AT THE pediatric ICU to find an almost-empty waiting area.

Elizabeth said, "It must be visiting time. I guess Lupe's already inside. We'd better wait."

"I know most of the nurses. They won't mind. What are a couple of extra relatives? Come on."

Joe and Elizabeth walked through the electronic doors into the pediatric ICU. As a consideration to Joe, the nurses had moved Joaquín into an empty isolation room near the entrance. It usually was reserved for babies with highly contagious infections, but since it wasn't in use, they let Joaquín have the private area.

Solid walls extended only to waist height. Clear glass continued to the ceiling. Joe could see Lupe standing, talking to a physician. The physician gestured toward the baby lying on the warming bed. Small wires connected the child to the monitor, and a plastic tube, connecting him to the ventilator, served as his lifeline.

The back of the physician appeared familiar. The doctor wore scrubs and a long white coat, unusual, not the typical pediatric doctor's jeans and polo shirt.

Wait! Joe recognized the doctor.

Joe slammed into the glass door sending it crashing against the wall. "What in hell are you doing here?" he said to the visitor.

Elizabeth followed close behind.

Lupe answered the question even though it wasn't directed to her. "José, Dr. Carlisle came to check on Joaquín."

"I asked you what you're doing here." Joe moved to within inches of Carlisle's face. "You should be consulting your attorneys, concocting some explanation of why you were messing with the cardioplegia solutions, killing De la Toure's patients in the OR."

"To be accurate, Joe, not all the patients died in surgery. Some actually made it to the ICU. They had strong hearts, but a little hypoxia goes a long way. No one survives without oxygen."

"You turned off those ventilators?"

"Now, Joe, why would you think that?" Carlisle chuckled and then stepped to the side in order to move around Joe, but a cut-down tray on a rolling stand blocked his path. Carlisle pushed it away so that he could leave the room. "You've been causing a lot of trouble when you should have been watching out for your boy."

Carlisle's lips tightened and the smirk stretched across his face. He nodded to Joe as he got to the door.

"Wait," Joe said. He grabbed Carlisle's arm and pulled him back into the room.

Carlisle tried to jerk free but Joe shoved the taller man into the wall. Joe's left forearm pushed against Carlisle's chest, pinning him up against the glass. "Did you do something to Joaquín?"

"Oh my God," Elizabeth shrieked as she ran to their child's side.

In response to the commotion, Amy's replacement, Corinne, rushed into the room. "Dr. Carlisle, Dr. Morales, are y'all OK?"

Obviously, neither Corinne nor his mother had heard of the destruction of Carlisle's reputation. But how could they? It hadn't even been an hour before.

"Yes, thanks," Carlisle answered. He pushed Joe back a step. "I was just leaving."

Corinne seemed unsure, but she headed back to the workstation.

"You're not leaving, Dr. Carlisle." Joe brought his elbow up and slammed it into Carlisle's jaw. It knocked his attending's head against the glass. With Carlisle stunned, Joe turned partially so he could reach the cut-down tray behind him. There, he found what he needed.

A scalpel.

Joe put the knife blade to Carlisle's face. For a moment, he thought of stabbing it through one of the bastard's eyes.

Elizabeth screeched, "No!" The high-pitched, blood-curdling sound bounced off the glass and reverberated around the room. Joe imagined everyone in the ICU was watching this real-life drama.

304

"Joe, what are you doing?" she asked, rushing toward him.

"Stay back, Elizabeth." With his left forearm pushed against Carlisle's chest, Joe pinned Carlisle against the glass. His right hand held the sharp stainless steel against Carlisle's throat, precisely positioned over the carotid artery.

"Did you do something to my boy?"

"I didn't—."

Joe pushed the knife in until it broke skin. Blood trickled down, staining the surgeon's starched, white, coat collar. "Carlisle, I swear to God, I'll kill you. Right here. Right now. You got away with Lourdes's death, but I won't let you hurt my boy—."

Corinne threw open the door into the room. The glass vibrated within its frame, threatening to shatter.

"What's happening?" she shrieked.

"Call security," Carlisle pleaded.

"No! Corinne, listen to me. Do as I say or I'll kill Dr. Carlisle." Joe's eyes searched the room. An IV was dripping fluid into a small vein that the pediatric resident had cut down on in Joaquín's ankle. "Stop the IV. Now! I think Dr. Carlisle put something in there."

Slowly, Corinne moved over to Joaquín's bed, nervously looking to Lupe and Elizabeth, obviously unsure of Joe's mental status.

"Please," Elizabeth said. "Do what he says."

Corinne turned off the intravenous pump. "OK. It's off."

While he kept Carlisle pushed against the wall, Joe turned his head and examined Joaquín's monitor. Heart rate: 85, good; Rhythm: sinus, excellent; Blood pressure: 120/80, perfect. Yet Joe couldn't find his son's oxygen saturation. He was frantic.

"Corinne, where's the O2 monitor? It doesn't seem as if Joaquín's breathing."

She gestured to a small, stainless steel table on rollers. "The monitor is over on the—."

"Madre de Dios," Joe said. "His saturation is only 55%."

"V-tach," Corinne screamed. "He's in V-tach. Oh my God, we need to call a code."

"Your boy's dying, Joe," Carlisle said. "Isn't that sad. Aren't you sorry you messed with me?"

Elizabeth tried to push to the side of the nurse to touch her baby, but Lupe held her back.

"Joe, you have to do something," Elizabeth screamed. "Our baby. He's going to die!"

Joe reached deep inside his being. He'd been so focused on his own life, his dreams, his career. Now, Carlisle was going to kill his child and Joe had let it happen. Joaquín was dying and Joe couldn't stop it.

NO!

He could. He was in control and he knew what to do. He was the only one in the room who could save his son.

"Corinne, listen to me," Joe said.

"Code blue, pediatric ICU," boomed overhead.

Joe spoke louder; his forceful orders demanded compliance. "Grab the ambu. Use the wall oxygen. Bag him. Now!"

Corinne took the egg-shaped plastic ambu from the emergency cart and began to ventilate Joaquín by hand. With each squeeze, she pushed oxygen into his lungs.

Joe watched the oxygen monitor immediately respond, the flashing display indicating the rising concentration of oxygen in Joaquín's blood: 65% . . . 75% . . . 85% . . .

"What's going on here?" asked a security guard as he entered, panting, trying to catch his breath.

A code team followed behind, the crowd unable to get inside the room.

"He's trying to—," Carlisle started.

"Shut up, Carlisle." Joe pushed the knife deeper into the side of Carlisle's neck until blood flowed freely. "Now what did you do to my boy?"

"I'm telling you, I didn't do anything."

The guard pulled his gun and ordered Joe to drop his knife, but Joe ignored the command. The officer raised the weapon and pointed it at Joe.

"No!" Elizabeth shrieked, but the security guard kept his gun aimed at Joe. "Please, Officer Riggers. Don't shoot. Joe won't hurt Dr. Carlisle."

Joe kept the scalpel immobile. He had broken skin and penetrated the first layers of connective tissue. The tip of the blade was less than a centimeter away from Carlisle's carotid artery. With a gentle shove, he could end Carlisle's life. He just might do it. But first he had to save his son's life. Elizabeth had read the guard's nametag. Using someone's name was supposed to help in negotiation. Maybe. "Officer Riggers, please do not shoot me. If you do, I'll fall into Dr. Carlisle and this blade will sever his carotid artery. Do you understand?" The guard didn't respond, but no one moved and Joe took that to mean he had some time. "Corinne, the ventilator. Tell me, what is it set on?"

She examined the big blue box, the front of which contained multiple knobs and gauges that controlled every aspect of the patient's breathing.

"Rate is off, oxygen is off, and the alarm is off," Corinne said, her voice rising through the sentence. "Someone has changed these settings. This baby is paralyzed. He can't breathe for himself until the vercuronium wears off."

She reached for the dials, but Joe shouted, "Don't touch the machine. Keep bagging him. We know he's getting oxygen from the wall outlet. The oxygen saturation is up to 95%, and he's back in sinus rhythm. Have someone get a fresh bag of IV fluid and take down the other one. Get pulmonary to bring a new ventilator. Then, we'll know he's safe."

"Yes, sir, Dr. Morales," Corinne said as she executed Joe's instructions.

"Shoot him," Carlisle screamed. "He's going to kill me."

Joe thought about doing just that. Carlisle was pure evil. Who would blame Joe if he slipped and let the scalpel stab the artery? It'd be an accident. Joe was only defending his infant son from a murderer.

Joe looked at Joaquín. Taped over his bed, the holy card with the image of Our Lady of Guadalupe. She had protected his son. And now, his heavenly mother wouldn't want him to take another's life.

Joe turned to the security guard. "No, I'm not going to kill this low-life scum." Joe looked to the door. "Officer Riggers, I was holding Dr. Carlisle for you. This is just a flesh wound." Joe slowly pulled the bloodied scalpel away from Carlisle's throat. "I'm going to step back. Don't let either of us leave until you can get the Houston police here. This man is a murderer, and he just tried to kill my little boy."

He took a sudden step straight back, leaving Carlisle to fall to the floor.

Joe held both hands up, just as he'd seen on TV, and dropped the knife. It clanked on the floor.

Carlisle regained his composure and righted himself. One of the other nurses handed him a gauze sponge, which he used to apply pressure to the neck wound. As he started for the door, he spoke to the guard. "Thanks. You saved my life. I'll go to the ER and get stitched up."

"Don't let him leave," Joe said to the guard, whose gun was still pointed at Joe.

"Don't be ridiculous, officer. What's your name? Riggers? You know me. I'm Dr. Victor Carlisle, cardiovascular surgeon, associate to Dr. De la Toure. You saw what this lunatic tried to do." Carlisle released the pressure over the wound and blood trickled down his neck.

"Stop him," Elizabeth said.

"Officer Riggers, Dr. Morales may be right," added Corinne who was still bagging the child. "Someone changed this ventilator. This child's grandmother and Dr. Carlisle were the only ones here."

"I don't have to listen to any more of this. Corinne, I'll report you to Mr. Hackett. Officer, I'm leaving."

The security guard took Carlisle's arm.

"Perhaps we should wait for the police. Take a seat, doctor."

CHAPTER FORTY-FIVE

JOE AND ELIZABETH SAT IN THEIR CAR PARKED IN front of St. Anne's' church. It was February tenth, the feast day of Our Lady of Lourdes, a celebration of one of the apparitions of the Virgin Mary.

The notion that the mother of Jesus appeared to a peasant girl in a remote French village, even some Catholics found it difficult to believe.

Yet Joe wondered. Did he receive a visitation?

Elizabeth reached over to him, stroking the side of his head, gently pushing a few errant strands of hair behind his ear.

"You look nice, sweetheart."

"Well, you're ravishing. Motherhood definitely agrees with you. Should we tell Lupe today?"

"No, let this be Joaquín's day."

Joe looked at the rearview mirror, at Joaquín sitting in the rear-facing car seat behind him. He turned and patted the top of his head. His boy responded with delightful babbling. Joe was convinced he was trying to say 'dad.'

Joe turned back to face Elizabeth. "I wouldn't trade anything for you and Joaquín, or for that matter, baby Anne." He placed his hand on her abdomen.

"We don't know that it's going to be a girl."

"Oh, I'm sure."

Elizabeth gently touched his face again. "Thank you for saving my baby's life. You've been through a lot, and you put it all on the line. I would never have guessed Carlisle would go to such an extreme for revenge."

"Carlisle wanted so much, and he had to be the best. He thought if he could force De la Toure out of practice, he could lead the department in a new direction. He would be the most important surgeon in the state, maybe the nation. Then, he saw his whole life being stripped away. That's an awful feeling."

She laid her hand on his shoulder. "At least, Dr. De la Toure knows the problems in the unit weren't your fault. The cardiovascular fellowship should be yours without any question."

"Sweetheart, I've told you. No resident has ever received a CV fellowship without finishing the unit."

"Joe, that would be so unfair. He has to understand—."

"It really doesn't matter. Mamá always says 'health is our greatest blessing.' I have you, Joaquín, and little Anne. I may not have everything I wished for, but I have all I could have ever hoped for."

She turned away for a moment and wiped a tear from her eye.

When she looked back, he spoke. "Hey, let's go. We've got a baptism to get to."

* * *

THE GODFATHER, DR. MATT KEITH, held the infant over the baptismal font. In his large hands nestled Joaquín dressed in the antique-white, Spanish-lace baptismal gown that Lourdes had worn.

Next to him stood Lupe and by her side, Raúl, beaming. Joe imagined they thought of the day Lourdes was made a child of God.

As Father Wall poured holy water on the infant's head, he said the words to initiate Joe's son into the Church.

"Joaquín Keith Morales, I baptize you in the name of the Father, and of the Son, and of the Holy Spirit."

With deliberation, Joe made the sign of the cross and then brought a Rosary to his lips and kissed the crucifix.

The baptism completed, Joe took Joaquín from Matt's arms and walked with Elizabeth to the small side chapel. They knelt beside one another and Joe lifted up his child.

Just as Raúl and his mother had done on the day of Lourdes's and his own baptism, Joe prayed to the Virgin of Guadalupe, their protectress. "Virgencita, we dedicate our child to your Son. Please guide us. Make us good parents."

Joe pulled Joaquín close to his chest, holding him tight with his left arm. He placed his right hand on Elizabeth's abdomen. "And watch over our little one who's coming. May she be born in good health."

Joe followed this consecration of his infant with prayers of gratitude for the Virgin's assistance in the ICU. He knew she'd help him save Hank. He hoped she'd carry his prayers for the souls of those who didn't survive: Lourdes, Pops Duffey, Dr. Verney, Miss Pat, Coach Kubecka and the prince.

As St. Therese had said, "a whole lifetime is short indeed."

* * *

JOE'S TINY APARTMENT EFFERVESCED with partygoers from every economic, social, racial, and educational background. Spanish and English conversations mixed and marbled.

Friends, relatives, and co-workers gathered not only to celebrate Joaquín's baptism, but also to join together to restore normalcy to the Houston Heart Institute.

Masters, Allgood, and Chiu were grazing at the buffet table along with Amy and Corinne. Across the room, Joe saw Raúl talking with Lupe, Anita, Matt, and Ricky Gutierrez. Joe approached Raúl and held out his hand, looking him directly in the eye. He wanted to apologize for the hundredth time, knowing it would never be enough.

Instead of taking Joe's outstretched hand, Raúl embraced him tightly. "My Lourdes would be so proud of you."

Elizabeth swooped in with the baby.

Holding Joaquín, Elizabeth and Joe approached Eric and his wife.

"Howdy, neighbors," Eric said, his arms wrapped around his wife, just starting to show signs of her pregnancy, her face aglow.

"Hey," Joe said. "I'm glad you guys could come over." Joe hadn't thought they would, afraid that Eric's wife would feel like a traitor. Everyone knew that her father had been removed from the Lutheran board. And they'd fired Evan Hackett for his complicity, working behind the scenes with HealthTex to advance his personal wealth.

"We appreciate you including us," Eric's wife said. "Can I help?"

"Sure," Elizabeth said. She headed back to the kitchen with Elizabeth.

"Yup," Eric echoed. "Moving out of the big house was the best thing we ever did. You and Elizabeth are our inspiration. Given that we'll be right down the hall, you can teach me the baby duties, how to change the stinkies."

"Eagerly," Joe said. "We can start with you practicing on Joaquín."

"Hello, boys," Delia said as she approached with Bo, her hands locked around his bulging biceps.

Elizabeth had said to invite everybody. It was time for mending.

And like every individual, Delia was complex. She'd suffered her injuries and she had many good qualities.

The doorbell rang, unnoticed by most of the revelers who celebrated the baptism. In Elizabeth's kitchen, the light flashed to indicate that someone was at the front door.

"Joe, would you get it?" Elizabeth called out.

"I'll be right back," Joe said and maneuvered through the crowd. He opened the door. "Dr. De la Toure, Mrs. De la Toure, what a surprise."

"I hope you don't mind our coming by so late. Susan and I have a little present, in celebration of Joaquín's baptism."

De la Toure held out a beautifully wrapped box, Tiffany blue with a white ribbon.

"Thank you, sir."

Susan De la Toure stepped forward and hugged Joe.

"Thank you, Dr. Morales. You saved my husband's life. Thank you." The embrace lasted a few awkward moments before she released him.

Joe stepped back. "Please, won't you both come in? Dr. Masters is here. So is Dr. Sufi. Everyone from the Institute."

"Thank you, Joe," answered De la Toure. Turning to his wife, he said, "Susan, go on in. I want to speak with Joe for a minute."

Susan entered and Joe stepped out onto the landing.

"Joe, in a couple of years, we're going to need a new associate," De la Toure said. "I want him to be well trained. Of course, you know the best program is ours at the Houston Heart Institute."

"Yes, sir."

"When I return to work, I'm only going to assist in surgery. I've turned the department over to Dr. Masters, but I'll be in charge of the residency program. You know, we have never given a cardio-vascular surgery fellowship to anyone who didn't complete the ICU rotation."

"Yes, sir."

"I want you to return to the ICU next month."

"Thank you, sir. I'm flattered, but . . ."

Joe looked into the kitchen at Elizabeth holding Joaquín in her arms, little Anne growing in her womb. They were his three most prized possessions.

"I'm sorry," Joe said. "But I can't next month." He almost didn't believe his own words. Was he turning down the ICU rotation, the ticket to a cardiac fellowship and an associate position with Dr. Jacques de la Toure?

"I see." De la Toure viewed Joe's treasures. "I understand, but I still want you in my cardiovascular program. Can we talk about it later?"

"Yes, sir. Later would be perfectomundo."

WRITER'S NOTE

This book is a work of fiction. However, while the characters are entirely of my own creation, some aspects of the novel are based on real locales and real events.

Now it's time to separate fact from fiction.

Some characters in *FATAL RHYTHM* proclaim the authenticity of the Marian apparition to Saint Juan Diego. While the Church has deemed this apparition as worthy of belief and recent popes have proclaimed her Patroness of the Americas, we are prudent to recall the teachings of the Catechism of the Catholic Church (CCC 67). With respect to private revelations, the Church teaches, "It is not their role to improve or complete Christ's definitive Revelation, but to help live more fully by it in a certain period of history."

St. Anne Church and School in Houston is portrayed accurately. It is a wonderful community that successfully merges believers from different cultural and socio-economic groups. The celebration of Las Mañanitas is described to the best of my memory. Hundreds of worshipers gathered before dawn and processed into a darkened church, the only light coming from a single sanctuary light. As they each arrived at the altar, they placed a large votive candle on the floor of the apse. The candles made visible a large portrait of Our Lady of Guadalupe hanging from the rear pillars of the twenty-foot-tall baldacchino.

The Virgin appeared to Saint Juan Diego on Tepeyac Hill. At her direction, Juan took Our Lady's message to Bishop Zumárraga who asked for proof. On December 12, 1531, Our Lady instructed Juan to gather roses from the barren top of the hill, amidst the biting frost, and present them to the bishop. As Juan opened his cloak to display the roses, the image of the Virgin appeared imprinted on the ayate, a material made from the cactus-like agave plant fibers. She appeared as an Aztec princess, expectant with child, clothed by the sun and lifted by an angel. The bishop commissioned the construction of a church in her honor. The symbols of her image reflect the Virgin's concern for her children, Spanish and Ameri-Indian, but especially demonstrated her love for the new race that the mixture of cultures would create.

In the Nican Mopohua, Nahuatl for "here it is told," Don Antonio Valeriano transcribes the story of Juan Diego in Latin characters, mimicking the sound of Nahuatl, the language of the Aztecs. The Virgin spoke to Juan Diego as a gentle mother, calling him "my dearest, littlest, and youngest son." When he expressed concern about his uncle's health, she told him, "Listen, put it in your heart. Do not let your . . . heart be disturbed. Am I not here, I, who am your Mother?"

Bishop Zumárraga, Protector of the Indians, took responsibility for the safety of the indigenous population. At risk to his own life, he excommunicated the cruel Beltran de Guzman, who was President of the first Audiencia of New Spain, ruler of the Western Hemisphere. The bishop also sought the intercession of the king. Unfortunately, Bloody Guzman had forbidden direct communication with the court in Spain; so, Zumárraga hid a letter in a cask that was smuggled to King Carlos V.

At Bishop Zumárraga's request, King Carlos sent Cortes back to the New World to supervise establishment of the Second Audiencia, replacing Guzman with a new leader, one who would be kinder to the indigenous population. Unfortunately, Bloody Guzman extended his conquest west to the Pacific Ocean before he was arrested and returned to Spain in irons in 1537. I know of no Mexican family that relishes any connection to this sad part of Spanish history.

Our Lady appeared at this critical time, the beginning of a new relationship between conquerors and indigenous population. In the years following her appearance, it is said that eight million Indians converted to Catholicism. To this day, Mexicans embrace La Raza, a term coined by Jose Vasconcelos to reflect the mixture inherent in the Latino people.

We have documentation of the miracle of Guadalupe from contemporaneous sources. Don Antonio recorded Juan's story within approximately ten years of the event and the miraculous image is depicted on Codex1548. The image on the tilma, the agave-fiber cloak of Juan Diego, is remarkable in many ways. To mention a few: the ayate material would normally disintegrate within twenty years; no sizing was used to enable an image to be painted on the loosely woven fabric; the brilliance of the colors persist; and microscopic examination of the Virgin's pupils have demonstrated the reflected image of Juan Diego's presentation to the bishop.

Many have researched the authenticity of the image of Our Lady of Guadalupe and there are a number of excellent resources. Two that I find particularly helpful are *A Handbook on Guadalupe* by Franciscan Friars of the Immaculate and *Our Lady of Guadalupe: Mother of the Civilization of Love* by Carl Anderson.

FATAL RHYTHM takes place at the Houston Heart Institute. Not long ago, residents frequently worked 36 hours straight with only 12 hours off in between shifts. This schedule continued for months at a time without any vacation days. And in fact, there was a rotation with Dr. DeBakey where the resident lived in the hospital for two month of uninterrupted call. Currently, trainee hours are strictly regulated. The abuses described in this story would not be tolerated.

The Houston Heart Institute is a fictional place in the Texas Medical Center, and the setting is not intended to resemble The Methodist Hospital, St. Luke's Hospital, The Texas Heart Institute, Hermann Hospital, Ben Taub Hospital, or the Michael E. DeBakey V.A. Hospital. Each of these is an excellent facility with a successful heart surgery program.

The Texas Medical Center is the largest medical center in the world set on over one thousand acres near the campus of Rice University in Houston. The center includes twenty-one hospitals and three medical schools along with thirty other health institutions. The center has more than 100,000 employees and receives seven million annual patient visits.

In *FATAL RHYTHM*, the character of Jacques De la Toure is not based on Dr. Michael DeBakey. In the case of this true giant of medicine, the reality of his accomplishments tests belief. Just to mention a few: as a medical student he developed the roller head pump we now use in bypass surgery; he was the first to advocate for vascular repair of war wounds after WWII; he recommended establishment of MASH units in the Korean conflict; he was the first to suggest correlation between smoking and lung cancer; he performed the first carotid endarterectomy, the first aorto-bifemoral bypass and the first vein coronary artery bypass to treat atherosclerosis that leads to stroke, amputation, and heart attack; he performed the implantation of the first ventricular assist device and supervised development of the first artificial heart.

In the Journal of the American Medical Association, Mike Mitka wrote, "Many consider Michael E. DeBakey to be the greatest surgeon ever." I would concur. He performed more than 60,000 operative procedures. He was surgeon, educator, scientist, and ambassador. In the Michael E. DeBakey Museum and Library at Baylor College of Medicine, one can see photos that document the phenomenal development of the Texas Medical Center over the last sixty years and view exhibits that testify to the titan of surgery that was Dr. Michael E. DeBakey.

Dr. DeBakey established the first surgery residency program in Houston. Through the years the Baylor program was renowned for teaching patient care. The faculty would commonly ask, "Who is the patient's doctor?" The concept expressed by that question was that the surgeon was responsible for every aspect of the patient's care. The surgeon might consult with a myriad of specialists, but at the end of the day, he was captain of the ship and he felt a personal responsibility for his patient.

The Affordable Care Act, commonly referred to as Obama-care, is a complicated piece of legislation. It promotes many current trends in the delivery of medical care. As we evaluate these changes in medicine, it is of primary importance that we be intellectually honest. First, it strains credulity that we can provide better care for more patients for less money. Second, the measure of quality is very difficult. And the attempt to rate quality may encourage proactive patient selection to accomplish improved results. Third, in America, we generally assume a capitalistic incentive in the marketplace. Most presume that the more testing and procedures that are performed, the more money the doctors and hospitals will receive. If we are to adopt systems where the incentive is to provide fewer interventions, it is our obligation to inform our patients.

Our oath demands that we never do harm. Our patients rely on our commitment to that principle. May we physicians never violate that sacred trust.

ABOUT THE AUTHOR

R. B. O'Gorman grew up in Texas where he developed a devotion to Our Lady of Guadalupe. He obtained a PhD in Biochemistry from Rice University and studied cardiovascular surgery under Dr. Michael E. DeBakey. His debut novel, *FATAL RHYTHM*, is a medical suspense/mystery based on his training experience. Currently, he lives in Mobile, Alabama, where he writes, teaches, and practices medicine. He and his wife stay busy with their six children and first three grandchildren.

A CHANCE TO CUT
A TEXAS MEDICAL CENTER MYSTERY
BY
R. B. O'GORMAN

WITHIN EACH BODY—A TRILLION CELLS.

In each liver cell's nucleus—twenty thousand unique genes.

On one chosen gene—the DNA helix uncoils, exposing the sequence coding for HMG-CoA reductase, the enzyme that controls cholesterol production.

CHAPTER ONE

A CHANCE TO CUT IS A CHANCE TO CURE—

the surgeon's motto.

And I had a lot of chances on the day Senator Travis received the Democratic nomination for president. I'd finished three heart bypass operations, each lasting about four hours. Back to back to back.

Exhausted, I plodded down the hall to City Hospital's OR lounge. I could've found it blindfolded, following the scent of fresh popcorn and the calypso beat emanating from the microwave. Orville Redenbacher's and Diet Coke—OR staples. But that night, I hoped to find a remnant of the pepperoni pizzas I'd ordered for the staff. They'd worked straight through lunch. Voluntarily. We had a great crew.

After inhaling a slice of cold pizza and chugging a can of soda, I plopped on one of the seasoned, cracked-vinyl sofas and stretched out, my feet resting on the Formica-topped coffee table and my head leaning against the wall behind me. At the opposite end of the room, mounted high on the wall, the TV was turned to the CNN coverage of the Democratic convention. I offered a few cursory greetings to the random staff there on break, but all I wanted was to close my eyes for a few minutes before jumping on my Cannondale and heading across Hermann Park to my condo.

When I was a resident, I calculated that I could bike it faster than I could drive. On the way home, I'd hook up with Spike, my feline best friend and roommate.

"Dr. O'Keefe," Takisha called out. "Our patient is fixing to accept the nomination. The Reverend Jefferson is making the introduction."

I groaned.

As the lounge spontaneously filled with doctors, nurses, and aides, I opened my eyelids a crack, just enough to see the familiar corpulent African American amidst a sea of red, white, and blue. Even though I rarely watched the cable news shows, I recognized the civil rights icon.

"... the next president of the United States, Senator Austin Fondren Travis, IV."

Applause filled the lounge and bellowed from the TV's speakers. It seemed like the producers had cranked up the volume, the same way networks augment their advertiser's messages that interrupt my favorite shows.

The vibrant senator, appearing much younger than his fifty-four years, approached the podium with hands raised in mock gesture to quiet the crowd, knowing that the pundits had the stop-clocks running. They'd be counting the number and duration of each ovation interrupting his speech. I closed my eyes again in search of that respite.

After several minutes, the noise diminished.

I was drifting off when the senator started to speak, and Takisha turned up the volume. I didn't need to listen to the words. I could recite by heart the mantra, the compilation of a dozen or so sound bytes evoking human emotions of love, loyalty, and patriotism. The senator was pro-everything: pro-life and pro-family, but also pro-gay, pro-feminism, pro-universal healthcare, and pro-environment.

I'd never been particularly interested in politics, believing that the military-industrial complex runs the country according to its own manual, not limited by external constraints or votes. After all, half of the country believes our greatest president was Ronald Reagan, who took cues from his wife who was following the advice of a psychic. The other half idolizes one so flawed that he engaged in oral sex in the Oval Office while talking on the phone with congressmen.

So, I've never allocated much energy to partisan discussions. The fact that I'd operated on Senator Travis had been little more than an interesting footnote to my first year as staff attending.

In practice I always voted for the Democratic nominee. My father and my grandfather never voted Republican and I hadn't seen any reason to start. Until President Obama treated the Catholic Church with such disdain. After that, I promised I'd never vote for another Democrat, but that was before Senator Travis entered the presidential race.

"That arrogant asshole," Takisha said. "I could wish him some major chest pain right now."

I sat upright, abandoning my plan for a power nap. "Takisha, people are going to think you really mean that. Not to mention, you don't want to set off the Secret service."

Some of the other staff laughed robustly.

"Very funny, Dr. O'Cutie. Very funny. But seriously, he could've shown us a little gratitude. Not even your blarney could thaw that cold fish."

"Takisha, you got to let it go."

"Yeah. I mean, all we did was rescue his worthless butt. B.F.D."

Four years before, Takisha had been my assistant when I performed the Senator's bypass surgery. He had a heart attack while driving, and when he passed out, he wrecked that car. That bought his ticket into our trauma-oriented ER. It was lucky that Dr. Joe Morales, a medical student at the time, suspected the underlying cause of his accident was cardiac, one of those moments where we truly saved a life.

Senator Travis was grateful, but four days after surgery he transferred to Lutheran Hospital, a comparative Taj Mahal, and our surgery chairman Dr. Brannon assumed his care. When Travis' supporters hosted a celebration at the River Oaks Country Club, our invitations must've gotten lost in the mail and Takisha was major pissed. She'd brought in the society page of the Chronicle and pinned it to the bulletin board in the OR lounge. The sun hadn't set before the Senator had grown a goatee and horns.

I didn't think he was a bad guy. In some ways, he uniquely echoed my political persuasion, proving that pro-life liberal wasn't an oxymoron. No one thought he could win the nomination, but when Hilary Clinton's health became an issue, Travis filled the vacuum. He formed an unstoppable coalition of the young and minority with the pro-life and compassionate, much to the dismay of the party sovereignty.

Normally, Takisha would have been all over this guy, like a groupie after Denzel. Instead, she was a woman scorned. I could appreciate her hurt feelings, but it was no big deal. I doubted the Senator was even consulted on the invite list for the country club blowout.

"He just better hope he doesn't need heart surgery here again."

"Dr. O'Keefe, Dr. Jack O'Keefe," the page operator summoned over the speaker mounted in the ceiling.

I picked up one of the phone extensions and dialed for the operator. "This is Dr. O'Keefe."

"I have an outside call for you. One moment ..."

When the connection was established, a cacophony of sounds spewed from the phone receiver. Music, fireworks, bell horns, and voices: singing, chanting, shouting.

"This is Dr. O'Keefe," I said to identify myself.

No response.

"Hello?" I spoke louder.

"Dr. O'Keefe?"

"Yes," I said. "This is Dr. O'Keefe. Go ahead."

"This is Timmy Strong. Hold just a minute."

Sometimes I wondered how many cumulative hours I'd spent on hold. Surely enough for an extended vacation. And when I was tired, the lack of consideration made me angry.

The crowd noise oscillated from the receiver of the phone mirroring that coming from the TV, wave upon wave of jubilation. Finally, I heard a door close on the caller's end and the extraneous sounds muffled.

"Sorry," he said. "I didn't realize they'd put me through so quickly."

"No problem, but tell me again. Who is this?" I put my hand over the mouthpiece to knock out some of the OR lounge noise.

"I'm Timmy Strong, campaign manager for Senator Travis and Governor Rodriguez."

I motioned to Takisha to turn down the volume on the TV. "And why are you calling me?"

"Dr. O'Keefe, you operated on the Senator and I need to schedule some face time. How about tomorrow?"

"Unfortunately, Mr. Strong—."

"Call me Timmy."

"Look, I don't want to be rude, but I have no way to verify who you are and even if I did, I wouldn't consider discussing a patient with you, even if Senator Travis had been my patient."

"Cute."

"Excuse me?"

"Dr. O'Keefe," Strong said, "look, I understand the HIPPA privacy rules. I'll bring you a notarized release from the Senator if you want. But this is a matter of highest priority. The future of our country depends on your helping us. Now, when can we meet tomorrow?"

Guadalupe, one of the OR techs, stuck her head in the door. "Dr. O'Keefe, the cath lab has an emergency redo heart for us."

For a split second, I wondered how I could escape, but my partner at City Hospital was on extended leave in Russia. His mother was dying. I knew how difficult that process could be, so I'd told him to stay as long as he needed. As physicians we frequently deal with end-of-life issues, but it's entirely different when the life in question belongs to your mother. So, I was the only heart surgeon covering City Hospital and I had to man up.

"Mr. Strong," I said. "I gotta go."

"No—."

I looked up at the TV. Senator Travis and his running mate, Governor Rodriguez, grasped hands and thrust them in a victorious gesture for an adoring crowd of sixty-five thousand believers. They didn't look like they needed my help.

Then suddenly, the screen went black.